P9-CCL-166

Praise for Winnie Griggs and her novels

"Griggs delivers the perfect blend of romance, adventure and laughter. Her characters are charming, quirky and unpredictable."
—*RT Book Reviews* on *The Christmas Journey*

"Griggs really outdoes herself in her latest Texas Grooms story, with outstanding characters who are developed strongly."
—*RT Book Reviews* on *The Holiday Courtship*

Praise for Janet Tronstad and her novels

"An emotionally vibrant and totally satisfying read."
—*RT Book Reviews* on *Snowbound in Dry Creek*

"Janet Tronstad pens a warm, comforting story."
—*RT Book Reviews* on *Shepherds Abiding in Dry Creek*

Praise for Sara Mitchell and her novels

"This tender love story holds just the right blend of romance and sophisticated intrigue."
—*RT Book Reviews* on *Shelter of His Arms*

"Mitchell is an amazing, talented author who spins a tale of greed, love, family secrets and keeping the faith in oneself."
—*RT Book Reviews* on *The Widow's Secret*

Winnie Griggs is the multipublished, award-winning author of historical (and occasionally contemporary) romances that focus on small towns, big hearts and amazing grace. She is also a list maker and a lover of dragonflies, and holds an advanced degree in the art of procrastination. Winnie loves to hear from readers—you can connect with her on Facebook at Facebook.com/winniegriggs.author or email her at winnie@winniegriggs.com.

Janet Tronstad grew up on her family's farm in central Montana and now lives in Turlock, California, where she is always at work on her next book. She has written more than thirty books, many of them set in the fictitious town of Dry Creek, Montana, where the men spend the winters gathered around the potbellied stove in the hardware store and the women make jelly in the fall.

A popular and highly acclaimed author in the Christian market, **Sara Mitchell**'s aim is to depict the struggle between the challenges of everyday life and the values to which our faith would have us aspire. The author of contemporary, historical suspense and historical novels, her work has been published by many inspirational book publishers.

The Christmas Journey

Winnie Griggs

&

Mistletoe Courtship

Janet Tronstad
Sara Mitchell

HARLEQUIN® LOVE INSPIRED® HISTORICAL

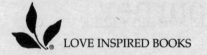

LOVE INSPIRED BOOKS

Recycling programs for this product may not exist in your area.

ISBN-13: 978-1-335-00542-7

The Christmas Journey and Mistletoe Courtship

Copyright © 2018 by Harlequin Books S.A.

The publisher acknowledges the copyright holders of the individual works as follows:

The Christmas Journey
Copyright © 2009 by Winnie Griggs

Christmas Bells for Dry Creek
Copyright © 2009 by Janet Tronstad

The Christmas Secret
Copyright © 2009 by Sara Mitchell

www.Harlequin.com

Printed in U.S.A.

CONTENTS

THE CHRISTMAS JOURNEY

Winnie Griggs

To my dear friend Joanne Rock,
who dropped everything to give me a much-needed
"fresh eyes" read and invaluable assistance in
brainstorming when I needed it most.

Delight yourself also in the Lord;
and he shall give you the desires of your heart.
Commit your way to the Lord, trust also in Him,
and He shall bring it to pass.
—*Psalms* 37:4–5

Chapter One

November 1892
Knotty Pine, Texas

"Hey!" The reedy voice coming from inside Wylie's Livery and Bridle Shop thrummed with outrage. "You can't take those horses 'til you settle up with Joe."

Ryland Lassiter halted outside the entry and swallowed an oath. Sounded as if a disagreement was brewing inside.

The last thing he needed was another delay. This trip had already taken too long. He wasn't about to sit cooling his heels, waiting for the railroad tracks to be cleared—not when he was this close.

Ry reached into his coat and fingered Belle's letter. There'd been an air of desperation in her plea to see him, a sense of urgency that gnawed at him. And the closer he drew to Foxberry, the stronger that feeling grew.

Pushing back the worry, he tugged on his shirt cuffs. Might as well wade in and do what he could to help settle matters. The quicker he could get going again, the sooner he could find out what was going on with Belle.

A burst of rough laughter from inside the stable added impetus to his decision. That first voice had been a boy's, but these sounded older and about as friendly as cornered badgers.

In the space between one heartbeat and the next, Ry stood inside the wide doorway. His jaw tightened as he spied a boy of ten or so squaring off against a pair of sneering thugs, looking for all the world like David before Goliath.

Unfortunately, this would-be giant-slayer didn't have so much as a sling to do battle with.

The larger of the two men, a barrel-chested brute with a scraggly mustache, shoved past the boy. "Outta my way, kid. Those are our horses and we aim to get 'em."

The man's heavy-handed move forced the boy back a step, but the youngster kept his balance and gamely thrust out his jaw. "You can't take them until you settle your bill," he insisted, hands fisting at his sides.

Ry silently applauded the boy's pluck.

But the pair of philistines didn't share his admiration. The second oaf, whose crooked nose and scarred cheek gave him a more villainous appearance than his partner, scowled. "Like we already said, we settled up with Joe this morning." The man's voice rasped like a dull saw on a stubborn log.

The boy crossed his arms. "Joe didn't say nothin' about it."

Mustache stopped in the act of opening a stall gate. "You calling us liars?" He swiveled toward the boy, jabbing his fist into his palm with a forceful *thwack*.

That did it. Ry couldn't abide bullies. And he was pretty sure the good Lord hadn't put him here at this particular moment just so he could stand by and watch.

Clearing his throat he strolled forward, casually nabbing a pitchfork from a pile of straw. "Good day, gentlemen. Is there a problem?"

The pair froze, then turned to eye him suspiciously. Ry held his genial smile as he mentally gauged his options.

As he'd expected, once they got a good look at his tailored clothes and "citified" appearance, their cocky grins reappeared. Better men than these had mistakenly equated polish with softness. His years at law school had added the polish, but he was still a born and bred Texan, able to stand with the best of them.

"No problem," Scarcheek finally answered. "The boy's confused is all. You just stay out of the way, and we'll be done in a minute."

Not likely. Another three unhurried steps placed Ry between the youth and the two men. He pulled out his pocket watch and flicked it open with his thumb.

As expected, both men's gazes latched onto the gold-cased timepiece with a covetous gleam.

"I don't know." Ry glanced down, then closed the heirloom with a snap. "It appears this is taking a good deal longer than a minute, and I've already wasted more time in Knotty Pine than I cared to."

Scarcheek met Ry's relaxed opposition with a lowered brow. "Unless you want to get them fancy duds and that pretty-boy face of yours messed up, you'd best stay out of matters that don't concern you."

Ry flashed a self-deprecating smile. "Well, now, that could be difficult. You see, it's an unfortunate failing of mine that I find there are so many matters that *do* concern me."

Scarcheek drew his pistol and pointed it at Ry's chest. "Don't know where you come from, Mister, but around here that's not a very healthy attitude."

Ry's smile never wavered as he coolly calculated his next step. Using the pitchfork to knock Scarcheek's gun out of his hand would be an easy maneuver. Handling Mustache, who was just out of reach, was a bit trickier. He'd hoped the sight of his watch would tempt the bully to step closer. Still, a few agile moves and a bit of finesse just might help him avoid a bullet while he disarmed the man.

He hoped to handle this without drawing his pocket pistol—the fewer bullets zipping around, the less chance of the boy getting caught in the crossfire.

Bracing himself, Ry shifted his weight and tightened his hold on the pitchfork. No time for doubts. But, as his mother had liked to say, there was always time for prayer.

Lord, I know I don't say it often, but Your help is always welcome, and right about now would be a good time to provide a distraction.

No sooner had Ry formed that thought than the metallic click of a cocked rifle sliced through the tense quiet of the livery. "What's going on here?"

"Joe!" The boy's shout signaled both relief and warning.

Then everything happened at once.

Scarcheek spun around, gun raised, just as the boy started toward the newcomer, putting himself directly in the line of fire.

Fueled by concern over the boy's safety, Ry swung

the pitchfork with a speed and force that surprised even him. The blow connected with Scarcheek's wrist, drawing a yelp and string of curses from the man as the gun went flying.

Before the gun hit the floor, Ry dropped the pitchfork and dove for the boy, tackling him to the ground. Covering the boy's back with his own body, he left the newcomer's line of fire clear to take care of Mustache if need be.

"Hands where I can see them." The rifle-wielding local's command carried the cold hardness of a marble slab.

With the sunlight at their rescuer's back, Ry couldn't make out many of his features. All he got was the general impression that this Joe fellow was a wiry young man who radiated a give-no-ground toughness.

Deciding it was safe to let the squirming stableboy up, Ry stood, though he kept a restraining hand on the lad's shoulder. Now that everything seemed under control, he was actually feeling a bit proud of the way he'd handled himself. He still had it in him, it seemed.

Joe's gaze shifted briefly toward the two of them. "You okay, Danny?"

"I am now." The boy rubbed an elbow as he glowered at Mustache and Scarcheek. "They was fixing to take off without paying what they owe."

"Is that right?" The inquisitor turned back to the surly pair, tightening his hold on the rifle. "You two planning to leave town without settling your bill?"

"Look here, no need to get all riled up." Scarcheek cradled his wrist against his chest. "Clete and I were just pulling the kid's leg a bit." He shot Ry a hot-for-vengeance look. "Before this stranger stuck his nose in, we was about to pay up."

Danny stiffened. "Hey! That's not—"

Ry squeezed the boy's shoulder, cutting off the rest of his protest. Joe was obviously in charge of the livery and it would be best to let him control the stage for now. Ry did, however, slip his free hand into his coat, palming his pistol. Wouldn't hurt to be ready if things turned ugly again.

He felt rather than saw Joe's gaze flicker his way. Apparently his movement hadn't been as subtle as he'd thought.

Then the livery operator's focus returned to Scarcheek and Mustache. "Well, you can hand over the cash now or decide which horse you're going to leave as payment."

Scarcheek scowled, then called over his shoulder. "Pay up, Clete."

Mustache reached into his pocket and pulled out some crumpled bills. He took a step forward, but halted when Joe shifted the rifle, pointing it dead center at his chest.

"Just set it on that barrel." There was a flash of teeth as Joe gave a wolfish grin. "Being as you two are such reliable souls, I'll trust it's all there."

Confident *and* cautious. Ry's assessment of the man raised another notch.

"Now, get your horses and gear, and move on." Joe lowered the rifle, but Ry doubted anyone in the stable thought he'd lowered his guard. "And don't plan on doing business here again."

With dark looks and muttered oaths, the men complied, and in short order were leading their horses into the street. The look Mustache shot Ry as he brushed by was pure venom.

Ry released his hold on Danny and the boy bolted to Joe's side.

The livery operator dropped an arm around the lad's shoulder never taking his gaze from the unsavory pair as they rode off.

Retrieving his hat, Ry brushed at the brim. He'd give them another minute to reassure themselves, then maybe he could finally get down to the business of renting a rig. Now that the little melodrama was over, he was more anxious than ever to be on his way. While Novembers in Texas weren't nearly as cold as those in Philadelphia, the days were every bit as short. He needed to make good use of what daylight was left.

Belle had said in her letter that he was her last hope—an ominous statement coming from the down-to-earth girl he remembered. She'd been like a sister to him back when they were growing up and he still felt that old tug to look out for her.

As he watched the man and boy, something about their pose niggled at him, like a faintly off-key passage in an otherwise flawless aria. What was it…

He shook his head, letting go of the puzzle. He was *not* going to get diverted again.

They turned and stepped into a pool of light, giving him his first clear look at the rifle-toting, overall-wearing, hard-mannered livery operator.

Ry stiffened and felt his world tilt slightly off-kilter. It couldn't be.

But the proof was there, standing right in front of him—barely perceptible curves under masculine attire, long lashes over flashing green eyes, ruddy but smooth cheeks that a razor had obviously never touched. And if he needed further proof he got it when Joe's hat came off, releasing a long, thick braid.

No, not "Joe," but "Jo."

He'd let a woman face down two brutes while he just stood by and watched.

Chapter Two

Josephine Wylie marched back inside the livery, still madder than a dunked cat. If those two mangy curs had done anything to hurt Danny—

Her eyes lit on the fancily-dressed stranger, and she suddenly had a target for her anger.

He stood staring at her with a dazed look—like he'd just swallowed a gnat. But then he smiled and stepped forward. "I believe introductions are in order. I'm Ryland Lassiter."

She ignored the hand. "You're also a flea-brained fool. What in Sam Hill did you think you were doing?"

He stiffened, slowly lowering his hand. "I was coming to the aid of that stalwart young man at your side."

Hah! Did he think he was going to win her over with his highfalutin talk and that toe-tingly deep voice of his? She planted her fists on her hips. "By going up against two gun-toting varmints with nothing but a pitchfork?"

"Now see here—"

She didn't give him a chance to finish his protest. "Mister, you might be the biggest toad in the pond where you come from, but that don't mean beans around here. If you want to risk your own hide, that's your business, but your blamed fool actions put Danny in danger, too. That's either pebble-brained stupidity or grizzly-sized disregard for others, neither of which I can stomach."

"Nor can I." The man's words were controlled but she didn't miss the flash of temper in his storm-gray eyes. "I also can't abide bullies. When I arrived, Danny was already trying to face them down. I only—"

"What!" Jo's heartbeat kicked up a notch as she swung around. "Daniel Edward Atkins, is that true?"

Danny's face reddened even as he thrust out his jaw. "They owed us for a week's feed and stabling. With Thanksgiving and Christmas coming up, we need that money."

This was her fault. She shouldn't have left him alone knowing those two polecats had mounts stabled here. He could handle a lot of the work right enough, but at eleven he just wasn't old enough to understand all the consequences of his actions. If anything had happened to him while she was at the feed store…

Jo leaned forward, baring the full force of her frown on the unrepentant boy. "I've told you before, nothing's worth getting shot over. If someone gives you this kind of trouble, let it go and we'll get Sheriff Hammond to handle it afterward."

The boy kicked at a clod of dirt. "I'm big enough to hold my own."

Jo blew the stray hair off her forehead with an exasperated huff. If only that were true. Someday, Danny would be old enough to take over and she'd finally be free to go her own way. But today's actions only proved how far away that day was.

Offering up a quick prayer for patience, she placed a hand on his shoulder. "Danny, I got to know you're going to mind what I tell you when I leave you in charge."

He gave a reluctant nod, then glanced past her, reminding Jo they weren't alone.

And that she had some crow to eat.

Someday, Lord, I'm going to learn to get all the facts before flying off the handle. Your teaching about thinking twice before speaking once is a sure-enough tough one for me to learn.

Squaring her shoulders, she turned to the gent who'd introduced himself as Ryland Lassiter. "Looks like I owe you an apology, Mister. And a big thank-you to boot." She thrust out her hand, not sure if he'd take it after the way she'd lit into him.

But he seemed willing to let it go. Taking her hand, he gave a short bow before releasing it. Well, wasn't he a fancy-mannered gent.

"Apology accepted. And there's no need for thanks. It's you who actually saved the day. Miss…" He cocked his head to one side with a questioning smile.

"Wylie. Josephine Wylie. But everyone just calls me Jo."

"Well, Miss Wylie, I'm glad I could be of service."

Miss Wylie—she couldn't remember the last time someone had called her that. Certainly not since her pa died and she took over the livery.

She was suddenly very aware of just how unladylike she looked in her overalls and boots. Certainly not like any of the prim-and-proper misses a fancy gent like him must be used to.

Jo turned and hung the rifle on a set of pegs near the

door, as much to hide her sudden discomfort as anything else. He probably thought she was a bumpkin who didn't know how a lady was supposed to dress or act.

Then she gave herself a mental shake. There was absolutely no reason why she should give a fig what he thought of her. He was likely just passing through Knotty Pine—she'd never see him again once he went on his way.

When she turned back around she was ready to look him in the eye again. But she glanced at Danny first. "Time you headed up to the house. Cora Beth has your lunch ready by now. And the train's been delayed, so we picked up a couple of boarders for tonight. I'm sure she's going to need your help getting everyone settled in."

With a nod, Danny turned to his rescuer. "Thanks for your help, Mister." He flashed a cocky grin. "We make a pretty good team, don't we?"

The man nodded with a smile. "I'd be happy to have you on my side anytime."

With a wave, Danny left the livery, whistling as he went.

Which left her alone with Mr. Lassiter.

Her first apology had been a bit grudging. Time to fix that. "Sorry I snapped at you. You stepped in to help Danny when you could've just stood by, and for that I'm beholden. No telling what those two snakes would've done if you hadn't come along."

He shrugged and gave her another of those let's-be-friends smiles. "I did what needed doing. Danny's more than just your stableboy I take it."

She nodded. "Foster brother."

"Well, he was brave to stand up to those thugs the way he did."

"Pigheaded, more like." She tilted her chin, irritation flaring again. "He might've gotten himself killed." Just the thought of what could have happened set her stomach churning.

"He's just a boy."

"But *you* aren't." Fool greenhorn. Didn't he realize how serious that little dust-up had been? Her hands fisted at her sides as she fought the urge to shake a finger in his face. "I know you mean well, and it might be different where you come from, but it's best you learn that in these parts there are men who'd as soon shoot you as look at you."

His jaw tightened. Probably didn't like getting lectured to, but it was for his own good.

"Where I come from," he said, each word dropping like a stone, "is Hawk's Creek Ranch, about eighty miles northwest of here."

Jo's head went up and her hands unclenched. He was a Texan? And a rancher to boot. Well, he sure as fire didn't look or dress like any rancher she'd ever met.

"And no," he continued, "as it happens, it isn't any different from Knotty Pine, at least not in the way you mean. I find bullies are pretty much the same wherever you find them."

Wherever you find them. She knew he hadn't meant anything by that, but the words still carried the bite of a scorpion sting.

"Now, if you don't mind getting down to business," he said, "I would like to rent a rig and I'm in a hurry."

Getting down to business sounded just fine to her. She leaned back against a stall and met his gaze head-on. "When do you need it, for how long and where are you headed?"

"The when is right now. The where is Foxberry and I'm not certain how long I'll be gone, but it will likely be about a week." He raised one brow. "Do you have a rig for lease or not?"

She had the feeling this gent was used to getting his way. Too bad she'd have to disappoint him. "Sorry. The buggy and buckboard are both leased out for the day. The buggy's due back by suppertime, though, if you want to wait."

He impatiently brushed a bit of straw from his sleeve. "I don't."

Jo straightened. "Look, I reckon you came in on the train. I heard there was a problem with the tracks up around Tatter's Gully. It's happened before. They ought to have it fixed by noon tomorrow."

"Like I said, I'm in a hurry." He ran a hand through his hair, mussing it just enough to take a dab of the polish off his dandified looks.

She approved of the change.

"If there are no carriages, what about renting me a horse and saddle?" He nodded toward the two animals still in the stable. His tone had been polite, but she saw the muscles in that square jaw of his tense. Impatience flashed in his see-through-you eyes.

She didn't much blame him for wanting to be on his way. She'd been dreaming of getting out of Knotty Pine for what seemed her whole life.

Jo retrieved the pitchfork and leaned on it, studying her would-be customer. He was a sure-enough puzzlement. Obviously well-heeled. And not a bad-looking man if you liked the broad-shouldered, smooth-as-worn-leather type. But he wasn't a too-good-to-get-his-hands-dirty gent either. Knew how to handle himself, too. That had been a slick move he'd made, knocking the gun from Otis's hand and then covering Danny's back.

"Let's see," she said, thinking out loud, "Foxberry is about a day's ride—assuming you're an experienced rider." She paused and he nodded stiffly. Not that she'd expect him to answer otherwise. "It's just past noon so you won't get there today. Let's say three days for the trip there and back then, and maybe five days' stay. That means you'd have the animal tied up for about eight days, give or take."

Jo rubbed her chin, ready for a bit of dickering. "That kind of time won't come cheap. You sure you wouldn't rather wait? My family runs a boardinghouse and I'm sure my sister has a comfortable room we can rent you for a fair price."

Mr. Lassiter pulled a wallet out of his coat. "I appreciate the offer, but no thanks. Name your price so I can get going."

Jo's knuckles whitened as her grip tightened on the pitchfork. He could just whip out that wallet of his and go wherever he wanted, whenever he wanted. And he didn't even seem to realize how lucky he was. Much as she hankered to get out and see something of the world, she'd never traveled more than twenty miles from Knotty Pine in her entire twenty-three years.

Lord God, it just ain't fair.

"One hundred dollars." The words were out of her mouth before she'd even realized what she was going to say.

"A hundred dollars?" His eyes narrowed. "I could practically *buy* the animal for that price."

Too late to back down now. "Not one as good as these. Besides, I don't have any guarantees you're going to return the animal, do I?" She ignored the way he'd stiffened. "Like I said, you'd be better off waiting for the train."

To her surprise, he pulled out a wad of bills. "Here. Anything to get on my way."

Realizing her jaw had dropped, Jo hurriedly closed her mouth. This fool was actually carrying that kind of money around with him? And a hundred dollars didn't even clean him out—the wallet was still plump when he stuffed it back into his jacket. "But—"

He'd grabbed her hand and the shock of that physical contact shut her up. He slapped the money into her palm, then moved to the stalls.

Guilt pinched at Jo's conscience. She'd expected him to haggle a bit—not actually agree to her outlandish price. It just wouldn't be right for her to take all this money.

She bit her lip, staring at his stiff back. How could she give some of it back without sounding like a henwit?

I know, Lord, it's my own fault for letting envy get the best of me.

Stuffing the money in her pocket, Jo followed him to the far end of the livery. "Of course," she said as casually as she could, "you'll get half of this back when you return the horse." Much as she tried, she couldn't stop the heat rising in her cheeks.

He shot her a look she couldn't read. Then he nodded and pointed to the larger of the animals. "I'll take this one."

"That's Scout." The knot in Jo's stomach eased as she settled back down to discussing business. "I'm afraid he's a bit fractious—doesn't take to strangers much. You'd be better off with Licorice."

He shrugged. "He's the better of the two horses. And I've handled more spirited animals before, both Texas-bred and foreign. I've even helped saddle-break my share. So I think I can manage Scout here just fine."

Jo clamped her lips closed. There he went, hinting about his travels again. That was the worst part about this job. Watching other people come and go, hearing about all the places they'd been or were headed to, while she just stood and watched life pass her by. Would she ever be able to act on the plans she and Aunt Pearl had made?

Without waiting for assistance, Mr. Lassiter began gathering tack. He moved with an ease and sureness she had to admire. But he also seemed in an awful hurry. Made you wonder if he was running *from* something or *to* something.

"You manage this place all on your own?" he asked, not pausing from his efforts.

"Yep. Lock, stock and barrel." Somebody had to support the family and for now she was it.

"Seems a mighty big responsibility."

She stiffened. "For a woman, you mean."

He glanced up and his expression reflected friendly curiosity, nothing more. "No offense, but I admit I find it an unorthodox arrangement."

Did he believe this was how she'd planned for her life to turn out? "It's a family business—my pa passed it on to me." She jutted her chin out. "Like you said earlier, we do what needs doing. I can handle it."

He grinned. "I don't doubt that for a minute."

For some reason that response bothered her more than anything else he'd said since they'd started this strange conversation.

She jammed her hands in her pockets. Did he think less of her because she wasn't some soft, helpless female who needed a man looking out for her?

Not that she gave a hoot for his opinion. After all, she barely knew the man.

Jo did her best to ignore the niggling voice in her head that chided her for not being completely honest with herself.

Chapter Three

As he saddled the horse, Ry eyed the livery operator from the corner of his eye. Why in the world was she so prickly?

True, he *had* mistaken her for a man at first, but she didn't know that. And he'd stepped in to defend her brother at no small personal risk. Why, he hadn't even haggled over the outrageous price she'd demanded for the use of her horse.

Still, he couldn't forget he'd actually let this woman—a member of the fairer sex for all her rough edges—face down a pair of armed thugs while he'd stood by.

His gut clenched every time he thought about it. It was an unforgivable act, going against everything he'd been taught about duty and honor. So he was willing to give her more than the usual bit of leeway.

He felt her gaze studying him as he worked, could almost see the questions forming in her mind.

Finally, she broke the silence. "I suppose you're anxious to get your business taken care of so you can spend Thanksgiving at home."

Home. Ry paused, patting the horse absently. Lately he'd been trying to figure out exactly where that was—in Philadelphia with his grandfather or Hawk's Creek with his brother and sister.

Sometimes he was torn between the two. Other times he felt as if he didn't belong in either place. And holidays hadn't felt special or festive in a very long time.

He gave himself a mental shake. Time enough to work through that problem after he saw Belle. And Miss Wylie was watching him curiously, expecting a response. "My family's not big on holiday celebrations."

That earned him a surprised frown, but no further comment. Instead, she moved across the stable and grabbed a bedroll. Retracing her steps, she hefted it onto the stall next to him. "Quinlinn is between here and Foxberry. You should reach it well before dark, but if you end up having to sleep on the trail you'll need this. Gets cold at night this time of year."

He grinned. "Believe me, this is mild compared to New England."

Far from setting her at ease, his words deepened her scowl. It had been a while since he'd found it so difficult to coax a smile from a woman. But it seemed he couldn't say anything to charm this one.

Well, so be it. The bedroll would come in handy since he wasn't planning to stop in Quinlinn. He'd push on as far as he could until darkness made traveling dangerous, then get up with the first lightening of the sky. The sooner he reached Foxberry, the sooner he could get the answers he wanted.

He had to hand it to Miss Wylie, though. He gathered she was her family's provider—a responsibility she appeared to take seriously. Even if life had set him on a different path, he could certainly respect that.

How big a family was it? He'd already met Danny and she'd mentioned a sister. Were there more?

"You got any kind of weapon with you?"

He raised a brow at her unexpected question, then reached into his coat and pulled out his pocket pistol. "I carry this when I travel."

She surprised him with an unladylike snort. "That peashooter won't be much protection on the trail." Moving with quick strides, she retrieved the rifle she'd wielded earlier. "Here, take this. Never know what kind of varmints you'll meet up with—and I don't mean just the four-legged kind."

Ry slipped his unjustly-maligned derringer back inside his coat. The double-barreled pocket pistol was more formidable than it appeared. "Don't you need that rifle yourself?" He wasn't about to compound his first blunder by riding off with her best means of protection.

But she shrugged off his concern. "I've got another one." A nod toward the far wall indicated a second rifle.

He studied her a moment, noting her earnest expression, the tightly concealed concern lurking in her eyes. It appeared she was making a peace offering and it would be rude to brush it aside.

He took the weapon. "Thanks. I'll return it when I bring the horse back."

She nodded. "Once you leave Quinlinn in the morning, it'll be an easy half day's ride to Foxberry."

"I'll be fine."

"I don't imagine you've had lunch yet." She fiddled with a straw she'd plucked from the pitchfork. "If you were of a mind to remedy that before you head out, you could head over to the boardinghouse. Just tell my sister I—"

Ry held up a hand. "Thanks, but I'll just purchase a few supplies from the mercantile and head out." The itch to be on his way had returned with a vengeance. He'd wasted too much time already.

He mounted the horse, gathered the reins and turned to say a quick goodbye. Then paused.

She'd shoved her hands in her overall pockets and stood watching him. For just a moment, despite her outspokenness, Ry sensed something wistful, something almost vulnerable about the unorthodox female. He had the strangest urge to climb back down and lift some of the weight from her shoulders.

Which was strange. She wasn't at all the sort of girl he was usually attracted to.

Then she straightened and her eyes narrowed. "You take good care of Scout, you hear. I raised him from a colt and I'd take it poorly if you let something happen to him."

So much for his instincts. There was nothing vulnerable about this woman. If he offered to help her she'd no doubt throw the offer back in his teeth. And Belle, who actually *wanted* his help, was waiting in Foxberry.

"Don't worry." He tipped his hat. "I'll treat him as if he were my own prize thoroughbred. See you in about a week or so." With that, he set the horse in motion.

Jo felt another stab of jealousy as Mr. Lassiter turned to go. What must it be like to just pick up and head out anywhere, anytime you took a notion to? Someday she'd find out.

Or so she prayed every night.

She rubbed the side of her face. *I truly am trying to be patient, Lord. But I'm twenty-three and not getting any younger.*

With a sigh, she let it go and watched Mr. Lassiter ride the short distance to Danvers' Mercantile. One thing she could say for the man, he sat a horse well. Seemed to have a knack for appearing both relaxed and in command at the same time.

Seemed he'd do all right with Scout, after all.

At least he wouldn't have the weather to worry about. November was one of those changeable months in these parts. You could have mild weather one day and frost the next. This was one of the sunnier days.

Jo watched him step past the table of pumpkins and gourds Mr. Danvers had set up out front and enter the mercantile. With a shake of the head, she decided she'd wasted enough time worrying about the stranger, and turned back to the livery. Then frowned.

Otis's and Clete's horses were hitched in front of the saloon. Now, why in blue blazes were they still hanging around town?

She retrieved the second rifle and carefully loaded it. They probably wouldn't be back to bother her, but it wouldn't hurt to be prepared. Especially if those polecats were getting liquored up.

Jo sat at her worktable where she had a clear view of the street, and picked up a harness that needed mending. From here she could watch both the mercantile and the saloon.

A few minutes later Mr. Lassiter stepped back out on the sidewalk. Sure hadn't wasted any time. He quickly attached a bundle to Scout's saddle and gathered up the reins.

Yep, something had definitely lit a fire under that man.

As if he felt her watching, he glanced up and his gaze locked on hers. Even from two blocks away, Jo felt the impact of that look down to the tips of her toes.

Land sakes—what was it about this man that could irritate her, confuse her and make her want to squirm all at the same time? And if he thought she would look away first he could just—

A wagon passed between them and the connection was broken. When Jo's line of sight was clear again, Mr. Lassiter had already mounted up and was headed out of town. Not wanting to be caught staring again, Jo managed to watch his progress without looking directly at him.

When he passed in front of the livery, Mr. High-and-Mighty Lassiter gave her a brief tip of the hat, but didn't bother to pause or speak. Which was just fine with her. She didn't care if he paid her any notice or not.

After he'd passed by, she slammed the bridle down with a *thunk* and stood, stretching her muscles. She suddenly felt restless, felt the urge to do something physical.

Then she stilled. Someone else was watching Mr. Lassiter leave town. Otis and Clete lounged outside the saloon, all but licking their chops, nudging each other like a pair of weasels who'd spied a way into the chicken coop.

Even after they stepped back inside the saloon, Jo couldn't shake the notion they were up to no good. And that Mr. Lassiter was their target.

She retrieved her lunch pail and absently picked at her meal, not tasting a single morsel.

Sure enough, ten minutes later Otis and Clete swaggered out of the saloon, mounted their horses and rode off in the same direction as Mr. Lassiter.

Otis glanced her way and the ugly smile he flashed sent alarm skittering up her spine like a frightened centipede.

She had to do something. But what?

Jo tugged on her earlobe. Business wasn't exactly brisk right now. She could likely afford to leave things unattended for a bit.

A few minutes later she was marching down the sidewalk, her pace just short of a trot, trying to figure out exactly what she'd say to Sheriff Hammond.

Otis and Clete had caused enough trouble in town lately that she was sure the sheriff would be inclined to believe they were up to no good. But she didn't really have any proof, other than a sick feeling in the pit of her stomach. And even if he agreed with her that Mr. Lassiter was in danger, would he be willing to take action now that they were headed away from Knotty Pine?

A few minutes later Jo marched back into the livery, as frustrated as a frisky dog on a short leash. Just her luck—Sheriff Hammond was out. No telling when he'd be back either. And she just couldn't shake the feeling that every minute counted.

She might be wrong about this whole mess, but fool or no she had to find out what Otis and Clete were up to. If those two varmints ambushed Mr. Lassiter she didn't have a whole lot of trust in his ability to hold his own.

Heavenly Father, help me figure out what to do.

She tugged on her ear again, trying to come up with a plan. A heartbeat later she spied a familiar towheaded boy on the sidewalk, and as quick as that made up her mind. "Tommy, I need you to do me a favor. Head up to the boardinghouse quick-like. Tell Danny I need him back here for a spell."

With a nod, the boy set off at a run.

Jo grabbed a saddle and headed toward Licorice's stall. She set to work, praying alternately that her suspicions were wrong and that she wouldn't be too late.

By the time Danny arrived she was ready to go.

She gave him a smile she had to force. "I need to ride out after that Lassiter gent. He forgot something." Like watching his back. "Think you can keep an eye on things while I'm gone? It might take a while to catch up with him."

Danny's chest puffed out. "You can count on me."

Jo ruffled his hair. "Especially when it means you get out of doing chores for Cora Beth, huh?"

Danny answered with a prisoner-set-free grin.

"Don't forget what I said about not getting into any dust-ups while I'm gone." She patted Licorice and casually retrieved the rifle.

Danny frowned at the firearm. "You expecting trouble?"

"Just being careful." Jo mounted up. "Mr. Lassiter's had a good head start so tell Cora Beth not to worry if I'm late for supper."

Before Danny could ask more questions she headed out.

As soon as Jo was clear of town, she nudged the mare into a trot. Otis and Clete hadn't seemed in much of a hurry to catch up with Mr. Lassiter. Even no-account slugs like those two would know better than to bushwhack the man too close to town. Sheriff Hammond would be on them like a hungry hound on a meaty bone.

No, more'n likely they were going to hold back for a while. Which meant she had a chance to—

Jo eased Licorice to a walk. To do what?

Otis and Clete were between her and Mr. Lassiter. What would she do if she caught up with them before they caught up to him? And how much time did she have?

She did some quick reckoning. They'd wait until they were well out of Knotty Pine, but would want to strike before Quinlinn. Up ahead a piece, the trail cut through a stretch of woods where there wasn't even a farmstead in hollering distance. Even though it was November, there were plenty of leaves left and the brush was thick enough to provide good cover if a body had need of it.

Past that the trees gave way to Whistler's Meadow. Just a small clearing really, but a spring cut through it, and most folks stopped to refill their canteens and water their horses.

The cowards could use the tree line for cover. Even if Mr. Lassiter didn't stop, just slowed a bit, they'd be able to pick him off, easy as shooting a penned colt.

Jo nudged Licorice into a trot again as a plan took shape in her mind. She'd hang back just a bit. But as soon as she got close to the meadow, she'd fire a few shots in the air, then hightail it for the cover of the woods. That ought to put Mr. Lassiter on the alert, make him aware he wasn't alone. For a man as sharp as him, that ought to be enough.

Dear Lord, please let me get there in time. And give that fool Samaritan the smarts to recognize the warning shot for what it is.

By the time she neared the meadow her back and neck were stiff with tension, and her head pounded with the effort to stay alert to everything around her. So far she hadn't seen any hint of a scuffle or heard any shots.

She slowed Licorice to a walk. The meadow was about a quarter mile ahead. Time to make her move if she was going to do it.

Jo pulled the horse to a full stop and lifted her rifle. The road ran nearly straight from here to the meadow. She stared hard, trying to make out what lay ahead. Otis and Clete weren't the smartest curs in the pack— not by a long shot. Surely she'd see some sign if they were there.

Nothing seemed out of place. A crow cawed in the distance, some squirrels scurried in the nearby trees— just normal forest sounds.

Had she imagined bugaboos where none existed? Had her own yearning for adventure set her mind to creating one for her?

Or what if she'd guessed wrong about where they would spring the ambush? If she fired now, would she be tipping her hand?

A second later she spied the glint of sunshine reflecting off metal. A gun barrel!

Praying again that her plan would work, Jo quickly fired off a shot. Two other shots rang out before the echo died.

A high-pitched squeal of pain followed closely behind the blasts. Her heart in her throat, Jo abandoned her plan to duck for cover. Instead, she urged Licorice into a gallop, full tilt ahead. Sounded like the man needed reinforcements.

If her shilly-shallying had cost Mr. Lassiter serious injury she'd never forgive herself. The least she could do was race in, fire a few shots to distract the bushwhackers, and then get out before they could react.

She refused to believe she might already be too late.

Chapter Four

$\sim$

Ry grimly took stock of the situation from his position behind the fallen horse.

He thanked God for the hunter who'd fired that shot. If the sound hadn't caught his attention it would likely be his blood staining the ground instead of Scout's.

The horse jerked, making a feeble attempt to get up. Ry patted the animal's back. "Easy boy." Scout's muscles quivered under his hand.

Ry's jaw clenched at the animal's struggle. Those gunmen had a lot to pay for.

But he couldn't collect on that debt if he stayed belly to the ground with only the horse for cover. His pistol wouldn't do him much good unless the highwaymen got a whole lot closer, something he'd rather they not do.

If he could just get to the rifle Miss Wylie had loaned him…

The scabbard was tantalizingly close, yet too far to reach without giving the unseen enemy a clear shot. Silently apologizing to Scout, Ry pulled against the saddle with one hand, tugging at the weapon with the other. The rifle slid a few inches, then stopped.

More shots rang out and a searing pain exploded through Ry's shoulder. With an oath, he flattened himself to the ground again.

A quick check revealed that the bullet had passed through the fleshy part of his upper left arm. Lots of blood and it felt as if a hot poker were pressed against his skin, but the wound probably wasn't serious. Leastways, not nearly as serious as things were going to get if he didn't yank that rifle free.

"He ain't firing back."

That sounded like Scarcheek's voice hissing across the clearing. So this wasn't a random attack.

"You reckon he's hit, or just playing possum?"

That had to be Mustache.

"Only one way to find out."

The gunmen didn't try to hide their approach. They'd be on him in a minute and he had no doubts about what would happen next.

He had to get hold of that rifle! If he could fire before they were on him, he might have time to get off two shots.

Keeping as flat as possible, Ry ignored the pain in his arm, grasped the rifle with both hands, and yanked for all he was worth.

But it was no good, not from this angle anyway. He pulled out his derringer and prepared for the worst. He wouldn't make this easy for them. *Sorry Belle, seems I'm not going to be there for you after all.*

A moment later, two man-sized shadows blocked the sun.

"Well, looky here. Pretty Boy done got all mussed up."

Ry twisted his neck to see the two men looming over him, their ugly grins and rifles pointed at his back. He slowly raised himself to a crouch, carefully keeping his pistol hidden. He might not live to see nightfall but at least one of these cowards was going down with him.

"That's right." Scarcheek made a menacing motion with his rifle. "Up where I can see your face and hands."

Tension coiled inside Ry. His muscles bunched, ready to spring. He had to make this move count.

It would be the only one he had.

"Ayyiiieeeeee!"

The shrill war cry shattered nerves already drawn taught. Scarcheek and Mustache whirled around as a wildman swooped into the clearing, riding at breakneck speed straight toward them.

Thank you, God.

Scout made another spasmodic attempt to rise and Ry dove for the rifle. Ignoring the pain in his arm, he jerked the weapon free an eyeblink before the horse collapsed again.

The mounted banshee fired two shots that missed their marks.

Mustache returned fire and the one-man cavalry charge leaned lower in the saddle. The rider's hat went flying and a tawny braid flapped free, whipping in the wind like the tail of a kite.

Miss Wylie!

Was the woman insane? He'd wring her neck over this fool stunt.

If they lived long enough…

Seeing the men take aim at his rescuer, Ry gritted his teeth against the throbbing in his arm and tried to simultaneously fire his rifle and position himself between the gunmen and Miss Wylie. His first shot found its mark and Mustache went down with a grunt.

But a second shot echoed his own and Ry whirled in time to see Miss Wylie's horse go down.

It was getting more difficult to hold the gun steady, but Ry pushed harder, moving between her and Scarcheek, firing again.

He swore when he took a misstep and his shot missed the mark. From the corner of his eye he saw the horse get up.

But not Miss Wylie.

At least he'd turned Scarcheek's attention back toward him. If only it wasn't too late…

Ry fired again. Or at least attempted to. Either the rifle chamber was empty or it had jammed.

Tossing the useless weapon aside, he dropped to one knee, barely dodging another bullet as he jerked out his derringer and fired.

This time there was a satisfying report.

Unfortunately, Scarcheek was a split second faster.

Jo shook her head, trying to clear it, as she pushed up from the ground with both hands. The fall had knocked the wind clear out of her. Her entire left side, from shoulder to hip, felt bruised and battered. Looking up, she spotted Licorice, tail high, galloping back toward home.

Bam! Bam!

She flattened again, twisting around to see where the shots had come from. She saw Mr. Lassiter's back first and then Otis beyond him. How had the greenhorn got himself between her and that snake in the few seconds since Licorice had stumbled?

As she watched, Mr. Lassiter went down, hitting the ground with a jarring thud.

No! Her heart stopped and then stuttered painfully back to life.

Dear God, please, let him still be alive.

It took her a moment to realize Otis had turned his attention back her way.

"Well, now," he said nastily, "first I get to give Pretty Boy the comeuppance he deserves, and now you land in my lap too. Must be my lucky day."

The words cleared the last of the wool from Jo's head and she frantically looked around for her dropped rifle.

He snickered. "Don't even try to go for it or I'll shoot you where you sit."

There! The rifle was just a few feet away. "Don't know that it matters much," she said, trying to give herself time to think. "You're just going to shoot me anyway."

"Maybe. Hadn't decided yet." He moved closer, keeping the gun pointed at her. She winced when he paused to give Mr. Lassiter's leg a vicious kick. "I thought we might have a little fun first." He licked his lip in a disgusting manner. "See if there's really a woman under all those man's clothes."

His leering words made the decision for her. She'd rather chance getting shot than endure the fate he was planning.

She scrambled on all fours toward the weapon, hearing Otis laugh as if at a bawdy joke, knowing she'd never reach it in time, but driven to try anyway.

As she dove the last few feet to the rifle, Jo braced for the bullet, prayed he'd miss, or if not, that it would kill her clean.

She flinched when she heard the anticipated shot, but felt nothing, not even the bullet's impact.

Had he missed?

Her hand closed reflexively on the rifle to the sound of Otis's screams and vile oaths.

She flipped onto her back with the weapon aimed and ready, but instead of finding the brute still bearing down on her, he stood clutching his side, blood streaming through his fingers, his rifle lying useless on the ground.

She looked past him and saw Mr. Lassiter, pale and unsteady on his knees, but blessedly alive and strong enough to aim his pistol at Otis. He'd apparently managed to get a shot off, one that had saved her life.

Relief washed through her in giddy waves as she got to her knees. If Otis had been able to carry out his threat—

She fought down the sour bile rising in her throat.

Otis, still spitting out a stream of curses, reached down for his rifle.

"Don't," Mr. Lassiter rasped.

Otis froze, his hand less than a foot from the weapon.

"The way I see it," her wounded hero continued, "is that no matter how good a shot you are, between Miss Wylie and me, one of us is bound to get you before you can get both of us."

Otis looked from one to the other of them, then slowly straightened, one hand still clutching his side.

"Smart move." Mr. Lassiter made a sideways motion with his weapon. "Now step away from the gun."

Otis moved back several paces.

"Far enough." Mr. Lassiter's eyes flickered her way briefly before returning to the low-down skunk still moaning over his wound. "Are you all right, Miss Wylie?"

"I'm fine." The way he insisted on addressing her so respectful-like after all her carryings on today struck her as oddly sweet.

Now why was she thinking on things like that at a time like this? That fall must have rattled her more than she reckoned.

She stood, trying not to wince at the pain from her bruised muscles. Nothing broken at least, but she'd be moving gingerly for a few days. "Just bruised up a bit," she reassured him.

"Think you can find something to tie up our friend with?"

"Be my pleasure." She started toward Scout, but kept a watchful eye on Mr. Lassiter. He held his gun pointed at Otis, but he didn't attempt to stand. His shirt was soaked with blood, his forehead was beaded with sweat, and as she watched he swayed, then leaned heavily back on his haunches.

The man had to be keeping himself upright by sheer willpower.

She pushed herself to move faster, trying to ignore the fire that licked at her ankle with each step. But she'd only covered half the distance when she saw his aim waver.

"Mr. Lassiter!" Changing course, she made a beeline toward him, but before she could reach him, his eyes fluttered closed. He swayed, then slowly crumpled to the ground.

Jo charged across the last few yards, her pulse pounding an urgent rhythm. This was her fault. She should have done more to warn him, should have intervened sooner.

He *had* to be okay. She would *not* have his death on her conscience.

An eternity of seconds later, Jo dropped to her knees beside him, braced for the worst. A part of her registered the sound of Otis's retreat, but he'd left his rifle behind so she let him go. Right now Mr. Lassiter's well-being was more important than getting vengeance on that bucket of pond scum.

Jo gently brushed the hair from his brow. The low moan that greeted her was the sweetest sound she'd heard in quite some time.

No time to savor her relief, though. He might be alive, but he was far from okay. He hadn't opened his eyes and his breathing was thready. The red stain that drenched his shirt was getting darker by the minute. Even more worrisome was the blood that matted one side of his head.

Gorge rose in her throat but she sent up a prayer for strength. This wasn't the time to act like some prim and proper twit—Mr. Lassiter needed help and right now she was all he had.

Jo gently probed his head where the blood seemed thickest. Yep, there was the wound. Nothing lodged there—best she could tell the bullet had grazed him, gouging a furrow as it went. No way to know how serious it was until Doc Whitman got a look at it.

Trying to remain alert in case Otis circled back, she turned her attention to Mr. Lassiter's arm. Using her pocketknife, she cut open his sleeve to get a better look. The source of all that blood was quickly found—a nasty hole in his upper arm, an ugly, gaping thing that oozed a sluggish stream of blood.

Tightening her jaw, she gingerly examined the wound.

When Jo found the exit hole on the other side of his arm, she swiped her sleeve across her forehead and got her breathing back under control. At least she wouldn't have to try to dig the blamed bullet out.

Now that the initial gut-churning shock was behind her, Jo's control snapped back into place.

First order of business—stop the bleeding. Between the two wounds, and pushing himself to defend the two of them, he'd lost entirely too much blood.

Had he really thrown his already-injured-body between her and Otis? The man was either the flea-brained fool she'd called him earlier or one of the most heroic men she'd ever met.

Maybe both.

If he hadn't stopped Otis—

Her mind rebelled, refusing to finish that thought.

Setting her jaw, she cut his now useless sleeve completely off, then did the same with his other one and both of hers. Taking a few precious minutes to wet one of the strips in the stream, she used it to clean his injuries as best she could. Then she formed pads with the remaining cloths and bound them in place.

Sitting back, Jo stretched her leg to ease the throbbing. She watched her unconscious hero closely for a few minutes, then nodded in satisfaction. The blood seemed stanched, for now at least. It would be nice, though, if he'd open those gunpowder gray eyes again, even if it was just for a moment. Long enough to assure her he'd be all right.

She took a quick glance around. They seemed to be out of any immediate danger. Otis was long gone and Clete hadn't moved from where he'd fallen.

She squared her shoulders and slowly turned to her

right. Like a coward, she'd been avoiding what she knew had to be done.

Rising heavily, she headed toward the fallen horse that had served as Mr. Lassiter's living shield.

Chapter Five

Scout had quit struggling, but his muscles quivered with each labored breath. It was obvious the animal's injuries were irreparable, his time left extremely painful. Jo felt the hot tears come as she knelt to stroke the horse's neck.

The horse she'd raised from a colt gazed at her with pain-filled eyes as she gently finger combed the tangles from his mane.

Heavenly Father, help me through this 'cause I don't think I can do it on my own.

"I'm so sorry," she said, her voice breaking on the last word. With a final pat, Jo wiped her eyes, stood and aimed the rifle.

A heartbeat later, it was over. She lowered the gun, still holding it with both hands. The weight seemed almost more than she could bear.

But mourning was a luxury she couldn't afford right now—time to refocus on the needs of the living. She paused by Mr. Lassiter's side long enough to assure herself he was still breathing, then, steeling her nerve, Jo limped over to where Clete lay. Doing her best to ignore the sick feeling in the pit of her stomach, she rolled the body over. A quick look was all it took. The beefy outlaw was quite dead.

Everything had happened so fast when she charged into the meadow. She hadn't aimed, just fired, trying to draw attention from Mr. Lassiter. Could one of *her* bullets have done this?

That thought broke the last thread of her control and she found herself on all fours, heaving.

It was several minutes before she could straighten back up.

Determined to be practical, Jo averted her gaze from Clete's unseeing stare and pulled out her pocketknife again. Making quick work of it, she cut large strips from his shirt. It felt like grave robbing, but it wasn't as if Clete had any more use for the shirt, and it was a sure bet she'd need additional bandages for Mr. Lassiter before this was over. And with evening coming on she couldn't afford to sacrifice any more of their own clothing.

She wadded up the swaths of cloth, then retrieved the dead man's rifle, using it to ease herself back up with a groan. Yep, she'd be feeling the effects of that fall for several days.

Playing a hunch, she studied the wooded area where Clete and Otis had hidden earlier. Catching a glimpse of movement, she gave a satisfied smile. Sure enough, a few minutes later she found Clete's horse, tethered to a low branch just inside the wood.

Thank goodness Otis hadn't bothered to take the animal with him. With Licorice halfway back to Knotty Pine and Scout dead, this horse would give them some much needed options.

Once she had the mare tethered near the stream, Jo returned to Mr. Lassiter's side, wiping his face with a damp cloth. It wasn't much, but it was all she could think to do at the moment. His breathing seemed stronger, but he was still unconscious and pale as moonlight.

She hated feeling so all-fired useless. He needed more than puny old wet cloths. He needed a doctor, and the sooner the better. But all she could do for now was make him as comfortable as possible.

Jo rubbed her calf, trying to ease a bit of the throbbing. Too bad there wasn't anyone here to see to *her* comfort.

Oh, well, like it or not, being the one to do the looking after had become her lot in life.

With a sigh, she stood and began gathering wood to make a fire, one that would not only ward off the coming chill of evening but would also create lots of smoke.

Whenever the search party came looking—she refused to believe that wouldn't happen soon—she wanted to make finding them as easy as possible.

Ry stirred, then grimaced. His head throbbed as if a judge were pounding a gavel in his skull, and there seemed to be a branding iron pressed into his shoulder. He shifted, trying to get more comfortable, then fisted his hands against the pain that shot through his leg. Thunderation! It felt like he'd been mule kicked.

Was that *grass* under his hand? Had his horse thrown him? He couldn't think straight—his mind felt thick as sludge. He tried opening his eyes, but only managed slits.

Then the memory of what had happened came stampeding back and his heart slammed in his chest as he

struggled to get up. He had to make sure Scarcheek
didn't get to Miss Wylie—

"Whoa there." A hand pressed him gently but firmly
down.

Relief surged through him. That had been her voice.
She was okay. *Thank You, Lord!*

But where was Scarcheek? He renewed his efforts
to get up. "My gun!" Was that croak really his voice?
"Where—"

She cut off his words by pressing him down again,
this time wiping his brow with a damp cloth.

"Easy. No need to get stirred up. We're in the clear
now."

Had his last desperate shot found its mark? If only
he could remember...

As if reading his mind she answered his unvoiced
questions. "Clete won't be bothering anyone—not ever
again. And Otis is long gone. High-tailed it out of here,
bleeding like a stuck pig, as soon as he saw you fall."

Realizing he'd obviously blacked out, leaving her
to deal with a hornet's nest on her own, he wanted to
howl in frustration and self-disgust. How long had he
been unconscious?

Whatever had happened, it was a good thing the
gun-wielding outlaw was gone. He couldn't even sit up
right now, much less fight off anything more threatening than a gnat.

He studied Miss Wylie, looking for signs of injury.
"What about you? Your horse fell—"

"Got bruised up a mite, nothing serious."

Her tone was light but the strain in her expression
told a different story. Was she hurt worse than—

The memory of Scarcheek's threat suddenly slammed

back into him. He grabbed her wrist. "Did he touch you? So help me, if he did there's no place far enough—"

"Whoa there, hero." Her smile was more genuine this time. "Otis never laid a hand on me. Thanks entirely to you."

Hero—hah! Ry suppressed a groan at her attempt to make him feel better. Still, he couldn't help but admire her courage and fortitude.

This woman was unlike any he'd ever met. How could she find something to smile about after all she'd just been through? Most women he knew would be hysterical, would be looking for him to comfort *them*.

Aware that he was still squeezing her wrist, he released her and leaned back. He realized there was a bandage on his head and another on his otherwise bare arm.

A woman of many talents, it seemed, and one who didn't let squeamishness get in the way of doing what had to be done.

She reached beside her and lifted a canteen. "How about a drink of water?"

At his nod she rested the canteen on his chest then twisted around, reaching for something he couldn't quite see. "First, let's try to get you propped up a bit."

A second later he realized she was maneuvering a saddle into place behind him.

"Easy now." She slipped a hand under his neck, supporting him while she nudged the makeshift prop under his shoulders. She was surprisingly strong. No doubt due to her work at the livery. Funny how nice those callused hands felt against his skin.

He tried to keep the wince from his expression as the movements dug the branding iron deeper into his shoulder. He wasn't going to add to her already piled-high worries.

"There now," she eased him back, "how does that feel?"

"Better, thanks."

"Good." She held the canteen to his lips, once more supporting his neck. The water tasted heavenly and felt even better going down. The liquid smoothed away the sawdust lining his mouth and throat. He couldn't get enough of it, as if he were a parched bit of earth that hadn't seen rain in months.

"Easy now," she repeated, a touch of humor in her voice, "There's a whole stream of this stuff over yonder so there's no need to worry we'll run out before you're quenched."

Her teasing surprised an answering grin from him. "Are you maligning my table manners, Miss Wylie?"

She shrugged, her expression bland. "Not me. I'm used to being around animals that drink from troughs, remember?"

Ry chuckled at her unexpected dry humor. At least the day's events hadn't robbed her of her spirit.

"And there's no need to be so formal, especially considering the fix we're in. Just call me Jo."

He hesitated, not wanting to offend her, but not certain he wanted to comply. The use of Miss Wylie had been a deliberate effort to make up for his having mistaken her for a man, even if she wasn't aware of his gaffe. Calling her Jo, a man's name, just didn't sit right with him after so ungentlemanly a blunder. But she didn't seem like a Josephine either. "What if I call you Josie instead?"

A flash of surprise crossed her features. But her only response was an offhand "I reckon that'll do."

"And of course you can call me Ry."

With a nod, she raised the canteen to his lips again. He took care to drink more slowly this time, taking the opportunity to look around. She'd built a fire while he was out, one that was emitting enough smoke to cure a side of bacon. A second saddle lay on the ground next to him and what looked to be the rest of the tack and gear from two horses was placed in neat piles nearby.

A whicker drew his gaze toward the stream. A horse stood tethered there. Not the horse she'd charged in on and certainly not Scout. How in the world had she managed to find another mount out here?

Then he spied what was unmistakably a body covered by a couple of horse blankets.

His gaze shot back to her.

Her smile was gone and her jaw tightened. "It's Clete," she said. "I thought covering him up was the decent thing to do."

Ry leaned back against the saddle, glad for its support.

Her fingers fiddled with the cap of the now empty canteen. "I didn't see him go down. I don't know which one of us—"

"It was my shot," he said quickly, realizing what she feared.

"Oh." She searched his face for a moment, then the tension in her eased. She stood and waggled the canteen. "Better refill this."

Ry shifted again, chafing at his weakened condition as he watched her limp toward the stream. She was hurt, yet she hadn't spoken a word of complaint. How long had she been sitting there, wondering if she'd been responsible for taking a man's life?

His opinion of her character rose another notch.

"How long was I out?"

"About thirty minutes or so," she called back over her shoulder. "Had me worried for a while."

Again, her light tone didn't quite cover the underlying strain. He knew it wasn't all due to the physical pain and exhaustion she must be feeling. The emotional turmoil she'd been through had taken its toll as well.

She paused to check on the horse before stooping with some difficulty at the stream to refill the canteen. Her action reminded him of what had happened to Scout. Had the animal died of its wounds, or had she been forced to deal with that, as well?

Either way, he had a lot to make up for. Starting now.

"Only thirty minutes, huh?" he said as she returned. "It appears you made good use of the time."

She shrugged. "I'm used to keeping busy."

That he could believe. "Well, you've set up a tight little camp here." Pulling on every ounce of strength he had, Ry propped himself up on one elbow. "I ought to be comfortable enough while you head back to town."

Her eyes widened. "What?"

"Take that horse and ride to town. You can send a wagon back for me. There's no point in us both just sitting here hoping someone will come along."

"Uh-uh. Whether we like it or not, we're in this together. I'm not leaving here without you, not after all the trouble I went through to save your hide."

"And you can finish the job by sending a wagon back for me."

"What if Otis comes back?"

Exactly. He had to make certain she was well out of harm's way. "Look, Josie, you said yourself Otis was long gone. Besides, I'm not hurt so bad that I can't hold my own for the time it'll take you to get to town and send help back. Just leave me one of those rifles and I'll be fine."

She snorted. "Fine my left foot." Thrusting a rifle at him, she walked off, positioning herself several yards behind him. "Okay, hero, I'm Otis. Defend yourself."

Ry struggled to sit up and at the same time swivel his body to face her. He failed miserably. On both counts.

"Might as well quit trying." The edge of irritation in her voice exacerbated the ache in his head. "If I was Otis you'd already be dead. And that's with lots of warning to boot."

She stood over him, glaring. "Hang it all, Mister, there's no shame in admitting you're hurt. It's just plain selfish, too—making more work for me. Look at you. All that tomfool twisting and turning set your arm to bleeding again. At this rate we're going to run out of bandages before we can get you to the doc."

Even if he'd had the energy to take offense, Ry knew she was right. For a moment he didn't even have the breath to speak.

He flopped back with a thud that amplified the pounding in his head. It was getting colder too. He couldn't suppress the shiver that racked his body.

Josie removed the rifle from his grasp, her brow furrowing. "How are you feeling?"

"Thoroughly useless."

She patted his hand, as if he were some wet-behind-the-ears kid who needed comforting. "Sorry I lit into you that way—ain't your fault you don't like being stove up. My ma used to say that trying times were God's way of keeping us humble and reminding us to look to Him for our strength."

She leaned back. "Just think of it as taking a bit of time off from all that rushing around you've been doing."

Belle! Hang it all, with everything that had happened he'd forgotten all about her cry for help. If only she hadn't been so cryptic about what she needed from him.

"Can't afford to take time off right now." He shivered again. So cold. So tired. "Belle needs me."

He closed his eyes to keep the spinning sky from drawing him into the maelstrom.

Belle. Josie. Different as night and day. In fact, the only thing they had in common was that they were facing big troubles.

And he was powerless to lift a finger to help either of them.

Chapter Six

Who was Belle?

Jo tried to ignore her curiosity and concentrate instead on keeping Mr. Lassiter from passing out.

His eyes drifted closed again and she chewed on her lip. How serious *were* his injuries?

"Come on, Mister—Ry—try to stay awake. Just until help comes. It shouldn't be much longer."

His eyes fluttered open. "Sorry. Feeling drowsy."

"Talk to me. Where you traveling from?"

"Philadelphia."

"Hah! I knew you weren't a rancher."

That got a reaction from him. "Not calling me a liar, are you? I said I was *raised* on a ranch. My family's still there."

"But not you."

"My grandfather lives in Philadelphia. I stayed with him while I went to law school."

"So which do you call home, the ranch or Philadelphia?"

His face creased in annoyance. "Too many questions."

She tried another tack. "So why were you in such an all-fired hurry to reach Foxberry?"

"Still am. Supposed to meet someone there, someone who asked for help."

"You came all the way from Philadelphia to answer a call for help? Must be an awfully good friend."

"She is."

She? Was it this Belle woman he'd mentioned?

He lifted a hand, then let it drop. "Sounded urgent. Hadn't heard from her in years. She must be desperate."

He shifted again and winced. "What makes you so sure help is coming?"

Jo threw another stick on the fire. "Whenever Licorice gets spooked she heads straight for home. As soon as she shows up without me, Danny'll put out the alarm."

"And if she doesn't get there this time?"

"My sister's the worrying type. By now she's started hounding the sheriff and won't let up until he sends someone out to look." If only she hadn't told Danny she might be late. No point worrying him with that little bit of information though. "Don't you worry, we'll get you to a doctor soon enough."

"Not worried. Just thinking we should make use of that horse."

"We already talked about that. I'm not leaving you here alone." She tugged on her ear. "I could try making a litter I guess. We have most of the materials— the bedroll, rope, leather from the bridle." She glanced toward the shrouded body and shivered. "I could even use the horse blankets if we needed 'em. Just have to try to cut a few saplings for the poles—"

"Or we could ride double."

She studied him. "Do you think you could mount up?"

His mouth tightened. "I might need a hand, but I could do it."

"I don't know if we should put you to the test until we have to. There's still time for help to get here before dark."

His jaw clinched and she could tell he wasn't happy with what he was about to say. "Look, I'll be honest. Right now I believe I have the strength to do this, with your help. But I'm not sure how long that'll last." He stared at her with fiercely determined eyes. "So if we're going to mount up, it had better be soon."

Jo glanced toward the trail from town. No sign of help. The temperature had already started dropping and it'd be dusk soon.

She also didn't care much for the flushed look of his face. If he developed a fever things could go from bad to worse in a hurry. He was right. Time to fish or cut bait.

The thing was, she wasn't just worried about getting him up on the horse, though that was going to take more than a bit of effort. Was he really up to the long ride back to Knotty Pine? He'd admitted his strength was fading. His wound could start bleeding again, or worse, he could fall off. If that happened they'd be worse off than before.

What a pickle!

Jo drew her shoulders back. Better to leave the hand wringing to Cora Beth. It wasn't a great choice but it was the only one they had. The last thing she needed was to be caught out here after dark, with Otis roaming around somewhere.

"Okay, let's give it a shot. You conserve what

strength you have while I put out the fire and get the horse ready."

He nodded.

"Just try to stay awake." Grabbing the fallen branch she'd been using as a makeshift cane, Jo levered herself up. She'd probably be sore for the next few days but she'd put up with worse aches before. And it wasn't anything like what Mr. Lassiter was dealing with.

She still had trouble thinking of him as just Ry. Funny thing how he'd insisted on addressing her as Josie instead of Jo. No one had called her that before. Ma had always used her given name of Josephine, and her nieces called her Aunt JoJo. But to everyone else she was just plain Jo.

Josie. Kind of had a nice ring to it. Not too frilly or fancy sounding, but definitely recognizable as a girl's name.

The thought struck her then that she would finally have a story of her own to add to her journal. Not that this was the way she'd wanted it to happen, but it was an adventure just the same.

Heavenly Father, I know I've been praying for an adventure and now that I've found myself smack-dab in the middle of a humdinger of one it don't seem quite right for me to be asking You to end it so soon. But I guess that's what I'm doing.

Mr. Lassiter don't deserve to suffer just 'cause I want some excitement. Especially since he pushed himself so hard to save me. So please, whatever it takes, keep him safe.

Ry roused to the feel of a damp cloth on his forehead.

He opened his eyes to see Josie staring down at him, her face creased in worry.

"You sure you want to try this? We can always wait a little longer for help to come."

"I'm all right. Just resting."

Doubt flashed in her eyes at his obvious fib.

"Let's see if you can sit up first," she temporized.

Determined to reassure her, Ry steeled himself and pushed up with his good arm, doing his best to ignore the spinning sensation. He gritted his teeth, chafing at this unaccustomed feebleness. If he hadn't had her hand at his back he might not have made it.

After a moment he felt steady again and took his bearings. He must have been out for more than the few seconds he'd thought. She'd managed to douse the fire without him even noticing.

"First we're going to put that arm of yours in a sling and secure it against your chest so we can keep from jarring it as much as possible. Won't do to have you bleeding to death on me."

Where had she found those strips of cloth? His eyes flashed to the blanket-covered body in sudden understanding. The woman not only had gumption but she was cannily resourceful.

"That was a mighty vicious kick Otis gave you," she said, bringing his gaze back around. "You sure you can stand okay?"

That explained why his thigh hurt so bad. "I'll manage."

"Have you ever ridden bareback before?" she asked.

"Yes, of course."

"Good. 'Cause I figure that's our best chance of getting the two of us on that animal."

Made sense. Riding double with a saddle was not a comfortable proposition.

"Problem is, without stirrups we need a mounting block. There's a fallen tree over where I've tethered the horse. If you use me as a crutch, can you make it?"

He eyed the distance separating him from the horse. About ten yards. Might as well have been a mile. "I'll make it."

"Good." She studied her handiwork with the sling. "How does that feel? Not too tight is it?"

"It's fine." Enough talk, time for action.

"Okay then. Whenever you're ready, put your good arm around my neck and I'll help you up, nice and steady."

Bracing himself, Ry nodded and did as he was told.

By the time he finally stood upright, he was as winded as a racehorse after a gallop and drenched in sweat.

Josie supported him, not saying a word or clucking over him in useless sympathy. He appreciated her patience and restraint.

He was also determined not to lean on her one jot more than necessary. He just needed her to provide an anchor when the waves of dizziness hit.

He'd be hanged if he'd let any of his injuries stop him. It was imperative that he get her away from here, and it seemed the only way to budge her was to go with her.

Lord, let me make it to that horse without giving this woman more troubles than she's already had.

He let her lead him across the short patch of ground, focusing on placing one foot in front of the other. And on not falling.

When they reached the makeshift mounting block

he paused, gathering every bit of energy he still possessed for the effort ahead.

Before he could move, she spoke up. "Now this is going to be the tricky part. I'll need to ride up front so I can guide the horse. That means I should mount first. Can you support yourself while I do that?"

Ry nodded. It had to be done, so he would do it. He'd always prided himself on his horsemanship—time to give it a *real* test. Mounting with no stirrups and only one good arm would be tricky under the best of circumstances. Doing it while he was weak as a babe and she was already taking up a good chunk of available space would ratchet it up to a whole new level of difficulty.

He moved his arm from her shoulders to the horse's back, aware that she kept her hand on him, ready to assist if he should fall.

"Steady now. Once you're ready I'm going to let go so I can mount up. I'll help you up after me as much as I can."

He took a deep breath. "Let's get this over with." Almost before he had time to draw a second breath she was up on the horse. She scooted forward then reached down. "I'll hold the horse as steady as I can. Take my hand so I can help pull you up."

The next few minutes were fragmented splinters of motion. He grabbed hold of her hand, then found himself chest first over the back of the horse, pain clawing through his injured arm and shoulder. The next thing he knew he had somehow gotten his leg over the horse without any memory of doing so, and was maneuvering himself into an upright position.

Which brought him face-to-face with his next dilemma.

"This isn't the time to worry about niceties," she said, obviously reading his mind again. "Ain't no way you're going to be able to stay on this horse without holding on to me. We're not budging from here until that arm of yours is around my waist."

She was right of course. Still, it felt like taking liberties he wasn't entitled to. "Yes, ma'am." He eased his right hand around her surprisingly trim waist, but managed to hold himself erect, keeping several inches between his chest and her back.

She set the horse in motion. "I'm going to try to keep a slow, steady pace. This probably won't be the most comfortable ride you ever took, but it'll be best if we go straight through without stopping."

"I agree." He swallowed an oath as the horse tossed its head before settling into a steady rhythm. "The sooner we get back to town, the better." He wasn't certain he could climb back up on this animal if he ever got off of it.

He'd just have to live with the fact that they were headed back to Knotty Pine and not toward Foxberry. For now, Josie's needs would come before his, and even before Belle's.

Jo wasn't ready to celebrate just yet. Getting him up on the horse had only been half the battle. The other half would be keeping him there until they reached town.

The man had a lot of grit, she'd give him that. Not many would have managed to come through that ambush and lived to tell the tale.

She'd been well aware of his efforts to spare her during their walk across the clearing, and again when he'd mounted up.

Even now, with his hand around her waist, she could feel his effort not to lean against her. If she'd had reason to question whether he was an honorable man before, she could set her mind at ease now.

Probably be best to keep him talking so she could gauge how alert he was. Besides, she liked the sound of his voice. "Tell me about that family of yours back on the ranch."

"I have a brother and a sister, Griff and Sadie." His voice had slowed and deepened, his Texas drawl coming out. And she could feel the warmth of his breath stir the hair at her nape.

She told herself the shiver that fluttered her shoulders was due to the dropping temperature. "I said tell me about them, not name them."

"What do you want to know?"

"The usual stuff. Are they older or younger than you? Are they married? What are they like?"

"Both younger—Griff by two years, Sadie by five. Neither is married."

He paused and she wondered if he would give her any more information.

"Griff takes after Pa—a rancher through and through. Hawk's Creek is in his blood and you couldn't pry him away with a crowbar."

So, was he implying that he himself wasn't so tied to the land? She could sure relate to that. God had made this world way too big to limit yourself to one little patch of it.

"Sadie's what you'd call impetuous. She's a bit on the clumsy side, but she doesn't let that stop her. She's as comfortable at a barn raising as she is at a ladies auxiliary tea."

Sounded like someone she'd get along fine with. "How often do you see them?"

"Two, three times a year."

It was like wresting a bone from a dog to get any information out of him. Did he hurt too bad to talk? Or did he just not like the questions she was asking? "Tell me about the ranch."

"Hawk's Creek? It's just north of Tyler. Covers about six hundred acres all told. My family raises some of the finest Hereford stock around. Not to mention cutting horses."

There was an unmistakable touch of pride in his voice. Sounded like he still had a fondness for the place. "So how did you end up going to law school?"

"Long story."

His voice was getting deeper, his words dragging. She had to keep him alert. "Seems we've got nothing but time. Talk to me."

"My grandfather's a lawyer and prominent member of Philadelphia society. Mother was his only child."

He paused and she leaned against him briefly. She could almost see him pull himself back together.

"She was the apple of his eye," he continued. "He didn't like it much when she up and married my pa and moved to Texas. Took it even harder when she died without ever moving back."

"And?" she prodded, placing her hand on top of his at her waist.

"Grandfather always wanted a son to follow in his footsteps. The year I turned sixteen, he asked my father to send one of us boys up to Philadelphia to spend a few months with him. Truth be told, I think Pa felt guilty over having deprived Grandfather of his daughter. Whatever the reason, he agreed."

"And you volunteered."

"It was only supposed to be for the summer."

That sounded almost defensive.

He shifted but his hand never moved from her waist. "When summer was over, Grandfather wanted me to accompany him on a trip to Boston. When we returned he needed help researching a major case. Then he wanted to show me his lodge up in the Adirondacks. The entire fall stretched out that way, one 'one more thing' after another, and it was Christmas before I made it home."

The offhand, almost resentful way he cataloged his travels, as if he'd just taken a not-too-enjoyable walk around the block, flabbergasted her. She'd give her eye-teeth to have such an experience. "Sounds like he went all out to give you a taste of what your mother's world had been like."

"I never thought of it that way." He seemed to ponder on that a moment before he went on. "Anyway, before I left Philadelphia, he asked me to consider returning to attend the university and perhaps enter law school. It was hard to leave because I knew he was lonely and that in a way I was a tie to his daughter."

"Is that the only reason you went back?" Surely life in a big city like Philadelphia would have spoiled him for something as simple as life on a ranch.

"Things had changed while I was away. Pa relied more on Griff to help run the ranch. Sadie was growing into the lady of the house. Pa spent more time with his work than with the family. Everything appeared to be running smoothly without me." He shifted slightly.

"I just seemed like more of an outsider there than I had at Grandfather's."

Much as Jo wanted to get away from Knotty Pine and see the world, there was something sad about his story. Family was so important. No wonder he hadn't answered when she asked which place he called home.

"Don't know why I just told you all that," he said gruffly. "Must be woozier than I thought."

"Is your pa still around?"

"No. He died two years ago. Griff runs the ranch now."

Did he resent his younger brother for stepping in to the oldest son's role? Or was he relieved not to have that burden?

They rode in silence for a while. Jo figured as long as his grip on her waist was firm enough he wasn't in any danger of drifting off.

And it definitely was firm, though not uncomfortably so. At least not in the usual sense. His hold wasn't the least bit inappropriate. He merely used her to steady himself. He'd have held onto a sack of flour the same way. Even so, something about the near-embrace made her feel safe, secure, protected in an almost intimate kind of way. She'd never experienced such feelings before.

She'd always done her best to discourage any thoughts the men in Knotty Pine might have of walking out with her. After all, she had big plans to travel some day, and marriage would only get in the way. She needed wings, not roots.

Not that the menfolk had lined up to come courting. She wasn't exactly the kind of woman men looked for in a wife. Too outspoken and independent, she supposed.

Funny, though, how that didn't seem to bother Mr. Lassiter...

She gave her head a shake, not comfortable with where that line of thought might lead. Time for more talk and less thinking. "So nowadays you spend most of your time in Philadelphia? Do you get to travel to other places?"

"Sometimes."

"Like where?"

"There's that hunting lodge in the Adirondacks my grandfather owns—we spend several weeks a year there. And I've been to most parts of New England at one time or another."

"Ever been to another country?"

"Once."

His one word answers were less than informative. "Where to?"

"Greece." He seemed to be speaking with an effort. "A client hired me to check on some legal aspects of an estate he'd inherited there."

Greece! She had a world map in her room, one of her dearest treasures. On it were pins marking all the interesting-sounding places various travelers had told her about. This was the first one from Greece. "The good Lord willing, I aim to do my own share of traveling some day."

"Is that so?"

She hadn't realized she'd voiced that thought aloud. No shame in it though. "Yep. Just as soon as Danny's old enough to take care of the livery on his own I plan to set out and see as much of the world as I can."

"By yourself?"

"Sure. Other women have done it. Look at Ida Pfeiffer and Nellie Bly and Isabella Bird. And my own Aunt Pearl."

"If any woman can, you..."

The slurred words drifted into something incoherent as his grip on her waist slackened.

"Mister!" She grabbed his hand. She had to keep him on this horse.

If he slid off there'd be no getting him back up.

Chapter Seven

The sharp command jerked Ry back to consciousness. There had been more than a warning in her voice, there'd been worry edged with outright desperation. And it was his fault.

On top of everything else on her plate right now she had to worry about keeping him on the horse as if he were some toddler astride his first pony.

"Sorry. I'm okay now." He hoped he sounded more confident than he felt.

"Lean against me if you need to. Just don't you dare fall off this animal."

"Yes, ma'am." Despite the seriousness of the situation, Ry found himself amused by her military general attitude. And also touched by her courage.

But he refused to let himself take advantage of her generosity any more than absolutely necessary. He'd keep himself upright under his own steam as long as possible. And he offered up a prayer that his "steam" would last long enough to get them where they were going.

"Tell me about this Aunt Pearl of yours."

"She was a really colorful woman. Spent most of her life as the personal companion to an opera singer. The two of them traveled all over the world and met lots of exciting people."

"Sounds like an interesting life." He tried to focus on her words, anything to keep the blackness at bay.

"Oh, it was. Aunt Pearl was fifty-one when Madame Liddy passed on, and she came to live with us. I was six at the time and used to spend hours listening to her stories."

She gave a selfconscious laugh, a surprisingly feminine sound that brought a smile to his lips.

"Aunt Pearl used to say she saw herself in me. Made me promise to not let myself get locked away in Knotty Pine, at least not until I'd tasted what the rest of the world had to offer."

"How old were you when you made the promise?"

"Eight. But I never forgot it. And I'm going to do it someday, too, even if it takes me another fifteen years to work out the hows and wherefores."

"I believe you." And he did.

They rode in silence for a while. Or maybe she did some talking. But his efforts were now wholly focused on staying upright and he didn't have room to pay attention to anything else.

Twice more he caught himself as he slumped forward. The third time she halted the horse and stared at him over her shoulder. The worry in her eyes cut as deep into him as any blade.

"I hope you're a praying man, Mister, 'cause we need some help from the Almighty to get us the rest of the way home."

She chewed on her lower lip a moment then seemed

to come to a decision. "I have to climb down to take care of something. If you can hold steady for just a bit, you can lean over the horse's neck as soon as I'm out of the way. Think you can manage?"

He nodded, then wished he hadn't. The world spun dizzily.

"Okay, we'll do this nice and easy." She moved his hand from her waist and he suddenly felt set adrift. But before he could flounder, her voice came to him from somewhere in the vicinity of his knee.

"Just lean forward. That's right, all the way. Take hold of the mane with your good hand."

Her tone was soothing, her words mesmerizing. Before he knew it, his chest rested against the horse's neck. It was a relief to let the tension ebb away, to not worry about burdening her with his weight or inadvertently taking ungentlemanly liberties. If he could just rest here for a few minutes, he should be able to hold himself together for another go at this when she mounted up again.

Ry tried to pry his eyes open, but they weren't cooperating. He couldn't seem to get his bearings, and was having trouble telling up from down.

How long had he been out this time? Couldn't have been too long—he could still feel the heat of the sun beating down on him, scorching him all the way to his core. Where was that cool breeze when he wanted it?

He could feel the movement of the horse, hear the plodding of its hooves. At least he'd managed to stay astride.

It was so hot! This felt like a Texas summer, not fall. "Water." The word came out as a raspy croak. Right now he'd give every bit of cash in his wallet for a sip of cool liquid.

"Try to hold out a little longer. I promise you can have all the water you want as soon as we reach town."

Startled, he realized the voice hadn't come from in front of him. Why hadn't he realized before now that he was still slumped over the horse's neck?

He managed to open his eyes enough to see Josie walking beside the horse, one hand on his thigh to steady him.

How long had she been walking? Had she ever intended to remount in the first place? He tried to sit up. "What are you—"

"Settle back down. You'll get that arm to bleeding again and I've run out of bandages."

Ry fought the returning blackness, tried to protest, but the words came out as garbled nonsense. He shut his eyes, pushing back the molten darkness swirling about him, trying to gather both his strength and his wits, focusing on the feel of her hand on his knee. The heat was sapping what little energy he had left.

He wanted—needed—to convince her to get back on the horse, but his mind couldn't form the right words.

"That's it," she said. "Just concentrate on staying up there. Don't worry, I won't let you fall. Why, we'll be back to town before you know it."

Her words turned into a pleasant buzzing, then nothing. For a time—he couldn't say if it was minutes or hours—he battled the boiling current, surfacing into a sort of smoke-filled awareness before being ruthlessly tugged back under.

He was so hot! He felt like the rich man of the parable, locked in torment, pleading for Abraham to send

Lazarus to slake his thirst. Was that it? Was this punishment for his failings?

No, he wasn't totally lost. Mercy had been granted. Someone was there, someone with calloused but curiously gentle hands, trickling liquid through his parched lips, wiping his brow with a cool cloth, providing relief until the next wave of searing darkness swallowed him again.

At one point Belle drifted in through the haze. He tried to reach for her, tried to apologize for not getting to her sooner. But no matter how hard he fought to reach her, the current tugged at him, held him back, and she stared at him with pleading eyes until the haze swallowed her again.

Through it all, those calloused hands and the sound of Josie's voice became his lifelines. Not that he understood much of what she said, but he knew when she was there and clutched at those moments of sanity. Sometimes her tone was soothing and gentle, other times it was coaxing or scolding. He even thought he heard her exhorting the Almighty on his behalf.

Finally the boiling eased, the current cooled and he floated aimlessly for a while. When the darkness came again, it approached as a friend, ready to wrap him in a blanket of peaceful sleep.

Ry roused reluctantly, trying to burrow back into the blessed painlessness of sleep. But his parched throat protested, urging him to full wakefulness.

He wasn't on the horse any longer. Instead he was lying on a nice comfortable bed. Where was Josie? Had she made it back okay?

He missed the nearness of her that had been his lifeline on that long nightmarish ride—the warmth of her hand on his at her waist, the earthy scent of her that had invaded his senses, the feel of her hair as strands fluttered back to tickle his face. And finally the comforting hand at his knee, connecting him to her, assuring him he was in good hands.

A rustling sound drew him back from his drowsy state. He couldn't see anyone, but it had to be his dictatorial rescuer.

"Water." Had that croak really been his voice?

"Goodness, you gave me quite a start."

Though definitely female, it wasn't the voice he'd expected. Ry pried his eyes open to find an apron-clad woman standing over him with a soft smile on her face.

Nope, definitely not Josie.

"It's so good to see you finally awake. And calm."

What did that mean? Vague images returned to him, images that he hoped were merely dreams. "Miss Wylie. Is she—"

"Don't you go getting all stirred up. Jo's just fine."

"I must have passed out again. I'm afraid I don't remember much about how I got here."

"I'm not at all surprised. Why, by the time the search party found the two of you, you were burning up with fever. You certainly gave us quite a scare."

Where exactly was "here?" Had he been dropped off at a farmhouse along the road back to town? "I'm sorry, Miss…"

"Collins. Cora Beth Collins. And it's Mrs." She reached for the pitcher on the bedside table and poured a glass of water. "I'm Jo's sister."

This was Josie's *sister?* He'd gotten the impression the livery owner was the provider for her household, that her sister would be younger, like Danny. But this woman appeared to be the older of the two by several years.

Mrs. Collins propped some pillows behind his head and then put the glass to his lips, cutting off any further questions. She, on the other hand, seemed quite happy to chatter on.

"I can't tell you how thankful we all are for the way you saved our Jo. You're a true hero."

Ry choked, sputtering precious drops of water. *Hero.* Didn't the woman know he was the one who'd actually put her sister in harm's way? And what all she'd endured to get him back to town?

Mrs. Collins dabbed his chin with a napkin. "I apologize if I was giving it to you too fast. Let's try that again, but slower this time." She held the glass to his lips again.

"After all that thrashing about," she continued, "I imagine you're hungry as a bear in springtime. But don't you worry none. I've got a nice pot of broth simmering on the stove and I'll fetch you a bowl just as soon as I leave here." She lowered the now empty glass, finally giving him a chance to speak.

"Your sister—" A fit of coughing sent a bolt of fire through his arm, making it impossible to finish his question.

His nurse-hostess made soothing noises and patted his hand until the coughing subsided. "There now," she said when he finally got his breath under control, "don't push yourself too much just yet." She set the glass down and straightened. "As for Jo, she's all right—thanks to you. Bruised up a bit, but she's not letting that slow her down."

Mrs. Collins smoothed the coverlet. "Speaking of Jo, I'd best send word you're awake. She's been worrying over you no end."

Disjointed memories surfaced again. Vague impressions of someone demanding he not be such a "pigheaded fool" and quit trying to get up because he'd fall flat on his face and how it would just serve him right if he did. He could venture a guess as to who'd delivered that acerbic advice.

His hostess stepped back. "You rest up for a bit while I fetch that broth."

"Thank you, Mrs. Collins. I certainly appreciate all you've done for me."

"Glad to do it. After all, you were there for Jo when she needed you."

Her words brought back another memory. How could he have forgotten? "I need to send a telegram."

"Of course. After I fetch your broth—"

"No, this is important." Her expression told him his words had come out too harsh, too abrupt. He fought to moderate his tone. "I'm sorry, but I must send word right away so the person I was traveling to see will know what happened."

Her expression changed into one of concern. "Of course. Your friend must be very worried. I'll fetch a pencil and paper right away."

"Thank you." Ry settled against the pillows and closed his eyes, but not to sleep. His racing thoughts wouldn't allow it. Had Belle given up on him, decided he'd let her down?

"Well, now, don't you look all comfy."

He opened his eyes to see Josie standing in his doorway, shoulder propped against the jamb. How long had she been there?

Wondering how much of his vague memories were real and how much a mere dream, he shifted uncomfortably. "Your sister's a good nurse. Hope I haven't been too much trouble."

A flash of emotion flickered in her eyes then disappeared. "Don't worry about Cora Beth. She's happiest when she has someone to fuss over. And I'm afraid I don't play the part of patient near well enough to satisfy her." She pushed away from the jamb. "Won't find a better mother hen anywhere in the county."

She crossed the room, holding up the paper and pencil she'd brought with her. "I just came in from the livery to check on things and Cora Beth said you were in an all-fired hurry to get a telegram sent off."

"Yes, I—" He frowned as he noticed the way she favored her right leg. "Should you be up and about?"

Her glare was fierce enough to stop a charging bull. "Don't you start in on that. I have enough with Cora Beth nagging at me until I'm about ready to move out and set up camp in the livery."

He sympathized with her sister if this was an indication of the kind of patient Miss Wylie made. "At least it appears your temper hasn't suffered any ill effects."

She grinned. "Sounds like yours is recovering too."

Another allusion to the fact that he might have been less than docile while he was out. "What time is it?"

"Almost one o'clock."

He grimaced. "So, I was out for nearly a day."

"Two. It's Monday."

Two days! And he wasn't likely to be fit for travel

today either. He certainly hoped whatever was plaguing Belle would hold off another few days.

Miss Wylie pulled up a chair next to his bed. "So, I suppose the telegram is for your friend in Foxberry. Guess she's probably worrying over what happened to you. 'Specially since the train started running again this morning."

There was likely an "I told you so" lurking in her words, but Ry decided to ignore it. "Which is why I need to send the telegram off as soon as possible."

She held the pencil over the paper. "Ready whenever you are."

"Send it to Belle Anderson—no, make that Belle Hadley—in Foxberry, Texas." He'd almost forgotten her married name.

Which brought up a question that had nagged at him since he first received her telegram. Where was her husband?

Chapter Eight

Jo scribbled the name and destination. She'd figured it would be this Belle person—he'd kept going on and on about needing to get to her the whole time he'd been locked in that fever. He'd even mistaken her for Belle once and tried to reach out to her.

She pushed that thought aside, feeling uncharitably annoyed by this woman she'd never even met. "What do you want it to say?"

"The text should read *Unavoidably delayed in Knotty Pine. Will resume travel earliest possible or send funds for you to travel here if you prefer. Please advise if there is anything I can do to assist in the interim. Yours, Ry*"

Jo kept her head down as she wrote down his message. Had he been carrying a torch for this woman all these years? Sure sounded like it was someone he was sweet on. And someone who needed a man to look out for her.

Well, *she* didn't need a man to look out for *her*. After all, she'd been taking care of this household for going on six years now without anybody's help.

And once she could ease out from under that yoke,

she was fully prepared to set off to see the world, just like Aunt Pearl, all on her own. No siree, she didn't need a man or anyone else looking out for her.

"Here we go." Cora Beth sailed into the room, carefully balancing a tray holding a steaming bowl of broth. Jo noticed there were also the fancy details her sister was so good at—like a crisply folded napkin and a pair of pansies arranged next to the bowl. A man like Mr. Lassiter probably appreciated such niceties.

Sure enough, he gave her sister a welcoming smile. "Mmm. That smells good."

"Cora Beth's broth is better than Doc Whitman's medicine for what ails you." Jo stood. "I'll stop by the telegraph office on my way to the livery and make sure Amos sends this right away."

Cora Beth set the tray down. "Actually, Jo, I was hoping you'd help Mr. Lassiter with his lunch. I'm doing some baking and can't leave things unattended for long. Besides, Mr. Lassiter has some questions about how he ended up here."

Jo held up the piece of paper. "But the telegram—"

"Don't worry about that." Cora Beth plucked the note from her fingers. "Uncle Grover'll take care of it. And he can let Freddie know you'll be a little late getting back to the livery." With that she breezed out of the room as if the matter were settled.

"Who's Freddie?"

Jo shifted her focus back to the man lying in the bed. "Freddie Boggs. He's the son of one of the local farmers. He helps out at the livery when I can't be there." A telltale rumbling lifted one corner of her mouth. "From the sounds your innards are making I'd say you're ready for this broth."

"It's that loud, is it?"

"Uncle Grover probably heard it clear down the hall."

He winced as he tried to sit up.

She put out a restraining hand. "Hold on. Let me help you."

"I'm not helpless," he grumbled.

"Wasn't saying you were, but no point overdoing it first thing out the chute." She grabbed a quilt from the foot of the bed and folded it into a large, plump rectangle. Then she slipped a hand under his back and provided some support and a little extra push as he sat up.

Once she had the blanket in place, she stood back. "How's that?"

"Comfortable. Thanks." His gaze scanned the room, pausing to study the large pin-covered maps decorating the far wall, before moving on to the mismatched furniture and the wooden train on the top of the chest of drawers.

Finally he turned back to her. "So just where am I?"

"I told you, you're at our place. The boardinghouse."

"But whose room is this?"

She could tell by the way he looked at her that he'd already guessed. There was really no reason for her to feel so selfconscious, but her cheeks warmed anyway. "Mine."

He frowned. "And where are you staying?"

"One of the extra guest rooms upstairs."

"So not only do you come to my rescue *twice* against those thugs, but you give me your room as well. Seems my debt to you keeps mounting."

If only he would stop staring at her so...well, so fiercely.

"Don't get to feeling you're getting special treatment.

The only reason we put you here is because it's on the first floor and saved us having to cart your delirious carcass up the stairs."

She pulled her chair closer and picked up the bowl and spoon. "And it's not like I haven't done this before. Whenever any of the family takes sick they end up in here. It's easier for Cora Beth to keep an eye on the patient when they're close to where she spends most of her days."

"And at night?"

How did he know just what questions to ask to get her all flustered? "We took turns sitting with you." Better not to dwell on how difficult the past two nights had been, how worried she'd been—they'd all been—over his condition.

Jo ladled up a spoonful of broth and gave him her cheeriest smile. "If you think this smells good, just wait until you taste it. Cora Beth is one of the best cooks in these parts."

He swallowed and smiled in agreement. "You're right. It's delicious."

"Like I said, Cora Beth has a real knack for cooking. Come Thanksgiving week, the whole house is going to fill up with some of the most toothsome smells you can imagine. Plumb makes my mouth water just thinking on it."

"Your sister introduced herself as Mrs. Collins. Where's her husband?"

"Philip died just on four years ago."

"And so you moved in with her to help out."

"You have that backward." Jo wasn't quite sure why his misguided assumption bothered her. "This is the home my grandfather built and where we grew up. My sister moved back in here with us." She ladled up another spoonful. "When Philip died, Cora Beth had a two-year-old kid, another on the way and not much in the way of funds."

"So you took her in."

She shrugged. "She's my sister and family takes care of each other. Besides, Ma needed help running the place, not to mention that she liked having her grandchildren close by."

"Liked?"

He sure didn't miss much. "Ma passed away a year after Philip."

"I'm sorry."

"Nothing for you to apologize for—it wasn't your fault. Besides, she got to see her youngest grandkids born and spend time with them. And her passing was easy. She simply went to bed one night and never woke up." Josie stirred the broth before offering him another sip. "Ma never was one to fear dying. Always said she was just passing through this world to get to the next."

He eyed her over the spoon, his expression like Uncle Grover's when he was studying a new kind of bug he'd stumbled on. "So," he said after he'd swallowed, "in addition to running the livery, you take care of a household that includes Danny, and your sister and her two kids."

"Three kids. Cora Beth's youngest turned out to be twins. Then there's Uncle Grover." She could feel the walls closing in on her just listing them all. She loved her family, but sometimes she wished they were a bit more able to fend for themselves.

"Uncle Grover?"

"He's actually Philip's great-uncle. A good man but kind of forgetful-like. Once Philip passed on, Uncle

Grover didn't have anyone else to watch out for him, so he just sort of tagged along with Cora Beth when she moved back here."

"And now he's part of the family too."

"Family's important. And it's not just made up of blood kin. It's like with Danny. When he was just a toddler, his family was passing through town and his pa got bad sick. They stayed here at the boardinghouse 'til he could get his strength back, but he never did. His ma passed two days after his pa."

"And your folks took him in."

"He didn't have anyone else. And he's as much my brother today as makes no never mind."

She thought she saw a shift in her patient's expression, but it was there and gone so quickly she couldn't be sure.

"Mind if I ask a question?"

She rolled her eyes. "Seems like you've done nothing but since you woke up."

He ignored her gibe. "Why did you come after me?"

She ladled up another spoonful. "I saw Clete and Otis ride out after you and something about the way they were acting just didn't smell right. I tried to get the sheriff to handle it but he wasn't around."

"So you decided to come yourself."

"Two against one just didn't seem fair." She lifted her chin. "Sorta like when you came to Danny's rescue."

He gave her a lopsided grin. "Not exactly the same thing. Even the Good Samaritan didn't go chasing after trouble."

"But he didn't shirk his duty, either."

"Even so, it was a brave, selfless act. You could have gotten yourself killed—very nearly did."

She shifted, uncomfortable with the direction this had taken. "But I didn't, thanks mostly to you."

He brushed her words aside. Then he crooked his head. "That first shot, just before the ambush, that wasn't a hunter, was it?"

"It was supposed to be a warning, but I was too late."

"Not too late to save me."

His voice had taken on that deep timbre again—the one that seemed to set an echoing vibration inside her. And he was staring at her as if trying to see deep into her mind. Whatever it was he saw there, his expression made her all fidgety feeling.

Time to change the subject. "So, with Thanksgiving and Christmas coming up, I suppose you'll be spending time at Hawk's Creek with your own family."

His expression closed off. "It depends on how long Belle needs me for."

She nodded sympathetically. "Nice of you to be willing to sacrifice your holiday to help a friend. But maybe it'll work out so you can do both."

He waved a hand, dismissing her concern. "It's not as if they're expecting me. My family doesn't do much to mark the holidays."

She fed him another spoonful of soup while she absorbed that surprising bit of information. "I guess every household has its own set of traditions. But holidays just seem sort of a natural time for gathering close to family."

His expression turned thoughtful. "Actually, it wasn't that way when I was growing up. My mother loved the holidays and started decorating the house in late November. She always gathered family and friends around on Thanksgiving and Christmas, especially those who

were alone. She made the day as festive as she could."
He paused a fraction of a second. "The year I turned
thirteen, though, she passed away two days before
Christmas."

Josie's heart went out to him and his family. "That
must have been hard on all of you."

He seemed to give himself a mental shake. "Naturally none of us felt like celebrating that year," he said
matter-of-factly. "The next year, Pa didn't want us to
bring out any of the decorations mother was so fond of,
or host any of the festivities. So we had a quiet day that,
except for the elaborate meal Inez insisted on cooking,
was barely distinguishable from any other."

For goodness sake! "Your pa should be ashamed of
himself."

"What?" His wrinkled brow told her it wasn't the
reaction he'd been expecting.

"I don't like to speak ill of someone I never met, but
the way he acted seems mighty selfish, to my way of
thinking. He robbed his children of the joy that comes
with celebrating the holidays. And what about the happier memories of your mother? Do y'all ever talk about
her?"

"I don't know how we got off on this subject." There
was a bit of a huff to his tone.

"We were asking each other nosy questions is how."

His brows lifted at that but then he grinned. "So
we were."

He leaned against the pillows as she set aside the
now empty bowl. "Thank your sister for the meal. I'm
feeling stronger already."

"Glad to hear it."

"When's the next train to Foxberry?"

"Tomorrow."

He nodded. "I might need some assistance, but I should be well enough to travel by then."

"Hold on there. I don't care if you have the Queen of Sheba waiting for you in Foxberry, you aren't in any shape to be getting on a train, not until Doc says you are. There'll be another southbound come through in three days. Your friend's waited this long, a few more days won't hurt."

His glare would have stopped a rearing stallion. "I think I'm the best judge of what I can and can't do."

"Oh, yeah. Like you were back at the meadow when you wanted me to head back to town without you?"

His jaw clinched. "That was different."

"Not by my reckoning. Don't think I don't notice the way you flinch every time you move that arm of yours. It's still paining you, and more than just a bit."

"I'll manage."

"Huh! You'll manage. What kind of tomfool statement is that? Doc says you lost a lot of blood and that fever didn't help much. You're weak as a day-old pup and have just about as much sense."

"I'm getting stronger by the minute and I have a whole day to rest. Besides, I don't need a functioning arm to ride a train."

She fisted her hands on her hips. "I didn't follow you all the way out to Whistler's Meadow, play nursemaid over you, and then haul your wounded carcass back here just so you could pass out on some train between here and Foxberry."

"Miss Wylie, I sincerely appreciate all you've done, but I have to get to Foxberry. And no offense, but I don't see as you've much say in the matter."

As if she didn't have enough responsibilities already, now she had a pigheaded patient to deal with. Fool man. He might have come to her rescue, but his shining armor was starting to tarnish.

How could a man who'd so bravely defended first Danny and then her not have enough sense to understand he needed to take it easy until he healed proper? Was it because he was so eager to play the hero for his precious Belle?

She glared down at him. "Oh, don't I? Let's see you get out of this room without your boots or pants."

That caught his attention. He glanced around the room, then back at her with narrowed eyes. "Where are they?"

"In the washroom. Cora Beth takes her duty as lady of the house very serious."

She grabbed the tray with enough force to rattle the dishes and headed for the door. The man ought to realize just how lucky he was. At least he *could* look forward to the day when he could leave. If she were in his place that alone would be enough to sweeten her temper a bit.

Of course, he was in a hurry to see this Belle of his. Jo paused at the doorway and gave him a narrow-eyed look of her own. "Your lady friend will just have to wait a bit longer. If she's worth her salt, she'd want you to take care of yourself first."

From the tightening of his jaw she saw she'd riled him. Well, sometimes that happened when you were looking out for folks. Being in charge of everyone else's welfare didn't always make you the most popular gal around.

And if someone else wanted the job, then by George she was more than willing to let them take over. But so far, no one had come forward to claim it.

Chapter Nine

Ry watched Josie exit the room, his irritation at her high-handedness tempered by a reluctant admiration, and maybe something else. The woman's concern for his well-being was misguided but genuine. She was such an intriguing mix—full of spit and vinegar, but with a generous heart that drove her to try to take care of anyone she thought needed her.

Like him.

He still marveled at the way she'd disregarded her own welfare to come to his rescue, then put herself through the grueling ordeal of getting him back to town. He hadn't felt that kind of focused, genuine concern in a long time, and he wasn't quite certain how to react. It was tempting to stay awhile and try to learn more about her.

But right now his priority had to be Belle. They'd been good friends during those four years she'd spent at Hawk's Creek before he moved to Philadelphia. In fact, she'd been like a sister to him. They'd lost touch after she married—the life of an itinerant preacher's wife wasn't conducive to regular communication. But he still felt that same sense of kinship and responsibility for her he had all those years ago.

What had driven Belle to send that dire-sounding telegram? He shifted restlessly, itching to climb out of bed and head for Foxberry despite Josie's admonitions to the contrary. Those three stark lines from her telegram had played relentlessly through his mind ever since he'd first read it.

SITUATION DESPERATE. MUST SEE YOU WITHOUT DELAY. PLEASE COME.

Why hadn't he thought to send Griff on ahead to see to her? Perhaps he should still—

"My, my, young man, whatever did you do to set Jo off like that?"

Ry turned to find a balding gentleman peering at him over horn rimmed glasses from the doorway. "Sir?"

"Jo. I just passed her stomping down the hall muttering something about 'stubborn, pigheaded fools' under her breath."

Stubborn, huh? Now there was a case of the pot calling the kettle black. "We had a slight disagreement over how soon I'd be well enough to be on my way."

"Oh-ho, I see." Ry's visitor chuckled and stepped into the room. "Jo's not ready to turn loose of her hero just yet."

There was that word again. What had that mind-of-her-own woman been saying while he was unconscious? "I'm no hero, sir. Far from it in fact."

"Jo seems to think otherwise, and she doesn't give praise lightly. I'm Grover Collins by the way."

So this was Josie's Uncle Grover. "Glad to meet you, sir. But you have the story backward. It's Miss Wylie who did the rescuing."

"Please, call me Uncle Grover. And no need to be modest, my boy. Between Danny's account of the fracas in the livery and Josie's telling of the shoot-out in Whistler's Meadow, we're all quite determined to declare you a bona fide hero."

Ry swallowed a groan. "Let's just say, then, that Miss Wylie and I rescued each other."

The older gentleman chuckled. "A man who understands when to dig in his heels and when to compromise. Yes, you'll do."

Do for what?

Uncle Grover, however, seemed ready to change the subject. "Do you like bugs?" he asked.

"Bugs?" Josie had said the man was forgetful, but was he addled as well?

The older man waved a hand. "You know, insects."

"I can't say as I've thought about it much."

"Fascinating creatures. Remarkable, really. Most are highly organized and amazingly efficient." He leaned back on his heels and hooked his thumbs in his suspenders. "People could learn a lot from the way bugs conduct themselves."

Ry relaxed as understanding dawned. "I take it you're an entomologist?"

The man beamed at him. "You're familiar with the science."

"Only in passing."

"Ah, well, we'll remedy that. Once you're feeling better you can accompany me on an entomological expedition. I dare say you'll be surprised at what exciting specimens can be found right here in the woods around Knotty Pine."

"That sounds fascinating, sir, but I'm afraid I'll have to be on my way as soon as I'm able to travel."

"Ah, pity. Well, perhaps you can stop by for another visit on your way back through here."

"Perhaps." Ry kept his response deliberately non-committal.

"Excellent. In the meantime, I'll let you rest. Jo left strict orders not to tire you out with a lot of talk. I'm sure we'll have a chance to chat again before you leave."

So, even though she thought him a "pigheaded fool," she was still worried enough to try to mollycoddle him.

Women sure were a tough lot to understand. Especially this particular, very hard-headed, very intriguing woman.

"Shh, Pippa, you'll wake him up."

Ry roused from a half sleep. Had that been a child's voice? Or was he hallucinating again?

"Is this what a hero looks like, Audrey?" The whisperer sounded doubtful.

Josie's nieces? He was starting to feel like the main attraction at a circus exhibition.

"Of course, silly." There was a definite note of authority in the response. Audrey was undoubtedly the ringleader.

"But he's just laying there."

"I'm glad. I didn't like it when he was carrying on. I thought he was gonna hurt Aunt JoJo."

Ry mentally winced. What had he done while feverish?

"He wouldn't hurt her, Lottie. He's a true enough hero. He got shot up saving her from the bad men, remember?"

Ry opened his eyes to find three little girls standing beside his bed. The two youngest, as alike as a pair of pennies, took an involuntary step back.

The oldest, however, who must be all of six or seven, graced him with a never-met-a-stranger smile. "Hello," she said brightly. "I'm Audrey."

Yep, definitely the ringleader. "Hello, Audrey. And who are your friends?"

"My sisters, Pippa and Lottie. Actually their names are Philippa and Charlotte, because they were named after our pa, Philip Charles Collins. But I wasn't named after anyone so I'm just Audrey."

A chatterbox in addition to being a ringleader. "Well, Just Audrey," he said, "to what do I owe the honor of this visit?"

Audrey giggled. "You even talk like a hero."

Ry resisted the urge to roll his eyes. Was he ever going to live down that appellation? "Why don't you just call me Mr. Lassiter? So, you were around when they brought me in?"

"Yes, sir. You sure were carrying on something awful, arms flying and mumbling about fire and rivers and bells. Momma said you were de-lir-us."

Ry winced at the reminder. And just what had he said about Belle? "My apologies, ladies, if I upset you."

"Oh, you didn't scare us or anything." The self-appointed spokeswoman glanced toward her sisters. "Well, maybe Pippa and Lottie, but only a little. We were just worried 'cause I heard Doc Whitman say you might die from the fever, and that upset Aunt JoJo a lot."

"What are you girls doing in here?" Cora Beth stood in the doorway, a fresh pitcher of water in her hands. "Scat now. Mr. Lassiter's supposed to be resting. And

Audrey, didn't Mr. Saddler assign you some lessons to go over?"

"Yes, ma'am." The three girls scooted past their mother, but not before Audrey gave him a friendly goodbye wave.

"I'm sorry if they disturbed you," Cora Beth said. "I should have known Audrey would head straight here as soon as she got home from school. And of course the twins take their lead from her."

"No need to apologize. They weren't bothering me."

"That's kind of you to say, but we don't want to tax your strength. You're still on the mend, after all."

"Actually, I'm feeling much stronger. Must be that wonderful broth of yours."

She beamed at his compliment. "Why, thank you. I do pride myself on being a passable cook. If you're still here next week for Thanksgiving, I'm planning quite a feast." She set the pitcher on the bedside table. "Still, you mustn't try to do too much too soon. I have enough of that with Jo."

He frowned. "Is something ailing your sister?"

"She got bruised up pretty bad when her horse threw her, not that she'd admit as much. I tried to talk her into taking it easy for a few days, but that sister of mine has a head harder than a brick. That's the only reason Danny hasn't been in to bother you, too—I sent him to relieve her as soon as he got home from school."

Cora Beth shook her head, a look of exasperation on her face. "Not only won't she take it easy, if anything, between watching over you the past two nights and spending all day at the livery, Jo's been working harder than before."

Ry frowned. He'd assumed it was Mrs. Collins who'd sat up with him, not Josie.

His hostess paused in the act of pouring a glass of water and gave him a guilty look. "Oh, dear. I didn't mean to imply—"

"That's all right, ma'am. I should be the one apologizing for the trouble I've caused. And I'm truly grateful to your whole family for all you've done. But you can rest easy—I promise I won't need any watching over tonight."

She gave him a generous smile. "You're a good man. I can see why Jo is so taken with you."

Taken with him? He certainly hadn't seen any signs of that in their last encounter. Other than that whole hero thing. Still, the thought made him smile.

Before she could try to lift the glass to his lips, Ry took it from her with his good hand.

She nodded approvingly. "I can see by the way you were talking to my girls that you're good with children, too. You're going to make a great father someday."

Ry barely avoided choking on his water. Was it mere coincidence that she'd conversationally tied him to both Josie and fatherhood in the matter of seconds? Surely she wasn't trying to play matchmaker between him and her sister.

Not that he had anything against Josie. Sure, she was more gruff than most ladies of his acquaintance, but she was also a bold, spirited woman with lots to offer some lucky man.

Just not him. The two of them would make about as good a match as a cougar and a wolf.

The muffled sound of a hail interrupted his thoughts.

"Oh, there's Dr. Whitmore," Cora Beth said. "He promised to check in on you this afternoon."

The doctor—good. Ry should be able to help convince these nice but overly cautious folks that he was strong enough to travel. It was a train ride after all—not a headlong gallop over rocky terrain.

It was high time he was on his way.

Jo marched down the sidewalk rolling her shoulders and neck to ease the stiffness. Her bruises were mostly healed now, though she still had a tender spot here and there. Not that she'd admit as much to Cora Beth. There was nothing her sister liked better than mollycoddling folks, and nothing Jo liked less than having someone think they knew better than she did what was best for her.

She'd be hanged if she'd pay someone her hard-earned money to watch the livery when she was capable of doing so herself.

"Hey, Jo." Amos stepped out of the telegraph office, waving a piece of paper. "That Lassiter fella's got a response already."

Well, that was fast. "Thanks, I'm just heading up to the house now."

Jo continued down the sidewalk, fighting the urge to unfold the note and read it herself. He'd said he hadn't seen the woman in over twelve years. Why the long separation? Had they had a falling out of some sort? Who'd done what to who?

Was Belle the sort of woman to play on a man's honorable nature to get her way? What if the message made him more anxious than ever to get to Foxberry? What if Belle had awful things to say about him being delayed?

Jo fingered the telegram as she paused on the front porch. The last thing Mr. Lassiter needed was more guilt heaped on his plate right now.

Her finger was actually between the folds when she got hold of herself. No matter her reasons, it was wrong to pry in someone else's personal business.

But so help her, if this Belle tried to make him feel the least bit guilty...

She found Mr. Lassiter's door open a crack, but knocked anyway. "Hello, it's me, Jo."

The bed creaked and then he said something she couldn't quite make out. Deciding it was an invitation to enter, she pushed the door wider. Then frowned as she saw him swaying on the edge of the bed.

"Just what in blue blazes do you think you're doing?"

"Sitting up," he said through gritted teeth.

"And a fine job you're doing of it, too." She marched across the room and set the telegram on the bedside table. "Here, let me help you back down."

It was an indication of how much the effort had cost him that he didn't protest. "Let me guess," she said as she straightened the coverlet over him once more, "you were planning to sneak out and walk to Foxberry."

The sideways look he cut her was a mix of exasperation and exhaustion. She suddenly felt sorry she'd fussed at him.

"Just testing my limits." His voice sounded forced.

"Is that what the doc told you to do?"

"He gave me the usual doctor talk about getting plenty to eat and lots of rest. He also said that, so long as I didn't overtax myself, I should regain most of my strength in short order."

"Looks to me like you're doing a bit of that over-taxing now."

He set his jaw. "Regardless of any ideas you have to the contrary, I plan to get on that train tomorrow."

They'd see about that. Rather than challenge him, though, she changed the subject. "Speaking of Foxberry, you got an answer to your telegram already."

His expression shifted, and the tension in his jaw was back. "Read it to me."

Jo lifted the telegram, hating herself for her eagerness to learn what it had to say. Then she hesitated. "You sure?"

He nodded.

She glanced down and read the first line.

REGRET TO INFORM YOU BELLE HADLEY PASSED AWAY YESTERDAY

Jo's hand went to her throat as the words sunk in. Dead!

She'd been so callous about his concern, had dismissed his impatience to get to his friend as mere eagerness to see her again. She should have been more supportive, should have believed in his instincts about the urgency of the matter.

The look on his face almost did her in. There was such self-recrimination, such loss reflected there.

"What else does it say?" The strain in his voice was painful to hear.

Her hands shook slightly as she read the rest of the message.

WILL ARRIVE ON NEXT TRAIN TO DE-LIVER VIOLA AND OTHER BELONGINGS LEFT TO YOU. REV EDMOND FIELDS

He'd been too late. And now Belle was dead.

How had she died? Was there something he could have done to prevent this? Is that why she'd wanted so desperately for him to come to her?

Why hadn't he left Philadelphia as soon as he received her telegram? That one afternoon he'd spent wrapping up his current case might have made all the difference.

"Mr. Lassiter, I'm so sorry. I had no idea…"

He gave himself a mental shake, trying to focus on the present. Josie had such a stricken look on her face. "It's not your fault."

"It's not yours, either."

The firmness of her tone surprised him. But he wasn't so certain his delay hadn't been at least partially responsible. He wouldn't know until he spoke to this Reverend Fields. At least he hoped the clergyman would have answers for him.

Why hadn't he done more to keep in touch with Belle?

"She was a musician?"

"What? Oh, the viola. Yes, Belle loved music. I suppose she must have acquired an instrument along the way."

"Want me to have someone meet the train for you on Wednesday?"

He shook off the memories. "I'd appreciate that." No point in pushing himself now. He'd have a two day wait to get his answers. Assuming this Reverend Fields *had* the answers he sought.

Ry felt her troubled gaze on him, sensed her uncertainty as the silence drew out. But he had nothing in him to say, no reassurance to offer right now.

Finally she set the telegram on the table and shoved

her hands in her pockets. "I'll see if Cora Beth has another bowl of broth ready."

He nodded. With one final searching look, she left the room.

The fact that Belle had left him her belongings tore at Ry's already shredded conscience. It spoke to the fact that she'd had no one else she felt close to there at the end.

And she hadn't even had him with her to ease her final hours.

Chapter Ten

R<small>y</small> spent what was left of the day being the perfect patient. He ate every bit of food sent his way. He played three rounds of checkers with Danny. When Uncle Grover brought in a collection of moths he'd acquired, not only did Ry admire them but he asked all the right questions to give the gentleman an opportunity to expound on their individual characteristics. He even got out of bed long enough to walk across his room and back.

In short, he tried to keep himself too occupied to dwell on the news about Belle. But that night he lay awake long after the last lamp was trimmed. All he could think about was that he'd failed Belle, without having any idea what she'd needed from him.

The next morning, Josie brought in his breakfast tray right after sunrise. "Figured you'd be up early. I thought I'd save Cora Beth the trouble and bring this in before I head over to the livery."

"Thanks." He managed to sit up without her assistance.

"How you feeling today?"

"Better." He was pleased to see the tray contained a

second dish. He'd had enough of his own company for a while. Josie pulled a chair up beside the bed, took a seat and lifted the extra dish. "Hope you don't mind if I join you." She wanted to gauge his mood this morning, to see how he was coping with what had happened.

"Company's always welcome."

She situated his plate in comfortable reach, then speared a bit of egg from her own dish. She decided there was no point beating around the bush. "What are you planning to do now that you don't need to go to Foxberry?"

He gave her a surprised look, then shrugged. "Wait for Reverend Fields to arrive and find out what happened to Belle."

"Then what? You going back to Philadelphia, or to Hawk's Creek?"

"I'll probably stop in at the ranch and visit with Griff and Sadie for a week or so."

Being around family would likely be good for him. "I'm sure they'll be right glad to have you home for Thanksgiving."

"I'm not certain I'll stay that long." He must have read the surprise in her face. "As I've said before, the Lassiter family doesn't expend much effort celebrating holidays."

That still didn't seem right, but she had something more pressing to discuss. "Do you want to talk about her?"

He paused, as if seriously considering her question. At least he hadn't taken offense.

"She was the niece of our ranch foreman," he said slowly. "The summer I turned twelve, her folks died and she came to live with him. Harvey was a good man and a great foreman, but he didn't know anything about raising kids, especially girls. And Belle was a city girl—she'd never lived on a ranch before."

"So you took her under your wing?" Seems he'd had that hero streak even then.

"It wasn't my idea." His voice sounded defensive. Then he gave a sheepish smile. "I was a twelve-year-old boy, after all."

He pushed around the last bit of egg on his plate. "Belle spent a lot of time in the kitchen with Inez at first, but Mother thought it would be good for her to have someone her own age to spend time with. So she suggested I give Belle riding lessons."

"And y'all became friends." Jo tried to imagine what twelve-year-old Ry had been like and felt a little stab of jealousy toward Belle.

He nodded. "Before long she was like a sister to me."

A sister, huh? Jo perked up a bit. "Thought you already had a sister."

"Sadie's five years younger than me." He pointed his fork at her. "When you're twelve, that's a big difference. Belle was my age."

He leaned back, his expression turning inward. "Once Belle was comfortable in the saddle, whenever I wasn't busy with chores, we took long rides all around the ranch. I showed her all of my favorite places. Taught her how to do birdcalls and how to fish. And I listened to her talk about what her life had been like before her folks died."

Yep, definitely a hero in the making. "I'm sure that meant a lot to her."

"It wasn't all one-sided. Her father had been a whip maker and had taught her how to use one. And she taught me." His expression turned sober. "It was about a year after she arrived that my mother died. Belle... well, Belle had been through that before. It was good to have her to talk to."

Jo placed a hand on his arm before she'd consciously formed the thought to do so.

He stared at her hand for a long moment, an unreadable expression on his face. Just as she started to pull away, he met her gaze, his eyes filled with something that looked suspiciously like gratitude.

A second later the expression was gone and he reached for his glass as she pulled her arm back. "So, is this Freddie you mentioned yesterday the only help you have at the livery?"

Ready to change the subject, was he? "He watches the place at night. Actually, he sleeps mostly. But it means someone is there to keep an eye on things."

"What about someone to help during the day?"

"Not necessary. I can handle most of the business that comes my way, and Danny helps out after school if I need him to." She gave him a dry smile. "And there's always Uncle Grover to help out in a pinch."

"Did I hear my name?" Uncle Grover stood in the doorway, smiling jovially at the two of them. He set his focus on Josie. "Cora Beth wanted me to remind you to stop at Mrs. Potter's and see how many pumpkin pies she wants for the Thanksgiving baskets this year."

"Will do. And you're just in time to keep Mr. Lassiter company. I need to head off to the livery."

Jo left the room, her mind rolling the conversation over in her thoughts like a river stone between her fingers. She'd learned a lot about the kind of man Ry was just by reading between the lines of what he'd said.

And she'd give a pretty penny to know just what it was that had shone in his eyes when he stared into hers a few minutes ago.

Remembering that look, something warm and soft seemed to unfurl inside her.

For once, Ry didn't mind seeing Josie go. It was high time he got out of bed, and accomplishing that would be a lot easier without her around to admonish him for trying to do too much.

Uncle Grover, on the other hand, was easily recruited to help him clean up a bit and shave.

With that taken care of Ry felt almost civilized again.

Uncle Grover stayed around afterward, apparently taking Josie's words to entertain him to heart. Ry was treated to a surprisingly interesting discussion on the various species of grasshoppers in the area and their feeding and migratory habits. At one point, the older gentleman left, only to return shortly with a board, affixed to which was a grouping of grasshoppers, carefully labeled and arranged by size.

In the course of their visit, Ry managed to slip in a few questions of his own about the Wylie household. He found the answers enlightening.

The older man left no doubt that Cora Beth was the domestic center of this household, fussing over everyone like a mother hen, keeping them well fed, clothed and healthy. But there was another thread running through the conversation, offhand references to Josie, that strengthened Ry's perception that she was the glue holding them together, the one they looked to for direction. A very capable woman with a lot of heart.

Like the way she'd listened to him talk about Belle

this morning. There'd been a moment of connection then, as if...

No, he was imagining things. It was just that they'd been through something intense together, that was all.

Which reminded him...

Ry penciled a note and had Uncle Grover promise to take it to the telegraph office. Assuming Griff followed his instructions, that would take care of one of the debts he owed Josie, whether she wanted repayment or not.

Shortly after Uncle Grover left, Cora Beth brought Ry his lunch. To his relief, instead of another serving of broth, it was a hearty bowl of rabbit stew. She offered to stay and help him eat, but Ry assured her he was capable of feeding himself.

"I'm glad to hear you're feeling stronger today. Call me if you need anything else." She flashed a teasing smile. "After lunch you'd better rest up while you can. When Danny and Audrey get home from school they'll be wanting to pester you some more."

"I don't mind their company," Ry assured her. And he meant it. The last thing he wanted right now was to be alone with his own thoughts.

But the early afternoon hours drew out interminably.

He pushed aside thoughts of Belle and his failure to reach her. What's done was done, and all the guilt in the world wouldn't change it. There were still questions to be answered, but those would have to wait until tomorrow.

It would be more productive to focus on resolving issues he still had control over. Like figuring out the answer to the question Josie had asked him.

Where *did* he call home?

It was a question that had begun to niggle at him with

increasing frequency since his father's death two years ago. He'd never intended to spend his life in Philadelphia, had always figured he'd return to Texas someday to open a law practice of his own. Somehow, though, the time had never seemed quite right.

Perhaps now it was.

Ry moved his injured arm, trying to ease into a more comfortable position. And realized he was no longer alone.

Two identical pairs of eyes stared up at him from the foot of his bed. "Hello."

"Hello," they answered in unison.

"Is there something I can do for you?"

Two pigtail-adorned heads nodded.

"And what might that be?"

One of the girls moved to the side of the bed where he could get a better look at her. She was closely followed by her sister, who kept both hands behind her back.

"Lottie needs a hero," the first child, obviously Pippa, proclaimed solemnly.

Uh-oh. This did not sound good. Why were they coming to him for help instead of their mother? He had absolutely no experience with children—especially ones in crisis. "And just why does Lottie need a hero?" he asked cautiously.

Lottie moved her hands forward, revealing one fist stuck inside a preserve jar. "It won't come off," she said, her voice ending on a sniffle.

Please, Lord, don't let her start crying, at least not before I can get her mother in here. "Does it hurt?" He kept his voice calm, hoping it would help soothe the child.

She shook her head, another sniffle escaping.

No pain—that was good. "Well, then, there's no reason to fret. We'll just get your mother to—"

"Oh, no!" Pippa shook her head violently. "We can't tell Ma. That's why we need a hero."

Ry eyed her suspiciously. "And just why can't you tell your mother?"

"Because we weren't supposed to be playing with Danny's things," she said in a rush of words. "But we didn't go in his room, honest. He left two of his marbles on the floor in the kitchen. We just wanted to play with them for a little while, then we were going to put them right back."

Ry hid a smile at her rationalizations. "What do Danny's marbles have to do with getting Lottie's hand stuck in the jar?"

"We put them there so they wouldn't get losted. But when Lottie tried to get them out, she got stuck."

"I see. Come closer so I can have a look at your problem."

Lottie dutifully moved forward and set her hand, jar and all, on the bed next to him.

"Did you try opening your fist?" he asked.

Lottie nodded.

"We pulled and pulled but it just won't come out," Pippa said, joining her sister. "Can you help us?"

He studied the small hand. It appeared swollen, but not injured. "I think so." He looked at Pippa. "Can you fetch me some lard from the kitchen?"

The child nodded.

"I need a great big spoonful."

With another nod, Pippa turned and raced out of the room, leaving Ry alone with the still sniffling Lottie. He sent a silent "hurry up" plea Pippa's way. "Don't worry," he said awkwardly. "We'll have your hand out of there in just a few minutes." Hurry Pippa.

Lottie gave him a wide-eyed, trusting look, and nodded solemnly. At least the sniffles had stopped.

Pippa returned, a spoonful of lard bobbing precariously in her hand. "Here it is."

"Good. Now, take some and smear it all around the part of Lottie's wrist you can reach and around the inside lip of the jar."

"This feels icky," Pippa complained. But she did as he'd instructed.

"All right, Pippa, that looks good. Lottie, I'm going to hold the jar and I want you to ease your hand out, nice and slow. Okay?"

Holding the base of the jar with one hand, Ry watched with satisfaction as the small, well-greased hand did indeed slide right out of the jar.

Both girls looked at him with bright, relieved smiles. "See, Lottie," Pippa said, "I told you heroes help people who are in trouble."

Ry handed the jar back to Lottie. "You girls put this back where it belongs, and I suggest you wash your hands as best you can if you don't want your ma to ask what you've been up to."

With a chorus of thank yous, they skipped out of the room.

Ry chuckled, relieved that their problem had been so easy to resolve.

Would that his own could be handled so easily.

Chapter Eleven

As predicted, Danny and Audrey both stopped by to visit once school was out. Neither visit was quite as dramatic as the one with the twins, though.

Audrey sat on the chair next to his bed, swinging her legs and telling him about her day, from the time she stepped into the classroom to the moment she came home. The highlight, apparently, had been when she received her assigned part for the upcoming Thanksgiving program. Thanksgiving, it appeared, was a major event in Knotty Pine.

"I'm going to be a gardener," she said. "I can tell everyone why I'm thankful for the sun and the rain and the seeds and the fruit and everything."

And for Audrey, "everything" would undoubtedly be taken literally.

Danny came by next and challenged him to another game of checkers. They played two, winning one apiece.

Once he left, Ry tried to sleep, and to his surprise, did drift off for a short nap.

When he woke up, he decided he'd been confined

long enough. It was time he tested his legs on something more ambitious than crossing the room.

Moving with care, Ry got dressed. He appreciated the use of Uncle Grover's sleep shirts but it would feel good to be in his own clothes again. Maneuvering his injured arm into the shirt sleeve caused more than one wince, but getting his boots on was even trickier.

Once he was fully dressed he had to sit again to get his second wind. He contemplated leaving off the sling, but then decided it was best not to ignore the doctor's advice just for the sake of his pride.

At last he stood and crossed the room, determined to prove to himself and the Wylie household that he was no longer an invalid.

Once in the hallway, Ry paused to get his bearings. His room—or rather Josie's—was situated on the far end of a long corridor. Based on the enticing smells emanating from the room across the hall, he'd guess that would be the kitchen. Which was probably a good place to start.

When he pushed open the door, Cora Beth looked up from the stove. "Why, Mr. Lassiter, whatever are you doing up and about? If you're hungry, all you had to do—"

He held up a hand. "No need to fret, ma'am. That is, I *am* hungry but that's not why I'm here. I figured it was past time I started doing for myself again. I've imposed on your hospitality long enough."

"Don't be silly." She wiped her hands on her apron. "While I'm glad you're feeling well enough to be up and about, you were a very undemanding patient." She turned to her oldest. "Audrey, please set another place at the table for Mr. Lassiter."

"Yes, ma'am."

Josie pushed through the door, brushing past her niece. "Cora Beth, if you have Mr. Las—" She stopped short when she saw him standing there.

"What in blue blazes are you doing up?" She fisted her hands on her hip.s "You should—"

"I'm fine," he said firmly. He rather liked the way her eyes flashed when she was irritated.

Cora Beth intervened before Josie could continue to argue.

"Jo, why don't you take him in and introduce him to everyone while I dish up the peas."

Seeing the stubborn thrust of Josie's chin, he thought she might refuse. But she finally gave a curt nod and headed back into the hallway.

Without saying a word or slowing her step, she escorted him past what appeared to be a large dining room and to a door near the front entryway. Ry followed her into a comfortably appointed parlor containing three unfamiliar persons.

"Mr. Lassiter," Josie said with uncharacteristic formality, "allow me to introduce you to Mrs. Beulah Plunkett, her daughter Honoria, and the town's schoolteacher, Mr. Odell Saddler."

Ry nodded a greeting to each in turn.

"Folks, this is Mr. Ryland Lassiter, the gent I told you about."

Mrs. Plunkett, an elderly woman whose figure and hook-shaped nose put him in mind of a plump parrot, spoke first. "So you're the young man who fought off those hooligans."

He bowed, hiding a grimace. "With Miss Wylie's help."

"Modest as well as dashing—an admirable combination. Don't you agree, Honoria?"

The younger woman, as slight and shy as her mother was broad and outspoken, flushed. "Yes, indeed, Mama," she responded, without ever quite meeting his gaze.

Mr. Saddler intervened, mercifully taking the spotlight from the younger woman. "Tell us, sir, where did you travel from?"

"Philadelphia."

"Really." The schoolteacher leaned forward. "How fascinating. Philadelphia is such a rich cornucopia of our nation's history." The man's face all but glowed with enthusiasm. "Have you advantaged yourself of the museums and exhibitions?"

"On a number of occasions."

"Ah, I envy you." He gave a self-deprecating smile. "I'm a bit of a history enthusiast."

Danny stepped in the doorway with a quick "Dinner's ready" announcement before disappearing again.

As they trooped into the dining room, Ry was surprised to discover everyone ate together, boarders and family, from Uncle Grover right down to Pippa and Lottie. But the double-sized room with the proportionally long table easily accommodated all of them, with room to spare.

Uncle Grover took a place at the head of the table and Mrs. Collins took hers at the foot. Ry had every intention of sitting next to Josie, but somehow found himself holding a chair out for Mrs. Plunkett instead.

The next forty minutes was an interesting experience for Ry. Conversations were lively and the subject matters wide-ranging. Everyone contributed, including the children, joining in or not as the mood struck them. Discussions ranged from how everyone's day had gone, to next week's Thanksgiving festivities, to the relative merits of this year's crop of pears versus last year's. Audrey chattered on about her role in the upcoming school program and Danny bragged about how he could have won the schoolyard game of mumblety-peg if the tip of his knife hadn't broken off in the last round.

It was chaos, but a comfortable sort of chaos, wrapping itself around Ry like a brightly-colored patchwork quilt on a chilly evening. This was what a family should be, he thought, what his *had* been before his mother died.

Ry found his gaze drifting to Josie time and again throughout the meal. He was glimpsing a side of her he hadn't seen before. Gone was the guarded, overly-responsible, got-to-fix-everyone's-problems personality she normally wore with him. Instead he saw a relaxed woman who laughed and teased and chatted comfortably with those around her, a woman who had the confidence that came with knowing she belonged.

He envied her that.

Jo kept a surreptitious eye on Mr. Lassiter throughout the meal. He seemed to be holding up well, considering all he'd been through. He was doing more observing than joining in, but that might have more to do with his being seated next to Mrs. Plunkett than with his recovery. The woman tended to dominate any conversation she took part in.

Still, he didn't show any signs he was ailing. In fact, he looked mighty good. She straightened, giving her head a mental shake. She'd meant from a health perspective, of course.

She glanced toward Pippa and Lottie, and felt herself soften again. When she'd arrived home this evening she'd caught them whispering, and in no time had gotten the story of the hand in the jar incident out of them. It seemed Ry was a hero in more than one sense of the word.

He glanced across the table just then and his gaze met hers. A slow, appreciative smile warmed his face and Jo's breath caught in her throat. Then his attention was captured by a comment from Mr. Saddler and his gaze released her, allowing her to breathe again.

She glanced down at her plate, confused. How could one fleeting smile from him leave her feeling so tingly and on edge? She must still be tuckered out from those nights spent watching over him, waiting for his fever to break. A good night's rest would put things back in proper perspective.

She was relieved when the meal finally came to an end. As usual, Mrs. Plunkett and Honoria retired to their rooms while Mr. Saddler stepped out for his evening constitutional.

Mr. Lassiter stood, looking uncertain about what to do with himself.

He had a big day tomorrow, one that was likely to be difficult for him. And regardless of how he looked, he'd already been up and about long enough for the first time out of his sickbed.

"Mr. Lassiter," she said, claiming his attention, "would you like Uncle Grover to help you back to your room?"

122 The Christmas Journey

He frowned. "No, thank you, I can manage on my own."

There was no need for him to sound so prickly. She was only thinking of his health. "Well, then, please don't let us keep you from your rest."

That annoyed frown made another appearance. Then he turned to Cora Beth. "That was a wonderful meal, ma'am."

"Why, thank you. I'm glad you enjoyed it."

"I wonder if you have any reading material I might borrow?"

"Sure do," Jo answered before Cora Beth could say anything. Did he think they were illiterate? "There's a bookcase plumb full of books in the family parlor."

"Why don't you show him where that is," Cora Beth suggested. "We'll get started with the evening chores."

Mr. Lassiter paused. "If there's anything I can do to help—"

"Don't be silly." Cora Beth waved him off. "You're our guest. Go on with Jo and find yourself something to read."

Now why did he take Cora Beth's concern with a smile while he frowned at hers?

Jo mulled that over as she dutifully led him to the family parlor, the one room their boarders never entered. She opened the door and waved him inside. "The bookcase is there on your left."

Leaning against the jamb, she crossed her arms while he looked over the titles. It might not be much compared to what he was used to, but she was certain there was enough there to satisfy his needs for today. There were Uncle Grover's insect books, Aunt Pearl's books about far-off places, Cora Beth's poetry books, some morality tales and lighter fiction, books about gardening and some of her father's books about carriages and harnesses.

He finally selected two volumes. "These should do for now. Thanks for the loan."

She straightened, shoving her hands in her pockets. "Feel free to come in here and fetch a book whenever you want."

They stared at each other awkwardly for a moment. Then he gave her a crooked smile. "Guess I'll head back to my room and put these to good use."

"Yes, of course." She stepped aside to let him pass.

But not quite far enough. His arm brushed against hers and she was startled by the way her pulse jumped in response. Had he felt it too?

She watched him walk away, absently rubbing the place on her arm he'd touched. There was no sign that his injuries were bothering him.

Or anything else, for that matter.

Chapter Twelve

Ry closed the book with a resounding *thunk*. He'd read the same page three times and still had no idea what it contained. Not that it was the book's fault. The part of the travelogue he'd managed to absorb proved both entertaining and informative.

Trouble was, he found himself unable to concentrate. Too many of his own thoughts crowded out the words on the page. He eyed the bed from his vantage across the room with a jaundiced eye. No doubt the same restlessness that kept him from enjoying the book would prevent him from sliding into an easy slumber.

Muted sounds of conversation and laughter floated in under the door. So, the Wylie household hadn't turned in for the night yet.

The sound was seductive, enticing.

It had been quite some time since he'd been in a true family setting. Life at his grandfather's was comprised of a string of formal interactions. On the few occasions each year when he returned to the ranch, he and his siblings interacted with each other like near-strangers.

And at supper he'd felt like one of the boarders. Allowed into the Wylie family circle for a time, but still an outsider. Sort of the way it was when he tried to pin down his own family life. Part of both worlds, belonging in neither. Was it something about him? Had he forgotten how to get close to people?

What would it feel like to be a member of a large, demonstrative family like the Wylies?

He shook his head, pushing away that thought. There was no point getting too close to these folks. Once he met with Reverend Fields tomorrow and found out what he could about Belle's last days, he planned to head over to Hawk's Creek. Probably never pass this way again.

For some reason, that thought didn't sit well with him either.

He dropped the book on a side table and stood. On the other hand, it wasn't as if he'd form any long-term attachments just from joining them for an evening.

Before he could change his mind, Ry headed for the door.

When he stepped into the kitchen he had a few moments to look around before anyone noticed him.

The Wylie family—blood kin and otherwise—were gathered around the table. Cora Beth sat at one end with some sewing, an oil lamp at her elbow.

Audrey stood on a chair nearby, reciting what sounded like lines for the Thanksgiving program with all the verve and passion of a seasoned thespian. Pippa and Lottie sat cross-legged at her feet, playing the part of rapt audience.

Halfway down the table, Uncle Grover and Danny were shelling pecans and having a lively discussion that had the older man gesticulating enthusiastically.

It was Josie, though, who caught and held his attention. Was she carving a pumpkin?

Then Danny said something Ry didn't quite catch and Josie, laughing, reached across the table, snagged a bit of pecan shell and tossed it at him.

The cozy family scene, complete with the scent of a pie in the oven and a warmth that came as much from the people as from the cook stove, sent an unexpected pang through Ry, one he refused to analyze too closely.

A moment later Josie looked up, and, predictably, greeted him with a frown. "Shouldn't you be resting?"

He ignored both her question and tone, turning instead to Cora Beth. "I hope I'm not intruding. It's too early for sleep and I'm afraid the book I chose didn't hold my interest as I'd hoped."

"Please, come on in," she answered with a warm smile. "You're more than welcome to join us."

Josie set her knife down and pulled a chair out. "Here, have a seat." It was more command than suggestion.

"Thanks." As he eased into the chair, the others resumed their activities.

"What's that you're working on?" he asked, nodding toward the pumpkin.

She shrugged, her face reddening slightly. "Cora Beth cleaned out this pumpkin yesterday to make some pies. I'm just tinkering around with the shell."

"Jo's being far too modest," Cora Beth interrupted. "She's a real artist with a carving knife."

Ry studied Josie's handiwork and found he agreed with Cora Beth. The top third had been artfully removed from the pumpkin, leaving a bowl shape with a fluted rim. But it was the design on the bowl itself that was truly remarkable. A dragonfly hovered above an almost-completed flower. The detail was amazing.

"Just trying out a new design I might use for the Thanksgiving Celebration." Josie sounded uncharacteristically hesitant. "Not sure yet if I like it."

"Well, I do." Ry's words earned him a pleased smile from Josie. "So what's this Thanksgiving Celebration?"

"It's like a big party," Danny answered. "The whole town gathers together. There's lots of food and games and contests. And the grown-ups dance."

Ry smiled at the sour face the boy made over that last bit.

"Don't forget the pageant," Audrey chimed in.

"Jo's pumpkins and gourds are used as decorations," Cora Beth paused mid-stitch to explain. "They hold fruit and flowers, and once evening sets in, they're used to hold candles."

"Does that mean you're going to be making a lot of pumpkin pies?"

Josie laughed. Ry decided he liked the sound of it.

"Most of the ladies around here donate the empty shells from their own cooking," she said. "By next week we'll be tripping over pumpkin shells and gourds around here."

"I'm sure that'll be a sight." Not that he'd be here to see it.

"Is this enough?" Danny held up the bowl of pecans for Cora Beth's inspection.

She put a finger to her chin as she studied his offering. Finally she nodded. "I suppose you've earned yourself an extra piece of fruitcake when we cut it."

Danny let out a whoop that echoed through the room.

"Must be some fruitcake," Ry said dryly.

"Yes, sir. Best you're ever gonna taste."

"It's a holiday tradition around here," Josie added. "Both for Thanksgiving and Christmas. Lot's of folks want one for their own table, and they fetch a handsome price. In fact she has two in the oven right now."

Ry noticed the pride in Josie's tone. "Sounds like quite a delicacy."

"That they are," she said. "Cora Beth takes a blue ribbon at the county fair every year."

"Now you all hush before you give me a big head. I'm certain Mr. Lassiter has been to any number of fancy restaurants that serve finer desserts than my fruitcake."

"Well, ma'am, there's been many a time when I would've traded those so-called fancy restaurants for good home cooking."

Cora Beth set her needlework aside and stood. "Then we'll cut one right now."

Ry held up a hand in protest. "Please, I wasn't angling for a taste. Especially if you have customers waiting in line." He didn't want to steal from their livelihood.

"Nonsense," she waved a hand dismissively, already taking saucers from the cupboard. "The family usually samples a few of them, anyway."

"Just to make certain she hasn't lost her touch." The crinkles at Uncle Grover's eyes belied his serious tone.

"In that case, I confess to being both curious and eager to try a bite."

"Hey, girls!" Danny set down his bowl of pecans. "We're going to slice into one of the fruitcakes."

Ry accepted the dessert-laden saucer and forked up a bite, aware that every eye in the room was on him. He mentally prepared himself to give them the reaction they expected, no matter what.

Because, as Cora Beth had said, he'd eaten at some of the finest restaurants in New England. And he'd dined at the homes of socially prominent hostesses who prided themselves on hiring only the best chefs for their kitchens. He'd be very surprised if this dessert could compete with their signature creations.

But as soon as the first bite entered his mouth, Ry found he didn't have to pretend. This was unlike any cake he'd ever tasted. It had a robust, burst-in-your-mouth flavor, both ambrosially sweet and slightly tart at the same time, without any of the heaviness usually associated with fruitcakes. And there was an underlying flavor he couldn't quite identify that added a tantalizing zest to the whole.

"Mmm. I understand why these are so popular."

"It's Cora Beth's own recipe," Josie bragged. "She uses a honey syrup and spiced apple cider and some other special ingredients. Ladies around these parts have been trying to pry the recipe from her for ages."

Ry eyed Josie thoughtfully. Even though he knew Cora Beth could drive her crazy, she hadn't stopped bragging on her sister since he'd entered the room. There was a deep bond between the members of this family that he found oddly touching.

He cleared his throat and refocused on the rest of the room. "So, are these only available to locals, or can anyone order one?" Purchasing some of the fruitcakes would be a way to repay part of the debt he owed the Wylies.

But Cora Beth shook her head. "If you're wanting one for yourself, we'll just consider it an early Christmas present."

"No, no. I was actually thinking of purchasing several as gifts. One for my brother and sister, one for the hands at the ranch, one for my grandfather, one for his law partner..."

Cora Beth laughed. "My goodness, if you keep adding on orders you're going to become my biggest customer ever."

"Absolutely." He pointed his fork at her. "Honestly, this will be a huge help to me. I never know what sort of gifts to get for my family and friends at Christmas, but each and every one of them will love this."

Cora Beth relented at once. "Well, of course, if you're certain you want them, just let me know how many and I'll add your order to my list."

"A dozen ought to cover it."

Cora Beth blinked, her eyes growing rounder. "My goodness, a dozen?"

"If that's not too much trouble."

He caught the speculative look Josie shot his way. Was she on to him? Had he overdone it?

"No, no, not at all," Cora Beth said. "I've just never had such a large order from one person before."

"In Philadelphia you'd have folks banging down your door, begging for the chance to order these."

"Hey, why don't we play the 'where in the world' game?" Danny had obviously grown tired of this talk of food.

"I don't know, Danny." Josie carried her own saucer to the sink. "Mr. Lassiter probably—"

"But we always play it when we have someone new at the boardinghouse," Danny protested.

"Mr. Lassiter isn't exactly a boarder."

Ry wondered if her reluctance had anything to do

with him. He leaned back. "What is this 'where in the world' game?"

"Jo made it up," Danny explained. "When someone new comes around, we ask them to name the most interesting place they've ever visited. Then they have to say what makes that place so interesting to them."

Ry gave Josie a considering look, remembering the maps covering the walls of her room, as well as the things she'd told him about her Aunt Pearl. "I see. Sure, I'll be glad to play."

Everyone took a seat and stared at him expectantly.

"Let me think—the most interesting place. Hmm. I'd say that would be New York Harbor."

Josie still leaned back against the sink, but even from this distance he could sense the keenness of her interest, almost feel the thirst she seemed to have for his words. And he suddenly wanted to paint the most vivid picture he could.

"Why there?" Danny asked.

"It's an energetic place," he answered, keeping his eyes focused on Josie. "I've never seen anything like it. It's busier than a stirred-up ant hill. People coming and going, speaking more languages than you would have heard at the Tower of Babel, goods from the most commonplace to the unimaginably exotic being loaded and unloaded on the docks, the smells of spices and smoke mingling with that of fish and brine. And everything moving at a pace that makes you dizzy just remembering it all." He looked around at each of them in turn, then returned his gaze to Josie. "But none of that is what makes it the most memorable place I've been to."

He paused, deliberately taking another bite, inexplicably wishing he could actually show her the sight that had so captured his own imagination.

"Then what is it?" Audrey finally asked.

Ry smiled and pointed his fork at the child. "The most amazing thing of all is the Statue of Liberty, standing tall and beautiful, guarding the harbor." His gaze slid back to Josie. "It's a sight that, once seen, can never be forgotten. She stands a little over three hundred feet tall and is majestic in a way that has to be seen to be appreciated. She's an especially stirring sight when one is returning home after a trip abroad."

The faces around him showed varying levels of interest, but in Josie's he saw a longing, an almost painful yearning that made him want to scoop her up and take her there straightaway.

"Three hundred feet." Danny whistled, breaking the spell. "Why, that's even taller than the church steeple."

Ry nodded. "Probably about ten times taller."

"Amazing." Cora Beth stood. "But we don't want to tire Mr. Lassiter out with all our questions. Girls, it's time for the three of you to get ready for bed. I'll be up to tuck you in and hear your prayers as soon as I clear these dishes."

"You go on," Josie offered. "I'll finish up for you."

Ry caught Cora Beth's look of surprise, quickly followed by a flash of understanding. "Thanks," she said. "Danny, please check the lamps on the landing. Uncle Grover, would you please lock the front door for me before you head upstairs?"

The older man stood. "Come along, Danny, my boy, it seems we have our marching orders."

In a surprisingly short time, Ry and Josie were alone in the kitchen. He should head back to his room, but he was strangely reluctant to leave. Instead, he stared at her back, watching her wash and rinse the dishes with the same efficiency she tackled everything she set her mind to.

He studied the carved pumpkin, noticing the delicate detail, the fine craftsmanship, so at odds with the impulsive, heavyhanded image she projected. The contradictions in this woman continued to intrigue him.

"I've seen pictures of the Statue of Liberty," she said, breaking into his thoughts. "I bet it's really something to see in real life."

"That it is."

"I plan to see it for myself someday, you know. That and lots of other places."

Something in her tone caught his attention, made him remember the yearning expression of a few moments ago. "Do you now?" he replied softly.

"As soon as Danny's old enough to take over the livery. I want to see the world, or at least as big a piece of it as I can."

"Because of the promise you made your aunt?"

She glanced over her shoulder with an annoyed frown. "I made that promise because it's what *I* want, not just to please her."

"You know," he said slowly, "I've done a fair share of traveling in my day, and after a while it loses a bit of its luster. There's plenty of folks who'd give anything to have what you have right here with your family."

He saw her shoulders stiffen. "How old were you when you set off from that ranch your family runs?"

"Sixteen. But I only did it to appease my grandfather. And I only intended it to be for a short time."

"You never really went back, though, did you? Not to stay."

Ry swallowed a wince as her words brought back his frustration over his current arrangement.

"Do you regret it?" she asked, not waiting for an answer to her previous question. "Going off to spend time with your grandfather, I mean?"

Did he? If he'd stayed at Hawk's Creek he'd never have gotten the first-rate education he'd received, never become a lawyer, never been able to appreciate all his mother gave up to marry his father. But he'd also never have found himself so alienated from his siblings.

"There's no simple answer to that question," he finally said.

That earned him an inelegant snort. "I think that's an answer in itself."

Ouch! Seemed her sympathy only extended to his physical injuries. One thing about Josie, she didn't have any problem speaking her mind. The proverbial thorn on the rose.

But he was beginning to believe the bloom was worth risking a few scratches for.

He stood abruptly. Better not to go any further down that path. "If you're certain you don't need my help, I believe I'll turn in."

"See you in the morning." She threw the response over her shoulder without bothering to turn around.

Jo resisted the urge to stomp her foot.

It wasn't fair that he had everything *she* wanted and seemed so discontented. Yet *he* judged *her* for daring to set her sights beyond Knotty Pine. He wouldn't think her life was so rosy if he were the one living it. Too bad they couldn't up and change places. If he had all her family responsibilities…

She stilled. What if he *did* have her responsibilities? It was obvious the family already liked him. And he seemed equally taken with them. If she could somehow make him an actual part of the family, he was the sort of man who'd do everything he could to provide for and protect those in his care.

Cora Beth admired him. She could see he liked her too. As for the rest of the family, after that ruckus in the livery Danny practically hero-worshipped him. Ry had shown he could deal with her nieces—why, he even got along with Uncle Grover. They'd all be in good hands.

As for Ry's part, what man wouldn't be attracted to Cora Beth? She had that sweet domestic air about her that drew men looking for a wife like bees to honey.

If Ry and Cora Beth were to get hitched, she would be free to leave Knotty Pine knowing the family was well cared for.

So what if she'd been doing a bit of daydreaming over him herself? It was just because he'd been so all-fired heroic the other day and, to be honest, handsome as all get out. But, even if the thought stung a bit, she was realistic enough to know a man like Ryland Lassiter wouldn't fall for a girl like her.

Besides, she didn't need a man to tie her down. Just the opposite—she wanted to cut her tightly knotted bonds to this place so she could fly free.

In that respect, Ry *was* the answer to her prayers. God's hand had been in the timing of his trip through Knotty Pine, she was certain of it.

Jo lifted her chin. If this tug of attraction she felt for him was a way of testing her resolve, she was more

than up to the challenge. All she needed for her plan to
work would be for someone to give Ry and Cora Beth
a little push.

And no matter how much her silly heart protested,
she was just the person to do it.

Chapter Thirteen

Ry watched the world outside his window shift from black, to gray, to the rosy shades of dawn. He probably hadn't slept more than three hours last night, and that only in fits and starts.

Today he'd get some answers about Belle—or whatever answers were available. Then what?

Last night with the Wylies—experiencing first-hand their closeness and shared sense of purpose—had strengthened the feeling that had gradually grown in him the past few months, that he was merely drifting through life.

He had family, of course. Sadie and Griff and Grandfather Wallace—his Texas family and his Philadelphia family.

The problem was, he didn't have strong roots in either place. He mattered to his siblings, but if he passed away tomorrow it wouldn't leave any big gap in their lives. And he mattered to his grandfather, but only as someone to carry on the Wallace family legacy. Griff would have done just as well if he'd been the one to go to Philadelphia that fateful summer.

But the fault lay with him as much as with his family—maybe more so. He'd never truly committed to either world.

It was time that changed. He was twenty-nine years old. Time he made some decisions, set down some deeper roots. Perhaps time he started a family of his own.

Family. Home. A sense of belonging and mattering to folks in a real way. Those were things that gave a man a sense of purpose.

For some reason, Josie's face popped into his mind on the heels of that thought.

The sound of someone stirring around brought a welcome interruption to his musings. Ready for something to occupy him besides his own thoughts, Ry quickly got dressed.

He found Josie in the kitchen, frying up some eggs.

"Good morning," she called over her shoulder. "I'll be out of your way in a minute."

"Take your time," he drawled.

She jerked her head around. "Oh, sorry. I thought you were Cora Beth." Her surprised expression changed to one of curiosity. "What are you doing up so early?"

He shrugged. "No point staying in bed once you're awake."

Without asking if he was hungry, she cracked a couple more eggs and mixed them up with hers in the skillet. "Worried about meeting with Reverend Fields?"

Ry smiled as he watched her quick, efficient movements. He was surprised but pleased that she assumed he would share a meal with her, and that she would go through the trouble of cooking it. "Not worried," he replied. "Just ready to get some answers."

She nodded. "Plates are in the cupboard above the sink."

No false platitudes from this one. He took down two of the plates and set them on the counter next to the stove. "Anything else I can do to help?"

"Coffee cups are in the next cabinet over. I take mine with just a dab of cream."

As he poured up the two cups of coffee he thought how comfortable this was, sharing the start of day in this relaxed, unhurried way with someone who didn't chatter on just to fill the silences and who seemed so attuned to his thoughts and mood.

Jo finished scrambling the eggs, never looking up but very conscious of his movements. Not that she could help it. He was such an imposing man—tall and broad shouldered, moving with a wholly masculine, wolf-like grace despite his injuries, and just out-and-out filling a room with his presence.

Her matchmaking job should be easy. How could Cora Beth *not* fall for him?

And of course, given time to get to know her better, he would fall for Cora Beth too. After all, her sister wasn't still single for lack of offers.

Jo dished up the eggs just as he set the cups of coffee on the table. She set the plates next to the cups, noting from its color that her coffee was prepared just the way she liked it.

They sat across from each other and ate in comfortable silence for a while. Finally, he wrapped his hands around his cup and looked up. "When does the next northbound train pass through?"

She paused with the fork halfway to her mouth. "Friday." Uh-oh, she hadn't thought about this part. Once he talked with Reverend Fields there'd be nothing to keep him here. And two days wasn't nearly enough time for her plan to take hold.

He nodded. "Well, I won't make you wait to get your room back. I'll move into one of the guest chambers this morning. Just let me know which one."

"Talk to Cora Beth about that. She's the one in charge here. I'm good at the livery business but not running a household. No sir, not like Cora Beth. That sister of mine sure knows how to keep this big ole place running as smooth as kitten's fur."

Seeing his puzzled frown, Jo realized she'd been babbling. Good heavens, best get out of here while she could, and think this thing through when she was alone. There had to be a way to keep him in Knotty Pine a bit longer.

Pushing quickly back from the table, she carried her dishes to the sink.

"Josie, are you all—"

"Gotta head over to the livery," she said, cutting him off. "Don't you worry, though, I still plan to meet Reverend Fields at the train station this morning. Uncle Grover's already agreed to watch the livery while I'm gone."

"That's not necessary. I can—"

"No problem at all. Glad to do it." She edged toward the door, ignoring his puzzled expression.

Cora Beth walked in, tying an apron around her waist. She paused when she realized she wasn't alone. "Oh, hello. Looks like I'm the slugabed this morning."

Jo felt a tiny pang as Ry smiled at her sister. Which was plumb foolish, being as that was exactly what she wanted. She was just rattled by being caught off guard by his question was all.

"Morning, Cora Beth," she said quickly. "Mr. Lassiter wants to move into one of the guest rooms. You don't mind helping him with that, do you?"

"Of course not."

"Good. Well, I better get going. Freddie'll be wondering what's keeping me." And with that she was out the door. She sucked in a deep breath, clearing her head.

With luck, Mr. Lassiter would keep Cora Beth company while getting breakfast ready for everyone else. That would give him a taste for how well her sister handled things and how comfortable she was to be around. And Cora Beth would certainly help him move upstairs. Another chance for them to be thrown together.

If only she had a few more days she was sure she could get them to see how right they were for each other.

And then, with such an honorable, hard-working man around, she would finally be free to keep her promise to Aunt Pearl.

She wasn't sure why that thought didn't put more of a bounce in her step.

Ry paced across the bare wooden floor in the Wylies' family parlor as he waited for Reverend Fields to arrive.

The guest room Cora Beth had assigned him was larger and better furnished than Josie's, and the extra window made it brighter as well. And Cora Beth had done everything possible to make him comfortable, fluttering about, adding a pillow here, a vase of flowers there, an extra lamp near the bed.

Still, he missed the other room. There had been

something homey and warm about it that his new one, for all its cheeriness, lacked.

Ry shoved that irrelevant thought aside as he plopped down in one of the wingback chairs. He wasn't ready to run a race yet, but he'd be fit for travel by the time the train came through on Friday.

His fingers drummed against the arm of the chair. How well had Reverend Fields known Belle? Would the man be able to answer his questions? What had happened to her husband? How long had she been on her own?

Josie and the reverend should be here any moment now. How had the minister reacted to being met by a female livery owner? He hoped her unorthodox dress and manner hadn't caused any awkwardness. Surely a man of the cloth would be slow to judge, would take the time to see beyond the overalls and workshirt to the strong, selfless woman inside.

Not that Josie couldn't fend for herself. Still, he sensed a hidden vulnerability in her. And he felt a tug to defend her from any snubs or slights that might be directed her way.

Which was only natural, he told himself, considering all he owed her.

The house seemed quiet, as if it too was holding its breath, waiting. The only discernable sound was the rhythmic beat of the parlor clock's pendulum.

After what seemed an interminable delay, the front door opened, letting in a gust of air strong enough to chill him where he sat. The tension inside him coiled a notch tighter and a muscle in his jaw pulsed.

The muted sounds of conversation slid down the hall as he stood. Was that another woman's voice?

A moment later, Josie ushered in not only the man he assumed to be Reverend Fields but a woman and a child holding tight to a cat. He hadn't counted on the reverend bringing his family with him. This might make it difficult to have a frank conversation.

Josie motioned his direction. "This is Mr. Lassiter." She seemed to be trying to convey a message with her eyes. A warning perhaps? But of what?

"Mr. Lassiter, you didn't need to stand on our account." Reverend Fields, a tall, spare man with a horse-like face, approached Ry with an outstretched hand. "Miss Wylie told us of your unfortunate accident." Ry managed not to wince as the reverend vigorously pumped his hand.

"Thank you, sir, but I'm better now." Ry remained standing. "And thank you for making this trip on my behalf."

"Under the circumstances, we thought it best not to waste any time in carrying out Mrs. Hadley's wishes."

What did he mean, "under the circumstances?"

"Mrs. Hadley insisted right until the very end that you would have come sooner if you could have," the reverend continued. "I'm pleased to see her faith in your friendship was not misplaced."

"Thank you, sir. I just wish—"

The reverend cut him off, drawing the woman and child forward. "Please, before we continue, allow me to introduce my wife, Mrs. Fields."

Ry made a slight bow, wondering how to signal Josie to take Mrs. Fields and her daughter into another part of the house. "Ma'am."

"And this, of course," the gentleman put a hand on the child's shoulder, drawing her forward, "is Viola."

Chapter Fourteen

Ry froze. Viola? Had he heard right? Surely this wasn't—

Trying to ignore the unease tickling the back of his neck, he studied the child, looking for an indication he'd read this wrong.

Instead, what he saw—the familiar mahogany-colored ringlets, toffee brown eyes and tip-tilted nose—proved just the opposite.

There was no mistaking that this was Belle's daughter.

What was going on? Why had Belle sent the child to him?

The little girl moved closer to Mrs. Fields and drew the cat to her chin. A trembling in her lower lip brought Ry back to his senses. Whatever Belle's intent, the child needed reassurance.

"Viola," he said, keeping his voice soft, "do you know who I am?"

She nodded. "You're Mr. Lassiter, my momma's best friend in the whole world. Except for me and my daddy."

Had Belle still thought of him that way? "That's

right. Your mother and I were very good friends. I knew her back when she was a little girl."

Viola nodded. "She told me."

At a loss as to what to say next, he glanced toward Josie.

And, as if waiting for his signal, she stepped forward and smiled. "Viola, I'll have you know my sister bakes the best honey pecan tarts in all of Texas. What do you say we head to the kitchen and find us a few to sample? And I can introduce you to my nieces, Pippa and Lottie. They're twins you know, alike as two blades of grass, and I know they'd love to meet your cat."

Ry was both surprised and grateful at the easy way she interacted with the child.

Viola hesitated a moment, glancing first at Ry and then at Mrs. Fields. Finally she took Josie's outstretched hand and the two exited the room.

As the door closed behind them, Ry scrubbed a hand across his face. "I'm sorry, Reverend, Ma'am, please have a seat."

Reverend Fields seated his wife on the sofa and then took a chair next to Ry. Ry finally sank into a chair himself.

The reverend leaned forward, studying Ry with a solemn expression. "I pride myself on being able to read people, and unless I'm mistaken, you were surprised by Viola's presence."

"Yes sir, extremely so. It's been over twelve years since I last saw Mrs. Hadley and I had no idea she had children."

"But surely you received my telegram?"

"I'm afraid I misunderstood. I assumed you were referring to a musical instrument."

"I see."

Ry took a deep breath and asked the question that had haunted him these past few days. "What happened to Belle?"

Reverend Fields steepled his hands. "Mrs. Hadley was passing through Foxberry when she had an accident. Broke her leg. It was bad, but for a while, she seemed to be recovering. Then an infection set in."

Ry's stomach tightened as he thought about the pain she must have suffered. Was there something he could have done if he'd gotten there in time?

"Dr. Holcomb counted it a miracle she survived as long as she did," the reverend continued. "I believe it was her desire to speak to you before she passed that kept her going."

And he'd failed her in that. "Did she indicate why she wanted to see me?"

"I assume it was to discuss Viola's future."

"Of course." Ry raked a hand through his hair, then winced as his fingers brushed against his injury.

He still hadn't quite absorbed what the child's appearance meant. "Do you know what happened to Viola's father?"

"Mrs. Hadley indicated he died of a snakebite. Happened a month or so before they arrived in Foxberry."

So Viola had lost both parents in a short time. "Did Belle leave instructions as to what she expected me to do for Viola?"

Perhaps she needed him to act as escort, to deliver the child safely to her new guardian, whoever that might be. Or maybe she wanted to have Ry provide for the child's future. It was the least he could do. He would see that Belle's daughter received a top-notch education, that she never wanted for anything—

"Mr. Lassiter." This time it was Mrs. Fields who spoke, her voice gentle but firm. "I don't think you quite understand. Belle named you as Viola's guardian."

Ry's mind rebelled at that thought. It was too big a responsibility. He was a bachelor. What did he know about raising a child, much less a daughter? What had Belle been thinking? *Surely* there was someone else—

"She gave this to me the day before she died." Reverend Fields held out an envelope. "She asked me to deliver it if you didn't arrive in time for her to speak to you. Perhaps it provides some of the answers you seek."

Ry took the envelope but didn't open it. He wanted to be alone when he read whatever Belle had written.

"Mr. Lassiter, please consider this carefully." Reverend Fields leaned forward, hands clasped between his knees. "This was obviously what Viola's mother wanted, but your wishes are important as well. Viola is a dear child who's experienced a great tragedy. She deserves the comfort and security of being raised by someone who truly wants her. If that person isn't you, there's no shame in admitting as much. And I assure you Viola would be well cared for. There are several families in Foxberry who would be glad to give her a loving, God-fearing home."

Ry was very tempted. Surely the girl would be better off with one of those families the reverend referred to? What if he failed the child the way he'd failed her mother?

"I only want what's best for Viola," he said slowly.

Reverend Fields nodded. "Of course, as do we all. Mrs. Fields and I plan to spend the night here in Knotty

Pine and return to Foxberry on tomorrow's train. It's not much time, I grant you, but I encourage you to use it to get to know the child a bit and for her to get to know you. And most of all to spend time in prayer, seeking the Lord's guidance, before you make such a momentous decision."

He motioned toward his wife. "We will pray for you, as well."

The woman nodded, her smile gentle, empathetic. "I have confidence this will work out according to God's plan."

Ry only hoped her confidence hadn't been misplaced.

Feeling like an intruder, Jo balanced one end of the tray Cora Beth had saddled her with on the hall table and rapped on the parlor door before opening it.

"Sorry for the interruption," she said as she entered, "but my sister thought you might like a glass of lemonade."

Ry's expression was that of a prisoner who'd just received a reprieve. "No need to apologize," he said quickly. "That was quite thoughtful of your sister."

As Jo set the tray down, he added, "Reverend and Mrs. Fields plan to stay the night in Knotty Pine. I suggested they take a room here rather than the hotel."

"Of course." Jo wondered if Ry was trying to toss a bit of business their way, or wanted to have the Fields close by to make it easier for Viola.

Either way, he was still living up to his hero image. "We have a very comfortable room available and I can promise you my sister sets a much finer table than any you'll find at the hotel."

Reverend Fields turned to his wife. "What say you, my dear?"

She nodded. "It sounds lovely."

Jo moved to the door. "That's settled then. Let me just step over to the kitchen and talk to my sister about getting the room prepared while you enjoy your lemonade."

She didn't miss the dazed look on Ry's face, and couldn't say she blamed him much. The poor man had been blindsided by Viola's arrival.

A few moments later Cora Beth bustled into the room. "Reverend and Mrs. Fields, I'm so pleased to have you as our guests for the night. Allow me to show you to your room so you can rest and freshen up a bit after your trip. We'll be serving lunch soon. I hope you like black bean and ham soup."

"That sounds delicious. We appreciate you taking us in on such short notice."

"Not at all." Cora Beth motioned for them to precede her. "And I've already sent over to the depot for your bags."

Reverend Fields turned to Ry. "The large trunk with our bags contains Mrs. Hadley's and Viola's things."

Ry nodded. "Thank you. I'll see to it."

After the others left the room, Jo studied Ry. "You okay? Want me to help you back to your room?"

"I'm fine." He shook his head as if to clear it. "Belle appointed me Viola's guardian." He rubbed his temple. "Heaven help that child."

"So you're going to take the job?"

"How can I not? I have to believe Belle had her reasons for doing this. Besides, it's not the kind of responsibility one can just walk away from. You of all people should know that."

"That's different. This is my family." Did he truly realize what he was taking on?

"And now it seems, Viola is mine."

She saw the determination reflected in his eyes. Well, it was his choice. She had to hand it to him, though. As much as he seemed bumfuzzled and downright scared spitless, he also appeared ready to step up and do what was required.

"Raising a kid is not an easy thing," she warned. "Especially for a man on his own. Even Cora Beth, as good as she is with young'uns, moved back in here when Philip died. It was just too much for her to handle by herself."

He raised a brow as one corner of his mouth kicked up. "You trying to change my mind?"

"Just want to make sure you know what you're taking on."

"Believe me, I know it won't be all sunshine and daisies. I suppose I'll wind up hiring a nanny."

That's right, he had money. Well, it was going to take more than money to raise that little girl. Leastways if he wanted to do it right. Which she was pretty sure he did.

But that's something he'd figure out for himself soon enough.

One thing for sure, whether he knew it or not, his traveling days were about over. If he went through with this, he was going to get a taste of what *her* life had been like the past six years.

Actually, this would work right into her matchmaking plan. With a kid of his own to care for, he'd be more likely now than before to be looking for a wife. And who better than Cora Beth?

Sure, Cora Beth had said she didn't intend to marry again. But Ry was the kind of man who could melt any woman's heart. In fact, if she wasn't careful, she could fall for him herself.

Jo straightened. That was not going to happen. Ry might be a good man—charming, handsome, heroic even—but marriage didn't fit into her plans for her future, at least not short term.

Time to put some distance between them. "If you don't need my help, I'd better head back to the livery. Don't want to leave Uncle Grover on his own for too long." She gave him a pointed look. "Viola's in the kitchen with Cora Beth and the twins."

After she'd gone Ry fingered Belle's letter. This was it—his best chance to find the answers he'd been looking for ever since he received her telegram.

Mentally bracing himself, Ry opened the letter.

My dearest Ry,
If you are reading this it means I did not survive to see you. And, knowing you, you are riddled with guilt for not getting here in time, but there is no need. I believe God is in control of all things and whatever comes to pass, all will be well in the end.

There is so much I wanted to say to you. But mostly I want to thank you for taking me under your wing at a time when I had no one else. You'll never know what your friendship meant to me— still means to me. You brought back joy and light into my life when both had been all but extinguished.

I took those memories with me when I left Hawk's Creek, and my life was the richer for it. Horace and I had a good life, truly blessed, and it was made even better when Viola came along. It was only after Horace was taken from us so unexpectedly that I realized what our child missed because of our nomadic way of life.

Viola has never had a permanent home, has no aunts or cousins, no close friends except for her cat. And now she will not even have parents.

She will be very much alone once I am gone— just as I was all those years ago when I arrived at Hawk's Creek. Which brings me to why I wrote this letter. I had hoped to take the little bit of money Horace and I had put aside and use it to give Viola a real home. It seems, though, that the Good Lord has other plans for me. So now I am asking you to do for my daughter what I cannot. I know this seems a heavy burden to hand you, but I would not ask it if I did not know firsthand how well suited you are to the task. And I feel in my heart that it will bring you an equal measure of joy.

Please do for her what you did for me. Bring joy and light into her life. Show her she's not alone, that someone cares for her. Give her a home. Teach her to see the beauty in the world around her. Allow yourself to take joy in her as well. And above all, raise her in the Word.
Yours in our Lord,
Belle

Ry slowly folded the letter, his mind churning, spinning from one random thought to another.

Belle didn't blame him for not making it to Foxberry in time. She saw God's hand in all that had happened. She had entrusted her daughter to his care.

There was no way he could turn his back on her dying request.

Ry squeezed his hands at his sides, praying fervently that he could live up to her trust.

Chapter Fifteen

When Ry pushed open the kitchen door, his gaze went straight to Viola. She and the twins sat cross-legged on the floor dangling a bit of yarn for the cat to play with. Pippa and Lottie were giggling but it was the smile on Viola's face that held his attention. It transformed her, turned her into the carefree child she should have been.

As soon as she saw him, however, the smile was replaced by a look of worry. She reached for the cat and hugged him tightly against her. Ry wasn't certain if she drew comfort from her pet or if she thought she was protecting the animal from him.

Cora Beth set her cooking spoon down. "Come along, Pippa, Lottie. I have something upstairs I need your help with."

When Viola started to rise, Cora Beth motioned her to stay put. "Not you, dear. You're our guest. You and Mr. Lassiter can visit while we're gone." She gave the girl an encouraging smile. "Why don't you pass him one of the pecan tarts?"

"Yes, ma'am."

Ry took a seat at the table, waiting for her to serve him. What in the world would they find to talk about?

Lord, please give me the words. Don't let me make her world scarier than it already is.

She handed him the tart and he took a bite. "Mmm-mmm. These sure are good."

Viola merely nodded, her gaze remaining fixed on her cat.

"I'm sure Mrs. Collins wouldn't mind if you had another one."

This time she shook her head. She certainly wasn't much for talking. Time for a question that couldn't be answered with a yes or no. "That's a mighty fine look-ing cat. What's his name?"

"Daffy."

"Daffy? Is that because he acts silly?"

Her eyes got rounder. "Oh, no. Daffy's a very proper cat, I promise."

Okay, no teasing about the cat. "So how did he get his name?"

"It's really Daffodil, because of his color. But Ma and I—" her voice wavered slightly then recovered "—Ma and I decided Daffodil wasn't really a good name for a boy cat so we decided to call him Daffy instead."

He nodded approvingly. "That makes sense. And how long have you had Daffy?"

"A long time. Ma said Pa gave him to me for my third birthday. But I don't remember that far back."

She finally looked up and met his gaze. To his dis-may, he saw unshed tears in her eyes. Had he said some-thing wrong already?

"Please don't make me give him away." Her voice wavered alarmingly.

Stunned, Ry sat up straighter. "Of course I won't make you give Daffy away. Whatever gave you that idea?"

She sniffed. "Annie Orr told me lots of men don't like cats, not for pets. She said all three of her uncles *and* her grandpa won't let them in their houses 'cause cats make them sneeze."

"Well, cats don't make me sneeze." He held out his hands. "Mind if I hold Daffy for a minute?"

She hesitated and he wondered if she'd trust him enough to comply.

"After all," he said, keeping his tone conversational, "if Daffy and I are going to be friends we should start getting acquainted, don't you think?"

She still looked apprehensive, but gave a slow nod and handed her pet over. He lifted the cat so they were at eye level. "Well, Daffy, what do you think? Will we get along?"

The feline's answer to that was an inelegant sneeze.

"Uh-oh." Ry wrinkled his brow. "Do you suppose he's trying to tell me something?" Then he gave her a mock-worried look. "I sure hope *he* doesn't try to keep *me* out of the house."

To his relief she gave him a you're-so-silly smile.

"Here," he handed her the cat, "you better take him back before he sneezes again."

Viola gave the cat another hug, then set him down where he commenced washing himself.

"I've been thinking," Ry chose his words carefully, "if we're going to become a family like your ma wanted, maybe we ought to get to know each other better."

"How do we do that?"

"Well, I could ask you some questions, and then you could ask me questions."

She nodded. "All right."

"You start. Go ahead, ask me anything you want to know."

"What should I call you?"

Her question set Ry back for a moment. "Father" or "Pa" didn't feel right and "Mr. Lassiter" was much too formal. "How does Uncle Ry sound?"

"Uncle Ry." Her nose wrinkled as if she were tasting some unfamiliar food. Then she nodded. "Okay." She rubbed her arms. "Your turn."

"So what should I call you?"

"My name."

"Ah, but which name? You have so many. Miss Hadley, Viola, Button."

Her nose wrinkled in surprise. "Button?"

"With that cute little button nose of yours," he said, tapping it lightly, "surely someone calls you Button?"

She shook her head, rubbing her nose. "That's silly."

"But it suits you. Now, your turn again."

She smiled at his teasing, but moved on to her next question. "Do you live here with all these people?"

"No. I'm just staying here until my arm heals."

"Then where's your home?"

That question seemed to come up a lot lately. "Actually, I have two homes. There's Hawk's Creek ranch, the place where I met your mother and where my brother and sister live. But I spend most of my time in a city back east called Philadelphia where my grandfather lives." What would his family think of his taking on the role of guardian?

"Oh." She seemed to think about that for a minute. "Then which place would we live at?"

"Hmm, I haven't thought about that yet. Maybe I could take you to visit both places and then we could decide together."

She nodded solemnly. "That would be nice. And I'll ask God about it in my prayers tonight, too."

"That's a fine idea. Now it's my turn again." He searched his mind for another innocuous topic. "How old are you?"

"Seven."

So young to have been through so much.

She chewed on her lip a moment. "How did you hurt your arm?" she asked at last.

How much should he say? No way he was going to lie to her, but he didn't want to frighten or worry her either. "I'm afraid I got in the way of a bullet. But don't you worry, it's healing nicely and should be good as new in a day or two."

He quickly moved on to another subject. "What's your favorite food?"

She didn't hesitate. "Strawberries with sweet cream."

"Ah, I admire a girl who knows what she likes. Your turn again."

Jo quietly moved away from the back door. She'd passed through the kitchen to snag a pecan tart on her way out earlier, and truth be known, to make sure Viola was settling in okay with the twins. Not that she needed to concern herself. She should have known Cora Beth would have it under control.

She'd paused on the back porch to pull on her work

boots. A problem with the laces had held her there a few moments longer.

When she heard Ry come in, her curiosity had gotten the better of her and she hadn't been able to resist the urge to eavesdrop.

She was glad she had. Despite his own doubts, she'd heard enough to decide Belle had made the right choice in naming him Viola's guardian. Ry would make a fine father to the little girl.

And wouldn't Cora Beth, who already had such great experience in the parent department, make the perfect mother…

When Danny and Audrey returned from school, Audrey latched on to Viola as if they were long lost friends. At supper, Viola was introduced to the other boarders, and Audrey promptly asked Mr. Saddler if Viola could accompany her to school in the morning.

"Of course," he answered. "Miss Viola is welcome to attend while she's here. That is, if Mr. Lassiter is agreeable."

Viola immediately looked to him for permission, an act Ry found unnerving. With blinding clarity, he realized this is what his life would become—making decisions, large and small, for another person who would trust those decisions unquestioningly.

Lord, please give me the wisdom to make the right ones.

He nodded agreement, guiltily relieved she would have something to occupy her for most of the day tomorrow.

Once supper was cleared, Ry and Viola joined the Wylies as they gathered in the kitchen.

He helped Josie shell pecans while Cora Beth mixed the ingredients for another of her fruitcakes.

Uncle Grover and Danny pulled out a chessboard. The twins sat on the floor, absorbed in a game of make-believe with a pair of rag dolls. Audrey and Viola played with a set of tiddly winks nearby.

Ry was encouraged to see Viola and Audrey were becoming fast friends. But he still worried that the child was too quiet and reserved for a seven-year-old. Had she always been this way? Or was it her current situation? Was there something he should be doing to make this easier for her?

"She'll come around," Josie said softly.

His head swung around, his gaze meeting hers. "What's that?"

"I said, she'll come around." Josie expertly separated the meat from the shell on the pecan she'd just cracked, and reached for another. "Give her time. She's just lost her parents, and now she's been plopped smack-dab in the middle of a group of strangers, in a place she's never seen before. That would be hard on anyone, but especially a youngster."

"I know." Her comment was reassuring. In the short time he'd known Josie he'd come to trust her judgment. "I only wish I was sure Belle made the right choice in naming me Viola's guardian."

"Seems to me she knew exactly what she was doing." Josie cracked another pecan. "In fact, I can't think of anyone who'd take the responsibility more seriously."

"Thanks. But it's my ability rather than my intent I'm worried about."

Josie tossed a pecan shell, startling him when it

bounced against his chest. "Have faith" was her only response to his questioning frown.

Ry stared at the ceiling, resigned to the fact that he'd spend another restless night.

This morning he'd lain in bed feeling guilty for failing Belle, and hoping to get a few answers. The only real problem in front of him at that point, though, had been deciding whether he wanted to call Texas or Philadelphia home.

Tonight he'd found himself the guardian of a much-too-somber seven-year-old and her cat. Sort of put things in perspective.

A sound from the hallway caught his attention. Was someone else having trouble sleeping?

Curious, he crossed the room and cracked open his door. It was dark on this end of the hall, but the stairway was gilded with moonlight from the window over the landing.

A child-sized form, a cat clutched in her arms, tiptoed toward the stairs.

Ry grabbed his pants and stepped into them. What was Viola up to? Surely she wasn't planning to run away? Alarmed, he grabbed a shirt and followed her, still working the buttons. He got as far as the bend in the staircase before he realized she'd sat down on the bottom tread.

He paused. Now what? Did he give her some privacy to work out whatever was on her mind? Or did he try to comfort her?

Before he could decide, Josie stepped from the kitchen and paused. "And just what are you doing sitting here in the dark, young lady?"

"Me and Daffy couldn't sleep."

Should he make his presence known?

"I see. Mind if I join you?" The tread creaked as Josie sat beside her.

Ry decided it would be less intimidating for Viola to have just one adult to deal with. And he trusted Josie to find the right words.

"So," Josie asked in a stage whisper, "do my nieces snore?"

Viola giggled. "No. Well, maybe just a little," she temporized.

"But that's not why you can't sleep, is it?"

The child raised the cat to her cheek as she shook her head.

"You know," Josie's tone was that of someone sharing a secret, "I lost my ma, too. It was three years ago but I still remember like it was yesterday. It left a big old hole right in the middle of my heart that hurt awful bad."

"Did you cry?"

"Sure did."

There was a bit of a pause, then she looked up at Josie. "Do you still cry sometimes?"

"No, not about my ma's passing. But it took a while. I had to get over being mad at God first."

Even from where he stood, Ry could feel the shocked surprise pouring out of Viola. It was pretty much a reflection of his own.

"You were mad at *God?*" The child's words were hushed, as if she were almost afraid to voice the question.

"Yep." Josie spoke as if such an admission was normal. "I mean, He already had my pa, why'd He need to take my ma too?

"But God is good." Viola appeared to be trying to reason with Josie. "You're not supposed to get mad at Him."

Josie leaned back against the banister. "Let me ask you this. Did you ever get a little bit mad at your ma when she wouldn't let you have your way?" She scratched the cat behind the ears. "That doesn't mean they're not good or that we don't love them anymore, just that we're angry with them. It's the same with God. Being angry with Him doesn't mean we don't love Him anymore, it just means we're hurting. And because He loves us, He understands. As long as we don't let our anger push us away from Him, as long as we keep talking to Him and letting Him know how we feel, we'll eventually get to a place of peace about whatever has happened."

"What do you mean?"

"For instance, my being angry about my ma's passing. After a while, I stopped fussing and fuming quite so much and started listening to what God had to say."

"What did He say?"

"Well, whenever I'd read my Bible I'd come across passages about the freedom from pain and sorrow to be found in heaven, and the unbounded joys of being with the Father, and about there being a season for living and for dying. Then I got to remembering how my ma always talked about dying as a homecoming. Of course, I'd known all along she was in heaven. Just like you know your ma and pa are too."

Viola nodded.

Josie placed a hand on Viola's knee. "I realized it was

selfish of me to be wishing she'd have to live one more minute down here when she could be enjoying all that glory has to offer."

"But don't you still miss her?"

"Of course I do. I think about her most every day. But I keep all my good memories close to my heart and I know that some day, when God figures the time is right, I'm going to join her up there in heaven and we'll be together again."

Ry closed his eyes, thanking God for putting Josie here to talk to Viola.

How had she done it? Opened her heart to Viola in such a simple, sensitive manner. He wasn't certain he could have handled the child's hurt nearly so well.

But he'd been hiding in the dark long enough. Ry started down the stairs, making certain his footsteps would be heard. "Well, hello, ladies. Are you two looking for a late night snack, too?"

Josie stood, studying him as he descended. He could tell she was trying to figure out how much he'd overheard.

She glanced at Viola. "That sounds like a good idea. I think there's a few pieces of Cora Beth's apple cobbler left from supper. What do you say we raid the pie safe?"

"Mmm." Ry patted his stomach. "Sounds like just what I need. How about you, Viola?"

The child nodded, stroking Daffy's back.

Ry helped Viola to her feet. He met Josie's glance over Viola's head and mouthed a heartfelt "Thank you."

She reddened slightly, but nodded as she took Viola's other hand and returned a silent "You're welcome."

They strolled into the kitchen, Viola between them, and Ry suddenly felt like things might just work out after all.

Chapter Sixteen

Ry strolled along the sidewalk, fighting the urge to whistle. It felt great to be outdoors again. He passed several people as he made his way to the livery, all of them strangers, all of them seeming to know his name and offering friendly greetings.

The sound of the train whistle carried to him from the depot, signaling the arrival of the southbound train. The Fieldses would be boarding soon, severing Viola's last link to her past, tying her irrevocably to him.

But that thought wasn't as daunting this morning as it had been yesterday. Seeing Josie with Viola last night had planted a seed in his mind, one that had taken root during the night.

Viola didn't need a nanny. She needed a mother.

A woman who was strong, caring, God-fearing. A woman who could help him love and guide Viola on the path to becoming a woman herself. A woman he'd be comfortable sharing his own life with.

A woman like Josie.

On that thought, he found himself once more at Wylie's Livery and Bridle Shop.

As soon as Josie spied him, she frowned. "What are you doing out here? And where's your sling?"

Was her concern a sign that she cared about him, even if just a little? "I'm fine without the sling. I thought it was time I took in some fresh air and saw what Knotty Pine has to offer."

"Well, now that you proved you're on the mend, set yourself down on that crate and give yourself a rest."

"Yes, ma'am." He was actually beginning to enjoy her tendency to fuss over him.

She studied him suspiciously but he maintained a bland expression and she finally went back to work, carving on another pumpkin. "Viola get off to school okay this morning?"

"Yep. Audrey had her by the hand, chattering away about all the fun they were going to have."

Josie shook her head. "I'm afraid Audrey inherited the bossier side of the Wylie family traits."

Ry suppressed a grin. He'd been thinking the girl was a lot like her Aunt Josie. "It'll be good for Viola. Being with other children will give her something to think about besides her loss."

Josie nodded. "Are there any kids running around that ranch of yours?"

Ry shook his head. "No. Even Inez's kids—she's our cook—are grown now."

"How about at your grandfather's place?"

"I'm afraid I'm the youngest one there."

"Then maybe you ought to think about staying around here for a spell." She kept her eyes focused on her work and her voice seemed a bit too casual. "Through Thanksgiving, anyway. Like you said, it'll be good for Viola to be around other kids. And you said your family isn't much for celebrating and such."

Ry's mood improved yet another notch. Without any prodding, she'd unwittingly helped him set his plan in motion. Now he'd have a legitimate reason to hang around, giving him time to do a bit of wooing and to convince her they'd be a good match. "Thanks for the invitation," he answered. "And you may be right. Spending Thanksgiving here, with all of you, will be a real comfort to her." And he was rather looking forward to an old-fashioned family Thanksgiving himself.

Josie gave him a pleased smile. "Good. That's settled then."

She glanced toward the sidewalk. "Hello, Sheriff. Something I can help you with?"

"Hi, Jo."

Ry sized up the tall man with the slow Texas drawl who was staring straight at him. He decided the seemingly lazy exterior hid something decidedly more formidable.

"I heard your new boarder was out and about today and I thought I'd come around and introduce myself."

Ry stood. "Hello, Sheriff. I'm Ryland Lassiter."

"Glad to make your acquaintance. Name's Mitchell Hammond."

They shook hands and then the sheriff stepped back, crossing his arms. "I put the word out on Otis. If he shows up at any town within sixty miles of here he'll be dealt with as he deserves."

"That's good to hear. If you need anyone to testify against him, let me know."

The sheriff nodded. "I've heard Jo's version of what

happened. When you have a few minutes, why don't you drop by my office and fill me in on yours."

Ry decided there was more command than suggestion in the invitation. "I'll stop in on my way back to the boardinghouse."

"Good, I'll be looking for you." He tipped his hat Josie's way. "Guess I'd better let you folks get on with your business."

Once they were alone, Ry rubbed the back of his neck, trying to decide what it was about the man that seemed so intimidating.

"Sheriff Hammond's a good man," Josie said as if reading his thoughts. "Easygoing most of the time. But he takes his job seriously and doesn't let anything stand in the way of his duty."

"I can see that." A movement in one of the far stalls caught his attention. "What do we have here?" Ry moved to the back of the livery where a horse and foal were penned. "You purchase some new stock?" Had she already taken steps to replace Scout?

"Those aren't mine. Miz Parsons left for Shreveport yesterday to visit her daughter and new grandbaby. I'm taking care of her horses while she's gone."

Ry leaned on the stall gate, studying the pair. The foal, a filly he could see now, couldn't be more than a week old. The mare was in good shape—not up to the bloodlines Hawk's Creek stables produced, but obviously well fed and cared for.

"Excuse me, ma'am. Is the owner around?"

Ry swung around at the sound of the familiar voice. It couldn't be—

But it was. His brother stood just inside the livery with their sister at his side. Both were staring at Josie with uncertain expressions, as if not sure what to make of a woman working in a livery, and one dressed the way she was.

Griff held the lead to a roan horse. So they'd delivered Kestrel in person—he hadn't figured on that. Watching them, he realized they hadn't noticed him standing back in the shadows.

"I'm the owner," Josie stated as she stood. He watched her size his siblings up.

They returned the favor, reacting to her announcement with barely concealed surprise. Sadie, especially, had her lips compressed in a disapproving line.

Josie crossed her arms. "Jo Wylie at your service. Something I can do for you?"

Ry had heard that tone before. He quickly stepped forward to help smooth things over. "Hello, Griff, Sadie. Nice to see you."

"Ry!" His sister raced forward and threw her arms around his neck. "Are you all right? I've been so worried."

"Hi, Sadie." Ry winced at the near collision, but gave his impetuous sister a one-armed hug. For someone whose head barely reached his chin, she sure packed a powerful wallop. "I'm fine. Or at least I was until you tackled me."

She released him immediately and stepped back. "Oh no. Did I hurt you? Are you injured?"

"Like I said, I'm fine. Nothing to worry that pretty head of yours over." He looked past his sister to his brother, who'd made no move to step forward. "Hello, Griff. I wasn't expecting you two to deliver the horse personally. Figured you'd send Red or one of the other hands."

His brother shrugged. "Coming wasn't my idea. When Sadie saw your telegram, though, there was no holding her back. And I certainly couldn't let her come out here on her own."

Ry frowned. "All I said was that I'd be here in Knotty Pine for a while and requested you send Kestrel."

"That phrase you slipped in about dropping by the ranch when you were 'able to travel' set our sister's alarm bells ringing. She was convinced you were at death's door."

"Nothing quite so dramatic." Was that Josie's snort behind him or one of the horses?

Sadie didn't seem the least convinced by his reassurances. "I was right to be worried. I told you, Griff. Look how pale he is." She shook a finger in Ry's direction. "Ryland Jeremiah Lassiter, don't lie to me. You're hurt, I can tell."

Ry raised his hand in mock surrender. "Okay, I ran into a bit of trouble, but I'm healing quite well, as you can see."

"More like he's too ornery to stay down."

Ry stepped aside, widening the circle to include Josie. "Speaking of which, I believe you've already met Miss Josephine Wylie. She's the one who saved my life."

"Saved your life!" Sadie plopped her fists on her hips. "I knew there was more to this than you were letting on. Will you *please* tell me what happened?"

Ry ignored her demand. "Josie, this overly-dramatic chit is my sister, Sadie, and the gentleman with her is my brother, Griffith."

Griff gave a short bow. "Miss Wylie."

Sadie didn't waste time with the amenities. "Josephine, did you truly save my brother's life?"

"Call me Jo. And your brother is exaggerating just a tad."

"Not at all." Ry enjoyed turning the tables and putting *her* heroics center stage for a change. "I stumbled into an ambush and she came charging to my rescue, guns blazing, in true hero form."

Sadie stepped forward and enveloped Josie in a bear hug, all her previous reservations forgotten. "Thank you so much for helping my brother. I'll be forever in your debt—we all will."

Josie blinked, a what-just-happened expression on her face.

Sadie stepped back with an arch smile. "Now, I know it must be a fascinating story and you're going to have to tell me all about it, because Ry will skip over the interesting parts."

Ry, deciding to leave Josie to deal with Sadie for the time being, turned to his brother. "How'd Kestrel make the trip?"

Griff led the horse forward. "No problems. You'd never know it was his first train ride."

Ry took the reins and gave the animal a careful once-over. "You've done a good job caring for him. He's turned into a fine animal."

His brother shrugged. "It was part of our agreement."

There was a time when he and Griff had been the best of friends. But somewhere along the way they'd lost the ability to speak to each other with anything but resentment.

Feeling a sense of regret, Ry turned to the ladies. "Josie, this is Kestrel. He's a three-year-old out of one of Hawk's Creek's finest stallions."

"He's a beauty." Josie stepped close enough to rub

the animal's nose. "If this is the kind of stock you're breeding I can see why you'd be proud of the program."

"Kestrel is Ry's prize," Sadie said. "He has big plans—"

Ry gave his sister a quelling look. "Actually, he's just one of Monarch's many offspring."

Sadie blinked, staring at him as if he'd said the animal had two heads, and even Griff wore a puzzled frown. Better barrel on through before they bungled this any further. He thrust the lead at Josie. "Glad you like him. He's yours."

Ry ignored the startled expressions from his siblings. He hadn't told Griff why he'd wanted the best three-year-old in his stable brought here. "I know Scout was special to you," he continued, focusing on Josie, "and it won't be easy to replace him, but Kestrel's a fine animal out of a strong line. He'll make a good work horse as well as a mount."

"But I can't—"

"Nonsense. I won't take no for an answer."

Her jaw set in a firm line. "This animal is obviously valuable and I don't accept charity."

"This isn't charity. It's repayment of a debt." He gave her his sternest courtroom look. "You of all people should know about repaying one's debts."

Josie stuffed her hands in her pockets and worried at her bottom lip. Finally she nodded. "All right. But only if you let me return the money you paid for the use of Scout."

"It's a deal." Ry's quick agreement seemed to surprise her. But he knew Kestrel was worth a great deal more than the hundred dollars he'd paid for the use of her horse. And he'd find other ways to provide cash to the Wylie family, ways that wouldn't infringe on Josie's pride.

Besides, if things worked out as he hoped, it would be all in the family before long.

Ry turned to his siblings. "You'll need a place to stay while you're here. Josie's family runs a boardinghouse and her sister's cooking rivals Inez's."

"Sounds perfect," Sadie said, her manners smoothing over her surprise. "That'll give us a chance to corner you for a nice long chat. In fact, why don't we all go over there now and Jo can tell us about this amazing adventure the two of you had."

Josie shook her head. "I need to keep an eye on the livery. But y'all go on. I'm sure you want to freshen up and rest after your trip."

"Nonsense." Sadie waved away Josie's objections. "We'd much rather pump you for information about what Ry's been up to. There must be someone who can take over for you for a bit."

"There's someone who watches the place at night. But he won't be by until nearly suppertime."

"Well then, we'll just find someone else. I insist that you join us. I know I won't get the full story out of Ry unless you're there to keep him from leaving out the exciting bits."

"You might as well give in." Ry gave Josie a mock-defeated look. "Sadie may appear demure, but once she gets the bit between her teeth there's no stopping her."

Josie looked from him to his sister. "I suppose I could check with Edgar from the boot shop across the street," she said uncertainly. "He might be willing to watch the place for a bit."

"Splendid." Sadie nodded as if the matter were settled.

"Y'all just go on up to the house and freshen up. Your brother can show you the way. I'll join you as soon as I have Kestrel here settled in and talk to Edgar."

Ry hesitated, then caught the speculative look in his sister's eye. No point tipping his hand just yet. "All right. We'll see you back at the house." Sheriff Hammond would just have to wait for that chat a bit longer.

Josie watched Ry leave with his brother and sister, then began settling in the horse.

There was definitely something going on with those three that she couldn't figure out. Like his obvious surprise that they'd come instead of sending one of the ranch hands. And the fact that he and his brother barely exchanged a handful of words even though it had been months since they'd seen each other.

That sister of his was quite the lady, though. She looked small and delicate as a honeysuckle bloom, even if she was a bit excitable. Her clothes were every bit as fine as those in the fashion magazines Cora Beth liked to pore over. And she had a bit of a pampered look about her.

Was that the kind of female Ry was used to keeping company with? Would his sister's visit have him making comparisons that weren't flattering?

Good thing she didn't care what he thought about her, not in that area at any rate.

As for Cora Beth, she could hold her own. What she lacked in polish, she more than made up for in her sweet temper and domestic skills. A man could do a lot worse selecting a wife than casting his eye toward Cora Beth. She only hoped Ry was smart enough to realize that. Because the sooner she could make this match happen, the sooner she could shake off her family obligations and follow her dream.

She'd already decided the first place she'd go, too. Ever since Ry had described New York harbor in such lively detail she'd had a hankering to see it for herself.

The thing was, every time she imagined the scene, she pictured Ry standing beside her.

Chapter Seventeen

"If you ask me, it sounds like you two saved each other."

Jo shot an exasperated frown at Ry's sister. Not that Sadie seemed to notice.

She and Ry had spent the last thirty minutes telling what had happened the day of the ambush in Whistler's Meadow. At least they'd tried to.

Seemed like every time Jo tried to paint a true picture of Ry's heroics, he interrupted, making light of his part and trying to paint her as the hero of the story.

And Sadie seemed inclined to accept Ry's version.

Griff, on the other hand, hadn't said much at all. He'd leaned back in his chair the whole time, listening to their story as if it had happened to some stranger rather than his brother.

But now that there was a pause in the conversation, he rubbed his jaw. "So, did you ever find out why Belle sent for you?"

That was the part of the story Griff wanted to focus on? Did anyone but her see the painful emotion flash across Ry's face?

"Because she was dying." Ry's voice betrayed nothing of his feelings. "Unfortunately, I didn't make it in time to see her one last time."

Sadie reached for her brother's hand. "Oh, Ry, I'm so sorry."

Griff's only reaction was a tightening of his jaw.

"Which brings us to another interesting twist to this story," Ry continued.

Sadie's hand went to her chest. "You mean there's more?"

Ry nodded. "Belle's husband also passed on, about a month before she did. And they had a daughter, Viola."

"That poor child. What's to become of her?"

Ry's lips twisted into a sort of half grin. "Belle named me as guardian."

"Oh, Ry, no." Was Sadie dismayed on Ry's behalf or on the child's? Either way, it wasn't the reaction Josie had expected.

"You can't be seriously thinking about raising a child on your own." Griff's reaction was even less flattering.

That did it. "I'll have you know your brother has done quite well with Viola so far." Jo glared at both of his siblings. "From where I'm sitting, a kid couldn't ask for a better pa."

She ignored Ry's startled look. Besides, she wasn't finished. "Viola's ma handed your brother this responsibility slap-dab out of the blue and he never so much as flinched. I'd think his family would be a mite more supportive of his efforts."

Three pairs of eyes stared at her with varying degrees of surprise. The silence in the room was deafening, surpassed only by the growing tension.

When Cora Beth and Uncle Grover entered the parlor, each carrying a tray loaded with goodies, it was like opening a steam valve and letting off the pressure. Everyone was suddenly keenly interested in the new arrivals and what they'd brought in.

"I'm sorry I took so long." Cora Beth set her tray on the low table in front of the sofa. "I had to take care of something in the kitchen." She turned to take Uncle Grover's tray. "I hope you don't mind that I invited Uncle Grover to join us."

"Not at all," Ry answered. "In fact, I'm pleased to be able to introduce him to my brother and sister."

After introductions were made and refreshments passed around, Cora Beth took on her make-everyone-feel-at-home hostess role, one she excelled at, and the conversation turned to tamer topics.

Jo let the discussion flow around her as she continued to mull over the strained relationship that seemed to exist between the Lassiter siblings.

Ry stepped into the hall as soon as he heard the front door open. Danny, Audrey and Viola spilled inside the house, cheeks pinkened from the blustery day, the two girls laughing at something Danny had said.

Daffy, who'd remained out of sight most of the day, trotted down the stairs right on cue, stropping himself insistently against Viola's legs.

"Hello," Ry included them all in his greeting. "Viola, how was your first day at Knotty Pine's school?"

"I like Mr. Saddler, and everyone was very nice."

"Except for Mary Alice Johnson," Audrey corrected. "But she doesn't count because she's not nice to anyone."

"Audrey Elizabeth Collins, what an unkind thing to

say." Cora Beth stood at the kitchen door, a large cook spoon in one hand.

"Sorry, Ma." Audrey looked suitably abashed, but Ry noticed her contrite expression didn't quite extend to her eyes. He decided to rescue her by turning the subject.

"Viola, I have some people I'd like you to meet."

"We have company?" Audrey tried peering past him into the parlor.

But her mother was quicker. "I need you and Danny in the kitchen. You can meet Mr. Lassiter's guests later."

Viola studied Ry as if scenting a trap. She picked up Daffy then straightened, seeming to brace herself for the worst.

"There's nothing to be alarmed about," Ry said, trying to reassure her. "You're going to like these folks." At least he sincerely hoped so.

He placed a hand on her shoulder as they stepped into the parlor. "Viola, this is my sister and brother, the ones I told you about yesterday."

"Hello, Viola." Sadie's voice held all the delight of a child who'd found a new toy. "I've been looking forward to meeting you all afternoon."

Viola stepped closer to Ry, as if for support. He rested a hand on her shoulder, feeling curiously touched by her gesture.

"Hello," she replied softly. Then she cocked her head to one side. "Does that mean you're my aunt?"

Sadie gave her a radiant smile. "Why yes, I suppose I am." She flashed a quick, delighted grin Ry's way, then turned back to the girl. "I'm your Aunt Sadie. And this," she said pointing to her other brother, "would be your Uncle Griff."

Griff gave a short bow, his stiff stance relaxing as

he too smiled. "Hello, Viola. You're just as pretty as your mother."

Ry was surprised at the change in his brother's demeanor. This was the Griff he remembered from his childhood. Was he only surly when it came to the interactions between the two of them?

"Did you know my mother too?" Viola asked.

Griff nodded. "I sure did."

"Oh." Viola smiled. "I've never had an aunt and an uncle before. Except for Uncle Ry, and I just met him yesterday."

"Well, you have us all now," Sadie said.

"Uncle Ry said you live on a ranch." Viola was obviously warming up to his sister.

"That's right. Would you like to come live there, too?"

Viola glanced up at Ry. "We haven't decided yet."

Sadie seemed put out at that. Before she could say anything, Ry stepped in. "I'll take Viola to Hawk's Creek for a nice visit. Then we'll go to Philadelphia so she can meet Grandfather. It'll be soon enough to decide where we'll call home once that's done."

"Seems like an easy enough choice." Griff's tone had regained that hard edge. "Especially since Belle lived at Hawk's Creek once. Of course you and I never saw eye to eye on that subject."

"Not all of us have as clear a vision of what we want out of life as you, Griff." Ry regretted the words as soon as they left his mouth. But there was no calling them back.

So instead, he smiled down at Viola. "Why don't you and Daffy see if Mrs. Collins needs help in the kitchen?"

With a nod, and a last uncertain smile at Sadie and Griff, Viola exited the room.

"Oh, Ry, she's adorable." Sadie clasped her hands together. "I can see how you formed such a quick attachment. And Josie was right—you *are* good with her."

That reminder of how Josie had defended him brought back an echo of that warm feeling deep in his chest. It was good to know she was on his side.

"Thanks," he told his sister. "I only hope you're right."

Griff's frown indicated he didn't wholly agree. "Just don't drag your feet deciding where to settle down." His glare carried something more than its usual fierceness. "Kids need roots, need to feel like they have a solid foundation that's going to be there no matter what." Griff's jaw tightened further. "Without that, they might just make a wrong turn and never find the way back."

Ry stared at his younger brother, wondering how much of what he'd said was prompted by concern for Viola, and how much was an indictment of the decisions Ry had made.

Sadie, never comfortable with the tension between her brothers, turned to Ry with one of her charm-your-socks-off smiles. "I'm certain you'll make the right decision when the time comes." She tugged him over to the nearby sofa. "Now, let's talk about your upcoming visit to Hawk's Creek. It's been a while since there were children in the house and I know Inez is going to be beside herself when she learns about Viola."

Ry let his sister chatter on, but it didn't quite drown out the memory of Griff's pointed comment. What he'd said about a kid needing roots made sense.

Right then and there Ry decided he'd select a permanent home for him and Viola—and hopefully Josie—by Christmas.

* * *

At supper that evening Ry was pleased to see that Sadie and Griff appeared to enjoy the boisterous, informal atmosphere.

Sadie sat next to Cora Beth and, as the ladies of their respective households, they found a number of things to discuss. Griff, who sat next to Danny, was drawn into a detailed discussion on the art of roping cattle. Danny hung on to every word with rapt attention, peppering Griff with questions whenever he paused.

Ry watched the way Griff not only tolerated but encouraged Danny's questions and remembered his earlier interactions with Viola. Was that the key—having children around? Would introducing Viola into the mix at Hawk's Creek lead to a more relaxed atmosphere there—not just at mealtime, but overall?

As for himself, tonight he'd managed to wrangle a seat next to Josie and had engaged her in a spirited conversation on the relative merits of quarter horses and Morgans. He found himself admiring the way her eyes lit up and her expression became animated when she discussed something she was passionate about. He could watch her like this all evening.

When it was time for dessert, Cora Beth carried in one of her fruitcakes and Ry rubbed his hands together, giving his brother and sister a grin. "Get ready, you two are in for a rare treat."

Sadie took one bite and her eyes widened in surprise. "This is absolutely delicious. I've never tasted a fruitcake so decadently rich and so delightfully light at the same time. I absolutely must have your recipe."

Cora Beth shifted uncomfortably. "Why, thank you. I—"

Ry tapped his sister's saucer with his fork. "You and

every other woman in town." He saw Cora Beth relax. "I'm afraid you're out of luck. The recipe is a closely guarded secret."

"But surely—"

"None of your pestering or cajoling, Sadie. Mrs. Collins has a small business selling the cakes to folks in these parts."

"Brothers!" Sadie made an unflattering face at him. Then she turned to Cora Beth. "I must say, that's very enterprising of you." She leaned in conspiratorially. "But if I can't have the recipe then I will content myself with purchasing several so I can serve them to anyone who visits for the holidays."

Ry shook his head, pointing his fork her way. "You mean have something new and different to lord over your neighbors. Rest easy, little sister. I've already commissioned Mrs. Collins to make a pair of them for you."

Sadie ignored his dig and clapped in delight. "Oh, Ry, you're so thoughtful. And Mrs. Collins, your cakes will be the centerpiece of our Thanksgiving meal."

Ry accompanied Sadie and Griff to the train station the next morning.

"I wish you were coming with us," Sadie said with a pout. "You certainly seem to have recovered well enough to travel."

He gave his sister's hand a squeeze. "Like I told you yesterday, Viola and I need to get more comfortable with each other before we go gallivanting across the country together."

Griff raised a brow. "Leaving will be harder on her once she's begun to form attachments to this place."

Ry was afraid it was already too late to worry about

that. Besides, he was counting on the attachments going both ways when it came to the Wylie family. "Perhaps. But she announced after school yesterday that she'd been assigned a role in the Thanksgiving program. I don't want to squash her excitement by saying she won't be here to participate."

"I'd hoped you'd be at the ranch for Thanksgiving." Sadie's pout grew more pronounced.

"Sorry. But I promise we'll be there soon after."

To Ry's relief, the train whistle signaled its imminent departure. He wrapped his sister in a hug. "Give Inez my love."

He turned to his brother and offered his hand. After a quick handshake, Griff picked up their bags. "Come on, Sadie," he said, "time to head home."

As Ry watched them go, it struck him that they called Hawk's Creek home when speaking to each other, but "the ranch" when speaking to him.

It seemed, for all their tugging at him to make a choice, they weren't quite certain where he belonged, either.

Chapter Eighteen

Ry straightened his shirt cuff and slipped on his jacket. There was only a slight twinge in his arm to remind him of his injury. Before long he'd be good as new.

He glanced out the window and smiled. It was a beautiful, clear Sunday morning and he and Viola were going to attend church services with the Wylie family.

Josie took Sundays off, which meant she'd be free all day. It was time to move on to the next stage of his plan. Her quick defense of him yesterday, coupled with her obvious affection for Viola, gave him hope that she would at least be open to his proposal. He just needed to lay a bit more groundwork.

Because she was a sensible sort of woman, he figured she wouldn't be swayed by fanciful, romantic notions. Which was fine by him. Keep it businesslike, that was the ticket, perhaps stress how much Viola needed her, and how she had all the qualities he wanted in a partner. He could even offer to take her on a trip from time to time to satisfy that itch she had to see the world.

Once downstairs, he found most of the family assembled in the dining room. Viola sat swinging her legs as she and Audrey exchanged whispers.

A quick head to toe glance confirmed she was neatly dressed and ready for church, for which he had Mrs. Collins to thank. Getting her ready would be his job soon, just one of the many responsibilities that made him break out in cold sweats at night.

He had to convince Josie to accept his offer. If not—

He glanced up as a door down the hall opened, and all other thoughts fled before the vision that greeted him.

Josie was wearing a dress.

What a difference it made in her appearance—one he definitely approved of. Gone were the baggy overalls and work boots. Instead she wore a soft blue dress that fit just as a dress ought to, and showed off her surprisingly trim waist. Sensible but feminine shoes peeked beneath the hem of her skirt and her normally ragged braid had been tamed into a soft coronet, with a few loose tendrils framing her face. He wanted to protest when she placed a bonnet on her head, hiding most of her hair.

"What's the matter?" Josie stopped in front of him, tying the ribbon under her chin with a bit more force than seemed necessary. "You didn't think I wore overalls *all* the time, did you?"

Ry blinked, trying to clear his suddenly jumbled thoughts. "No. Of course not. I just… I mean, you look very nice today."

His compliment—or was it the stammering delivery—earned him an irritated sniff as she moved toward the dining room.

"Sorry to keep everyone waiting. We'd best get going

if we don't want to be late." With that pronouncement, Josie turned and headed for the entryway. Ry barely had time to step ahead of her and open the door.

She walked past him with a swish of skirts, and he was left standing there while the others trooped out after her. And he still didn't know what he'd done to earn him that reaction.

Uncle Grover brought up the rear and he gave Ry a sympathetic smile. "I fear the workings of a woman's mind will forever be a mystery to us menfolk, son. Don't try to understand it. Better men than you have made the attempt and failed."

Ry smiled at the sage advice. As they joined the others, he remembered Mrs. Plunkett's attempts to flirt with his would-be mentor. Was Uncle Grover as oblivious to her advances as he appeared?

"Look, Cora Beth," Danny called out, "the sun is shining and it's not cold at all." He gave her a hopeful look. "Doesn't it feel like picnic weather?"

Before she could answer, Audrey took up the plea. "Oh please? Can we? I want to show Viola our special place."

Cora Beth turned to Josie. "What do you think?"

"I think we ought to take advantage of this weather while we can." Josie's gaze remained focused straight ahead. "December's almost here."

"Very well." Cora Beth smiled at the waiting children. "A picnic it is."

Danny let out a *whoop* as Pippa and Lottie clapped.

Audrey nudged shoulders with Viola. "Just you wait," she said. "Our picnics are the bestest ever."

Ry had planned to lend an arm to Josie on the short walk to church, but somehow he found himself beside

Cora Beth, as Josie linked arms with Uncle Grover and walked ahead.

He had no choice but to offer his arm to Cora Beth. "I want to thank you, ma'am, for all you're doing to make Viola feel comfortable here."

"No need for thanks." Cora Beth's smile was warm and sincere. "She's a sweet girl and she's good company for Audrey."

"For such different children, they do seem to get along well."

Cora Beth gave him a sideways look. "Don't you know it's the differences that add just the right glue to bind a friendship?"

Ry found his gaze wondering to Josie. "Guess I never thought of it quite that way."

"It's true. Take me and my Philip. I'm a fussbudget, pure and simple. Like to have things nice and tidy and I like taking care of folks. Philip, on the other hand, was a relaxed, take things as they come person. Not lazy, mind you, not by a long shot, just not too concerned about having things just so. Still, we suited well together." She sighed. "I did love that man."

Something caught her eye and she shifted immediately into mother-hen mode. "Philippa Louise, however did you get dirt on your sleeve? Come here and let me see if I can brush it off."

The little group paused while Cora Beth attacked the offending smudge. As they waited, Ry noticed a large building sitting off in a nearby field. Not a house, not a barn. It looked more like a warehouse.

"What's that over there?" He directed his question to Josie.

She followed his glance. "That's Knotty Pine's Town Hall."

"Town Hall? It's mighty big for a town this size."

"There's a reason for that."

He was relieved to hear she no longer sounded testy. Whatever had set her off this morning seemed forgotten.

"That land it's sitting on was owned by Mrs. Nora Stansberry," she continued. "Her husband died when she was quite young. Then her only child died in a swimming accident a few years later."

"Must have been terrible for her." Ry glanced at Viola, feeling the weight of that tragedy with new insight.

"Yes, it was. But Mrs. Stansberry didn't let it sour her. She was one of the most pleasant, generous women I ever knew. Anyway, when she passed away six years ago, she didn't have any family to leave her estate to. So she willed her land to the town, to be used for some purpose that would benefit the whole community."

"So y'all built a town hall."

"Yep. Took us a half dozen town meetings spread out over a couple of months to decide. But once we decided, everyone pitched in. We had a barn raising to construct it and the ladies went to work decorating it while the men built the furniture."

"So what do you use it for?"

She shrugged. "We hold town meetings there, of course, but it's also used for dances, holiday celebrations, school plays. Seems like there's something going on here all the time. It's been a real blessing to this town. That's where we'll have our Thanksgiving Celebration." She waved a hand in an inclusive gesture. "We use it for other things too. Last year, when the Helmon's home was struck by lightning, the family lived here until they could rebuild."

"Impressive."

Cora Beth signaled they were ready to move on and this time Ry was able to secure a spot beside Josie.

They reached the church just as the service was about to start and had to move quickly to take their seats. Once again, Ry found himself outmaneuvered without quite knowing how it happened. One minute he was ready to slide into the pew beside Josie and the next he had four little girls between the two of them and Cora Beth on his right.

Josie had orchestrated this, he was certain of it.

The question was, why? Had he read her wrong after all?

Jo pulled out the picnic blanket and gave it a shake. It felt good to be in her everyday clothes again. Though she had to admit, it hadn't been altogether unpleasant to see Ry's reaction to her being all gussied up.

It would have been a mite nicer, though, if he hadn't acted so all-fired surprised about it. Not that she should give a fig for his reaction when she was supposed to be doing her ever-loving best to get him to notice her sister.

But there had been a moment when his eyes lingered on her, a moment that set moths to dancing in her stomach…

Lost in that thought, she was startled when Ry grabbed the other end of the blanket. "Thanks, but I can take care of this," she announced. "Why don't you help Cora Beth with the basket?"

He held on to the cloth. "Danny's taking care of that."

Continuing to refuse his help would be silly, so she nodded and let him help her spread the square of cloth out on the ground.

"So, this is a family tradition, is it?" he asked.

"Yep. Goes all the way back to when my parents were courting." Jo anchored her two corners with fist-sized rocks while Ry did the same. "Pa proposed to Ma in this very meadow, under that tree over yonder. After they got hitched, they started coming here regular for picnics every Sunday, weather permitting."

"Sounds as if your parents were romantics."

Was he poking fun at them? A quick look at his expression satisfied her that it had been a simple observation. "My parents were very much in love."

"Well, that's one thing we have in common."

Her head shot up and her pulse kicked up a notch. What did he mean?

He stared straight into her eyes. "My parents were very much in love, too."

Of course. Jo stooped down, smoothing the blanket and hiding her face, which felt uncomfortably warm at the moment.

Uncle Grover wandered over just then and she could have hugged him for providing a distraction.

"Come along, my boy, you must see the millipedes I found near that fallen log. One of them is nearly five inches long."

Ry raised a brow. "Five inches, you say? That's something worth seeing."

They headed toward the site of the momentous find. "Of course," she heard Uncle Grover explain, "millipedes are not really insects, but I still find them fascinating creatures."

She saw Ry's nod and heard him ask a question about what millipedes fed on before they moved out of range.

With Ry gone, she sat back on her heels and took herself in hand. She had to push harder to get him and Cora Beth together if she ever wanted to see New York harbor and all those other places on her map. For Viola's sake too—that sweet little girl needed mothering.

By the time Ry and Uncle Grover returned, the meal was spread out and ready to enjoy, and Jo had herself back under control. Cora Beth asked Ry to say the blessing, and he did so after only the slightest hesitation.

Once the meal was over, Jo popped up and volunteered to keep an eye on the girls. "I thought we'd check out those persimmon trees over at the edge of the tree line. Mr. Lassiter, you don't mind helping Cora Beth clean up, do you?"

Cora Beth immediately protested. "That's not necessary. I can handle this on my own."

Ry, predictably, did the gentlemanly thing. "But you prepared this feast, Mrs. Collins," he argued. "It wouldn't be right for you to have to clean up after it, as well."

Jo strolled away with the girls, confident that having the two of them working side by side would set them on the road to a deeper attraction.

She returned forty minutes later to find Cora Beth knitting, Uncle Grover napping and Ry and Danny nowhere to be seen.

Her sister looked up with a smile. "Hello, girls. Any luck?"

"There's lots of fruit," Jo answered, "but none ripe enough to pick." She took another look around. "Where's Danny and Mr. Lassiter?"

"Oh, they wandered off about twenty minutes ago. Danny wanted to show him Fist Rock."

Jo plopped down next to her sister and hugged her knees in exasperation. All her planning seemed to have been in vain. But at least they'd had twenty minutes or so together. Maybe that had been enough to sow a few seeds of interest.

And it was hard to be angry with Ry. He was a good man, in the truest sense of that word. He allowed Uncle Grover his dignity. He got along well with the children. He was scrupulous in repaying even the smallest of debts. And he obviously had the means to support a large family.

He'd make a great husband for Cora Beth, no doubt about it. Her sister would easily adapt to life in his world, in fact would flourish in such a setting.

But Viola was the real key. Cora Beth had a soft spot for children and would be both willing and happy to add Viola to her brood. And of course Mr. Lassiter would welcome having someone as loving and capable as Cora Beth to help him raise his ward.

The plan was perfect.

So why didn't she feel as enthusiastic as she had earlier?

Jo gave herself a mental shake. She had to remember the prize she was aiming toward—her freedom. This was still her best shot.

Jo clicked her tongue as she gave the reins a flick. Somehow, despite her best efforts to arrange things otherwise, Ry sat on the front seat of the buckboard beside her.

She'd expected him to argue when she insisted on taking the reins. But to her surprise he'd merely nodded.

As they moved down the road, she was vaguely aware of Cora Beth and Uncle Grover chatting together behind them, but Ry's presence seemed to crowd everything else out. Not that he was doing much of anything. In fact he was leaned back all comfy-like, with his legs stretched out at an angle that brought his boots up close to hers. And he hadn't said a word since she'd set the horse in motion.

But there was something about his nearness, about the way he watched her with that little half smile, that made her all fidgety inside. Finally, she couldn't take it any longer. "What's the matter?" she groused. "I got dirt on my face or something?"

His smile widened. "Not at all." He tilted his head. "I was just trying to decide if the green in your eyes is closer to the color of spring clover or that of the hummingbirds that used to flit around my mother's flower garden."

His voice was pitched low enough that the others couldn't hear him without trying. The deep rumble of it spread through her like a cup of warm cocoa on a chilly day. Jo felt as if he'd trapped her gaze with his own. For the life of her she couldn't look away. No one had ever said such things to her, had ever looked at her the way he was now.

An endless heartbeat later she got hold of herself and abruptly faced forward. She was reading too much into his words. Besides, those were the kinds of things he should be saying to Cora Beth, not her.

The slight hitch in her breathing was merely surprise and frustration, nothing more.

Before she could figure out how to respond, he changed the subject. "Thanks for including me and Viola in your outing today. I think she really enjoyed herself." His voice had returned to normal, his expression nothing more than friendly. It was as if the past few moments hadn't happened. For some reason that didn't improve her mood any.

"Glad to hear it." Thank goodness her voice was steady.

"It was a good day for me as well." Something about his tone made her glance up but his expression gave nothing away.

"I've been thinking about your invitation to stay through Thanksgiving," he continued. "I think we ought to set a few conditions."

Uh-oh. The man and his conditions—what was he up to now? "And those are?"

"First, you let me pay for our board, just like any of your other customers."

She thought about that a minute. It didn't sit right with her, being as he'd saved her life and all, but if it was the only way to get him to stay...

She nodded. "That sounds fair. But since Viola's sharing a room with Cora Beth's girls, you only pay half price for her."

Had his lips twitched? What did he find so all-fired funny?

"Agreed." His tone made her wonder if she'd imagined that grin.

Better move on. "What else?"

"You agree to let me help out around the livery and the boardinghouse. I get bored just sitting around doing nothing."

She could understand that. "All right, but only if you promise not to do anything to set your healing back."

It was his turn to look surprised at her agreeable response. Thing was, she figured having him do a few chores around the house would give Cora Beth something else to admire about him.

"Then it looks like Viola and I will be availing ourselves of your hospitality through Thanksgiving."

And if her plans worked as well as she hoped, for quite some time after as well.

Fifteen minutes later, Jo stopped the buckboard in front of the boardinghouse. "Everybody out," she ordered. "Danny, make sure you grab the hamper and blanket." She rested an arm on her knee while the kids scrambled out of the back and Uncle Grover helped Cora Beth step down. "I'll take care of the wagon and horse. Just make sure you save me some supper."

Ry made no move to step down. "I'll lend you a hand." He turned to Cora Beth. "That is, if Mrs. Collins would be so good as to watch Viola for a bit."

Before Jo could protest, Cora Beth nodded. "It would be my pleasure."

"Thanks but I can handle this just fine." Ry was supposed to be spending time with Cora Beth, not her.

He raised a brow. "Remember our bargain. Not backing out on me already, are you?"

Feeling outmaneuvered, she grimaced and set the wagon in motion.

He thought he was so clever but he hadn't seen clever yet. She was already making a mental list of chores that would keep him way too busy around the boardinghouse for him to even think about working at the livery.

She didn't need him messing with her mind the way

he'd been doing lately. She was so close to achieving her dream, nothing, or nobody, was going to change her mind now.

The wheel hit a bump, causing his shoulder to brush against hers, and her pulse jumped in response.

So much for her self-control.

Heavenly Father, this man sure does present a powerful temptation. Please give me the strength to see this through to its proper outcome.

Chapter Nineteen

Ry wiped his brow with the back of his wrist, then leaned against the handle of the pitchfork. "So, tell me about this Thanksgiving festival. I take it it's a big to-do."

Josie examined a piece of leather she'd just trimmed. "Just about the biggest doings in these parts," she answered without looking up. "The whole town takes part, or them that can, and the celebrating goes on all day."

Ry tossed a forkful of hay in the middle stall. He'd spent the morning mucking them out and now he was spreading fresh straw. Seemed Josie had taken him at his word when he said to put him to work.

"So exactly what does this celebrating entail?" It was like pulling teeth today to get her to talk to him. Had he been too forward on the ride home from the picnic yesterday?

"It pretty much follows the same pattern every year." She leaned back in her seat and finally faced him. "Folks start arriving around eight o'clock. Reverend Ludlow preaches a short service to kick things off on the right note. Then there's games and competitions, like horseshoes, wheelbarrow races and pie eating contests. 'Round about eleven o'clock everyone troops inside and the kids put on their program."

She stretched out her legs and tipped her chair back. "Afterward, everybody sits down for the best-tasting, button-popping, belt-loosening meal you ever did eat."

"And that's it?" Of course he knew it wasn't, but he liked listening to her unique way of describing things.

Josie gave an unladylike snort. "That's just the morning. The early afternoon is more games for those who have energy to burn, and visiting or table games for those who prefer something quieter. At some point the men's quartet will serenade us. Later in the day, someone will pull out a fiddle, the center of the floor will get cleared and we'll have us a foot-stomping dance."

She gave him a wickedly amused smile. "I have to warn you, you'll be in high demand once the dancing starts."

His alarm was only partially feigned. "Surely you're joking."

"Not a bit. You're new in town, you're eligible, and you can be passably charming if you put your mind to it." She flashed a teasing grin. "All highly desirable qualities when it comes to claiming a dance partner."

Did *she* think they were "highly desirable qualities?" "So it has nothing to do with me personally? Just that I'm a fresh face and my ma raised me to be polite?"

"That's about the size of it."

"Sounds like a fun time will be had by all."

She laughed at his dour expression, just as he'd intended her to. Actually the thought of dancing, as long as it was with her, was rather appealing. What would it feel like to hold her and twirl her around the dance floor? Could he tease one of those beautiful, light-up-her-eyes smiles from her?

The family gathered in the kitchen after supper again that evening. Funny how in such a short time he'd come to consider himself and Viola almost a part of the family.

He glanced toward his ward and smiled. She was practicing her lines for the Thanksgiving program alongside Audrey. It was the most animated he'd seen her since she'd arrived five days ago.

"Mr. Lassiter, I want to thank you for fixing that loose baseboard." Cora Beth spoke without looking up from the pie crust she was making. "I've been meaning to tend to it for ages."

"Seems the least I could do after all you folks have done for Viola and me." Ry cast a surreptitious glance Josie's way. Had she taken note of how much use he could be to her and her family?

So, Ry had helped Cora Beth around the place after he left the livery this afternoon, had he? Was her sister starting to notice how nice it would be to have him in her life permanently? She'd be a fool not to. Any woman would be lucky to have a man like Ry.

"What are you doing?" Ry was watching her with a puzzled frown.

She raised a brow. Wasn't it obvious? "I'm peeling apples."

"But why are you taking such care?"

"Just practicing." She grinned at his puzzled look.

"Jo wins the apple peeling contest every year," Danny added.

"Apple peeling contest? If you're trying to be the fastest—"

"Not the fastest." Josie picked up the peel from the last apple she'd worked on. "It's to see who can get the longest unbroken piece."

"Ah, I see." Then his expression took on a challenging glint. "And can anybody enter this contest?"

Thought he could take her, did he? "Yep. But I'm warning you, it's not as easy as it looks."

Ry reached for an apple and a knife. "We'll see about that."

Josie stood at the back of the buckboard Thursday morning, carefully loading her carved pumpkins and gourds as Audrey and Viola carried them from the house. It was a beautiful day for the Thanksgiving festival, clear and crisp without being too cold. The trees all around, the ones that still had leaves at any rate, were sporting bursts of yellow, orange and red. And the air fairly crackled with excitement. Groups of townsfolk were moving toward the town hall, children skipping ahead of the adults.

Ry interrupted her thoughts as he lifted his fifth hamper into the buggy. She frowned, worried he might be putting too much strain on his arm.

"You'd think your sister was feeding an army," he groused.

"She is." Josie studied him carefully but saw no sign of discomfort.

"Didn't you say *everyone* brings food?"

"They do." She smiled at his raised brow. "All the food is set up together on long tables across one side of the room, and folks try to sample a little of everything.

It's a matter of pride amongst the women to bring the most popular dish." She took the pair of gourds Audrey and Viola handed her, the last of the lot. "Besides, most folks will eat both lunch and supper there."

Ry lifted first Pippa and then Lottie into the back of the buckboard, easing them gently in amongst her pumpkins. "You girls are in charge of guarding your Aunt Josie's masterpieces," he said with a solemn expression. "Do you think you can handle the job?"

Two heads bobbed in unison, while their hands made cross-my-heart motions.

His lips turned up in that heart-stopping smile. "I knew I could count on you."

Honestly, she didn't know why the man worried so much about how he would get on with Viola. He was obviously fine father material. Cora Beth would be lucky to have him.

For some reason her mind skittered away from that thought as she dusted her hands on her skirt.

Cora Beth, Audrey and Viola stepped out of the house, shaking Josie out of her jumbled thoughts.

"I do hope I haven't forgotten anything," Cora Beth said, snuggling one more jar of relish into the largest hamper.

"Doesn't matter." Josie rolled her eyes. "We couldn't fit another thing in the buggy."

Danny scrambled into the front seat beside Uncle Grover and gathered the reins. The rest of them would walk.

Ry turned his collar up. "Shall we, ladies," he said, with a bow and a flourish of the hand.

Always so gentlemanly. Made a woman feel special. Pushing that thought away, Josie quickly took hold of Audrey and Viola's hands, leaving Cora Beth to walk with Ry before she forgot she was trying to push the two of them together.

As they strolled down the sidewalk, Ry did his best to pay attention to Cora Beth's chatter while surreptitiously watching Josie walk ahead with the girls. He hadn't missed the deliberate way she distanced herself from him. Again. What was she up to?

A moment later, Cora Beth halted in her tracks. "Audrey Elizabeth, come here a minute please."

The little girl obediently trotted back to her mother's side. Cora Beth spun her around and fiddled with the tie at the back of her pinafore.

When they resumed walking, Ry made certain he was by Josie's side this time while Cora Beth and the girls took the lead.

They walked in silence for a few minutes, then Josie finally gave him a sideways look. "This'll probably be a letdown from the fancy parties you're used to."

"Actually, I'm looking forward to this shindig. Most of those so-called fancy parties are rather stuffy." He was certain there'd be nothing stuffy about this gathering.

She didn't appear convinced. "I've seen pictures of fine ballrooms filled with orchestras and crowds of people gussied up all fancy-like. Must be something to see."

"It's a sight to see, all right."

"I knew it." Apparently she'd missed the sarcasm in his tone. He could see her imagining some exotic, fairytale-like scene.

Once they arrived at the town hall, the morning passed much the way Josie had described it, and Ry enthusiastically joined in. He and Viola took third place in the wheelbarrow race and the child proudly wore her yellow ribbon the rest of the day.

Ry was also stood shoulder to shoulder with Josie as they cheered Danny on in the pie-eating contest. The boy didn't take a ribbon but he seemed pleased with his showing, anyway.

And Ry gave Josie a run for her money in the apple peeling contest. She ultimately won, but her winning apple peel was less than an inch longer than his.

After the ribbons were awarded, Viola touched his arm and studied him with concerned eyes. "Don't worry, Uncle Ry, you did your best and I'm proud of you."

Ry was touched by her words, even though he knew she was likely parroting something overheard from the adults. He stooped down so their faces were level. "Thank you, Viola. It means a lot to me that you were in my corner."

She gave him a sheepish grin. "Actually, I was rooting for both you and Miss Josie. That's okay, isn't it?"

He laughed and gave her a squeeze. "Absolutely." So she *was* forming an attachment to Josie. Things were definitely looking up.

After Viola ran off with Audrey and some of the other girls, Ry discovered Josie had disappeared. After several minutes of searching he finally found her inside the building, selecting tidbits from the vast array of food set on tables around the room.

"Trying to sneak in a few bites early," he accused.

She started, twisting around with an affronted frown. "Nope." Then she grinned. "Though it's mighty tempting."

Ry agreed. The tables were laden with dishes sumptuous enough to please even the most finicky hostess. The meats included platters of the traditional turkey, chicken, ham and roast, along with game such as venison, rabbit and fowl. Large pans of dressing sat alongside bowls containing sauces and gravies. Next came a dizzying array of vegetables—beans, potatoes, corn, carrots, onions and mixtures of the same. They were cooked in every imaginable way—baked, stewed, roasted, creamed. Farther along were colorful relishes, pickles, fresh baked breads, cheeses and fruit spreads.

But the real eye-catcher was the row upon row of elaborate desserts. Pies, cakes, cobblers, cookies, tarts—the women had truly outdone themselves.

Her laughter brought his gaze back around. "I declare, you look like a hungry dog who's spied a soup bone."

He grinned back, unabashed. "Said the woman pilfering from the food table."

"I'll have you know," she said, her tone haughty, "that I'm actually performing my good deed for the day."

"Is that a fact?"

"Yes sir, it is. I'm in charge of packing the shut-in baskets this year." She lifted the hamper looped over her left arm.

"Shut-in baskets?"

"If someone's not able to join us, we fix up a basket of goodies and bring it to 'em so they don't feel left out. This year Cora Beth and I get to handle the delivery."

"I see." That caretaker streak ran deep in her. "Here, let me help." He reached for the basket.

"No need. I—"

But he'd already snagged it. "Now you have both hands free." He tried for a guileless smile.

She frowned suspiciously, then nodded. "We have two families this year. Mr. Clawson owns a small farm just outside of town. His mare's about ready to foal and he didn't want to leave her."

She added another thick slice of ham to the basket before moving on to the vegetables. "Then there's Mrs. Willows and her daughter, Myra. Mrs. Willows has been doing poorly the past few years. I hear tell she barely gets out of bed these days. And Myra, bless her heart, looks out for her ma and younger sister now that her older sisters have moved on." She nodded toward a group of younger folk. "The girl over yonder in the blue and yellow dress, the one flirting with Cecil Jones, is her sister, Dolly."

The girl looked all of fifteen and seemed not to have a care in the world. "So, why isn't she taking care of her mother and sister's basket?"

Josie shrugged, but Ry didn't miss the disapproving purse of her lips. Family was important to Josie, and she obviously didn't approve of those who shirked their duty in that area.

At the dessert tables, Josie slipped two pies and a dish of cookies in the hamper, then gave a satisfied nod. "That ought to do it."

She didn't move to take the basket from him as he'd expected. Instead she cupped her chin. "You know," she said slowly, "being as you want to be so helpful, why don't *you* deliver these with Cora Beth? That way I can help get the stage ready for the children's program."

She was up to something. But before he could form

a response Cora Beth bustled up, closely followed by Sheriff Hammond.

"Thanks for packing the basket while I helped Iris," she said, then indicated her companion. "And Sheriff Hammond has volunteered to go in your place. Wasn't that kind of him?"

"Actually, I need to speak to Stan Clawson anyway," the sheriff added. "Thought this would be as good a time as any."

Ry hid a grin at Josie's thwarted-plans expression. "How fortunate you should offer. Josie here was just saying she had some other matters to attend to."

"Well, that's that then." Sheriff Hammond took the basket from Ry and turned to Cora Beth. "Shall we?"

As the two made their way out of the building, Ry turned to Josie. "Now, what is it we need to do to get the stage ready?"

Chapter Twenty

As the children made their way to the makeshift stage, Josie was acutely aware of Ry sitting shoulder to shoulder beside her in the crowded hall. In fact, the man had barely left her side since mid-morning. Not that she hadn't enjoyed his company. But how was she supposed to get him and Cora Beth to see how perfect they were for each other if they didn't spend some time together?

It should be Cora Beth sitting here beside him, watching how he smiled encouragingly when Viola cast an anxious glance at the audience, inhaling his unique, spicy scent, experiencing how very safe and comforting it felt to be at his side.

Josie caught herself on that last thought. She'd had way too many thoughts like that recently. It was Cora Beth who was a match for Ry, not her. What she wanted was freedom to travel, just like Aunt Pearl. There'd be time enough to think about settling down once she had a few adventures.

The children's program went off with only the normal snags—five-year-old Amy Dobbs took one look at the audience, burst into tears, and ran off the stage. A couple of the other kids forgot or stumbled over part of their lines. Joey Lofton stubbed his toe. But they were all given enthusiastic rounds of applause.

Audrey, of course, said her lines with a great deal of melodrama. When Viola's turn came up, Ry straightened in his seat. Josie was oddly touched as she felt equal parts pride and concern vibrating from him. When the little girl got through without a misstep he clapped louder than anyone in the audience. Just like a proud father.

How could her sister not fall head over heels for a guy like this? Why, if she wasn't so dead set against putting down roots, she might even find herself falling for him.

"Looks like you're quite the strategist, son." Uncle Grover rubbed his chin as he studied Ry's latest move on the chessboard.

Ry leaned back in his chair, keeping his gaze peripherally focused on the entry, just as it had been for the past few hours. He'd looked around for Josie after lunch without success and he was beginning to wonder if something had happened to her.

Uncle Grover made a triumphant sound in the back of his throat as he moved his bishop. "Let's see what you can do with that."

Ry shifted his gaze to the chessboard, then paused and turned back to the doorway. Sure enough, there was Josie, strolling in as if she hadn't a care in the world. She spared only a quick glance his way before heading across the room to join a small group that included her sister and several neighbors.

Trapped by the chess game, it was fifteen minutes before Ry could extricate himself.

As he stood, she threw back her head and laughed at something Sheriff Hammond had said. Ry wondered irritably why he couldn't draw that same kind of relaxed, unguarded reaction from Josie.

Surely she wasn't sweet on the lawman? Ry frowned at Sheriff Hammond's back. Any fool could see the man was all wrong for her. She needed someone who understood her spirited nature, who would encourage her rather than try to rein her in.

His jaw muscles tightened as he tried to navigate his way through the room in long, quick strides.

But the sound of someone tuning a fiddle ricocheted through the building before he could reach his goal. Suddenly everyone was in motion and Ry was drawn into the mix. Game boards and sewing baskets were put away. Tables and benches were dismantled and moved from the center of the room. Napping children roused and looked for ways to demonstrate their renewed energy.

More fiddlers took their places on the platform and in short order the room was filled with lively music. A moment later, couples began pairing off and making their way to the makeshift dance floor. Even those who preferred to sit on the sidelines joined in by clapping to the music.

Ry smiled as he saw Audrey drag Viola to the edge of the crowd and begin an enthusiastic if not graceful bit of whirling. And they weren't the only youngsters on the floor.

This was like the barn dances from his youth. He'd forgotten how family oriented they'd been.

"Do you dance, Mr. Lassiter?"

He smiled in pleased surprise as he turned to find Josie at his elbow, Sheriff Hammond nowhere in sight. Was that an invitation? "I do when I find the right partner."

She pulled her sister forward. "Then you should ask Cora Beth. She loves to dance."

Having little choice in the matter, Ry gave Josie's sister a bow. "I'd be delighted." He offered his arm. "Shall we?"

With a smile, Cora Beth allowed him to lead her onto the floor.

They'd barely taken their first turn when she met his glance with an amused twinkle in her eye. "I do believe my sister is trying to do a bit of matchmaking," she said demurely.

Ry almost missed a step. He hadn't realized she'd caught on to Josie's scheme, too. And how in blue blazes was he supposed to respond without insulting her or her sister or both of them?

She laughed. "Don't look so worried. You're not in any danger from me."

Good grief, had his trepidation been that obvious? "My apologies, ma'am, I—"

Her smile broadened. "No offense, Mr. Lassiter, but while I do enjoy your company, I'm not looking for another husband just yet." She tossed her head, for all the world like a saucy schoolgirl. "And if I ever do start looking, I'm afraid you and I just would not suit."

Ry wasn't quite certain how to take that. So he veered away from a direct response. "Shall we tell her that we're on to her?"

"Oh, heavens, no. I wouldn't want to spoil her fun. Besides, this fits nicely with some plans of my own."

"Ma'am?"

"Oh, nothing for you to concern yourself with."

Ry was beginning to believe there was the merest touch of lunacy running through the Wylie family, at least in the female members. "Whatever you say."

The song ended and he escorted her from the floor.

"Now, see if you can convince my sister not to spend all night playing the wallflower." Cora Beth leaned in conspiratorially. "She'll try to convince you she doesn't dance but I know better."

Ry spotted Josie talking to Sheriff Hammond again. He started toward her but was hailed by Dr. Whitman who inquired about his arm. The good doctor in turn introduced Ry to his daughter, Lucy. Good manners dictated that Ry invite her to dance.

Afterward he was twice more put in the position of escorting virtual strangers onto the dance floor. Josie hadn't been far off the mark when she said he'd be in demand. Once, in an effort to forestall yet another attempt, he asked Audrey and Viola to stand together as his partners. Delighted, the girls each took one of his hands and giggled their way through the entire song.

With some expert maneuvering and a good sense of timing, he managed to land beside Josie when the music stopped. "Ladies," he said with a formal bow to both girls, "I thank you for a most enjoyable dance."

The comment earned him another set of giggles.

"Did you see us, Aunt JoJo?" Audrey asked.

"I certainly did." Josie's eyes strayed to his as she answered, and he saw approval mixed with some softer emotion. "And a fine group of dancers you made."

"Come on, Viola." Audrey latched onto the other girl's hand. "Let's see if there's any lemonade left."

Josie smoothed her skirt. "Looks like you're popular with the ladies this evening."

"As you said, I'm just a novelty." He studied her, trying to figure out what was going on in that scheming mind of hers.

"You and Cora Beth looked pretty good out there. From the way y'all were smiling at each other it appeared you were enjoying yourselves."

Did he detect a touch of jealousy? That thought cheered him up. "Your sister is both a fine dancer and good company."

She gave him a sideways glance. "But you only danced with her that one time."

He shrugged. "She hasn't lacked for partners tonight. I didn't want to monopolize her time."

"She's popular because she's such a good catch. A fellow would be mighty lucky to be able to claim her for his own."

"I agree." But he was tired of discussing Cora Beth's virtues. "I noticed you haven't been out on the floor yet."

Her expression closed off. "I don't dance."

"Don't? Or won't?"

This time she crossed her arms and didn't quite meet his gaze. "Doesn't matter. I'm not getting out on that floor."

"That's where you're wrong." Ry took her hand and tugged her toward the area where couples were forming for the next dance.

Josie dug in her heels. "I said I don't dance."

He turned to face her. "I have it on good authority you're actually a very good dancer. I think it's high time you gave it another go."

He saw the mutinous look in her eye. "I'd count it a personal favor," he said quickly, "if you'd allow me to take the woman who saved my life for a spin around the dance floor."

He felt her hesitation, sensed the weakening of her resolve and decided that was as good as an agreement.

Placing a hand at her waist, he took her other hand in his and stepped forward as the music started. He smiled when he realized they were playing a waltz.

For a moment or two they simply danced, each adjusting to the other's movements. And they moved surprisingly well together.

She wasn't soft like other women he'd danced with. Years of hard work in the livery, doing the job her father had done before her, had given her firm muscles and rough, callused hands. But there was also a well-honed grace, a sureness of movement that he found much more appealing.

The dress she wore was plain, with none of the fripperies most girls seemed to enjoy—no bows in her hair, no lace on her bodice, no ribbons at her waist. Strangely, none of that detracted from her femininity, not tonight.

Holding her in his arms as they moved around the dance floor stirred all manner of unfamiliar, protective, tender feelings. And when one of the movements of the dance brought them unexpectedly close, the catch in her breath set his heart pounding with a beat he was certain she could hear.

This moment—holding her, inhaling her unique scent, trying to fathom the secrets locked in her eyes—was one of the sweetest things he'd ever experienced.

This felt oh, so right.

* * *

This was all wrong! Jo's heart hammered in her chest. Her breath caught in her throat every time she met Ry's glance. She felt plumb light-headed, and it wasn't just from spinning around the dance floor. That moment when they'd come so close together, she'd felt an unaccountable urge to kiss him, which was just plain chuckleheaded. What in the world had gotten into her?

She should never have allowed Ry talk her into this dance. How could she let herself get all besotted over him? He and Cora Beth were supposed to end up together, she had it all planned out.

She had to pull herself together. She was just letting her imagination get the best of her. Besides, he couldn't possibly be sweet on her. No man had shown the least bit of interest, at least not in that way, since she'd taken over the livery when her pa got so bad sick.

No, someone like Cora Beth was much better suited to a man like Ry.

She looked up and found herself staring into his smoky gray eyes, and her step faltered. The way he was looking at her was so…"tender" was the only word that came to mind.

Father, help me please, I think I'm in trouble here.

The song finally ended but they didn't move apart immediately. It was only when they were jostled by another couple leaving the floor that the spell was finally broken.

Josie took a deep breath, feeling as if she'd forgotten to inhale for the past few minutes. She sure didn't remember a simple dance getting a person so all-fired flustered.

Not that she would call what had just happened a "simple dance."

Ry took her elbow and moved toward the door. "You look flushed. Let's step outside for some fresh air."

Not trusting herself to speak, Josie nodded. They wended their way through the crowd, pausing to speak to others along the way.

What was he thinking? Had she given away any of her thoughts? That would be too mortifying to even consider. When they stepped outside, she took a deep breath of the cool evening air and let her jangly nerves settle a bit.

Ry motioned toward a bench set against the outer wall of the building and with a nod, she took a seat. He settled beside her, leaving a respectful distance between them. She refused to look at him, but was keenly aware of his presence, of his gaze on her.

Better to concentrate on the other things around them.

Murmurings of conversations mingled with the music of the fiddles from inside, making a pleasant backdrop of sound.

It wasn't quite evening yet but the overcast sky had made it necessary to light the lamps around the building, including the one directly over the bench she and Ry shared. A few other folks milled around outside, braving the cold to escape the crowded dance floor. Even so, situated in their own pool of light, Josie felt as if they were somehow enclosed in one of those water globes Mr. Miller had on display over at the mercantile, visible yet separate from everyone and everything around them.

She leaned against the building and stared up at the

lamp, watching as the glass-enclosed flame flickered in a solo dance of its own.

Was he going to say anything? Or just sit there and stare at her? Time to turn his thoughts in a different direction.

"You know," she said, staring out at the road to town, "Knotty Pine might look like a backwater, but it's growing."

"Is that so?"

She wished he'd quit staring at her so intently. "Yep. Why, just last year Mr. Danvers added three new rooms to the hotel and Mrs. Jefferson opened a dress shop. And two new families have moved into the area since spring."

"Impressive." He picked up a penny-sized rock, rolling it between his thumb and forefinger as he continued to watch her.

She wasn't comfortable with the loud silence hanging between them. "You ever thought of doing something besides lawyering?"

"I always liked working with horses." He smiled as if he'd just admitted wanting to fly. "Once upon a time I thought I'd like to start a horse ranch. Wanted to raise and train the best cutting horses in the country."

Interest piqued, she finally turned to face him. "So why didn't you?"

"Because horse ranching and being a lawyer don't exactly mix."

Was there a hint of regret in his words? "So I guess you like lawyering better than raising horses."

He was silent for a time, seeming to ponder her words. Finally he looked up. "I honestly don't know."

He reached for her hand, and she felt her heartbeat

kick up a notch as they connected. "Josie, if you've been trying to convince me that Knotty Pine has a lot to offer a man, there's no need. I'm already convinced. In fact—"

"No!" She saw the confusion in his eyes, the pulling back, and it hurt. But she couldn't let him finish what she sensed he'd been about to say.

"Pardon?" His expression was guarded now and he'd released her hand.

She missed the warmth of his touch. But this was no time to mince words. "I like you, you know that. But you have a kid to take care of now and you're looking to settle down. Don't get me wrong, I admire you for doing it, but that's not what I want from life right now."

"You still want to see the world."

At least he'd been paying attention. "Yes."

His expression was solemn. "I'm afraid the world may disappoint you."

"That's a chance I'll take." She swiveled around to face him fully. "You need to understand, this is something I have to do."

"But there's nothing that says you have to do it alone."

How could she make him see how she felt without having it sound like she resented her family? "I've been looking out for other folks for most of my life. I want to have some time where the only person I have to worry about is me. I know that sounds selfish, but for once I want to experience what it feels like not to be weighed down by other folks' wants or needs."

She took a deep breath, forcing herself to say what needed to be said. "If you want someone to settle down with, if you want to find a good mother for Viola, you'll have to look elsewhere."

He crossed his arms. "Is that why you keep pushing me at your sister?"

She winced. Had she been so obvious? "I'm not pushing." Her conscience wouldn't let her stop at that. "Well, not exactly."

His only response was a raised brow.

"Besides—" she hated that defensive note that had crept into her voice "—would marrying Cora Beth be such a bad choice?"

"Only in the sense that it wouldn't be the *right choice* for me. Or your sister, for that matter."

She stood abruptly, hating that he couldn't understand, hating that things couldn't be different.

She stared down at him with clenched fists. "You are the most stubborn, selfish man I have ever met. Can't you see what a choice like this could mean to Cora Beth and to Viola and to—" She halted, realizing she'd almost said too much.

But judging by the way his expression hardened, it was already too late.

"To who, Josie? To you?" He matched her stance. "Is that what this is all about? Marrying your sister off so you can feel free to go your merry way with a clear conscience? Even if marriage isn't what she wants?" His eyes narrowed. "Now who's being stubborn and selfish?"

His words were a slap in the face. How could he say such ugly things? She only wanted what was best for everyone. He didn't know how much she'd already sacrificed, how much she'd given up.

But she would *not* let him see how much his words had hurt.

She thrust out her chin. "I've had enough partying for one day. Please let Cora Beth know I've headed to the livery to check on a few things. I'll see y'all back at the house later tonight."

He raked a hand through his hair, a look of frustration on his face. "Look, I'm sorry. Sometimes I don't think before—"

She held up a hand. "No apology needed. I said some things I shouldn't have, too."

He moved back a half step, as if he knew she needed room. "You don't have to leave. I won't broach the subject again tonight—you have my word."

Josie shook her head. "I really should check the livery. The buggy's already been loaded up so I'll drop off the supplies at the house first. You'll probably need to help Cora Beth carry the twins home." That last comment would ensure he stayed put.

As Josie moved away, she found herself trying to stuff her hands in pockets that weren't there. Was he right in what he'd said? Was she being stubborn and selfish?

No! She was just being true to her dream.

Father, help me to be strong. I know this is the answer to my prayer if I'll but stand firm.

Ry watched her leave, giving himself a mental kick for his clumsy handling of the whole situation. Why had he pressed so hard? Her dream of escaping the confines of Knotty Pine was deeply felt and a driving force with her, probably all the more so since she'd had to put it on hold for so long. He'd known that.

She was a wild pony, yearning to trade the lush grasslands and security of the herd for a pair of wings. If only she could see those wings came with a price—a view of the world from a lonely distance, being at the mercy of the wind to chart your course, and sometimes, living life in a cage—gilded or otherwise.

Well, if her dream was that important to her, then he'd find a way to give her a taste. A journey of some sort—it would be his Christmas gift to her. But he'd do it in such a way that she would have a safety net. And in the process, maybe help her see how wonderful her life here was by comparison.

He'd just have to figure out a way to do it so she wouldn't feel as if she were taking charity from him.

Chapter Twenty-One

❦

"I want to hire you."

Jo looked up from her workbench to see Ry standing just inside the livery, his expression unreadable.

Had he said *hire* her? "What's that?"

"Viola and I will be leaving day after tomorrow."

She fought back the jolt of denial. It would be so strange not to have him here, not to see him sitting across the table from her at supper or look forward to him wandering in here every morning to lend a hand with whatever chores were on her list.

More importantly, she told herself, was that this spelled the end to her matchmaking scheme.

"We'll stop at Hawk's Creek first to visit Sadie and Griff for a few days, then move on to Philadelphia to see my grandfather."

She had herself back under control. "So what do you want to hire me for?"

"The thing is, I'm not ready to take on sole responsibility for Viola's care, especially on a long trip. It would be better if I had someone to help watch over her." His gaze drilled into hers. "Preferably someone Viola's already comfortable with."

Jo's heart thumped painfully against her chest. Was he really offering to take her with them?

"Since I know how much you want to travel, and since Viola is comfortable with you, I thought your joining us might be a good solution for everyone."

Did he know what a prize he was offering her?

Of course he did. He was doing this as part of his misguided effort to apologize for the words they'd exchanged last night. Not that his reason mattered. This was the opportunity—

Reality crashed back in. "I can't."

"Why not?"

Because I'm already half in love with you. Because my resolve is not as strong as I thought. Because I'm already close to throwing away my dream to be with you.

"Because I need to run this place, that's why. There's no way I could shut it down for that length of time."

"I'm not suggesting you do. I said I wanted to hire you. I plan to pay enough to cover the cost of hiring someone to watch the place while you're gone." He shrugged. "You wouldn't make much profit off the deal itself, but you'd get a chance to see other parts of the country. And I promise to get you back here in plenty of time to spend Christmas with your family."

He eyed her thoughtfully. "Unless you don't care for the idea of playing nanny-companion to Viola."

"You know I've taken a liking to her. She's like one of my nieces." Closer in some ways. There was something about the way Viola held part of herself back, the way she didn't quite fit in with the other kids, that Jo identified with on a gut level.

It was so tempting, but was it the right thing to do? Would having just this little taste make her even more discontent with her lot when she returned to Knotty Pine? Or would it make her work even harder to make it a permanent way of life?

Besides, if Ry escorted her back here for Christmas, it would give her a last chance to throw him and Cora Beth together.

Ry gave her a crooked smile. "Funny, I thought you'd jump at the offer." Something flickered in his eyes. "If it's me you're uncomfortable traveling with, I assure you—"

"No, of course not." The heat rose in her cheeks. "I mean, Viola will be with us, so of course there's nothing improper about it. It's just…"

She rubbed the back of her neck, trying to sort out her thoughts. Surely she could keep her feelings for him in check. After all, with new places to see she'd have other things to occupy her mind. "It's not just the livery," she said slowly. "I have responsibilities to my family. I need to talk this over with Cora Beth, make sure she's okay with taking charge while I'm gone."

"Perhaps this will let her test the waters a bit. After all, if you do eventually set out on your own, it would be good for both of you to know how everyone will fare."

Josie mulled that over. "I guess that makes sense."

"Then you're willing to take the job?"

Was she? A finger of excitement traced its way up Josie's spine. She grinned. "Yes, I suppose I am."

As familiar landmarks came into view, Ry felt the stirring of eagerness and dread he always felt when returning to Hawk's Creek. It was home. But a home where he felt more guest than resident.

"The house is around this bend and over the next hill," he said to his companions.

Viola and Josie straightened. They'd arrived at the Tyler depot almost an hour ago. He'd enjoyed pointing out some of the town's features to Josie, both the commendable and the notorious, as they'd passed through. She'd latched on to every novelty, every new sight or sound as if she could capture and pin them to a board to re-examine later, like Uncle Grover with his bugs.

Of course, once they'd left Tyler, the scenery hadn't offered anything different from the countryside around Knotty Pine.

For the past ten minutes, they'd been cutting through Hawk's Creek property, land that had been painstakingly cleared by his grandfather and further expanded by his father.

As they topped the rise, the main buildings came into view. The arched ironwork sign at the head of the drive informed the traveler that this was indeed Hawk's Creek Ranch. Beyond that, the sprawling two-story house shone a gleaming white, and proudly welcomed visitors with a well-maintained front drive and an expansive porch. The bunkhouse, barn and stable were just beyond.

Josie's reaction was just as he'd expected. Her eyes widened and she leaned forward to get a better look. Viola, however, clutched Daffy and wore a worried expression.

Was something bothering her?

"Do you think they'll mind if Daffy comes inside?"

Puzzle solved. "Not a bit," he reassured her. "When

I was a kid we had dogs running in and out of the place all the time. What's one little cat compared to that?"

His answer seemed to appease her.

They'd barely turned into the drive when Sadie rushed out the front door, waving excitedly.

"I thought you'd never get here," she exclaimed as soon as the buggy stopped. "I was just thinking I'd saddle Dusty and ride out to meet you."

Ry shook his head as he stepped down from the buggy. "Impatient as always." He grabbed Viola around the waist and swung her down before offering a hand to Josie.

"Manny will get your bags," Sadie said. "You just come on inside and make yourselves at home."

Was that a slip of the tongue? Did his sister truly think of him as a guest or was that more for Josie and Viola's benefit?

"We have refreshments ready." Sadie chattered on, taking Viola's hand. "I hope you like strawberry tarts, because Inez cooked up a fresh batch this morning."

Viola nodded. "Strawberries are my favorite."

"Mine, too!" Sadie said that as if it were the most wonderful of coincidences. "That's another thing we have in common."

Ry and Josie followed, apparently left to their own devices.

"Your sister is quite…enthusiastic," Josie commented.

He grinned. "A regular Texas whirlwind."

Inside, Sadie paused at the foot of the staircase. "I imagine you'll want to freshen up." She nodded Ry's way. "Your room is ready, as always. And since your letter stated that Josie and Viola would share a room, I had the large guest suite prepared."

She gave them a broad smile. "Ry, if you'll show them the way, I'll help Inez with the refreshments."

He swept an arm toward the staircase. "Ladies, after you."

He watched Josie eye the elaborately carved banister and the elegant stained glass window at the top of the landing. Then there was the chandelier hanging high above them. Not your usual furnishings for a ranch house. They were all touches his genteelly raised mother had added after she'd moved here.

"So, this is where you grew up," Josie said thoughtfully.

"In all its glory." They reached the second floor and he motioned to the right. "Your room is this way."

It was his turn to play host, to have her sleep under his roof, and it felt good. "This will be your room." He stood aside to let them enter the guest chamber, noting with approval that a small bed had been brought in from somewhere. It was placed near the roomy bed that anchored the center of the room.

He wanted Josie and Viola to feel comfortable and at home here. Because, if things went well on this trip, Josie would help him decide whether to call Hawk's Creek or Philadelphia home.

"Here comes Manny with your bags now." He took a step back. "My room is three doors down on the opposite side of the hall. Let me know if you need anything."

Josie wanted to hug herself and twirl around the room. The train ride, her very first, had been exciting. She'd stared out the window, drinking up the quickly passing countryside the way a thirsty horse lapped water. With each passing mile her dream drew closer to reality. At long last she was putting into motion all the plans she and Aunt Pearl had concocted, was fulfilling the promises she'd made to her aunt before she passed.

The town of Tyler had been an eye-opener, as unlike Knotty Pine as a woodshed was from a barn. It was a large, bustling city with lots of buildings and people milling about.

Ry had instructed the driver to take the long route through town and she knew it had been for her benefit. He'd been the perfect tour guide, pointing out people and landmarks, telling her and Viola interesting tidbits, bringing the place vividly alive.

And now this place. She'd visited ranches before but nothing to match Hawk's Creek. It operated on a scale far grander than anything she'd ever seen.

Even the house was deceptively simple-looking. Everywhere she looked were quiet signs of elegance. This huge room, with its fancy furnishings, its roomy padded window seat and large framed mirror, spoke of a level of comfort she wasn't used to.

Josie tried to picture Ry growing up here, to see the little boy he'd been—racing down the stairs, climbing that tree outside her window, roaming free across the wide expanse of this place.

The sound of Viola talking to Daffy brought Jo's attention back to the present. She checked her appearance in the vanity mirror one last time. No overalls for her on this trip. Cora Beth had outdone herself, producing several new dresses in the two days she had to plan her trip. Jo was more grateful to her sister than she would ever know. Now Ry wouldn't have to feel embarrassed by her appearance in front of his family and friends.

She held out her hand to Viola. "Ready for some of those strawberry tarts?"

As soon as they stepped into the hall, Ry's door opened. Was it coincidence or had he been listening for them?

He met them at the head of the stairs. "I hope the accommodations were acceptable, ladies."

Josie walked by him with a head-high nod. "They'll do."

She heard his chuckle as they descended the stairs and the deep bass thrummed inside her with a tingling sensation that was becoming all too familiar.

Chapter Twenty-Two

Ry followed Josie and Viola downstairs, smiling at Josie's unexpected quip. At least she hadn't left her down-to-earth humor behind in Knotty Pine.

When they reached the first floor, he swept an arm to his left. "This way."

Sadie waited for them in the parlor. The low table in front of her was covered with trays of pastries and preserves and his mother's china teapot. His sister played hostess with much fanfare, making certain everyone's tea was prepared just as they liked and heaping their saucers with a generous variety of treats.

"Now tell me," Sadie said as they settled down to enjoy their refreshments, "did you have a pleasant journey? Trains can be so stuffy and uncomfortable. Did you get to see much of Tyler when you passed through?"

Ry let Sadie's babble wash over him. Most of it was directed at Josie anyway. Instead he sat back and really studied his sister for the first time in years. She was twenty-four now, and still unmarried. Why? Surely there were plenty of good men around here who'd be happy to have a wife as personable and outgoing as Sadie, even if she did seem a bit flighty at times.

Was she too particular? Was she too tied to this place to want to leave it? Had someone already stolen her heart and failed to return her affection? Would his brother know the answer?

There was a short pause in the conversation and he set his now empty cup on the table. "Where's Griff?"

"Out in the east pasture." Sadie fiddled with the handle of her teacup. "He and the men are constructing a new barn out that way. But he should be home soon."

"That's a lovely upright you have," Josie interjected.

"Why, thank you." Sadie pounced on the change of subject. "It belonged to Grandma Iris. It was one of the first pieces she bought when Grandpa Jack finished the house. Do you play?"

"Afraid not. But I do admire a nice tune."

"I can play," Viola offered.

Ry straightened, surprised she would volunteer such information. "Can you now, Button?"

"Yes, sir. Momma taught me. She could play real nice."

Ry saw the way her eyes studied the instrument hungrily. "I remember. She could sing well too."

Viola's face lit up. "Pa said she had the voice of an angel."

Her smile surprised him. He'd assumed discussing her mother would only sadden her. Had he been wrong? Did she want someone to talk to, to remember with? "Would you like to play for us?"

The child immediately slipped from her seat and headed for the instrument, Daffy at her heels. In short order she was playing a simple melody. And doing it quite well.

Ry made a mental note to install a piano wherever they eventually landed. If Viola was like her mother, music was an important part of her life.

A heartbeat later he noticed Josie studying Viola as well, a soft smile on her lips. Was she finally coming to realize that the people she surrounded herself with were just as important as where she was? If so, his battle was half won.

When Viola finished, she stood and offered a curtsy to the sound of their applause, then let out a yawn.

Josie gave her a caught-you grin. "Looks like somebody's ready for a nap." She stood and held out a hand. "Why don't we go upstairs and lie down for a bit."

Sadie popped up from her seat. "Oh, please, let me take her. I have a beautiful picture book we can read together. And I'm sure Ry would be happy to give you a tour of the ranch." She drew her lips together in an uncertain line. "Unless, of course, you'd like to take a nap as well."

Josie shrugged. "I've never been one for sleeping when the sun's up."

"That's settled then." Sadie held out her hand. "Come along, Viola. Time for our beauty sleep."

Once they were gone, Josie turned to Ry. "Your sister seems to like kids. I'm surprised she hasn't started her own family."

He smiled at the way she'd echoed his own thoughts. "I guess she just hasn't met a man who's a match for her yet." He moved to the door. "Would you rather see the rest of the house or look around outside?"

"Is there any reason we can't do both?"

Direct as always. "None whatsoever."

He led her to the room next to the parlor and opened the door, moving back to allow her to precede him. "This was Mother's favorite room."

Josie stepped inside, halting after only two steps. Two of the walls were lined floor to ceiling with books. In one corner stood a piano, much larger than the one in the parlor. A flute and harpsichord were displayed on a nearby wall shelf. Across the room a desk, proportioned for a woman, sat next to a large window.

"I can see why she liked it. I don't think you'd find this many books in the whole of Knotty Pine."

"I thought you might find this of particular interest." He waved a hand to his right and Josie spied a large, colorful globe on a floor stand.

She stepped closer, studying it in awe. She'd seen such a thing in a catalog once, but it was so much more impressive in person. She reached out a hand then caught herself.

"Go ahead." There was an amused undertone in his voice. "Touch it all you like."

He stepped beside her, so close his shoulder brushed against hers, sending warmth radiating down to her fingertips.

"Here's where we are." He traced a course eastward. "And here is Philadelphia."

She forced her focus back to the globe. "It's a shame we can't stop at any of the places between here and there." Then she caught herself. "I'm sorry. I didn't mean to sound ungrateful. This trip is wonderful, just the way you have it set up."

He grinned. "That's all right. I doubt this is the last

time you'll travel this route. Perhaps next time." He moved toward the door. "Ready to see more?"

Still feeling slightly rattled, she nodded and followed him into the hall.

He pushed open another door. "And this was my father's domain."

This room was very different from the other. Not only was it more masculine with its heavy desk and leather chairs, but it had a more rugged, less polished feel. No attempt to soften anything here.

"This has actually been Griff's domain since Father passed," Ry said.

Josie wondered again what had happened to alienate the two brothers. Something in his tone, in the very lack of emotion, whenever he mentioned Griff, indicated he was clamping down on some deeper feeling. Was he even aware he did it?

"How did your pa die?" she asked.

Ry rested a hand on the leather chair behind the desk. "He and Griff were climbing into a gully where a calf had gotten tangled up. Pa lost his footing and fell, hitting his head on a rock. As quick as that he was gone."

"I'm sorry."

"It was how he would've wanted to go. One minute he was doing the work he loved, the next he was together with my mother again."

Ry straightened and moved to the door. "Come on. I want you to meet someone." He led her to the back of the house, past several other closed doors. "You've seen the heart of the house and its muscle. Now I'll show you the pulse point." With a flourish, he pushed open the kitchen door.

"Mr. Ry! Welcome home!" A short woman with a

salt-and-pepper bun on top of her head bustled around the table, wiping her hands on her apron. "I wondered if you were going to pay me a visit."

Ry wrapped her in a bear hug that lifted her feet clear off the floor. "Inez, Inez, how could you doubt me? Didn't I always say you're the love of my life?"

She laughed and swatted at him to let her down. "Ah, that's what you say, but then you stay away for months at a time."

"Yes, but the thought of your cooking always draws me back."

Josie smiled at their affectionate teasing.

The older woman patted her hair. "Now, use those manners your mama taught you and introduce me to your lady friend."

"Inez, this is Josephine Wylie, the woman who saved my life. Josie, this is Inez Garner, the world's best cook and the person who keeps this entire household running smoothly."

"Mrs. Garner." Josie extended her hand. "It's so nice to finally meet you. Mr. Lassiter always has such wonderful things to say about both you and your cooking." She smiled. "And after tasting those teacakes this afternoon I can see why."

The cook took her hand. "Now, I'll have none of this Mrs. Garner nonsense. You just call me Inez like everyone else." She gave Josie's hand a squeeze. "Sadie told me what you did to save our Ry from those awful men. As far as I'm concerned, you're one of the family now."

Josie was taken aback and could only stammer out a "thank you."

Inez brushed aside her thanks and crossed her arms over her ample bosom. "So you're the sister of the woman who made that wonderful fruitcake Sadie brought home."

"Yes, ma'am. It's Cora Beth's specialty."

"I can't say as I don't covet that recipe a bit more than the Almighty would smile upon, but I understand how a cook wants to keep her secrets. You tell her, from one cook to another, that I think her cake is one of the best desserts I've ever tasted."

"Thanks. She'll appreciate that."

Inez turned back to Ry, placing a hand on top of his where it rested on the counter. "I was sorry to hear about Belle's passing. It doesn't seem all that long ago that you and her and Griff sat here in my kitchen, begging cookies off of me."

Ry nodded, accepting her sympathy.

Inez gave him a thoughtful look. "So she left you her daughter to look out for?"

"Her name's Viola. Spitting image of her momma."

"I always thought Belle was a smart girl."

Ry gave her a crooked smile. "You think putting Viola in my care was a *smart* thing?"

"Of course I do." She waved her apron at them. "Now, you two get out of my kitchen. I have a meal to prepare and I'm sure you can find something more interesting to do than watch me cook."

Jo followed Ry out onto the back porch. "I like her."

"Inez is a special lady. She's more than a cook, though she insists on keeping the line drawn between family and hired help." He moved toward the steps. "She's been at Hawk's Creek since before Pa brought my mother home from Philadelphia. I couldn't imagine this place without her."

He waved her forward. "Come on, I'll show you the stables."

Most of the ranch hands they passed greeted Ry with a quick wave, some asked him how long he was staying. All of them greeted her with a polite tip of the hat and a friendly smile.

As they stepped inside the stables, Jo paused. Her livery and bridle shop could fit inside here four times over.

But Ry didn't give her much time to look closer. He led her straight to a large stall near the middle of the building. "This is Monarch, Kestrel's sire and the pride of my stable."

"Oh, Ry, he's magnificent. I can see where Kestrel gets his size and lines from."

Ry opened the stall gate and ran a hand along the stallion's back, whispering soothing words as man and animal got reacquainted. Amazing to watch the way the two interacted, almost as if they understood each other. How could she have ever doubted his ability to handle Scout?

He glanced up as if just remembering her presence. Giving Monarch a last pat, he stepped out of the stall. "Ought to head back. I want to be there when Viola wakes from her nap."

As they left the stable, a group of men rode toward them across the field. Josie recognized the lead rider as Griff. She immediately sensed a change in Ry. Some of the relaxed air evaporated, replaced by a sense of caution, withdrawal.

They waited there until the men arrived and dismounted.

"Hello, Miss Wylie." Griff removed his hat and tugged at his work gloves. "Sorry I wasn't here to greet you when you arrived but I'm sure Sadie made you feel welcome."

"She's been very hospitable. And what I've seen of Hawk's Creek has been nigh on perfect."

He smiled and the expression transformed him. "Nigh on perfect, is it? I can see you're a woman of keen insight."

When he turned to Ry, the smile disappeared. "Looks like you found your way back okay."

Ry's expression matched his brother's. "Monarch is looking in top shape. Thanks for seeing that he's taken care of."

Griff nodded. "If you two will excuse me, I need to see to my horse and get cleaned up."

Supper that evening was an interesting experience—starting with their seating arrangements. The two brothers did a masculine dance around who would sit at the head of the table, both insisting it was the other's place.

"For goodness sake, Griff." Ry's exasperation made his deep voice harsh. "That's where you sit when I'm not here. There's no reason to change things up when I come around."

"You're the oldest." Griff sounded just as determined. "It's yours by right."

Josie felt Viola's hand tighten on hers as they listened to the brothers argue. After a few minutes more of the bickering, she decided enough was enough. Chin jutted out in a don't-mess-with-me attitude, she marched forward and pulled the head chair out herself. "Being as neither of you gentlemen care to sit here, I'm certain you won't mind if I do."

Ignoring the identical frowns flashed her way, she

sat and indicated Viola should take the seat to her left. She glanced across the table to find Sadie staring dumbfounded at her.

However Inez, who'd brought in a platter of food, gave her an approving wink. Josie's confidence bounced back and her shoulders straightened.

The brothers, with nothing left to argue over, took seats across from each other.

When it came time to say the blessing, it looked as if the same argument would erupt, but Josie gave Ry a pointed frown, nodding toward Viola. This time, thankfully, he took the hint. Bowing his head, he asked the blessing over the food.

Once the meal started, things turned civil, but Josie noticed that the brothers never spoke directly to each other.

Since Griff sat to her right, he did his part to make polite conversation. He became quite animated when she asked questions about the livestock and the workings of the ranch. When he wasn't talking to or about his brother he could be downright charming.

During a lull in the conversation, Sadie turned to Viola. "I'm afraid we don't have a pony on the ranch, but we do have a horse who's gentle as a lamb. Her name's Poppy and she'd be perfect for you if you care to ride while you're here."

Viola shifted in her chair. "I don't know how to ride."

"You don't?" Ry sounded shocked.

She shook her head.

Recovering, he gave her a reassuring smile. "Well, we'll just have to remedy that. What do you say we have a riding lesson tomorrow morning?"

Chapter Twenty-Three

Josie leaned against the paddock rail, elbow to elbow with Sadie, watching as Ry gave Viola a riding lesson. It had rained during the night, making the ground slick and muddy, but Ry seemed perfectly at ease, ignoring the dirt caking his boots and splattering his pants, standing with a sure-footedness that conquered the slippery ground.

"I remember when Ry gave me riding lessons." Sadie's voice was soft and dreamy. "I was not quite six and he was eleven. You'd think a boy that age would resent having to take care of his baby sister. But not Ry. He was the most patient teacher, just the way he is with Viola right now."

"Why didn't your pa teach you?"

"Pa was much too busy that summer clearing the west pasture, and I was too impatient to wait. Besides, Ry was more than capable, even at that age."

"He mentioned once that he enjoyed working with horses."

Sadie laughed. "An understatement. He has a way with horses, an affinity for them. It's almost like he can understand what they're thinking. Pa said he was a natural."

"And he still keeps horses here."

Sadie nodded. "Monarch is his prize. Ry painstakingly bred several bloodlines through four generations until he was satisfied that he had just the right animal to sire superior bloodstock. And he's carefully chosen a number of quality brood mares from all around the country."

"Sounds impressive."

Sadie nodded. "The foals coming out of his stable now are highly coveted. Whenever word goes out that he's ready to sell one there's a line a mile long waiting to snatch it up."

She turned back to study what was happening in the paddock. "A pure pleasure to watch, isn't it? And he obviously loves doing it. Makes you wonder why he'd want to work in some stuffy office back east when he could be here, doing this."

Josie could think of a few reasons. "They have horses in Philadelphia."

"Yes, of course. But this is where he's set up his stable. Kind of telling, don't you think?"

Josie wasn't sure how to answer that, so she didn't. "How does Griff feel about that?"

"He appreciates a good horse, but he's a cattleman. To him, horses are tools, a means to get his job done."

Josie worded her next statement carefully. "I might be out of line for saying this, but I couldn't help noticing your brothers don't get along very well."

Sadie grimaced. "It wasn't always like that. There's only two years separating them age-wise you know, and they were really close growing up—sort of like those twin nieces of yours. If you saw one, you knew the other was close by."

"What happened?"

"Grandfather." There was a wealth of distaste in that word.

"How so?"

"One summer he came for a visit. Stayed for a very long two weeks." She cast Josie a sideways look. "Pa and Grandfather didn't get along well, though they both tried to put a good face on it when we were around."

She turned back to the paddock. "Anyway, the day before he was supposed to leave, he announced he wanted to take one of his grandsons with him to Philadelphia."

"Grandsons? Not grandchildren?"

Sadie laughed. "Grandfather wasn't looking to replace my mother, he was looking for someone to follow in his footsteps."

"Oh."

"Pa didn't like it, but he sent Ry along. After all, Griff would have been like a squirrel in a rabbit hutch if he'd gone to the city—completely out of place." She rested her chin on her fists. "And it was only supposed to be for a couple of months."

She cut her eyes Josie's way. "That was the sticking point, that Ry chose to stay rather than return to Hawk's Creek once the summer ended. It seemed such a betrayal."

"Is that how you feel?"

Sadie looked away. "After Pa died, Griff asked Ry to decide if he wanted to come back and take his rightful place on the ranch or if he'd rather have the kind of life Grandfather offered him. Ry keeps saying he has to weigh all the options and consequences." She dropped her hands. "I don't understand why he has so much trouble choosing. I just want my brother back."

"Aunt Josie! Aunt Sadie!" Viola's excited cry saved Josie from having to answer. "Look, I'm riding."

"Wonderful!" Josie said, while Sadie clapped in admiration.

Sadie obviously loved her brother, Josie decided. But it was just as obvious she didn't understand him.

Then it struck her that Inez, who wasn't related to Ry by blood, was the only person who'd truly acted as if he belonged here, rather than as if he were merely a guest.

Ry lifted Viola from the saddle, pleased with the progress they'd made. She was a quick learner and hadn't let her fears get in her way. With a bit more practice Viola would make a good rider. He'd get her a steady, well-mannered pony when they found a place to settle. Maybe by Christmas?

He carried her across the muddy ground, handing her over to Josie when he reached the fence. The action had such a natural feel to it. Did Josie sense that as well?

"Did you see me, Aunt Josie?"

Josie gave her a hug before setting her down. "I sure did, sweetie. Are you certain you haven't ridden before?"

"No, never."

"Well, you sure took to it mighty fast." She glanced at Ry. "Must have been the good teacher you had."

Viola nodded. "Uncle Ry told me just what to do. And after I got used to being up so high, it wasn't scary at all."

"I think we should celebrate your achievement." Sadie offered Viola her hand. "Let's go inside and clean up, then see what Inez has in the kitchen." She paused to glance back his way. "You're going to join us, aren't you?"

"You ladies go on while I take care of Poppy. Just tell Inez to save me some of whatever she's cooked up."

"As if I have to tell her." Sadie turned to Josie with a mock-pout. "Ry always was her favorite."

Josie grinned as she took Viola's other hand, then looked back over her shoulder. "You might want to hurry with your chores," she warned. "Those clouds look ready to burst anytime now."

He touched the brim of his hat. "Yes, ma'am."

Ry watched the three of them head back toward the house.

Sadie was laughing, probably at something she herself had said. There were times when she seemed as playful as a child. And she'd certainly taken to Viola. Yet it was Josie's hand Viola clung the tighter to, her skirts the child drew closest to.

The bond between those two was growing stronger. Had Josie noticed? If so, would that bond mean enough to her that she would reshape her dreams to embrace it?

Chapter Twenty-Four

"We're pulling into the station." Ry had pitched his voice to a whisper. No point waking Viola just yet. The child was curled up on the seat beside him, her head snuggled against his side.

The trip from Tyler to Philadelphia had taken four and a half days and even Josie had grown tired of the experience.

She blinked, then focused on his face. He saw her chagrin when she realized she'd dozed off. "Sorry."

"No need to be." In fact he'd enjoyed watching her nap, had admired the soft, relaxed look of her, had wondered what it would be like to kiss those generous, full lips.

What would she think if she knew of his highly inappropriate thoughts? Would she be affronted? Or pleased?

With an effort, he pulled his thoughts back to the present. "Grandfather should have a carriage waiting so we won't have to stand around for long."

Josie nodded and folded her lap blanket. He saw her gaze stray to the window, saw the eagerness creep into her expression.

He couldn't blame her. She was about to take a giant step toward realizing her dream. And he aimed to see that he did everything he could to give her her fill over the next week or so.

Only then could he bring up the subject of settling down again. He just hoped he'd guessed right about knowing where her heart truly lay. And that she figured it out for herself—soon.

He roused Viola and once he'd found a porter to take care of their bags, he picked her up, carrying her off the train. He didn't want to take a chance of her getting lost in the crowd on the windy platform. From her height, the mob of travelers rushing to get in from the cold was no doubt a daunting sight.

Josie, however, was another matter entirely. Her eyes gleamed with excitement as she drank in all the sights and sounds. Was it living up to her expectations?

He led them into the modern, bustling station building. A minute later, he spied a familiar face and lifted a hand in greeting. "Nichols, I trust you've been well."

"Yes, thank you, Mr. Lassiter."

"This is Miss Wylie and Miss Viola."

Nichols bowed to Josie, then turned back to Ry. "All is ready for you and your guests. You'll find the carriage right outside the main door and there are hot bricks inside to ward off the chill. Let me see to your bags and we'll be on our way."

Hefting Viola a bit higher on his hip, Ry placed his free hand at Josie's back and moved toward the exit.

Please, Lord, don't let me lose her to the tug and drama of the city. You know how much Viola needs her. How much I need her.

* * *

"Ladies, this is my grandfather, Mr. Roland Wallace. Grandfather, this is Miss Josephine Wylie and my ward, Miss Viola Hadley."

His grandfather gave Josie a slight bow. "Miss Wylie, welcome to Philadelphia."

"Thank you, sir." She looked around, her eyes seeming to drink everything in. "Your home is beautiful. And with all the greenery and ribbon draped about, it looks so festive."

"Ah, yes. Getting ready for the Christmas season and all that. Glad you like it." Then he turned to Viola. "And what is that you're holding on to so tightly, young lady?"

"This is Daffy, my cat. He won't be any trouble, honest."

"I'm certain he won't. You must keep him in the nursery wing with you and Miss Wylie, though. He might get lost in this big house if you let him roam around." He gave her cheek a pat. "I'll make certain he has a bowl of cream every morning and evening. He'll like that, won't he?"

"Yes, sir."

"I thought so. Now, I know you ladies want to freshen up. Brigit, escort Miss Wylie and Miss Viola to their rooms, please."

The maid curtsied and indicated they were to follow her. Ry gave Viola an encouraging wink, before turning to his grandfather.

"Glad to have you back, my boy. With so little warning before you left, the office has been in a bit of turmoil, but we'll set things to rights in no time now that you've returned."

Ry resisted the urge to apologize, and after a moment

his grandfather continued. "After you take a few minutes to settle in, why don't you come down to the study. I want to hear more about your trip, and there are a few things I want to catch you up on regarding our cases."

Ry straightened at that. "Anything in particular?"

"The Bergmon case, for starters. It took an unexpected turn and I thought some fresh eyes might see something we're missing."

Ry nodded. He'd put a lot of hours in on that case before he left, so he was familiar with the particulars. "I'll be down in fifteen minutes."

Ry climbed the stairs, hesitating at the second floor landing. Should he check on Josie and Viola? Deciding they were probably resting, he turned to the east wing, where his set of apartments were situated.

Fifteen minutes later, he was seated in one of the brown leather chairs that faced his grandfather's desk.

His grandfather poured a glass of port, then offered Ry one. Ry held up a hand in refusal.

"So," his grandfather said as he replaced the stopper, "will Miss Wylie be Viola's permanent governess or will she return to Texas once you and the child are settled in?"

Ry stiffened. "You mistake the situation, sir. Miss Wylie is not Viola's governess, nor is she a servant of any kind. I would consider it a personal favor if you would refrain from making her feel in any way inferior."

His grandfather held up a hand. "My mistake. But, if I may ask, in what capacity *is* she here?"

Ry considered that for a moment. He wasn't ready to let his grandfather realize how truly important Josie was to him just yet. Time for that when matters were more settled between them. "She's a friend," he finally said. "One I'm deeply indebted to. She helped me fight my way out of an ambush, her family took me in and nursed me when I was too weak to take care of myself, and she very kindly agreed to accompany Viola and myself on this trip so I'd have someone to help care for the child's needs."

His grandfather raised a brow. "Sounds like a remarkable woman."

"She is that."

The older man took his seat behind the desk. "Naturally she will be treated as an honored guest while she's here." He took a sip from his glass. "Just how long might that be, by the way?"

"I promised to have her home in time to spend Christmas with her family."

"Ah. It's good to have one's family around at Christmas." He leaned back in his chair. "Now, tell me about this misadventure of yours. How's the arm doing?"

Ry raised his arm and rotated his shoulder. "No lingering effects." He spread his hands. "As to the story, I was waylaid by a pair of hooligans. Fortunately, with Miss Wylie's help, we were able to gain the upper hand."

"Sounds like quite a dust-up. But I supose that sort of thing is to be expected when you travel in the less civilized parts of the country."

Ry set his jaw. "You can encounter unsavory types in any locale."

His grandfather made a noncommittal sound, then moved on to another topic. "Too bad things didn't work out the way you wanted with that Hadley woman. My condolences."

Ry nodded.

"It must have been unsettling to discover she named you to be her daughter's guardian."

"At first. But the longer I'm in Viola's company the more certain I am this is the right thing to do. I've grown quite attached to her." An understatement. "Which reminds me. I would like for Viola to take her meals with us."

"Is that wise?" His grandfather's brow furrowed. "Surely the child will be more comfortable in the nursery."

"Viola is accustomed to mingling with adults in small family gatherings." Ry spread his hands. "But if you're concerned, Miss Wylie and I can take our meals with her in the playroom."

"No, no, that won't be necessary." His grandfather waved a hand. "I only thought to spare her some tedium." Then he gave Ry an approving smile. "I'm glad to see you're taking your responsibilities to the child seriously. It's time you considered settling down and starting a family." He raised a brow. "This isn't exactly how I envisioned it, but what's done is done."

Ry didn't bother to hide his annoyance. "Pardon my bluntness, sir, but when and how I start a family is my concern, not yours."

"Yes, of course. I'm only anxious for you to find the same happiness I found with your grandmother." He set his glass aside. "And speaking of family, it's fortuitous you were able to combine this bit of business with a trip to Hawk's Creek. How are your brother and sister faring?"

"They're both well."

"Good, good. By the way, the Havershams have invited us to their home for Christmas dinner. I hope you don't mind, but I've told them we'd be there. I didn't think you'd want to travel back to Texas that quickly since you've only just returned."

Ry shook his head. "I'm afraid you'll have to send my regrets."

"What do you mean?"

Was that a touch of annoyance in his voice? "As I mentioned, I promised Miss Wylie I would make certain she got home before Christmas. I certainly can't expect her to make the trip alone."

Grandfather waved a hand dismissively. "We can always send one of the servants with her."

Not a chance. "I consider Miss Wylie's welfare my personal responsibility."

"I see." The older man drummed his finger on his desk, then sighed. "Well, I suppose it can't be helped. We'll put the Havershams off until New Year's."

"Perhaps you should hold off making any plans that include me for the time being."

"Oh?" There was a definite chill in Grandfather's tone.

"I've been thinking for some time that I need to decide just what course I want my life to take." Ry steepled his fingers, meeting his grandfather's stern gaze without blinking. "That includes whether I should remain in Philadelphia or return to Texas—full time." He interlaced his fingers. "Acquiring a ward has made that decision all the more pressing."

"After your recent, near-fatal misadventures I would think the answer would be obvious." If anything the chill had deepened. Grandfather leaned back in his chair.

Griff had also said he thought the answer was obvious. Of course, he'd been referring to a completely different conclusion.

Grandfather tugged at his vest. "Here she will have access to fine educational institutions, museums, theaters, symphonies. There are modern medical facilities and electricity to light our homes safely. Can Hawk's Creek offer her anything comparable?"

"Perhaps not. But there are other things to consider."

"Such as?"

"Such as being among people and settings one feels comfortable in. Such as being allowed to act rambunctious the way a child should without worry about being disciplined. Such as having a backyard comprised of acres rather than feet and a whole forest to explore as your playground."

"I take it you don't believe those things can be found here."

"I didn't say that." Ry wasn't going to be browbeaten into making the wrong choice. "What I said was that I need to consider both options before I decide."

His grandfather nodded. "Deliberate, as always. That's why you're a superb lawyer. Which reminds me, there are a few case files I'd like you to take a look at. I hope you don't mind going into the office tomorrow."

"Actually, I thought I'd spend tomorrow showing Viola and Miss Wylie some of the sights around town."

"The Bergmon case *is* rather urgent—we go to trial in two days. But I'll be glad to keep the ladies company—Sanderson can fill you in on all of the particulars of the case."

Ry nodded reluctantly, knowing his grandfather was right, on this point at least. He'd been gone for almost a month—time to get back to work. There'd be other opportunities to show Josie around in the days to come.

Besides, it would give him an opportunity to review his client files and assess what would need wrapping up if he left the firm.

Viola slipped her hand into Josie's as they descended the staircase to the first floor. Josie didn't blame her, she felt a bit intimidated by all the opulence herself.

She smoothed her skirt. It was one of the new dresses Cora Beth had made, but she still worried it wasn't good enough. She didn't want to embarrass Ry in front of his grandfather. Maybe she and Viola should have taken their meal in the playroom.

Just as they reached the foot of the staircase, Ry and his grandfather stepped out of a nearby room.

"My, my," the older man said, "don't you ladies look lovely?" He stepped forward and offered Josie his arm. "Allow me to escort you into supper."

His admiring smile eased her fears. She lifted her head and placed her hand on his arm. "Thank you."

Ry offered his arm to Viola, and Josie hid a grin as she saw the little girl follow her example.

As they settled into the meal, Ry's grandfather turned to Josie. "I understand this is your first trip outside of Texas."

"Yes, sir. I'm looking forward to exploring everything your city has to offer."

He laughed. "My dear, it would take a lifetime to explore the entire city. But we'll see if we can show you the best parts."

"That would be wonderful." Josie couldn't suppress

the flutter of excitement. Aunt Pearl would be so proud of her.

"Since my grandson will be busy at the office tomorrow," Mr. Wallace continued, "I would consider it an honor if you would allow an old gentleman like myself to show you around."

Josie's enthusiasm dimmed a bit. She'd expected Ry to be the one to show her around, to share in her discoveries. It wouldn't be nearly as much fun without him.

"That's mighty kind of you, sir." She turned to Ry. "But do you really need to get to work so soon? Couldn't you join us for our first excursion?"

He shook his head regretfully. "Sorry, but I was away longer than expected. There's work on my desk that's already waited too long."

Josie sat back. "If you'd like us to postpone—"

"Nonsense. No point wasting any of your time here." Ry nodded toward the head of the table. "Besides, Grandfather knows more about Philadelphia than I do. I'll join you another time."

"That's settled then." Mr. Wallace cut into his steak. "There are some wonderful shops on Market Street. And there are museums and libraries we can visit, if you prefer. We can plan trips to Independence Hall and Washington Square for later in the week."

Just listening to him name the places they would visit set Josie's pulse racing again. It was too bad Ry wouldn't be there to share it all.

Then she had another thought. Was he deliberately distancing himself? After all, it was one thing for him to spend time with her in Knotty Pine. But he was back in his world now. Did he see her as too countrified in these surroundings?

Maybe that was just as well. Didn't she keep telling herself that she didn't *want* his affections?

"How about you, young lady?" Mr. Wallace had turned to Viola. "Would you care to tour the city with Miss Wylie and me? I know a candy shop we can visit."

Viola's eyes widened. "Oh, yes, sir, that would be very nice." Then she turned to Ry. "Won't you be able to have any fun at all, Uncle Ry?"

Josie saw the concern on the child's face. Amazing how close she and Ry had become in the short time they'd been together.

Before Ry could respond, his grandfather spoke up. "Of course he will. In fact, why don't I purchase a pair of tickets to the theater for your Uncle Ry and Miss Wylie?" He glanced at Josie. "There's a comedy playing at the Walnut Street Theater that I hear has been well received."

"What about me?" Viola asked.

"Oh, I'm afraid it'll be way past your bedtime." Ry's grandfather pointed with his fork. "But don't worry. Brigit will keep you company."

Viola turned to Ry. "Will you tuck me in when you get back?"

"I wouldn't be able to sleep if I didn't, Button."

She nodded solemnly. "Me neither."

That seemed to satisfy Viola, and the conversation moved on to small talk. Later, when the dessert course was brought out, Mr. Wallace studied it with a frown. "What's this? I thought I requested a burnt custard for tonight."

"It was my doing," Ry explained. "Miss Wylie's sister bakes fruitcakes that are absolutely superb."

Mr. Wallace looked prepared to object, then seemed

to think better of it. "Well then, let's have a go at it." With a smile, he took a large bite and his eyes widened in appreciation. "You weren't exaggerating. I don't think I've ever tasted a fruitcake quite this delectable." He raised a glass to Josie in salute. "My compliments to your sister."

"Thank you. I'll be certain to pass your compliment on to her."

"You know, I'll be hosting a small holiday gathering for the law firm's staff. Do you think I could convince your sister to ship a few of these here? I'd pay her for them, of course."

Josie waved a hand, dismissing his offer of payment. "I'm sure Cora Beth would be glad to oblige. But I can't accept your money. Think of it as repayment for your hospitality." It was a little thing, but it felt good to be on the giving rather than receiving end for a change.

The next afternoon, Ry headed straight to the nursery wing when he returned from the office. It had felt good to dive back into his work, but part of him had been distracted, wondering what Josie and Viola were doing.

"Uncle Ry!" Viola ran to greet him as soon as he entered the playroom. "We visited the most wonderful shops today."

He stooped down to give her a quick hug. "Is that right?"

"Uh-huh. There was one that had nothing but candies. Shelves and shelves filled with chocolates and taffies and rock candies and, oh my goodness, everything!"

"Amazing." He felt a little pang that he hadn't been there to experience it with her.

"And the store next door had dolls and mechanical toys and music boxes."

"I wish Danny and the girls had been with us," Josie added. "They would have loved it."

Ry smiled. Was Josie missing her family? "And did Aunt Josie find anything to catch her interest?" His question was directed at Viola, but he kept his gaze on Josie.

"Oh, she looked at some clothes and hats." Apparently fashion did not rate as high on Viola's list as did sweets and toys.

Josie laughed selfconsciously. "Your grandfather was kind enough to introduce me to a lady at a very fancy dress shop." She smoothed her skirt. "Mrs. Richoux was very polite, but I got the impression this dress doesn't quite match what ladies here consider stylish."

Ry fought back a frown. Was his grandfather trying to be helpful or make her feel out of place?

Viola crossed the room and took her hand. "I think your dress is real pretty, Aunt Josie."

"As do I," he chimed in.

"Well, thank you both." Josie curtsied. "But I decided to splurge and get one nice new gown." She gave Ry a selfconscious look. "I didn't want to embarrass you when we went to the theater tonight."

He took both her hands in his. "I would never be embarrassed to have you on my arm, no matter what you wore." To his surprise, her cheeks pinkened, and a smile teased at her lips.

Perhaps he should offer her compliments more often.

That evening Ry decided Josie had made excellent use of her shopping time. When she came down the stairs in her new gown she looked absolutely radiant.

The dark green fabric matched her eyes perfectly, and the elegant lines lent her a sophisticated air. But her most flattering accessory was the sparkle in her eyes and the flush of excitement in her cheeks.

There'd be more than one man tonight who would cast envious glances his way.

Josie rested her hand on Ry's as he helped her into the carriage outside the theater. Truth be told, she could have floated in without any asstance whatsoever. The play had been wonderful, the elegantly dressed ladies and gents impressive, and the theater marvelous. And Ry had been flatteringly attentive, introducing her to his acquaintances with a touch of pride in his voice.

There was nothing to match this in Knotty Pine.

Ry settled into the seat across from her, an indulgent smile on his face. "Did you enjoy yourself tonight?"

Josie nodded. "It was the perfect ending to a wonderful day." She lightly touched his knee. "Thank you so much for bringing me here. I know this is old hat to you but to me it was magical."

"There's no one I'd rather have with me."

She felt the light wool of his trousers under her hand and her cheeks heated with awareness. She removed her hand quickly, but the warmth of him remained on her fingertips. She shivered slightly, as much from some too-uncomfortable-to-explore emotion as from the temperature, but his smile immediately changed to a look of concern.

"You're cold. Here, allow me." He moved across the space to sit beside her, unfolding a lap blanket and settling it over her skirt. "How's that?"

"Just right. Thank you."

The carriage hit a rut in the road, throwing her against him. His arm reached out, encircling her protectively. For a moment they were so close their noses nearly touched. Their breath mingled, weaving an invisible cord that bound them together. Her breath caught in her throat as she saw his eyes darken. He stared into her eyes as if she knew some secret he was driven to learn…as if he couldn't look away. As if she truly mattered to him.

The cord tightened and his face drew closer. He was going to kiss her.

And she was going to let him.

Chapter Twenty-Five

The kiss was warm, surprisingly gentle and absolutely unlike anything Josie had ever experienced. Everything else melted away. For this one moment in time she knew she was cherished and safe and part of something truly wonderful. She felt his strength as well as his restraint, his willingness to keep her safe against all harm, and most of all a tenderness that in no way equaled weakness, all channeled through that one marvelous kiss. It was a heady sensation that turned her whole world topsy-turvy.

When he drew back she wanted to cry out in protest. But his gaze captured hers again, intense, searching.

Was he looking for signs of outrage or regret? If so, he wouldn't find any. Instead, she stroked his cheek with the back of her hand. The firm, rugged feel of it brought an appreciative smile to her lips.

With a strangled sound that was part growl, part her name, he captured her hand with his own and brought it to his lips. Then he smiled like a man who'd just conquered the world, and pulled her to him, tucking her head against his shoulder.

It felt like coming home.

* * *

Later, Josie lay in bed, too fidgety to sleep.

After that turn-my-world-upside-down kiss, the rest of the carriage ride had passed in pleasantly charged silence, as if both of them were afraid that speaking would shatter the perfection of the moment.

He'd accompanied her to the nursery wing just long enough to check on Viola, then parted with a squeeze of her hand, a chaste kiss on her cheek and a softly uttered good-night.

Now she stared at the shadowy ceiling, reliving that carriage ride, trying to figure out what it meant, how it affected her dreams and her future.

Because it *had* changed things. She could no longer deny her attraction to Ry, could no longer pretend she wanted him to marry Cora Beth.

But was she really ready to settle down, to give him the kind of wife he wanted, the kind of mother Viola needed? If not, if she needed more time, would he give it to her? Could she ask him to? He already had so much turmoil in his life—torn between Hawk's Creek and Philadelphia, at odds with his brother, trying to be a father to a five-year-old who still grieved the loss of her parents—how could she add to that?

Her hand stole to her lips, feeling again the sweetness of his kiss. Who would have guessed that the mere joining of lips could stir such a hornet's nest of emotions?

He had put so much tenderness, so much of himself into the gesture. Perhaps there really was a chance for them to be happy together, a way to combine their needs and dreams and build something altogether beautiful.

Philadelphia was a wondrous place. And there were other amazing places to see within a day's ride. A per-

son could live here for a very long time and find something new to do or see nearly every day. Ry must see
that, as well. Surely, when it came down to it, he would
choose Philadelphia over Hawk's Creek.

Maybe she could reshape her dream. Maybe she
didn't need to be in a rush to see the whole world.
Maybe she should take time to really savor this one
exciting piece of it for now.

Josie snuggled down under the covers, thinking that
she could be quite happy with that.

As long as she had the right person to share it with.

Ry shrugged out of his coat and sat down to remove
his boots.

Heaven help him, holding her had felt so good, so
right. He could have held her like that forever. When she
looked at him with those shining, trusting eyes he would
have happily slain a dozen dragons for her. When she'd
smiled with wonder in her eyes and stroked his cheek,
he'd wanted to howl at the moon in sheer exuberance.

If nothing else, tonight had proven—to both of
them—that she felt the strong tug of attraction between
them, too. Because he was ready to admit that this was
no longer about finding the right mother for Viola. He
loved Josie, had for quite some time.

He wouldn't fool himself that the battle was won.
She'd held on to her dream too long to let it go over-
night. But it was a start. And a solid one at that.

He was determined that by the time they returned
to Knotty Pine for Christmas, she'd realize she needed
something deeper, something richer, than experience
for its own sake.

* * *

Josie woke the next morning to a cold dose of reality. What had she been thinking last night?

She groaned and buried her face in her pillow. That was the problem—she hadn't been thinking, she'd been feeling.

If the two of them stayed here in Philadelphia, who would see to the livery? If he'd married her sister, he would have taken responsibility for her kids as well. And Danny and Uncle Grover were an extension of that. But it wasn't the same thing at all if she and Ry got hitched. She couldn't expect him to take on the whole clan just because he married her.

Oh, she had no doubt he'd send money to her family if she asked him to, but that wasn't the kind of arrangement she wanted. And without her there to keep the livery running, her family wouldn't have the means to support themselves.

She sat up and hugged her knees. There was no getting around it. She'd have to go back. Alone.

Ry belonged here. She'd seen how much his lawyering meant to him, how eager he'd been to get back to work almost as soon as they'd arrived.

Heavenly Father, I truly do appreciate You giving me this little taste of what the world outside Knotty Pine holds for me. It's all I dreamed of and more. And I know it's plumb selfish of me to want this and a life with Ry and Viola, too. But I just got to believe You put them in my life for a reason. Please, if it be Your will, help me find a way to make things work out for us.

Feeling only slightly better, Josie threw off the covers and got dressed.

How was she going to face Ry this morning? What

was he thinking after that kiss? Had it affected him as much as it had her? On top of everything else, what if she'd read too much into it? Here she was, wondering how to answer a proposal that might not even come her way. After all, he was a man of the world. He'd likely kissed lots of girls. It didn't mean he was ready to ask her to marry him.

When Brigit informed her Ry had already eaten and headed out, Josie didn't know whether to be relieved or insulted. Was he avoiding her? Did he have second thoughts about last night?

Then the young maid handed her a note, accompanied by a red rose, and Josie's emotions took another swing.

She opened the note and couldn't stop a smile. The handwriting was as bold and firm as the man himself.

Sorry I won't be joining you for breakfast, but I wanted to get to the office early so I'd be able to spend time with you and Viola this afternoon. I'll be back by two o'clock to take you out for a carriage ride.
Ry.

So she had a reprieve until this afternoon. Josie inhaled the scent of the rose and slowly walked toward Viola's bedchamber.

Chapter Twenty-Six

Ry strode down the sidewalk to his grandfather's house, ignoring the cold wind that tried to snatch at his hat. He'd been looking forward to this outing ever since he awakened this morning. He'd finally have the chance to show Josie and Viola some of *his* favorite places in the city.

The memory of how sweet, how wistful she'd looked last night had kept a smile on his face most of the day. She was coming 'round, he could feel it. His patience was finally beginning to bear fruit.

He took the steps up to the front door two at a time and tossed his hat on the hall table, shrugged out of his coat and headed for the nursery wing.

When he pushed open the door to the playroom, Viola bounced up and ran to greet him. Her greetings were becoming less reserved, more enthusiastic as each day passed. Something squeezed at his heart when he thought of the reliance and affection she'd entrusted to him.

"Hello, Uncle Ry." She gave him a hug as he stooped

to greet her. "Aunt Josie told me all about the play you went to last night. It sounded wonderful."

"That it was." Ry met Josie's gaze over the child's head. "I especially liked the ending."

Josie blushed and broke eye contact as she stood. "Come along, Viola. Let's get you bundled up for our outing. We'll meet Uncle Ry downstairs."

Ry rubbed his chin as he watched the two of them hurry off to Viola's bedchamber. Was it his imagination or was Josie a bit stiff, evasive? Was it just embarrassment over last night's kiss? Or something else?

As he made his way to his own rooms to change clothes, some of the optimism he'd felt earlier slipped away.

The outing that afternoon only slightly lessened his sense of unease. He took them ice skating at Eastwick Park, a novel activity for the Texas-born-and-raised pair. Viola took to it with the quickness of a child, ready to try it on her own after only a few turns around the ice. Within a short time, Ry was ready to hand her over to Nichols while he turned his attentions to Josie.

It took Josie a bit more time to get the hang of it. Not that Ry minded. Having the opportunity to hold her while they glided across the ice was pure enjoyment. Helping her up when she lost her footing, hearing her laughter and seeing the elation on her face when she gained enough confidence for him to take her flying across the ice, his arm at her waist, was exhilarating.

And the cups of hot cocoa afterward were a definite hit.

Viola chattered excitedly about their excursion during the carriage ride back. Josie smiled and nodded and added her own enthusiastic observations, remarking how much her family would have enjoyed the outing, too. But Ry sensed a returning tension in her, a brittleness, that while subtle, was threaded through every glance, every overly bright smile she cast his way.

He bided his time, planning to take her aside for a quiet talk after supper, but she pled a headache and excused herself early.

The next day was no different—Josie was pleasant but distant and deftly avoided every attempt he made to get her alone for a few moments.

By the next morning, Ry rose determined to get to the bottom of whatever had made Josie so skittish. He wasn't going to let her put him off any longer. He'd leave the office early today and be back in time to have lunch with his two girls. Then, once Viola settled down for her nap, he'd corner the evasive Miss Wylie, and find out just what was going on.

Dear Lord, whatever problem Josie's conjured up in that wonderfully fertile mind of hers, please let me find the words to help her see that, with Your help, the two of us can handle anything together.

Ry marched into the nursery wing at noon to find Brigit setting out Viola's lunch. Josie was nowhere in sight.

"Uncle Ry!"

The way Viola's face lit up at the sight of him gave Ry's mood a boost. He couldn't imagine life without her now. "Hello, Button." He stooped down to accept and return her hug. "I thought I'd have lunch with you and Josie today."

"Aunt Josie went out with Grandfather Wallace this morning."

Ry tried to hide his disappointment. "Well, then, I'll have lunch with you, if that's okay."

"I'll fetch another plate right away." And with a quick bob, Brigit hurried from the room.

Ry let Viola chatter about her morning while the meal was brought in and set up. He tried to give her his full attention, but his mind kept turning impatiently to thoughts of how soon Josie would return.

Once Brigit left them to their meal, Viola quieted down. It took Ry a few minutes to notice the pensive edge to her expression.

"Something the matter, Button?"

She pushed the peas around on her plate. "I was just wondering if you decided where we would live yet?"

Now she had his undivided attention. "If I recall correctly, I promised you we'd make that decision together." And lately he'd hoped that Josie would have a part in making that decision as well. "I take it you've been giving this some thought."

She nodded, looking at him with large, somber eyes.

He reached over, placing his hand on hers. "Well, let's hear what you're thinking. And keep in mind, whether it's Philadelphia or Hawk's Creek, I want us to have our own house."

Her face brightened. "I've never had my own house before."

Ry leaned back, struck by the poignancy of her words. "Well, you're going to have one now." He cleared his throat, pushing the gruffness away.

She smiled, then cocked her head to one side. "But can we still go back to Knotty Pine for Christmas?"

He smiled, and made a cross-my-heart sign. "Yes, ma'am." Then he leaned forward. "I promised we would, remember? And if I give you my word about something, I will always, *always* do my very best to keep it, no matter what. Do you believe me?"

That earned him a solemn nod. "And I promise to do my very best, too."

Her earnestness touched something deep inside him. Then he straightened, returning to the matter at hand. "Let's talk about Philadelphia first, since that's where we are. You've had a good time here, meeting Grandfather Wallace and seeing some of the sights and shops of the city, haven't you?"

She nodded.

"And there are plenty of other things to see and do. Like museums and markets and parks. Then there's a fine school where you could be with lots of children your own age. And of course, if we stayed here we would get to see Grandfather on a regular basis."

He watched her carefully for some sign of what she was thinking, but for once he couldn't read her expression.

Time to discuss the other option. "As for Hawk's Creek, if we lived there we wouldn't be so crowded, there's lots of room to spread out and do whatever we want, a place to keep a horse of your very own, and Sadie and Griff would be close by so we'd get to see them whenever we wanted." It was the choice he was leaning toward. But again, there was no obvious reaction from Viola. What was she thinking?

She finally looked up and met his gaze. "Are those our only two choices?"

Her question caught him off guard. Didn't she like either place? "The thing is," he said slowly, "Philadelphia and Hawk's Creek is where my, *our*, family is. And

I think it's important to be close to family." The Wylies had taught him that. He wanted that kind of closeness, that sense of acceptance and nurturing and belonging, for Viola. And for himself too.

Viola traced a circle on the table with her fingertip, not looking up at him. "Once, when I was sad about not having any family left, Audrey told me that family isn't just the folks who are blood kin to you. It can include others, too. Like the way Danny and Uncle Grover are part of her family."

Ry covered her hand with his, hurting for the sense of aloneness she'd felt. "Audrey was absolutely right. You are part of my family now, just as sure as if you were my own daughter. And that makes all of my family—Sadie and Griff and Grandfather Wallace—yours as well."

She nodded, still not looking up. "The other thing Audrey told me is that, if we wanted to, she and I could call ourselves sisters. Or at least cousins."

Yep, Audrey was very much like her Aunt Josie. "I think that's wonderful."

This time she did look up. "Then, aren't they part of our family, too? Couldn't we move to Knotty Pine?" She spoke all in a rush now. "I like it there, Uncle Ry, a whole lot. I miss Audrey and Mrs. Collins. And I liked going to school there and the Thanksgiving Celebration. There's going to be a Christmas program too." Her eyes pleaded with him. "Couldn't we at least think about living *there*?"

Ry leaned back as her words sunk in. Move to Knotty Pine? A place where he could set his own path without constantly bumping into reminders of his grandfather's and siblings' expectations? And they'd still have "family" around to give Viola the support and sense of belonging she needed.

Setting up a law practice in Knotty Pine wouldn't be much more challenging than doing so at Hawk's Creek. And as Josie had pointed out once before, Knotty Pine was growing. If they didn't already need a lawyer, they would someday. In the interim, he'd have time to focus on building a home for Viola and perhaps establishing a horse ranch.

The one fly in the ointment would be Josie's reaction. He knew she wanted to travel, but surely she'd had enough to hold her for a while. And he'd seen some signs that she missed her family. Perhaps she was finally coming around to realizing what a great life she'd left behind in Knotty Pine. And it wasn't as if they couldn't travel from time to time.

The more he thought about the idea, the more he wondered why he hadn't seen it himself. "Viola," he said, tapping her nose, "you're a genius."

Her face brightened immediately. "Does that mean we can live in Knotty Pine?"

"I'll need to work out some things, but I do believe you've hit on the perfect plan."

"Oh, Uncle Ry, thank you." She ran around the table and hugged his neck for all he was worth.

Thank you, Lord, for bringing this child into my life.

Josie could hardly contain her excitement. With the help of Ry's grandfather, she'd found the answer she'd been praying for. Having both her dream and a life with Ry and Viola actually seemed possible now.

Ry crossed the room and took her hands in each of

his, smiling softly into her eyes. "Looks like someone had a fine time this morning."

"Oh, you have no idea."

"So tell me."

She laughed and pulled her hands away, savoring his attention yet too excited to hold still. She set her gloves down and twirled around to face him, eager to share her news. "Your grandfather had the most wonderful idea."

"And what was that?"

She heard the caution in his tone but brushed it aside. "We were talking about our favorite foods, and he mentioned how much he'd enjoyed Cora Beth's fruitcake. Then he suggested Cora Beth and I start our own business, *selling* her fruitcakes. Isn't that the most wonderful thing you ever heard?" The words burst from her like a spark from a flint.

Ry's reaction, however, was more puzzled than enthusiastic. "Sell fruitcakes? But you both already have businesses—the livery and the boardinghouse. Why start another?"

Didn't he understand what this meant? "This is different—it's something she and I can do together. She'll make them and I'll handle the business end. Your grandfather knows the right people to help us get started. He says folks will pay good money to buy them."

She paused, giving in to the one nagging worry she had about the scheme. "Do you really think that's true? He wasn't just being nice, was he?"

"Your sister's cakes are fabulous. I think people will line up to buy as many as she can produce."

It was going to work! Impulsively Josie threw herself at him, wrapping her arms around his neck in an enthusiastic hug. "Oh Ry, this is so exciting. Everything is finally coming together."

He held her, his warm breath tickling her neck, his arms a safe harbor. A moment later Josie pulled away, her cheeks warming. "I'm sorry, I—"

He touched her face with the back of his hand, smiling that crooked smile she found so endearing. "Don't you dare spoil a perfectly good hug with an apology. I've been wanting to do that myself for some time now."

He took her hand and drew her to the sofa. "And there's something else I've wanted to do for a while—something I need to ask you."

Josie's heart fluttered. There was a banked intensity in his gaze, a promise shining there that sent an anticipatory shiver through her.

He angled his body toward her, their knees nearly touching. "I realize we haven't known each other very long, but it's been more than enough time for me to know my heart. And lately I've had reason to hope you return some portion of my affection."

More than "some portion." Much more.

"I know you've always had your heart set on traveling the world, but—"

She touched a finger to his lips. "I don't need to see it all right away." The past few days, contemplating her life without Ry in it, had taught her that dreams could change, evolve. It wouldn't be such a sacrifice to make Philadelphia her world, at least for now. She could take time to explore it in detail, to truly savor each experience, experiences made all the sweeter by having Ry and Viola at her side.

And unlike Knotty Pine, Philadelphia was close to

other, interesting, exciting places. They could take the occasional trek along the coast from here.

Even Aunt Pearl couldn't find much to fault with that.

She saw the flare of relief—and something deeper— in Ry's expression, and knew she'd made the right choice.

Then he went down on one knee and her heart threatened to pound its way clear out of her chest.

"Josephine Wylie," his deep, strong voice sent a thrumming deep inside of her, "would you do me the very great honor of agreeing to be my wife?"

The joy surging through her was almost overwhelming. "Oh, Ry, yes."

Between one heartbeat and the next he was beside her again, pulling her to him in a fierce hug. Then he took her face between his hands and leaned in to kiss her.

This kiss was different from the first—this one spoke of claiming and being claimed, of a future together, and of the rightness of this moment.

When at last they parted, Josie rested against the crook of his arm with a contented sigh. "I never thought I could be so happy."

He squeezed her shoulder. "I promise to do everything I can to make certain you stay this happy."

She glanced up, meeting his gaze. "Everything has come together so well. You can't help but see God's hand in all of it."

"Amen."

Josie gave a contented sigh. "We're going to be so happy here. You can continue to work in your grandfather's law practice, and I can sell Cora Beth's fruitcakes so the family won't miss the income from the livery."

She felt Ry stiffen, felt his subtle withdrawal. Had she said something wrong?

He pushed away from her just enough to stare into her eyes. "You don't understand," he said slowly. "I'm not planning to stay in Philadelphia."

Josie blinked, feeling her brow furrow. Surely she hadn't heard right. "What?"

"I don't want to make our home here." His tone was firmer, as if he could convince her he was making sense just by sounding more assured.

She shrugged out of his embrace. "You decided on Hawk's Creek?"

"No."

Hope mingled with the confusion in her mind. Somewhere else then. A new place. "Where—"

He took her hand. "Josie, I want to settle in Knotty Pine."

No! She hadn't heard right. He had to be pulling her leg. But he looked so serious… "Knotty Pine?"

His earnest expression seemed to beg her to understand. "All this time I've been trying to decide between Philadelphia and Hawk's Creek. It was like trying to choose between Grandfather, and Griff and Sadie, between being a lawyer and being a horse breeder." He spread his hands. "It never occurred to me, until I talked to Viola this morning, that there were other options, that there was a way to live a fuller life."

"But Knotty Pine?" She pulled her hand away from his and stood. "You have the whole world to choose from."

He stood, watching her pace. "Viola likes it there.

She misses Audrey and the rest of your family. And I think she's more comfortable in a small town than in a city like this. As for me," he paused, as if gathering his thoughts, "well, I like the idea of a fresh start. And I like Knotty Pine and the people there just fine."

Easy for him to say, he'd already seen something of the world.

"Most importantly, though, is that I want Viola to have family close by while she's growing up."

She stilled. "You don't have family in Knotty Pine."

He smiled. "Oh, but I do. Someone once said family isn't restricted to the folks you're kin to. Viola reminded me of that again today. That wonderful, eccentric, generous household who resides at the Knotty Pine Boardinghouse is very much family. They—you—took me in and made me feel welcome. You all cared for first me and then Viola, accepting us for who we are, and generously welcoming us into your midst. That's the kind of people I want in my life and in Viola's life."

He stepped closer. "But it won't be complete unless you're one of those people."

She raised her hands, palms out. "Stop! I finally have a chance to taste what I've been dreaming of my whole life. I was even willing to compromise, to set down roots *here*. It's not fair of you to ask me to go back to the life I had before."

"But—"

"No!" She wouldn't take the chance that he would talk her into this ridiculous scheme. "Starting this business means I won't be chained to the livery any more." It was her turn to reach for his hands. "Don't you understand? I'm willing to give up my desire to travel, to settle down *here* with you and Viola."

His jaw worked. "But not in Knotty Pine."

She squeezed his hands, trying to let her determination flow through to him. "Have you really thought this through? Are you ready to give up lawyering? There's not enough business in all of Knotty Pine to keep even one lawyer busy full time."

"I don't plan to be a full-time lawyer. Sure, I'll open an office and be available to anyone who needs my services. But I intend to find a suitable piece of land and move my stable from Hawk's Creek."

She dropped his hands, feeling suddenly brittle as glass. "So, you have it all figured out so you can have everything you ever wanted."

"I was hoping it would be what we both wanted."

She turned away. "You were wrong."

There was a long moment of silence.

"Yes, I suppose I was," he finally said.

The heaviness in his voice tore at her and she turned back around. Surely they could get through this, could still find a way to make it work.

But his expression was closed, remote. "Will you at least be returning with us for Christmas?"

He was still leaving? "Does what I want mean so little to you? Can't we take some time, see if we can make it work *here*?"

His jaw tightened. "If it was just me, I would say yes. But I have Viola to think about now, and while she'd adjust, I don't think she'd be truly happy here. I won't compromise her happiness for my own." His gaze intensified. "Don't ever doubt, not even for one minute, that your happiness is important to me. That's why I'm not going to press you any further to come with us."

Her stomach churned. "When are you leaving?"

"The day after tomorrow. You didn't answer me—will you come with us?"

Just like that, he and Viola would be out of her life. "Your grandfather thinks I should spend Christmas here." She traced the scrollwork on the mantel with her finger. "The holidays will be the best time to get folks interested in buying the fruitcakes." She jutted out her chin. "Of course, I plan to go back for a visit after the new year."

A muscle in his jaw jumped. "I see." He gave her a short bow. "If you'll excuse me, I have some business to attend to."

Josie stared at the door after Ry left, wondering for a moment if she'd made the right choice.

He'd proposed, for goodness sake. This wonderful, generous, God-fearing, more-stubborn-than-a-balky-mule man had gotten down on one knee and asked for her hand. He'd looked at her with such love in his eyes that just remembering it was almost her undoing.

She did love him, more than she'd ever believed possible. And Viola too. So much so that the thought of being separated for a long period from them was like being kicked in the gut.

But he'd asked too much of her. Why couldn't he have met her halfway? She'd spent her whole life putting the needs of other folks first. It was finally time to think of herself.

So why did it feel so awful?

Josie sank down onto the sofa, crossing her arms over her chest, trying to hold the hurt inside. *Dear Father, give me the strength to get through this. You've taken me so far on the road to achieving my dream, opened so many doors to me that I never even imagined ex-*

*isted. Help me to see the good in this too and not focus
on the things I can't have.*

She buried her face in her arms and let the tears flow.

Ry went straight from the parlor to his grandfather's
study.

"Well, hello, my boy. I didn't realize you were home."

"I've come to let you know Viola and I are leaving
for Knotty Pine in two days."

His grandfather raised a brow. "Not Miss Wylie?"

"Miss Wylie has decided, based on your advice, I believe, that it would be best for her new business venture
to remain here for now in order to establish herself."

Grandfather nodded. "She has a fine head on her
shoulders, that one. I can see why you're so taken with
her." He leaned back. "But if she's decided to stay here
through the holidays, surely there's no need for you and
Viola to leave."

"You misunderstood. We're not returning to Knotty
Pine merely to spend Christmas. I plan to establish a
permanent residence there."

His grandfather stiffened. "You can't be serious."

"I assure you, sir, I've never been more serious in
my life."

"Ry, think about what you're doing. How can you
throw away your career, the connections you've established, to bury yourself in some backwater town that
won't appreciate your talents?" He narrowed his eyes.
"You're making the same mistake your mother made,
and look what happened to her."

Ry was done tiptoeing around that particular issue.
"What happened to her, sir, is that she lived fully and
joyously, at the side of a man she loved and who loved

her deeply. She bore three children and did her best to instill in each of them a spirit of self-confidence, integrity and grace."

Remembering he was talking about his grandfather's only child, Ry tempered his tone. "The fact that she died young is something that grieves me as much as it does you. But I truly believe she wouldn't have traded the life she had for even one extra day on this earth."

His grandfather's face reddened alarmingly. "Are you saying she preferred that uncivilized, heathen outpost to life with me?"

"I'm saying she wasn't afraid to leave the comforts of home to embrace the life she wanted. And that I aim to follow her example."

With that, Ry turned on his heel and left the room.

And then the irony struck him. Josie, in her own way, was attempting to do the very same thing. He rubbed his jaw as some of the anger drained from him. She had a right to pursue the life she believed would bring her the most joy, even if he didn't agree with her choice.

Still, he couldn't help but mourn the loss of the life they could have built together.

Josie shifted in her chair as the second course was served. She'd thought about pleading a headache and having dinner in her room, but she'd never taken the coward's way out, and she didn't aim to start now.

For Viola's sake she tried to pretend all was well, as did Ry. But the girl sensed something was wrong and it didn't take her long to figure out just what was at the heart of the matter.

"Aunt Josie, aren't you coming back to Knotty Pine with us?"

She gave Viola a regretful smile, doing her best to avoid direct eye contact with Ry. "Not right away, sweetie. I have some business to take care of here in Philadelphia."

"She's going to keep me company," Mr. Wallace added. "I'll get mighty lonely with you and your Uncle Ry gone."

"Oh." Viola chewed on her lip, then nodded.

Ry speared a piece of potato with his fork. "So what are your plans for the livery? Sell it?"

It was the first comment he'd directed her way all evening. "I couldn't do that," she responded. "I always planned for Danny to take it over when he got old enough."

Ry raised a brow. "Are you sure that's what *he* wants?"

Josie was taken aback by the question. "Of course. I mean, it's what we planned, even before Pa passed on." But had Danny ever said it was what he wanted? She couldn't remember.

Ry let that question go and returned to his original one. "If you're not planning to sell it, and you're not coming back to run it, then what *are* you planning? Surely you don't think Danny's ready to take it on by himself yet."

Was he baiting her? "Of course not. He needs to stay in school."

"Actually," Mr. Wallace intervened, "I suggested she take on a partner, someone who's willing to run the place and split the profits with her."

"I see." Ry nodded. "So the family continues to receive a stream of income, even if somewhat reduced."

"Yes." She felt a need to explain, to make him see that she knew what she was doing. "But there'll be one less mouth to feed, and there'll soon be an additional source of income from the new business."

"Have you got someone in mind?"

"I have some ideas. I—"

"Let me make this easy for you. *I'll* be your partner."

She dropped her wrists to the table. "You don't have to do that." Was he offering her charity?

"I know I don't have to. I want to. And this has nothing to do with you."

Josie hoped her flinch didn't show.

"Once I have my stable established, I'll want to make certain the bridle shop is well run."

"You're planning to work there yourself?"

"You doubt I could do it?"

He was twisting her words. "Of course not. I just thought—"

"At any rate, that'll be my worry, not yours. Do we have a deal?"

"If you're sure that's what you want."

He nodded. "I'll draw up the papers tonight and establish an account at a bank here in town. The initial funds will be transferred before I leave."

Josie didn't know how to respond so she merely nodded. The sound of Mr. Wallace clearing his throat reminded her they weren't alone. She pasted on a smile and turned to Viola. "Aren't the carrots flavorful tonight?"

Viola nodded, but Josie didn't miss the troubled look she gave both her and Ry.

Ry pulled off his boot and tossed it across the room, mentally berating himself. How could he have let his temper get the best of him at dinner tonight? Especially in front of Viola. It was unforgivable.

He pulled off the other boot and set it aside. At least he'd partially redeemed himself. By getting Josie to agree to his becoming her partner in the livery, he now had a legitimate reason to keep an eye on the Wylie household and a way to know Josie had enough money to see her through the next few months.

He scrubbed a hand across his face. Why couldn't Josie see what she was giving up? Didn't she realize what a treasure she had in her family, how much he envied her their closeness? Her decision was not only short-sighted, but hurtful to the family she was leaving behind.

His grandfather was using her own dreams, and her sympathy toward his alone-in-the-world state, to manipulate her. Maybe the man wasn't doing it consciously or maliciously, but it was happening nonetheless.

The thing was, the man had no one to blame for that aloneness but himself. He'd never once invited Griff or Sadie to visit, had never made an effort, with that one eventful exception, to travel to Texas to visit them.

The man wanted family around him, but on his own terms.

But he could never explain that to Josie—it was something she'd have to learn for herself. He just didn't understand why such a normally sharp woman hadn't figured it out already.

Ry paused in the act of unbuttoning his shirt.

Hadn't he allowed himself to be manipulated in the same way?

Is this how Griff had felt? Betrayed and disappointed? Had his father gone to his grave believing Ry preferred what his grandfather had to offer over the legacy he'd built with his own hands?

Ry moved to the window, leaning one arm against the frame, staring unseeing at the night sky.

He owed Josie an apology. She wasn't making the choice he'd wanted her to, she wasn't even making the choice he believed would make her happy. But she was staying true to her dream, standing up for herself, the same way he'd stood up to his grandfather this afternoon.

And, if he *really* loved her, he should trust her and not try to make her feel miserable for doing it.

Still, he couldn't help but mourn the loss of the life they could have built together.

While he was being so honest with himself, he might as well admit that Josie wasn't the only one he owed an apology to. In fact, he owed Griff much more than an apology. He hoped Viola wouldn't mind a slight delay in their return to Knotty Pine, because a stopover at Hawk's Creek was definitely in order.

Father, forgive my arrogance and the hurts I've inflicted on others, both the deliberate and the negligent. Help me exhibit the patience and humility I'll need in order to mend fences with Griff. And most of all, look after Josie, help her find the happiness and fulfillment she seeks, wherever that may be.

Josie's pulse jumped as the train whistle sounded. The bitter cold she felt came as much from inside her as from the weather.

Ry set down his bag and took her hand, staring deep into her eyes. "I want you to know, while I don't agree with your decision, I understand about needing to follow your dreams. I wish you nothing but the best and will be praying every day that you find what you're looking for."

"Ry, I'm so sor—"

He touched a finger to her lips. "I know. It's okay. And don't worry about Cora Beth and the others—I'll keep an eye on them."

She nodded, doing her best to swallow the lump in her throat. "Thank you."

He squeezed her hand. "Just please, if you ever change your mind, don't let your pride, or anything else for that matter," he glanced toward his grandfather, "get in your way."

The whistle sounded again and Josie bent down to give Viola one last fierce hug while Ry shook his grandfather's hand. "Take care of your Uncle Ry for me, okay?" she whispered in the child's ear.

Viola nodded. "I wish you were coming with us."

"Don't worry, sweetie, I'll be back for a visit real soon. And I'll write lots of letters."

"Time to go." Ry lifted Viola with one hand and within seconds the two of them had disappeared inside the train.

Josie pulled her cloak tighter across her chest, shivering as she watched the train pull out of the station. Up until this very moment she'd thought—hoped—Ry would change his mind and decide to stay.

"Don't worry, my dear." Grandfather Wallace patted her arm. "That boy loves you—it's obvious to anyone with eyes in his head. He'll see the light and come back to you."

Josie smiled, but her heart wasn't in it. Somehow, she didn't feel as confident as he did.

Chapter Twenty-Seven

"You did a marvelous job selecting a tree." Cora Beth held the door open while Ry and Danny dragged in the large fir.

"Thank you, ma'am." Ry let down his end and rolled his shoulders. "But I just did the chopping. The kids picked it out." And with each of them eyeing a different specimen it took quite a bit of finesse to steer them to one everyone could agree on.

"Well, then, good job everyone." She clapped her hands the way a schoolmarm would. "Girls, while Mr. Lassiter and Danny set the tree up in the parlor, you can help me get down the box of decorations." She gave Ry and Danny a stern look. "And see that you mind my carpets."

Ry turned to Danny, flexing his muscles with exaggerated display. "You heard the lady. We have work to do."

While working together at the livery and sharing some of the heavier chores around the boardinghouse, he and the boy had developed a close relationship. Ry found himself teaching Danny some of the things his own father had taught him.

Like how to handle an ax properly and how to fix loose shingles on the roof. Like how to select the best rocks for skimming across a pond and how to tell a dog's tracks from a fox's. Like how a man looked out for those in his care and how important a man's word was.

But for today, they were merely two menfolk exchanging indulgent expressions while following orders from their womenfolk.

Twenty minutes later the tree was standing tall and proud in the parlor and the box of ornaments had been ceremoniously opened. Sitting on the very top was a stack of paper snowflakes, some looking fairly new, others yellowed with age.

"It's a family tradition," Cora Beth explained. "Each of us has our own special snowflake that we hang on the tree every year."

Audrey lifted the elaborately cut paper decorations out of the box. "We each get one of these our very first Christmas," she explained. "It has our name and the day we were born written right on it."

She lifted one from the stack. "See, this one's mine."

Cora Beth fetched two similar decorations from the mantle. "I hope you don't mind," she told Ry, "but I made one for you and Viola last night. I thought, since this is your first Christmas here and you're like part of the family now, it was only fitting."

Ry saw Viola's face light up and offered Cora Beth his heartfelt thanks.

"Think nothing of it. The tree will look the nicer for the addition." She handed them the lacy bits of paper. "Now, let me get you something to write with."

As Ry added his name and birth date to the center of the snowflake, he noted that five of the ones taken from the box remained on the table, unclaimed. One of them would be Josie's.

Was she missing this or any of the other holiday traditions her family celebrated? The tree at his grandfather's was more grand but the trimming of it much less personal than this little ceremony.

Still, spending Christmas with Josie would have made even the most sterile of decorations shine. He couldn't believe how much he missed her, how many times he had a thought he wanted to share, a decision he wanted her opinion on. Would the hole she'd left in his life ever heal?

Cora Beth brought his thoughts back to the present as she gathered up the leftovers. "All right now, Pippa, I believe this is your year to hang the star on the top, so we'll let Lottie hang your father's snowflake. Audrey, you can take Grandma Emma's and Danny, you take Grandpa Bert's. I'll take Aunt Pearl's." She held up the last one and her smile drooped for a second. Then she turned to Viola. "Would you like to hang Jo's for her?"

Viola nodded, accepting the somewhat rumpled decoration with the care one would afford a fragile piece of crystal.

"All right then, let's get the snowflakes up and then we'll tackle the rest of these."

Once the snowflakes were duly hung, the rest of the tree trimming took place with a great deal of playful teasing. Danny and Audrey argued over whose snowflake showed to the best advantage. Pippa and Lottie tended to place any ornaments they hung at the very bottom of the tree and called foul whenever anyone tried to rearrange them. Viola placed her ornaments with a precision that earned her her own share of teasing.

And the adults were encouraged to admire the youngsters' handiwork, and listen to them as they shared bits of stories that had become part of the history of each ornament—the lacy dragonfly that Cora Beth had made for Uncle Grover, the silver rattle that had been found in Danny's belongings, a clay angel that had gotten chipped when Audrey dropped it four years ago, a small wooden train engine Josie had purchased from a tinker when she was twelve.

That last sent Ry's thoughts in a direction he had to force himself to turn back from.

When it came time for Pippa to place the star at the top, Ry was enlisted to lift her up.

"Isn't it beautiful?" Audrey asked.

"I have something I'd like to add, if it's okay," Viola offered tentatively.

"Why of course, dear." Cora Beth gave her an encouraging smile. "It's your tree too."

Viola took Ry's hand. "I need to get something from Ma's trunk."

"All right." Ry led her upstairs and into his room. She went immediately to the trunk and, after a few minutes of rummaging around, pulled out a battered hatbox. "Here it is."

Curious, Ry followed her back to the parlor.

"What's that?" Audrey asked.

Viola opened the box, to reveal a rough-hewn wooden nativity set. She lifted out the figure of Joseph. "My pa made these before I was born. Every year at Christmas, we would set them out under our tree."

"How lovely." Cora Beth fingered one of the pieces. "Your pa was very talented."

"Can I help set it up?" Audrey asked.

Ry watched the two girls with heads bent together, adjusting the pieces until they thought each one was placed just right.

How could Josie possibly want to trade this away for some other life?

Josie walked downstairs, feeling out of sorts this morning and not quite sure why.

The business was going well—almost too well. She'd already had requests for more cakes than Cora Beth could possibly produce. Ry's grandfather had counseled her not to be afraid to turn down orders. It gave the product a feeling of rarity, he'd said, of exclusivity, that would only add to the demand for it.

But he also advised her to write to Cora Beth and work out how they might increase production in the future. Once their reputation was set, it would be good business to take advantage of at least a portion of that increased demand.

And she'd had another new experience this week— snow. Not the dusting of flakes they sometimes got back home, but a true, piled high, sink your feet into, perfect for making snowballs, snowfall. Her first thought had been how much Danny and the girls would enjoy playing in it. Grandfather Wallace had listened to her chatter excitedly about it with a sort of amused tolerance for the first few minutes, but then returned to reading his paper.

So she'd gone out by herself, finding a few of the neighbor's children outside to share her enjoyment.

Which was fine, really. She'd always known, once she was able to travel, that she'd look to the locals for company.

So why wasn't she happier about how things were going? She was just at loose ends, she supposed.

Josie stepped into the parlor, then halted on the threshold. A large tree was set up by the window, decorated with beautiful glass ornaments. Cora Beth would love their fragile beauty and the gaily colored ribbons all tied in perfect bows. The girls would "ooh" and "aah" over the gilded angels. And wouldn't Danny just love the tin soldiers?

There was no popcorn garland hung on this tree. Instead it was draped in strings of pearl-like beads.

Who had set it up? And when?

The housekeeper appeared in the doorway. "Good morning, Miss. Mr. Wallace asked me to inform you that he would be down shortly to join you for breakfast."

"Thank you, Mrs. Hopkins." She halted the woman's exit with a raised hand. "By the way, I was just admiring the tree."

"Yes, Miss. Quite lovely, isn't it?"

"Very pretty. Who decorated it?"

"Why, me and the rest of the staff, just like always. We did it early this morning."

"And who picked out the tree?"

"Mr. Nichols, same as usual."

"Well, you all did a wonderful job."

The woman gave her a bright smile. "Thank you. I'll be sure to tell Agnes and Nichols you said so."

Josie studied the tree again, feeling deflated. She supposed every family had their own traditions. But this seemed so impersonal, so...empty. There was no searching until you found the perfect tree. No teasing as you hung the ornaments. No reminiscing over Christmases past. *No sharing.*

She supposed they'd put up the tree at home—after all, it was only six days until Christmas. Had Danny cut it this year? He was certainly old enough to handle the job. She'd probably have turned it over to him soon enough anyway.

This would be Ry and Viola's first Christmas together. How were they doing? She felt a soul-deep longing to be there to share it with them.

Cora Beth had said in her letter that they were staying at the boardinghouse for now, but that Ry had started laying the groundwork for his own place. Things seemed to be moving along nicely without her.

"There you are, my dear. Sorry to keep you waiting." Mr. Wallace looked past her. "Ah, I see the tree is up. What do you think of it?"

"It's quite impressive."

He seemed pleased with her answer. "Glad you like it.

"I hear you had a busy day yesterday," he commented as he escorted her in to breakfast.

"Yes, sir. I've actually turned away several orders."

"What did I tell you? The cake practically sells itself."

"I'll admit, the price you advised me to set seemed mighty steep for a cake. I wasn't sure anyone would order it for that sum."

"You must put a high value on your product if you expect others to do likewise."

She pushed the food around on her plate, feeling at loose ends. "I find myself free today."

"I'll tell Nichols to put the carriage at your disposal. Perhaps you can visit some of the shops on State Street."

Not the answer she'd hoped for. She tried a different topic. "How do you usually spend Christmas day?"

"Well, we'll attend church services first. Then afterward the Havershams have invited us to join them for their Christmas dinner and the Caldecotts have asked us to stop by for a small evening gathering."

"Don't you have your own holiday traditions?"

He gave her an indulgent smile. "Sentimentality is not my strong suit, I'm afraid. But if you'd like to host a holiday gathering, I can get Mrs. Hopkins to help with the preparations."

That wasn't at all what she'd been thinking. Besides, she didn't really know anyone here. "No, no, it was just idle talk."

"As you wish. But speaking of Christmas, the Havershams are a bit stuffy I'm afraid, but Joseph Haversham has been a faithful client for thirty years, so I wouldn't dream of offending him. And as for Charles Caldecott…"

Josie listened with half an ear as he talked about the two households they would spend Christmas with. After breakfast, he headed directly to his office. Not wanting to face that too-perfect tree again, she bypassed the parlor and returned to her room.

She stood at the window, staring at the snow-covered street. Perhaps she would visit Independence Square today, or maybe the market. She felt the urge to be outdoors, to see trees and breathe fresh air, even cold and damp as it was.

A passerby stepped onto a patch of ice and waved his arms, barely avoiding a fall. It put her in mind of the afternoon in Eastwick Park. Closing her eyes she recalled the invigorating feel of skimming across the ice with Ry holding her safe at his side.

Maybe she'd go back there today, practice up so that the next time Ry—

She stared at her reflection in the glass, studying the unhappy-looking stranger staring back at her. There wouldn't be a next time with Ry. And skating alone held no appeal for her.

Josie plopped down on her bed as she had a sudden, sickening moment of clarity. What had she done?

Heavenly Father, I'm an ungrateful wretch. Here You've given me all I asked for, and I'm still unhappy. I just never realized how lonely I would be. Maybe I'm not as much like Aunt Pearl as I thought. Because I finally figured out what Ry meant when he said it's not where you are so much as who you're with.

Your word says You have plans for us, plans to give us hope and a future. So I'm figuring that maybe Your plans included me learning this lesson. Trouble is, now that I've figured it out, I don't know what to do about it. I already threw Ry's proposal back in his face so I'm the last person he wants back in his life. And Cora Beth and the others are probably not real happy with me, either. My showing up in Knotty Pine right now would be plumb awkward for everyone.

So You see my puzzlement. Please help me figure out the right thing to do.

Chapter Twenty-Eight

Ry watched as Cora Beth settled everyone around the tree. They'd just returned from the church service and the children were eyeing the stack of presents with more than mild anticipation. He smiled at the glow in Viola's face. She was thriving here, in the middle of this warm, loving family. Thriving in a way she never would have in his grandfather's home or at the ranch.

This was how Christmas had been celebrated when his mother was still alive—everyone gathered in the parlor, laughing, exchanging gifts, bursting with anticipation and excitement. He didn't realize how much he'd missed this kind of interaction, how big a hole it had left in his life, until now.

At least he and Griff had started the healing process. He and Viola had stopped off and spent a day at Hawk's Creek on their way back to Knotty Pine.

He'd ridden out alone with Griff and they'd talked about a lot of things—about cattle and horses and the weather.

Then Ry had talked about that first year with his grandfather, how he'd come to make the decisions he had, how that had affected everything he touched from then on. He hadn't tried to gloss over any of it, hadn't made excuses or tried to place blame. And he'd apologized to Griff.

Afterward, when they were all together again, Ry had started talking about the good memories he had of their mother. Before long, Griff and Sadie had joined in with memories of their own. And they'd found themselves laughing in a way they hadn't in years.

The breach hadn't been completely healed when he and Viola left—it had been there too long for that. But they'd made a start and Ry was confident that he and his brother would become friends again.

Pippa handed him a package, bringing Ry's attention back to the here and now.

According to Wylie family tradition, each person in turn, starting with the youngest, handed out the presents they were giving the others. Once Pippa sat, everyone tore into their gifts.

The youngest of the clan had drawn pictures for everyone—his was of a stick man chopping down a large, oddly shaped tree.

Lottie handed hers out next—cutouts of paper butterflies for the female family members and paper snails for the males.

Audrey gave each person penny candy. She'd selected licorice whips for him.

Viola, whom he'd helped shop for everyone else in the room, gave him a wooden carving of a horse. Had Josie helped her select this?

Danny gave him a belt he'd made himself from strips of leather at the bridle shop.

As he added Danny's gift to the pile at his side, Ry

heard the distant wail of the train whistle. He glanced at the little red engine hanging on the tree.

How was Josie faring with her first big-city Christmas? Was she enjoying the parties? The elegant decorations and sumptuous foods? Was she exploring Philadelphia, planning excursions to nearby cities?

Had she found the happiness she'd sought?

"She'll come around."

Ry looked up to find Cora Beth standing in front of him, holding out a package.

"What do you mean?"

"Just what I said, she'll come around. Josie can be mighty stubborn sometimes, but she's a smart girl."

He smiled, touched by her attempt to reassure him. "I'm sure things will turn out just as they ought." What he wasn't certain of was if he'd be happy with that outcome.

She handed him the package. "Here, this is for you."

Ry opened the gift to find an intricately stitched sampler, the center of which read Home Sweet Home.

She smiled. "I thought you could hang it in your new home, once you move in."

How many hours had she spent stitching this? Did she blame him at all for taking her sister away? "Thank you. This was mighty thoughtful." He stood. "Now, it's my turn."

He reached under the tree and pulled out a stack of packages. He'd purchased some of the gifts in Philadelphia—a steel-handled magnifying glass for Uncle Grover, a new pocketknife for Danny, and multicolored hair ribbons for Audrey. But the others he'd made himself. For Cora Beth he'd made a bookstand suitable for holding her husband's family Bible, and for each of the twins he'd made building blocks in various sizes and shapes.

It had felt good to do it. When he was growing up they'd always made gifts for each other at Christmas. Somehow, though, as he'd gotten older, it had just become easier to purchase something.

For Viola he'd done both. He'd bought her a brass flute from a music shop in Philadelphia and he'd made a carved wooden box to put it in. Cora Beth had helped him, taking care of the satin lining inside. And because he knew it would mean something to Viola, he even made a new collar for Daffy, complete with a small silver bell at the throat.

He looked down at the last parcel, the one that contained Josie's gift. He should've shipped it to Philadelphia, but somehow he'd hoped—

"Looks like I missed most of the fun." Ry's head snapped up at that sound of that oh-so-familiar voice.

"Josie!"

He wasn't certain which of the girls squealed her name the loudest.

Suddenly there was bedlam as everyone scrambled to their feet.

Everyone but him. He couldn't move, couldn't take his eyes off her. She looked beautiful. Cheeks red from the cold, a slight breathlessness emphasizing the rise and fall of her chest, the green and gold of her traveling suit enhancing the sparkle of her eyes. And it was those eyes that held him captive, those eyes that seemed to be saying something only to him.

Then she dropped her parcels as she was mobbed, everyone eager to welcome her home, everyone full of questions about what had changed her mind.

He'd like to know the answer to that one himself.

Josie attempted to answer them over the din, but her gaze remained fixed on his.

Ry slowly stood but didn't approach her, afraid to move in case he'd just conjured her image from his wayward thoughts.

Finally, Cora Beth got everyone's attention. "I know we're all excited to see Jo, but let's give her a chance to catch her breath."

Josie gave a nervous laugh, still not looking away from him. "Sorry I didn't give y'all more warning. It was a sudden decision and I was so anxious to get the earliest train out of Philadelphia, there was barely time to think everything through."

Why had she come? How long did she plan to stay? The questions tumbled through his mind but still he held his peace.

"We're just glad you're here to spend Christmas with us." Cora Beth gave her sister a hug. Then she stepped aside and looked from Josie to Ry and back again. "Children, let's go check on that goose I have in the oven. Uncle Grover, I could use your help as well."

Her maneuvering was a bit heavy-handed, but at this point Ry didn't care. He tried to keep his expectations in check, to simply enjoy the moment. She'd probably just come home for the holidays.

Stop just staring at her and say something. "So, you decided to spend Christmas with your family after all."

She nodded, then wet her lips. "I hear you bought the old Rodgers place and are building a house."

His turn to nod. "I hope to have everything ready by the first of the year. Though Viola is going to miss living here."

"Sounds like you're serious about sticking around here."

"The town has a lot to recommend it." But not nearly as much as when she'd been a part of it. When were they going to get past these inanities? "I even bought the Boggins Building to use as my law office."

"Any clients yet?"

He shook his head. "No, but I only put out my sign two days ago." *Enough of this. Ask her.* "So, how long do you plan to stay around?"

"That depends."

He fisted his hands at his sides in an effort to keep them from reaching for her. "On what?"

Josie's insides fluttered. This was it. Time to make herself vulnerable. She'd never been so scared in her life. "On how long you want me to stay."

Ry stared at her for a long minute, not saying a word. Her senses were suddenly so acute it hurt. She heard the dishes rattling in the kitchen, heard the wind whooshing in rhythmic puffs that rattled the window panes, heard the sound of her own heartbeat. The smell of pine and roast goose and silver polish assailed her nostrils, making her want to sneeze. But mostly it was her vision that threatened to overwhelm her as she stared straight into his eyes, his pewter-gray, honest, beautiful eyes.

Why wasn't he saying anything?

Then suddenly he was across the room, taking her in his arms. "If that's the case," he whispered huskily in her ear, "then you're never leaving."

She threw her arms round his neck, wanting to laugh and cry at the same time. "Oh, Ry, I'm so sorry, I should have listened to you, should never have—"

"Shh. No more of that. You figured things out a lot

quicker than I ever did." Then he disengaged her arms from his neck and led her to the sofa. He seated her but remained standing himself. "Are you absolutely certain this is what you want? No regrets?"

"Absolutely." She took his hand and pulled him down beside her. "Oh, Ry, you were so right—the finest place in the world is empty and lonely without the people you love to share it with. When it snowed, I wanted Danny and the girls to play in it with me. When I tasted something new and exotic, I wanted Cora Beth to have a bite as well. When I visited the Academy of Natural Sciences, I wanted Uncle Grover to show me around and explain what I was looking at."

She touched his cheek, savoring again the rough, masculine feel of it. "And there wasn't a place I visited that I didn't wish you and Viola were there beside me to share it."

He pulled her to him again. "Your wish is my command."

Several minutes later, he popped up and marched to the tree, returning with a large package.

"What's this?" she asked.

"Your Christmas present. Open it."

She gave him a curious look, then unwrapped the package. When she lifted the lid her lips formed an *O* of surprise.

With his help, she lifted out the desk globe. "Oh, Ry it's beautiful."

"There's something else."

She peered inside the box and pulled out another, smaller box that rattled when she shook it. What in the world…

Opening it, she found several dozen colorful tacks. Her gaze flew to his.

"I don't want you to give up your dreams completely, Josie," he said solemnly. "This is my real gift to you. Every year, you get to stick one tack in the globe—wherever you want—and we'll plan a trip there."

Tears welled up in her eyes. "Oh, Ry, I don't deserve this."

"Probably not."

His words caught her off guard, until she saw his grin. A relieved chuckle bubbled out of her.

"But it's the only thing I have," he continued, "so you'll just have to take it."

She threw her arms around him again, and this time refused to let go.

"Merry Christmas, Josie," he whispered. "And welcome home."

* * * * *

Dear Reader,

Thank you so much for taking the time to read Ry and Josie's story. I always enjoy the challenge of starting with two people who seem very different and taking them on a journey that shows ultimately how perfect they are for each other.

As always, this story started with a few "what if" questions. What if a man crossed the county to come to the aid a childhood friend and was somehow delayed until it was too late? And then what if he found he had been named guardian to the child of this now deceased friend, a child he never knew existed? Once I had the hero identified, I needed to find a heroine who would challenge him on all levels.

Where Ry was well-to-do and polished, Josie was not only working class, but worked at a job normally held by men. Where Ry was disconnected from his family, Josie's world revolved around her family. And where Ry had reached a point in his life where he was ready to set down roots, Josie was looking forward to the day when she could fly free.

Bringing these two to their happily-ever-after offered a number of challenges, but I hope you enjoyed following their often bumpy journey as much as I enjoyed writing it.

Wishing you love and blessings,
Winnie Griggs

MISTLETOE COURTSHIP

* * *

CHRISTMAS BELLS FOR DRY CREEK
Janet Tronstad

&

THE CHRISTMAS SECRET
Sara Mitchell

CHRISTMAS BELLS
FOR DRY CREEK

Janet Tronstad

May the bells always ring for both of you.

In memory of Judy Eslick and Jim Jett.

Though I speak with the tongues of men and of angels, and have not charity, I am become as sounding brass, or a tinkling cymbal.
—*1 Corinthians* 13:1

Prologue

Montana Territory—January 1880

Noise spilled into the darkness as Virginia Parker opened the saloon's back door. She braced herself as she took a few steps out into the cold while wiping her hands on her damp apron. Ordinarily, she would have searched the alley to be sure no one saw her leave at night, but she was too upset even to think of her reputation right now. It wasn't the gossips in town who were bothering her anyway. It was *him*.

Colter Hayes had interrupted her dish-washing and asked her to come out here. The saloon owner hadn't said what he wanted to talk about, but she knew it could only be one thing—he must be getting ready to fire her. When he stood there and didn't speak, she wondered if he was trying to find words to soften the blow. That's when she realized why—the man pitied her.

Please, God, leave me with some dignity, she prayed.

She couldn't believe someone from here would pity her. She might be living in this small Montana town now, but she would find her way back to where she belonged. She would never get used to the coyotes that slid through the streets of Miles City in the dark. Or the wide-brimmed hats the men wore low on their heads to protect themselves from the bad weather that plagued this land.

Back east in her beloved home, the days were pleasant. Servants banished any difficulties. And the music—ah, the sounds she'd heard. She had learned to play the piano looking out at the green trees surrounding the house where she'd lived for most of her twenty-four years. She'd never become the concert pianist her father wanted, but she longed to go back and play for the trees again even though he wouldn't be there to hear her.

She wondered if pity had been the reason for the brooding expression she sometimes saw on Colter's face as he watched her at the piano. She had thought it was because he had other, more tender, feelings for her. She blushed and lowered her head. Obviously, she'd been wrong about that.

"It's a little busier tonight," she finally said with a sideways glance at him.

It wasn't any more comfortable to look at him than to stare out into the icy wind thinking about him. He kept his face clean-shaven and his dark hair neatly trimmed, but that did little to offset the rough-hewn strength of him. It was rumored he had been a gunfighter and, looking at him in the shadows just now, she believed it could be true.

The man nodded. "Danny needed help washing the glasses tonight. Thanks."

"You're welcome," she answered cautiously then brushed her hand over her forehead as strands of blond hair blew across her face. The dusting of snow on the ground had grown whiter and more flakes were falling. Now that Christmas had passed she couldn't expect Colter to keep paying her to play the piano for his customers, not with business the way it was. She was helping Danny with the dishes partly to show she could do other things to earn her wage.

"It's chilly out here," Colter announced with a frown as he took off his wool coat and held it out to her.

"I'm fine—"

"You're shivering." He stepped closer and draped the coat around her shoulders. She felt the warmth of it seep into her even as she refused to let it soften her. The garment smelled of damp wool. And him. She had to admit she sometimes had stared at him, too, when he wasn't looking. He wasn't a gentleman like her father, but he was compelling nonetheless.

Thinking of her father reminded her that she would sorely miss the magnificent Broadway piano in the saloon. She had despaired of ever playing a piano that fine again after her parents had died of the flu and she had been forced to move west to live with her brother. Everyone said it had been left in the saloon when Colter bought the building and it must be so because he didn't pay it any attention. It was scandalous to see an instrument like that ignored.

"You certainly don't need to pay me for working this evening," she said. The decision to tell the men they couldn't drink anything but coffee in the afternoons when she was working had been Colter's. She was a lady, he said, and would be treated as such in his establishment. She knew he lost business because of it.

"Don't be ridiculous. I'll pay you."

When Colter had found her in the street that first day,

with her bonnet dripping from the rain and desperate tears in her eyes, she'd already been turned down for a job by every respectable shopkeeper in Miles City. The Broadwater, Bubble and Company Mercantile had no work. Neither did the bank. Nor the school. Even the man with the laundry shook his head. Just last week she'd asked everyone again and they all said the same thing. When the North Pacific Railroad came to town, there would be work for everyone. But it hadn't even made it to Glendive yet.

"I know how you must feel about businesses like mine," Colter finally said and Virginia reluctantly pulled her mind back to the conversation.

"You run an honest place." She didn't want to add that he held himself like a leader so men naturally trusted him. The white shirt he wore had been pressed at the laundry down the street and it had the sharp creases she liked. He was holding his hat and running his fingers around the brim.

She had never seen him look nervous before. His jaw was strained, too.

"You don't need to worry," Virginia finally said. She didn't want to feel sorry for him any more than she wanted him to feel sorry for her. "I'll get by. I'm truly grateful for the time I've been able to work here."

When the army patrol her brother was on had been ambushed by Indians, she didn't even have time to finish mourning his death before the officials at nearby Fort Keogh informed her she would need to move. Her job with Colter was all that enabled her to afford a room at the boardinghouse.

Virginia turned to go inside.

Colter reached out to touch her arm. "I never should

have hired you in the first place. Ever since I answered the preacher's call, I've been uneasy. It's not right for you to be working in a place like this. People talk."

If people were talking, it was about him. She had been as surprised as everyone else when Colter had walked down the aisle after Reverend Olson called for those who were repentant to come forward last Sunday.

"It's okay." She reached out meaning to pat him on the arm, but then she stopped and let her hand fall to her side. "No one seriously thinks I'm doing anything in your saloon except playing the piano. Everyone can hear the music when they walk down the street. You've paid me a fair wage. You've done all that man or God requires."

"But I—" Colter looked at her and hesitated for a moment. "The problem is you shouldn't be working anywhere. A lady like you shouldn't have to wash dishes or boil water or anything. That's why I'm going to leave enough money for you to hire someone to do the rough work around here."

Virginia blinked. "What?"

"I know I'm not saying this right." Colter took a deep breath. "I need to go away."

"I don't understand."

"I have some business to take care of—family business." He looked uncomfortable as he stared out at the night. "I'm asking you to take care of my place while I'm gone. Not to run it, of course. But to see to the boy—Danny. He's finally in school and I don't want to take him away from his learning. I'll pay you, of course."

"You're leaving?"

Colter nodded and turned back to her. His dark eyes

studied her as if he was trying to decide something about her. Then a flash of something else—regret perhaps—flickered over his face and he looked away before continuing. "You'll have to close this place as a saloon, but I thought maybe you could use it to give your music lectures while I'm gone—you know talking about that Beck fellow."

"Bach," she corrected him. A few times, when the loneliness had overcome her, she had played some of the classical music she loved and told the men about the composers. She was pleased he'd remembered some of it.

Colter looked at her with a smile.

She wanted to be sure she understood. "You're planning to leave your property in my hands? For me to use?"

He nodded. "If you'd like."

"Of course, I'd like that. I could give real music lessons." Her days would be filled with joy. "I can't thank you enough."

"You don't need to thank me." He stepped closer. His eyes searched hers again for a moment and then he gently tilted her head up so she was looking at him. "All I ask is that you don't get married before I can get back."

The sight of his tawny eyes so close and warm distracted her. By the time she realized what he had said, his face was closer still. That's when he bent down farther and kissed her—quick and hard. She felt a jolt of awareness and then he pulled away.

"Why, I—" she sputtered.

"I know," he whispered. "Me, too."

She'd scarcely gathered enough wits to fully protest when he walked back through the door and into the saloon. What did he have to kiss her for? A gentleman asked before he kissed someone. It was disrespectful not to. Then it suddenly struck her. If her father were still alive, he would never let a man as brazen as Colter court her. Or kiss her either. In fact, her father would have known the man was going to be trouble long before now.

Chapter One

Eleven months, five days later

The place was on fire. Virginia whipped the wet blanket over her head and beat down on the last of the embers glowing along the blackened floor of the saloon. Then she swung again.

Her pulse was racing. When Colter had left his building in her hands, he'd hardly expected her to let it burn to the ground. No matter that he was taking his sweet time in coming back to it. The air had been freezing when he left and it was just as cold outside now.

All summer she'd expected him and here it was almost Christmas again. She'd put her brass bells on the piano with some red ribbons strewn around them for color and Danny had dragged in a small pine tree that he'd set in the corner. Everything had looked so fresh this morning and now it was all coated with gray.

The smoke stung Virginia's eyes, but she wasn't crying. She was too angry. Someone had deliberately doused the floor with kerosene and set it ablaze. She'd been in the back room putting some potatoes on to boil for dinner when she'd smelled the fire. Fortunately, Danny was still in school. Someone looking in the door would have thought everyone was gone. If they had been, then the saloon would have burned down for sure.

Virginia was just hearing the cries of *"Fire"* outside. Enough smoke had escaped into the winter air that someone down the street had finally noticed it.

She hit the smoldering floor one last time. She didn't know who would do this. She should go next door and ask Lester Duncan if there had been any strangers in town. Since Colter had closed his saloon, Lester's was the most likely place for a misfit to turn up. She couldn't believe anyone who lived in Miles City would set fire to any of its buildings.

She let the blanket fall to the floor so she could arch her back to relieve the mild pain that had come as she beat down the fire. When she thought about it, she really didn't want to face Lester today either. The fire would just make him more protective of her, which would probably lead to him asking her to marry him again. Then she'd have to soothe him with some words of comfort while making it clear she planned to follow through on her application to teach in the school in Denver.

A few months ago, she wouldn't have worried about dashing any hopes he'd had. But her feelings about him had been changing since he'd started bringing over the letters his sister wrote to him. He'd read portions of the letters to her. The affection between the brother and sister made Virginia long to be part of a family again.

And then the sister had mentioned that she looked forward to hearing Lester play Bach on the violin again. When Lester read what his sister said about the beauty of his playing, Virginia began to wonder if she'd found a man who could understand her. Her father would have approved of Lester. A man who could cause such rapture on any musical instrument was a man worthy of marriage. Maybe she should say yes to his proposal.

The memory of Colter's kiss, of course, had long since turned sour. Apparently, it was all very well for her to remain single while he romanced his Patricia— if he hadn't been married to the woman all along. Just last week Virginia had gotten a cryptic telegram from the man. "Arriving soon. Leaving Helena. Coming by wagon with Patricia. Many trunks."

Virginia hadn't even heard of the woman until the telegram came and she couldn't warm up to the sound of the name. *Patricia.* The woman was probably cold and critical. And well-dressed with all those trunks. Virginia hadn't felt stylish since she'd left the east coast. She now wore her hair in a simple bun and had given up her corset. Which, she just realized, was very fortunate. A woman in a corset wouldn't have been able to beat down a fire the way she'd just done.

Virginia heard the pounding of footsteps coming closer on the street so she walked over and swung the two doors wide. "It's all right. The fire's out."

She nodded a greeting as the men stomped inside and then, one by one, stared at the black scar on the floor. They needed to see it themselves. Most of the men were old customers so they had probably been next door in Lester's saloon. She recognized Petey and Shorty.

"Smells like kerosene," one of the men she didn't know said suspiciously. He had wide black suspenders holding up his wool pants and a beat-up Stetson on his head. He had the look of a miner about him.

Virginia nodded and wiped the hair out of her eyes. She'd have to rinse her hair for a week with rosewater to get rid of the smell of it. People said her blond hair was her crowning glory and she needed all the confidence she could dredge up to welcome Colter back to town with his Patricia.

The men just stood and stared at her and then back at the floor.

"You didn't do anything?" Petey finally asked. "On account of Colter coming back with this woman—"

It took Virginia a moment to realize what he was asking her. She drew in her breath indignantly. "Set a *fire!* Of course not!"

"Now, don't go getting upset," the first man said. "Petey was only asking because he's been thinking of calling Colter out when the man gets back. We've been talking, and it ain't right him leaving you like this and taking up with some fancy woman. You had a claim on him first. We're miners—we understand if you're stirred up mad. It is claim-jumping, pure and simple. Man or gold—it doesn't make any difference."

Virginia wished the fire had burned a hole in the floor big enough for her to hide in. She should have known the telegraph operator would spread the news that Colter was coming back and that he had company. "First of all, I have no claim to Colter. He's just my employer. He's free to marry anyone he wants. Just as I am free to marry anyone." She glared at Petey. The older man knew about Lester. He didn't approve for some strange reason, but he knew they might be coming to an understanding. "No one needs to call anyone out."

She didn't add that she didn't want Petey's death on her conscience. She'd grown fond of these old men during the past year. Even if Colter wasn't a gunfighter anymore, she had no doubt who would win a contest between the two men.

"Still, it ain't right," Petey repeated stubbornly. "A man can't leave his business with a woman and expect her not to get ideas. Now that your brother's gone, it's up to us to make sure you're treated with respect."

"A woman earns her own respect," Virginia said. She was only beginning to understand that herself. She'd learned a lot this past year taking care of Danny and giving a scattering of music lessons. "Besides, I'll do fine. You know I have plans."

Even though the men were not drinking at the saloon anymore, they stopped by to talk, especially around dinnertime. She always set a couple of extra plates around the poker table. She found the table did just fine for dining if she draped a cloth over it. She'd even convinced the men to eat with the proper utensils.

"We know all about your plans," Petey said. "And we're going to be at the church for the Christmas Eve service so we can applaud you and the Wells girls, but what if it just doesn't work out?"

Petey didn't need to say any more. Virginia heard her father's voice in her head continue the litany. *What if you aren't good enough? You missed that note and your timing was off there. Do it better. It's not good enough.*

She glanced over at the piano that stood in the corner of the room. She'd waxed it until it shone and kept it covered with a cloth so nothing would damage the top wood again. She liked the way the bells looked on it, too. She had not been able to bring a piano west with her, but she had brought her mother's treasured set of ten brass ringing bells, wrapped in linen and packed in her trunk.

"We must have faith," she finally said. She'd first heard about the banker's sister, Cecilia Wells, from his daughters, who were her students. They were the ones who'd mentioned that their aunt was looking for a music instructor at her academy for young ladies in Denver. If Virginia wanted, they said, their father would contact his sister about Virginia. Of course, she told him to write.

All she needed to do now was to impress Cecilia when she came to Miles City to attend the Christmas Eve service. The woman remembered bell songs from a trip she'd made to England and had said she'd be happy to consider the performance as an audition for the position at her school.

"She's sure to want to hire you when she hears you and the girls play them bells," Petey said proudly. "I've never heard anything like it. The sound puts me in mind of home."

"Everything reminds you of home."

"But what I mean to say is that even though she'll want to hire you, maybe she won't be able to," Petey continued. "Maybe she will already have promised the job to someone else before she gets here. Or maybe she won't have money to hire another teacher. Or—"

"We just need to have faith," Virginia repeated. She refused to consider defeat. The echoes of her father's criticism had stayed in her mind all these years, but she had thrown herself on God's mercy. Surely He would help her get this job. It wasn't as though she was asking to be invited on some European concert tour. She knew she wasn't good enough for that. Her father had been right to say it. But she could teach children. She knew that in her bones.

"Well, if the school lady doesn't hire you," Petey continued. "Lester says he'll let you sing over at his place. He doesn't have a piano, but we can get a rousing song or two going. And we'll promise not to drink too much while you're working either."

"Thanks," Virginia murmured. But Colter had been right about drinking and ladies. The next step to what Petey suggested would be for her to lift her skirts and dance. She shuddered at the thought. This was how young ladies were ruined.

"We can even help you clean this floor up." Petey turned to scowl at the men behind him and they eventually nodded.

She looked around the main room of the saloon. Most of it was intact. She'd gotten to the fire before it spread beyond the middle of the floor. The tables were fine even though the big mirror behind the mahogany bar would need another good cleaning. And the walls she'd just washed were now slightly gray.

"It is a mess, isn't it?" Virginia said. And then she heard the door open again so she turned to look over her shoulder. It was probably Lester. The winter sun was starting to set so it streamed right in the open door so she couldn't see clearly. She wanted to rub her eyes. It couldn't be. But there, standing in the middle of the doorway, was the last man she wanted to see right now. Fortunately, the men standing around her put themselves to good use and, quicker than she thought possible, she was hidden behind their shoulders and broad hats.

Colter hadn't expected to see half of his old customers standing in the saloon when he came back. The place was supposed to be closed. He looked over at the bar and saw there was no lineup of liquor bottles. He looked back at the men. They were all looking guilty, except for Petey, who looked as though he was going to erupt with something.

That's when Colter smelled the smoke. "What's happening here?"

The last thing he needed was more problems. He had enough of a challenge with Patricia. But he could see something was wrong. Then, as he watched, someone quietly pushed their way from behind the men to stand in front of them.

"I take full responsibility," Virginia said.

Colter's heart almost stopped. With her blond head held high, Virginia was beautiful. He hadn't remembered her being quite so breathtaking.

"I'd like to know your intentions." Petey stepped out from the rest of the men and walked around until he was standing in front of Virginia.

Colter looked at the man in surprise.

"Really, Petey, he doesn't need to—" Virginia said as she tried to step around the man.

It was obvious that Petey intended to stay in front because he took a step closer.

This could go on forever, Colter thought, *back and forth.*

He held up a hand. He'd had enough of people dancing around their opinions. It never made anything go smoother. "Let Petey talk." He turned to the older man, who had been one of his best customers. "What's the problem?"

Colter wondered if somehow Petey knew where he'd been and the trouble he was bringing back with him.

"I need to know what you intend to do about Miss Virginia here, now that you're back," Petey said with some heat to his words. "She doesn't deserve to have her heart broken."

"My heart's not—" Virginia protested.

"Tell me the man's name," Colter demanded before he remembered he'd sworn off using his guns. Being a Christian was harder than it had sounded, especially when it came to a man dealing with his enemies. He'd find something to do, though, to make the man sorry he'd dealt unjustly with Virginia. His fists would work fine for a fool man like that.

There was silence in the room.

"Well," Colter demanded as he looked the men over. They might not be as bad as the scoundrel he intended to face down, but there wasn't a man in the room good enough for Virginia, himself included.

Then Colter glanced at Petey and wondered what he was missing. The man's eyes were bulging out as if he'd swallowed something with a pit in it.

"Oh, for goodness' sakes," Virginia finally said. She stepped around the older man and looked Colter straight in the eye with a snap of annoyance he found rather endearing. "They think it's you."

"Me? What'd I do?"

"Well, you up and got married," Petey stammered, finding his voice finally. "A woman like Virginia naturally expected—"

"I'm not married." Colter heard Petey talking, but he kept his eyes on Virginia. She had turned pink and it was the most beautiful sight he'd ever seen. It was too bad about the two of them. He had hoped to be back months ago while the memory of that kiss would be fresh in her mind. Now, of course, everything was different.

"What about your Patricia?" Petey finally finished.

And that, Colter thought to himself, was where his life now began and ended. He turned around. "This is Patricia."

Chapter Two

Virginia looked at the open door of the saloon in consternation. There was no woman standing there. A few more men from the saloon next door had drifted in and there was a boy she didn't recognize standing beside the doorjamb. It was late afternoon and the boy was probably waiting to see Danny when school let out. She thought she knew all the boys in town, but she had missed this one.

"Patricia must have left," Virginia said as she turned back. She was relieved. She knew she'd have to meet the woman eventually, but she'd rather not do it when she had soot on her face. And her hair was coming undone. This was no time to meet anyone. Besides, she had been prepared to be polite to Colter's wife, but she wasn't sure how she was supposed to act now that she found out he hadn't even married the woman he brought back here. Virginia felt sorry for her. No wonder she was embarrassed to face everyone. At least Lester would never shame a woman this way, Virginia thought to herself in satisfaction.

"Come say hello, Patricia," Colter repeated calmly.

Virginia wondered if she should say something to Colter about being more patient with his—she hesitated—his friend. After all, he was putting the woman in an awkward situation. She was probably just outside the door waiting for him to come out again.

"I got nothing to say," the boy Virginia had seen earlier spoke up. She no sooner noticed that than she realized his voice sounded suspiciously like a girl's.

"This is Patricia?" Virginia whispered as she realized what it all meant. Now she really did want to crawl into a hole somewhere and wait for the awkwardness to pass. She looked over at the men who'd come in earlier and they were all gawking at the child as though she was a changeling. But it was clear that the woman was a girl, which meant—Virginia had been wrong.

"You must be thirsty," she said gently as she took a step toward the child. Now that she was more focused, she could see unmistakable clues that it was a girl inside those rough clothes. The girl's nose was feminine and her dark eyelashes curled. A beaten-up old hat was pulled down over her hair. Her eyes might be defiant, but they were a lovely shade of green.

"I have some tea ready to brew in back." Virginia offered with a smile. She'd heated the water when she was peeling the potatoes.

"It's a fine thing to drink," Petey said, adding his voice to the murmurs from the other men. They'd all had her tea at one time or another. She added a little cinnamon to it. And sometimes honey. "It'll warm you right up."

"I'd rather have whiskey," the child said, taking a step forward into the saloon as if she expected to get it.

"Surely, you don't—" Virginia gave a horrified glance at Colter.

Colter had seen looks like that before. When the good church women of Helena had realized that the saloon boy they knew as Patty was really a little girl named Patricia, they'd decided that Colter wasn't a fit parent for her.

He couldn't fight them on that, but he still didn't like their judgmental nature. On one point he was firm though. God had lots of people to care about Him. Patricia only had Colter. Even the women in Helena, as indignant as they were, hadn't stepped forward to take care of the child.

Colter refused to look over at Virginia. She was no doubt planning how to scold him. He knew a saloon was no place to raise a child. But he didn't have time to worry about it, not right at this minute anyway.

"Little girls don't drink whiskey." Colter repeated the words he'd had to say a few times already.

That made the girl look up, her eyes defiant. "My mother lets me have whiskey when it's cold outside. For my bones. I have thin bones."

Colter didn't answer. He didn't need to. He saw the dawning misery spread in Patricia's eyes. Her mother, Rose, had done a lot of unfortunate things in her life, but the worst of them had been to abandon her daughter.

Rose had sent a letter to Colter saying he was the father of a ten-year-old and he'd better come to the Golden Spur and pick up the girl or she would likely starve. Rose didn't even wait for Colter to get there before she took off with some miner named Rusty Jackson, who had struck it rich in one of the gulches outside of town.

"You've got to have whiskey," the girl continued, her voice clipped to show she didn't care about the other. "You own this saloon. Mama told me."

Colter walked over and put his arm on her shoulder. He supposed Rose had embellished everything to make it sound as though he owned the biggest and richest saloon west of the Mississippi. Rose had been like that. She would have promised her daughter anything if it meant Patricia would do what she was told.

Colter had been one of the woman's many admirers years ago when he'd been hired to keep the peace in the Golden Spur. He'd been fast with his guns back then, having more bravado than common sense. Rose hadn't been his only mistake.

Colter supposed at some time he would need to tell all of this to Virginia, but he could see from Patricia's face that now was not the time to talk about anyone's mother.

"I might not open up the saloon again," Colter settled for saying instead. He could ignore the problem if that's what Patricia wanted. "Especially not after the fire here."

"I plan to fix the floor," Virginia said stiffly.

Colter looked up. "You don't need to do that."

"Of course I do. It was my job to take care of things. You need the building now that you have another child to care for." She nodded toward the girl.

He could see by the set of her jaw that Virginia had a rush of emotions that she was keeping inside. She looked distressed, which surprised him. Most women looked outraged with him, especially when Patricia said she wanted whiskey to drink. He looked at Virginia more closely. She appeared tired, as though she hadn't been sleeping well. And she was thinner. He didn't like to see that. She must be worried about something.

"A burnt floor won't trouble Patricia," Colter said. "Not after what she's been through."

"That's why she needs a home," Virginia persisted. "I bet she doesn't even have a pillow to sleep on."

Colter relaxed. He recognized a mothering instinct when he saw it. "She needs a family more than anything."

Virginia nodded. "You've been good to Danny since he started living with you. I'm sure you'll do fine with Patricia, too."

Her approval felt like a blessing poured over him. It made him relax inside.

"I'd do better with a wife," he said without thinking. He hadn't meant to blurt it out like that. What was wrong with him? Now of all times, he couldn't afford to forget everything he knew about women.

Virginia blinked. "What?"

The men from the saloon had started to walk to the door, but they all stopped in midstride to look back at him.

"There comes a time to get married." Now that Colter had started, he decided it was worse to back down than to go forward. It probably didn't matter how he said things anyway. He hadn't had much hope even before he left here that Virginia would agree to marry him; he'd half expected her to be someone else's wife by the time he got back. Besides, he'd been a different man when he kissed her. A man with children had to think more about marriage than a man alone.

"Do you have—" Virginia started.

By now the men were all gathered around again as though this was even more entertaining than a blaze threatening to burn down the town. He supposed it was.

Colter tried to ignore his audience. "Every man has dreams."

He looked directly into Virginia's eyes, willing her to understand what was in his heart. Maybe if he hadn't been staring at her so intently he would have noticed his daughter's reaction earlier.

Patricia had walked into the middle of the circle of men and then glanced at Colter in triumph. "He means my mother."

It took a moment for the words to make it to Colter's brain. *"What?"*

Where had Patricia gotten that idea, he wondered?

"My mama's his dream. He's pined away for her for years and years. She told me she's going to come and marry him someday." Patricia jerked her thumb at Colter. "That's why I'm with him. We're just waiting until she comes."

It must have been the letter Rose left for her, Colter thought in dismay. Trust Rose to saddle him with the explanations. He'd tracked the woman down to San Francisco just to talk to her so he knew she had no intention of marrying any man. Not even her Rusty.

No one spoke for a moment. And then Petey burst forth. "You mean you aren't marrying our Virginia here?"

Everyone's eyes turned to Virginia.

"I— No—" Virginia sputtered. "Of course, he needs to marry the girl's mother. They have a child together. Besides, I have plans. And there's Lester— I—"

Colter wished he could set everyone down and explain. But before he did, he asked, "What's this about Lester?"

"Oh, you know women," Petey said with a marked lack of enthusiasm. "If there's one bad apple in the barrel—"

"Lester is not a bad apple. Just because Lester is a sensitive musician—"

Petey snorted. "That's why I'm hoping you get that job in Denver. Maybe some time away from Lester will do you good."

"Virginia's going to get a job at some fancy school in Denver." Petey turned to Colter and informed him. "Teaching music."

"So she's not getting married?" If he'd known Virginia was going to take up with Lester, he wouldn't have left her here. Now if it was a banker or a shopkeeper, he'd wish her well. Maybe even a railroad man if any of them ever got here. But Lester? There was something he didn't trust about that man. And it had nothing to do with music.

"A woman can have a job even when she's married," Virginia replied tartly. "Besides, who I marry is my own business."

Colter's heart sank. She had that look about her that said she was rattled over some man. He should have followed his impulse and asked her to marry him before he left. She hadn't loved him, but she might have married him. And, once she did, she'd stand by her word.

When he was driving the wagon over from Helena, he'd kept thinking that things between him and Patricia would go more smoothly once there was a woman like Virginia around. He'd been captivated by her during all those days when she'd played piano for the men in his saloon. She might have been exasperated with them at times, but she always looked at them with kindness. Even if she wouldn't marry him, he'd thought on the way here, she might be able to help Patricia adjust to her new life.

Not that he could ask Virginia to do all of that now. She was so caught up with Lester that—he looked around and his eyes settled on the piano in the corner. She'd been polishing the wood, he could tell that even with all of the soot that had filtered down to the piano's surface. And she had some fancy brass bells set out like Christmas decorations.

"Even if you are getting married," Colter said in a rush, "you're the best music teacher around and I'd like you to give Patricia piano lessons. I'll pay you your usual fee, of course."

"There's no need to—" Virginia said.

"I'm not gonna—" Patricia muttered.

"Double your fee," Colter interrupted them and kept going. "Triple even. I know it might take extra lessons since she's a beginner, but she doesn't need to be able to play any of those classical songs. Just some carols— maybe before Christmas."

That seemed to leave both Virginia and Patricia speechless, although he wasn't sure whether it was the price he was offering or the speed with which he was hoping for results.

"That's not even a week away," Virginia finally said. "If she's not already playing the piano, I don't think— I mean she's awfully young to—"

"A teacher like you can handle it," Colter said.

"Nobody wants to listen to any carols—" Patricia

protested with a touch of scorn. "Babies get born in mangers all the time in that part of the world." She gave a vague wave of her hand. "It's no reason to go out and play a song about it."

That made Virginia turn to the girl. "You might want to surprise your mother," she said as she knelt down so she was eye level with Patricia. Virginia got a soft look on her face that made Colter regret he didn't have more to offer her. "Parents always like to hear their children play music."

Colter would have pointed out that Rose wasn't coming so she wouldn't hear anything, but he didn't want to interrupt the two.

"Not my mother—" Patricia shook her head. "She says that all Christmas is good for is getting people to give you things 'cause they feel sorry for you. So the best thing to do is look sad so people give you nice things. Or money. She never mentions any songs."

With that, Patricia wrinkled her face up until she did look pathetic.

Colter turned and saw Virginia's mouth tighten in disapproval.

He knew then that she was going to teach Patricia. But just to be sure, he said, "You'll need some money even if you get that job in Denver. You'll need to travel. And, once you get there, you may need to stay in a hotel for a few days."

Before Virginia could answer, there was a noise as the doors opened and Danny stepped inside.

"What's for din—" the boy began as he looked around the saloon. Then he saw Colter. "You're back."

The boy's face lit up, and, for the first time in months, Colter had hope that he might make an adequate parent. After all, neither Danny nor Patricia had anyone else to look out for them. He was better than nobody.

Then he got a second look at the boy. What had happened to him? He was cleaned up until he shone. He was wearing a shirt with a collar instead of that sack-like thing he'd been wearing when Colter left. And his hair was cut proper. His ears were probably even clean.

Colter hoped Danny didn't blame him for leaving him with a lady who insisted on that much soap.

"Welcome back, sir," Danny finally added as he took a step closer to Colter and put his hand out.

Ordinarily, Danny welcomed him back with a grunt or two, but Colter took the boy's hand and shook it. Something had changed and Colter wasn't sure it was for the better. His misgivings evaporated though when the boy left him and went to Virginia, who opened her arms and gave him a hug. Colter couldn't remember anyone ever hugging Danny. If Virginia was willing to do that, then she could scrub the whole place as much as she wanted. He'd even supply the lye for the soap.

"What's burning?" Danny said as he stepped away from Virginia.

"Oh, no," the woman muttered and started to run out of the room. "I forgot the potatoes."

Colter decided that the burnt odor of the potatoes made the smell of the kerosene-soaked floor better somehow. It proved this was still their home. He was going to need to find out who had tried to destroy his saloon, but first he'd help Virginia find something for them to eat. It had done his heart good to see the affection she had for Danny. The boy hadn't been so happy since he'd wandered into the saloon a couple of years ago. Colter hoped soon Virginia would feel the same way about Patricia. That's what his two children needed most. If Virginia insisted in leaving, he'd have to find someone else to marry. His children needed a mother.

Chapter Three

$\sim$

Virginia had never seen a young girl with so many trunks. There were three dull black ones with worn brass hinges. Patricia had opened one slightly and the bright colors peeking out made Virginia blanch. She recognized the dresses. Well, not the exact dresses, but the style. The shiny ones sparkled like the dresses from the women working the saloon next door. Virginia hoped somewhere in the trunk was a dress suitable for a ten-year-old girl.

Patricia didn't seem worried about it though. The most immediate need was for something for her to sleep in and there was a threadbare night shift stuffed on top of the dresses in one of the trunks.

The night showed through the upstairs windows and it would be time to go to bed soon. They had all eaten a dinner of fried potatoes and canned peaches before they started to settle Patricia into the room upstairs that had belonged to Danny. Virginia offered to move back to the boardinghouse so the boy could have her room, but he seemed pleased to be invited to bunk down in the storeroom with Colter. The room was by the back door and they were going to stand watch tonight in case the man who started the fire came back to finish the job.

Virginia was careful not to mention any of that to Patricia. The girl had enough to worry about already.

"Maybe we can just hang up the dresses that you'll want to wear in the next few days," Virginia said. "We'll want to take our time and press them."

Patricia looked up in alarm. "I'm not going to wear them. I'm just saving them for my mother."

Virginia nodded. Of course. Now she understood why Patricia had treated the trunks with so much reverence. She had even refused to let Danny open the one with the bent latch for her.

Just then there was a commotion downstairs.

"Maybe that's my mother," Patricia said, springing up in excitement and racing for the door.

Virginia didn't get a chance to say she hadn't heard a woman's voice. Fortunately, the sounds didn't seem like trouble, so she walked over to the door and stepped out into the landing leading to the stairs. She looked down and saw it was Lester. He was wearing his black suit and holding his hat.

"There you are," Lester said as he looked up at her.

She hadn't noticed before that his hair was thinning on top of his head. The strands were kind of colorless to begin with as well. Not that it mattered. Physical attraction wasn't what drew her to the man.

She was glad she'd had a chance to clean some of the soot and grime off her just in case he cared about such things though.

"I didn't expect you," Virginia said as she smiled down at Lester.

"I was worried," he said.

Patricia went back into the bedroom when she saw who the visitor was. Briefly, Virginia's eyes scanned the saloon. Colter was sitting at a table and reading something. No one else was around. She couldn't help but notice that the top of Colter's head was covered with thick, softly curling dark hair. Not that it meant anything to her. It was just interesting to observe what a person could see from a height.

Virginia looked down at Lester and waited for a telltale skip in her heartbeat. She had always expected to have a rush of feelings when she imagined touching the man who might one day be her husband. Her heart just kept up its regular beat though. She supposed thoughts of hair and hearts belonged more to girls like Patricia than to her. She was a grown woman now and knew love was rooted in steadier things than thick hair.

Lester smiled up and she started to walk down the stairs. Truly, it was best that their relationship was a practical one based on a shared love of music; it would make it easier for Lester to understand her desire to teach. If they did marry, she hoped to convince him to move to Denver with her so she could take the teaching job if it was offered to her. Lester had talked of becoming the governor of Montana when it became a state, but until that happened, Denver would be a good place for him to meet important people. She'd told him about all the politicians her father knew, but there was no way to meet any of them in a place like Miles City. Her working for a school in Denver should help with that though.

Of course, she wouldn't be considering marriage to him if she hadn't seen from his sister's letters that he had a lifelong faith in God as well. She trusted the sister's words. Who knew a man better than his sister?

When Virginia reached the bottom of the stairs, she tilted her right cheek and offered it to Lester, who gave it a quick kiss. The sweetness of the moment was spoiled by a disbelieving grunt coming from the left of her.

Virginia looked over and caught Colter's eye. He'd glanced up from the book he was reading. She hoped the look she gave him rivaled the one her mother had given impertinent tradesmen when they tried to peddle old fish. The greeting between her and Lester was none of *his* business.

"Sorry," Colter said, looking no such thing as he gave her a wink. "It's just that men out here don't even bother with a puny kiss like that."

Virginia sensed Lester tensing up beside her so she put her hand on his arm. She'd handle this.

"A kiss on the cheek is a time-honored way of showing a woman respect," Virginia said, looking closer. Was that a Bible he was reading?

"Back east maybe," Colter agreed. "But out here a man knows how to kiss a woman."

Lester muttered something at that, but Virginia didn't hear it.

"It doesn't hurt any man to use good manners," she continued. Lester did have the sensitive soul of a violinist even if he'd left the instrument with his sister until he could send for it. "East, west, north or south. Besides, the Bible talks about a holy kiss."

Colter looked stunned as he held up the Bible in his hand and then sighed. "I haven't got to that part yet."

Lester started to chuckle. "You haven't got to a lot of things yet."

With that, Lester turned to Virginia and tipped her

head back before leaning down to kiss her fully and possessively.

Virginia tried to make him stop. She needed to breathe and—well, she just didn't like the way he was kissing her. As if he was proving a point. She pushed at him a little, but that only made him more determined. Finally, she pushed him harder.

Colter had never cared for a man abusing a woman and he grabbed Lester by the back of his collar. He'd do the same to a stray cat that had wandered into the wrong bowl of cream. Lester came away sputtering and looking mad enough to fight, but Colter wasn't worried about him.

"You all right?" he asked Virginia. Her hair was in disarray and she was gasping a little for breath. He'd seen enough women who'd been well-kissed to know that Virginia wasn't too happy with her beau.

"Of course she's all right," Lester answered for her. "She's my fiancée."

"I've never exactly said yes," Virginia snapped at him.

That answer made Colter feel pretty good, but he could see it didn't make the lovebirds too happy.

"I'm not going to wait for you forever, you know," Lester said as he started for the door, forgetting Colter still had a hold on his shirt.

"I think you should apologize to the lady," Colter suggested.

Lester choked a little and stopped abruptly.

"I don't need to—" Lester began and almost lost his wind altogether.

Colter nodded. "A man doesn't need to do much in this life, not even breathe."

Lester's face was turning pink so Colter had pity on him and untwisted his collar a little. "Next time you have a shirt tailored, you might want to have them make the neck a little bigger."

"Aargh," Lester muttered as he pulled himself up to his full height.

"Really, you need to let him go," Virginia commanded as she stepped closer.

Colter looked at her to be sure she meant it. Then he released Lester completely. "I suppose I do need to let him talk. Anyway, I've been meaning to ask him why he wasn't over here this afternoon when everyone thought there was a fire."

"I have a business to run," Lester said as he straightened the front of his shirt. "I can't be stepping outside every time the men decide to go look at something."

"The men do get excited about things. I think they make bets," Virginia said with disapproval in her voice. "Sometimes it's a horse race. Sometimes when the stage will get in."

Colter thought a minute. "I don't suppose any of them would bet on how long it would take for a saloon to burn down."

"Oh, absolutely not," Virginia protested. "They read the telegram about you coming back and—"

Colter nodded. He knew there were rumors about his gun days. Not many of the men around would challenge him. Although, he realized, the man with the match didn't exactly leave a name. Lester was coward enough to do something like that. So he looked back at the man. "Do you have any kerosene stored in that shed in back?"

Lester's face darkened at that. "Anybody could have gotten some from there. I'll bet that's what happened."

Colter grunted. "Well, I guess we're not going to figure it out tonight."

Now that Lester was free to leave, the man didn't seem too eager to go. Which made the man a fool as well as a coward in Colter's eyes.

"Is there something you want to tell me?" Colter finally asked. After what had happened today, he'd only lit a few of the lamps around, so the shadows were deep in parts of the saloon.

"A man has a right to say good-night to his fiancée in private," Lester said.

Colter shrugged. "He does if he's saying it in his own establishment."

What was it about Lester that reminded him of a rooster? Maybe it was the way his neck stretched when he got indignant.

"It's still snowing out there," Lester protested. "I can't ask Virginia to walk outside just to say good-night."

Colter nodded. "I suppose not."

"You can say good-night here," Virginia said as she reached out her hand to Lester.

Colter had to respect the woman for not letting the man kiss her after his earlier performance.

Lester still didn't look any too happy, but he finally shook Virginia's hand before saying good-night and shuffling out the door.

When the other man had left the building, Colter turned to Virginia. He figured she would want to thank him for coming to her rescue, but he didn't want her to fuss over it. He would do as much for any woman who was in trouble.

"What did you think you were doing?" Virginia turned to him and demanded.

Her voice wasn't as grateful as Colter had been expecting and it turned him cautious. "I—ah—"

"I had it perfectly under control," Virginia continued without letting him answer. "If you'd waited, I would have explained to him how a gentleman should behave and—"

"I don't think he was set to listen," Colter added mildly.

"I would have explained how he should behave," Virginia kept on going. "And then we would have been of one mind on how to be when we're together. We'd have had an understanding."

Colter was flabbergasted. "I interrupted all that?"

"Yes, you did," Virginia declared and then she sat down in a chair and burst into tears.

Colter was silent for a bit. "I could go get him and bring him back."

"I don't want him back," Virginia said, as she lifted her tear-streaked face and then hiccuped. "But he plays the vi-oo-lin."

She hiccuped again.

"Breathe easy now," Colter said as he moved close and patted her on the back.

Then he stepped over to the bar and brought back a cup of cold coffee. "Here, take a swallow of this."

Virginia took the cup and drained it. They were both quiet for a minute, but she didn't have another hiccup. Colter had never listened so intently to another person's breathing though, and he began to have some sympathy for poor Lester. In the light of the lamp, Virginia's skin glowed and her hair shone and—

"That holy kiss you were talking about," Colter finally said, his throat thick enough he was afraid Virginia would know his thoughts by the way his voice sounded. "Is it something like this?"

God was going to have to forgive him, Colter thought as he leaned down and touched his lips to Virginia's. He was a doomed man.

"That's not right," Virginia whispered against his lips.

Colter moved his head back.

She cleared her throat and continued, "A holy kiss is for church." Her face was flushed pink, but she was smiling a little.

"It's almost Sunday," Colter said as he straightened up and smoothed Virginia's hair back. "I don't recall any kissing in church before I left here. 'Course I didn't get a chance to go more than a few times before I left."

He had wished he had time to talk a little more with the pastor before he was called away to get Patricia. He'd been reading the Bible alone to try to make sense of things, but he had some questions.

"I've been taking Danny with me."

"I appreciate that," Colter said and then realized something. "I haven't paid you yet for taking care of everything. And the bank's closed now."

"Monday's fine," Virginia said as she stood up, too.

Before he knew it, she had said good-night and walked back up the stairs.

Colter supposed it was for the best. Virginia deserved a newly minted penny, not an old beat-up coin like him.

So far, he was doing all right by Danny and Patricia, but they had even fewer expectations of life than he did. Someone like Virginia was different though. She'd grown up with china dolls and tea parties—and those pianos she talked about. She should marry a man who could give her those things again. She hadn't talked much about her life back east, but he'd noticed she had a way of doing things that showed she'd known some fine things in life. She was very precise in her movements.

She'd certainly never had much to do with ex-gunfighters who were trying to be fathers. That much Colter could guarantee. He was better at trail grub than normal meals. He'd been meaning to get Danny a regular shirt, but he'd never quite made it to the mercantile to do it. Frankly, he wasn't even sure how he was supposed to make a home for the two children he was taking on. He'd been raising Danny in this saloon here, but it wasn't suitable for Patricia. Besides, he didn't have a taste for that kind of life anymore himself.

Maybe in church tomorrow he'd talk to Jake Hargrove, his old friend who lived over by Dry Creek. Jake had gone from a trapping life to raising his nieces and it hadn't seemed to hurt him any. Of course, he'd convinced Elizabeth to marry him shortly after his nieces came to live with him so he was probably making out just fine. A wife would make all of the difference.

Chapter Four

Virginia woke up and almost screamed. Thin streaks of morning sun were coming in the window and a purple bird was staring down at her. She blinked to clear her vision and noticed the bird had odd feathers. And a little girl's nose was sticking out of its beak, quivering with excitement.

"Well, who do we have here?" Virginia leaned up on an elbow so she could be eye to eye with her visitor. "I wonder if anyone wants fried chicken for breakfast."

That made the nose and the beak shake even more with barely stifled giggles.

"This looks like a nice plump bird," Virginia continued, pretending to consider the idea. "I bet it tastes good."

With that, Patricia put down the feathered mask that must have come from her mother's trunks and giggled freely.

"Are you finished trying to terrify me?" Virginia asked as she stretched.

"You weren't scared. You were hungry. My mother would have screamed."

"I'm sure she'd have swooned from fright," Virginia agreed.

Patricia was silent for a minute. "Sometimes she liked to play if she wasn't busy."

Virginia nodded. And sometimes purple birds came to visit at dawn. No matter how much Patricia loved this mother of hers, Virginia didn't think much of the woman. She reached out to sweep a stray feather out of Patricia's hair.

Then she pushed the covers off and swung her legs around to the floor. "If you get dressed, I'll show you how to make a sock doll this afternoon."

The girl shrugged. "Okay."

Patricia was leaving the room when Virginia remembered. "And put on your best clothes. It's Sunday today and we're going to church."

Patricia turned around. "My mother doesn't take me to church."

Now why aren't I surprised? Virginia thought.

"Well, it's time you went then," was all she said.

Virginia knew it wasn't really her decision to take the children to church. Colter was their parent. He should make that decision. But since she was going to church regardless of who else did, she decided she would wear her best gray wool dress with the brass buttons trailing down the front and the small bustle in the back. And, of course, her black hat and gloves.

Even when she was giving lessons to the Wells girls, she dressed like a lady. She was afraid to relax her standards for fear she wouldn't fit into her world anymore when she was able to return. Being caught without a corset yesterday was lazy on her part. A lady had to put the proper effort into dressing. Her father, she couldn't help thinking, would be appalled if he could see her now. He had expected more from her.

Virginia heard Patricia's footsteps going down the stairs while she put the last pins in her hair. If she knew Danny, the boy was already up and dressed for going to church.

When Virginia got to the stairs, she looked down and wondered what had happened. By the smell of things, pancake batter was burning somewhere and a gray barking dog was chasing an animal—it must be a cat—around the tables. Colter had just opened the doorway coming in from the back room. He was holding a wooden spoon in his hand and ignoring the smoke starting to billow out behind him. He must have heard the children. Danny was sitting in one of the chairs laughing as a wild-haired Patricia threatened to throw a small spittoon at him. If it was the spittoon from the bar, at least it was clean.

Virginia walked down the stairs and over to the piano. She didn't have much experience with chaos, but she did know sound. She reached for one of her deepest bells and rang it sharply. The pure sweet note floated over the saloon. Then Colter shut the door to the back room, closing the cat and dog in there. Patricia sat and gazed up at the bell with a look of rapture on her face. Even Danny had stopped laughing.

There was blessed silence in the room.

Now how did she do that? Colter asked himself as he walked over and set his spoon down on a table. When he'd gotten up this morning, he'd figured he'd make some pancakes for breakfast just like he used to do every Sunday morning for him and Danny. Two more people to feed didn't worry him.

But then Patricia had come down and opened the front door to get her morning breath of fresh air, something she claimed her mother always advised. A gust of wind made her hair blow this way and that. Then, Danny started to laugh at her hair and the cat ran inside, trying to escape that dog following her. Before Colter knew it, everything was out of control.

With one bell ring, though, Virginia had brought it all back to normal.

He hadn't realized until this very minute that he was a fool to think he was ready to be a father to two children. When it had just been him and Danny they had done all right. But how would he manage with Patricia as well? He didn't know anything about girls.

"How'd you do that?" Patricia was demanding of Virginia. Colter needed to sit down. He'd faced ambushes with less panic than he was feeling right now. How did ordinary men manage to raise children like these? A person couldn't just put them in a corral like spring colts. Or let them scatter like chickens. Could he?

Fortunately, Virginia rang the bell again and Patricia walked slowly over to the piano.

Life was full of surprises, Virginia thought to herself. Who would think that a slip of a girl more familiar with a spittoon than a musical instrument would be blessed with such an exceptional ear for music. By the look on her face, she figured the girl had also heard the slow slide of the bell tone. Most ears didn't pick that up. "The note's a D. It can also do this."

By hitting the bell slightly differently, Virginia made a lighter sound.

"It's beautiful," Patricia said as she stopped in front of the bells and reached out to touch one of them reverently.

"My mother's father had them engraved." Virginia smiled as she stepped closer to the girl. The etched cross was surrounded by curls on the front of the brass bell. "He was a change ringer with a cathedral guild in England. Very proud he was of it, too."

Virginia handed a bell to Patricia and the girl ran her finger around the rim of it.

Virginia guessed that, even if they hadn't started lessons, the girl was now a student so she should tell her more. "My grandfather's job was to mark the hours of the day and other important times and places. The different series of rings were called changes. He was most grateful for these small bells because he could use them to practice at home in front of the fire instead of in the church's cold bell tower. He left them to my mother when he died and she left them to me."

"I wouldn't have minded the cold," Patricia said.

Virginia smiled. "If you turn the bell over you'll see a mark. That means they were made by the Whitechapel Bell Foundry in England."

Virginia loved to teach about music. She picked up a couple of more bells and rang out part of a scale.

"Does the church here have bells?" Patricia asked. "I didn't know churches had bells."

"We have an organ, too. We're not planning to ring the bells until Christmas Eve. And we're not doing any changes, we're playing 'Silent Night.' But the organ plays every Sunday."

"Then I'm going," the girl said simply.

Virginia nodded. She knew what the love of music could mean to someone. It was too bad that Patricia couldn't go back east and discover the richness of the music there. Virginia sighed. She wished her father could have met the girl. It might have made up for some of his disappointment with her if she could have brought him a student with a natural talent for music that might even have rivaled his.

Colter felt his heart ease as he watched Virginia talking to Patricia. Maybe he wasn't as alone as he had thought. Virginia sounded as though she was willing to help Patricia. The girl needed affection almost more than she needed musical training, but he wouldn't tell either one of them that yet.

The only reason he knew how barren the girl's childhood had been was because he'd gone to Rose before he'd brought Patricia back here. That woman was drunk when he talked to her or she probably wouldn't have admitted she hadn't been sure he'd go to the Golden Spur, especially when the girl wasn't even his daughter. Rose had laughed like crazy at that, saying he should have asked the girl her birthday. He'd remembered Rose as being irresponsible, but he hadn't known she could be cruel until then.

On the ride back to Helena, he had decided he wouldn't mention birthdays. Or tell Patricia what her mother had said about him leaving her if he wanted. Colter figured God had tapped his shoulder to help the girl and that was that. He'd already learned with Danny that feeling like a father didn't always have much to do with the facts of the matter.

Colter shook his head as though to clear it. Patricia was safe with him now and, in time, her mother would become a distant memory. A little smoke was still in the air so he excused himself and went into the back room. The door to the outside had been pushed open by the escaping cat and dog so most of the smoke had left as well. He decided he'd just make oats for everyone for breakfast. If they were all going to church, he wouldn't have enough time to make pancakes now anyway.

He put the water on to boil and went back into the main room.

"Braids," Patricia was demanding. "I want braids."

"I think brushing your hair will be enough." Virginia was proceeding to do just that.

"But it tangles," Patricia protested. "Unless I wear my hat."

"No hats," Virginia said.

"Why not? He's wearing his." Patricia eyed Danny.

Colter noted that the boy did have his hat on. That was unlike him. He was probably making sure no one took a comb to him though. Or a spittoon.

"Oh, but you have such pretty hair. We don't want to cover it up," Virginia said to Patricia as she untangled everything.

Colter wondered when Virginia would notice they had bigger problems than Patricia's hair. He hadn't truly seen how ragged her clothes were until she sat next to Virginia. As near as he could tell, Patricia was wearing a cut-down man's shirt cinched in with a piece of cowboy rope. Her trousers were made of coarse wool and were starting to fray at the seams.

"You'll have to sit by me in church," Colter told Patricia. People wouldn't notice her clothes so much if she was sitting by him. At least they would be less noticeable than if she sat by Virginia.

How did that woman manage to always look so good anyway?

"I think there's a community dinner after church services today," Virginia remarked as she started to guide the brush through the girl's hair. "Elizabeth Hargrove is making her doughnuts, too. She passes those out between Sunday school and church."

"My mother made doughnuts once," Patricia said with longing in her voice. "She said doughnuts are the way to a man's heart."

"Yes, well—" Virginia hesitated and looked up at him. "If it's all right with Colter, we'll invite the Hargroves here some afternoon and make doughnuts with Elizabeth and Spotted Fawn. I don't know if they'll make their way to any man's heart, but they sure are good."

Patricia started to frown. "Spotted Fawn? Is that an Indian name?"

Colter wondered if he should have said something to Patricia earlier. He'd grown so accustomed to the Hargrove girls now that he often didn't remember they were part-Sioux.

"She'll be in church?" Patricia asked.

"We hope so," Colter said.

Patricia frowned as she looked up at him and then back at Virginia. "My mother won't let me sit down with no Indians. They can't even get whiskey at her saloon. They're no good. Everyone says they're a regular bite upon the face of the earth."

"The word's *blight* and it's not true," Virginia said with some heat.

Patricia still looked undecided.

"Spotted Fawn is a lovely girl. And you'll treat her politely." Virginia looked over at Colter. "That is, if your father agrees."

"Of course I agree," Colter said, wondering what was going through Virginia's mind. "You don't need to ask me if I agree with every little thing."

"They're your children," Virginia said.

"Well, yes, but—" He stammered to a halt. He could hardly admit he was adrift in that particular job and wasn't sure he could be trusted to decide all of those questions.

"I don't know if we can fix any of my dresses to fit you, but we can try." Virginia bent down to say to Patricia.

"I have my own dress." Patricia stood up. "I'll show you."

Colter watched as his daughter ran toward the stairs. "I should have bought her a dress before I left Helena."

Virginia got a worried look on her face. "Her mother must have given her the dress then."

Colter shook his head. "Everyone at the saloon there thought she was a boy. I doubt she has a dress."

Virginia was aghast. If she was ever so fortunate as to have a daughter, she wouldn't deny the girl her birthright. "Tomorrow morning I'm going to take her to the mercantile and let her pick out a dress. Any dress she wants. If they have any that will fit, I mean—"

Virginia stopped. The realization sank into her bones that she was only a temporary guest in this girl's life. Or Danny's life. She'd already made the mistake of getting too attached to both of them. And, before she knew it, Patricia's mother was going to come here and expect to marry Colter.

She looked up at the man in annoyance. "You need your hair cut, too. It wouldn't hurt to set a good example for your children."

"I've been making breakfast," he defended himself and then stopped to groan. "Ach, the oats are probably burnt, too."

With that, he rushed back to the cookstove in the other room.

The air inside the saloon was gray again and Danny had removed his hat and was trying to swat a fly with it. But Virginia felt as if her heart was pounding a little too fast. Nothing unusual was even going on. Except for the fact that this morning she'd been part of a family.

She went over to the table where a stack of bowls and some spoons were lying and began to arrange them for the four of them.

Music had been so central in her family's life that she had seldom sat down just to talk with her parents and brother. She'd spent hours practicing in hopes she would wake up one day with the miraculous talent her father kept saying she must have inside her since he had such a gift. She had been consumed with the search for that talent, only to be disappointed time and time again.

She could not remember a single day in her childhood when there had been the kind of chaos she had experienced this morning. She wouldn't have thought she would enjoy it. But something about Colter trying to take care of his two wards melted her heart. She felt a longing to be a mother.

She sighed. That led her back to Lester. Maybe he

would be back to normal by today. She needed to be patient; she supposed any man needed some training to be a good husband. It wouldn't hurt for them to sit together after church and talk a little more about their future. She'd welcome a chance to tell him about the concerts that they could attend in Denver. Maybe they'd even attend the opera if there was a performance in the town.

She smiled. Patricia's mask would make a worthy prop in an opera. Maybe the girl could come visit them when they were settled in Denver. And Danny, too, of course. She thought for a moment and then frowned. Somehow she couldn't picture Colter with them, sitting in her parlor and drinking tea with Lester and her. No, she couldn't see him doing that at all. She supposed that meant the children would need to be older before they could come. She frowned. She didn't like that thought at all.

Chapter Five

Virginia would not have guessed that Patricia was shy. Maybe she hadn't been when she was dressed as a boy, but now, in her girl clothes, she was as demure as a flower sitting beside Virginia. The snow still blew outside and the wood-plank floor inside was covered with wet splotches from the heat of the cast-iron stove melting the ice from the men's boots. Next year, the town planned to build a proper church, but until then they were using the schoolhouse for religious services, which meant they sat squeezed together on benches made for children.

Virginia was glad Patricia at least had good button-up shoes. They had chosen to sit on a front bench so they could see the organist play. The tips of the girl's shoes peeked out from beneath her clothes in a perfectly polite way. Colter had given them a quick polish before they had all left the saloon. Unfortunately, there wasn't room for Colter and Danny to join them on the bench so they were several benches behind them.

"This is Patricia," Virginia said for the tenth time as people filed past. Reverend Olson had said the final prayer and church was over. "She's moved down from Helena and she'll be in school when it starts up again after Christmas."

Everyone smiled and said hello while the girl beamed. Virginia had decided not to mention that Patricia was Colter's daughter. She would let him give that explanation; she only hoped he mentioned that he was planning to marry the girl's mother when he told people. Marriages around here were often irregular, but everyone seemed more comfortable when children were set in proper families.

Fortunately, they had been able to dress Patricia so she looked like the other children. The girl did have thin bones and none of Virginia's dresses would fit her, not even when they were tucked and hemmed. The dress Patricia thought of as hers was much too large, being cut down from one of her mother's saloon dresses and being too flashy by far for any respectable woman, let alone a school girl.

Virginia had a white apron, though, that wrapped around the girl's waist several times before they tied it and, with one of Danny's new white shirts and a few pale blue ribbons, she had emerged from her upstairs bedroom looking almost like the other girls. When she pulled Virginia's gray shawl around her shoulders, no one could tell that what she was wearing had been pieced together.

The people started going outside and Virginia saw Lester walk over to her.

"I don't know why you have to introduce her," Lester muttered as he sat down on Virginia's left side. "She's *his* daughter."

Virginia turned just in time to see the scowl Lester sent toward Colter's back.

"Would you like to go up and see the instrument closer?" Virginia bent to ask Patricia.

The girl nodded.

"Go ahead then."

Virginia waited for Patricia to walk away before she turned to Lester. "It's no trouble to introduce her to people around here."

Virginia had decided during the sermon to work on improving Lester's manners, but she hadn't wanted to say anything in front of Patricia. Children, she believed, should look up to the adults in their lives.

Virginia noticed Lester hadn't even turned to look at her. Instead, he was continuing to stare at the other man's back.

Colter must have sensed someone looking at him, because he turned and started walking right toward them. Virginia couldn't help but think that he was coming to her rescue once again. Maybe it was the way he walked, balanced and sure on his feet as though he wouldn't back down from any trouble—not even the trouble he clearly could see on the horizon if his frown was any indication. As he got closer, she noticed his scowl disappear and his eyes start to sweep her with warmth. Then it became more than warmth. Really, a man shouldn't look at a woman like that in a church, she thought to herself as her face heated up. Or anywhere else either.

"Who does he think he is?" Lester hissed in Virginia's ears. "You're practically my fiancée."

"He's only smiling," Virginia said quietly to Lester. She was sure Colter didn't know the way his eyes were shining anyway. If she meant to train Lester, the lessons might as well begin now. "A gentleman doesn't cause a disturbance in church anyway. A soft answer turns away wrath."

"I'm not going to just let—" Lester started, but by then Colter was standing right in front of them.

Virginia didn't think it was advantageous to remain seated while Colter stood over them, so she rose to her feet as well. My, she realized as her stomach flipped, his eyes did speak to a woman, whether she wanted to hear him or not. Maybe if she could demonstrate, Lester would see the value of being polite in public places regardless of what other people were doing though.

"Wonderful sermon, wasn't it?" Virginia said to Colter as she gave him just the right kind of social smile. Not too cold, but not warm either. Just very correct.

Lester stood to his feet, too.

Colter ignored the other man and kept his eyes on Virginia. "When the reverend was preaching about all that squabbling over who was supposed to be first, it made me think back. I've seen gunfights started over less."

"I don't think they had guns back in the Bible days." Virginia thought the conversation was going fairly well so she added, "Which is most fortunate, don't you agree?"

"People just killed each other with rocks," Lester interrupted to say, his voice deeper than usual.

The fact that her would-be fiancé sounded menacing when he delivered his observation was only accidental, Virginia told herself. Some men just needed to develop the art of social conversation.

Colter grunted as though to prove her point.

"People aren't so easy to kill with rocks," Colter

added. By now he'd taken his eyes off Virginia completely and they were boring into Lester.

Virginia was getting ready to say that this was the very reason that public conversation was to be kept neutral when she noticed that Lester's neck was getting pink.

"Well, the reverend clearly said Christians were to be the peacemakers." She tried to remind them both of the point of today's sermon. "All people need to do is—"

"You got a gun on you?" Lester interrupted to ask as he kept glowering at Colter. "I figure you've got one hidden someplace."

"My goodness, there's no need to speak of guns!" Virginia was appalled. Her explanation must be lacking something.

"Of course there's no need to talk of guns," Colter agreed smoothly as he pointedly ignored Lester again. "We're in church, getting ready to have dinner with our friends and neighbors." Colter smiled down at Virginia. "I'll go find us all a place to eat. They're putting some tables up by the window on the side."

"Virginia will be sitting with me for dinner," Lester said from his position to her left. He'd said the first to Colter, but then he turned to Virginia. "You can't ignore me forever. I'm going to apologize, you know. For last night."

Virginia smiled at him proudly. He seemed to be learning.

"You're more than welcome to join us," she countered Lester's invitation. There was no reason to have divisions in church. "Isn't he, Colter?"

Virginia appreciated that Lester had brushed his suit and shined his shoes, too. How could she refuse to forgive him when he'd gone to so much work? All men and women probably had disagreements before they married.

"I plan to sit with you *alone,*" Lester responded. His face was flushed and he ran his finger around the collar of his white shirt.

Virginia was torn, but she knew what she needed to do. After all, the children and Colter were only temporary family in her life. She hoped Lester would become permanent. He needed a little more work, but she remembered her mother saying how much trouble she'd gone through to teach her father his manners. And her father was flawlessly polite even when something displeased him.

"Virginia?" Colter asked.

She smiled up at him. "Lester and I do have a lot to talk about. You'll be fine with the children, I'm sure."

Colter's heart sank with her words. Of course he'd be fine with the children. The fact that it was the children and not him on her mind told him he was in trouble though. He never used to have a problem charming women. And then it struck him—he'd never even tried to impress a churchgoing woman before. He'd liked more ankle and flash. Women like Rose had been the ones he wanted to be around.

This agreement he'd made with God was turning him inside out and shaking him upside down at the same time. He'd come to peace with the fact that being a Christian had changed his gun-carrying ways. But women? He hadn't particularly expected it to make any difference in regards to women. At least not in ways that affected his heart. And he'd long since realized that it was his heart leading him toward this particular woman.

"You and Lester have a good dinner," Colter said, although he almost choked on the words. One thing he did know was that God intended for him to respect a woman's wishes. "As you said, the children and I will be fine."

With that, Colter turned and walked away. He would find Danny and Patricia and get them both settled at a table with him.

Virginia watched Colter walk away. "Maybe I should just help him find the children."

"I never get to spend time with you," Lester complained softly at her side. "Let him take care of his bas—"

Virginia gasped and shot him a look of horror. They were standing in the middle of the schoolhouse, but fortunately no one else had heard. She sat back down on the bench.

"His children," Lester continued as he sat down with her and then added defiantly, "I don't care what anyone calls the girl. I just know she's not your concern."

Virginia looked around to see that no one was walking close enough to them to hear their words.

"Of course she's my concern," Virginia said quietly. "She's only a little girl who needs some help adjusting to her new home. What's wrong with you lately anyway?"

Lester had been so pleasant those evenings when he'd sat and read her the letters he'd received from his sister. Maybe that was it. "You haven't had bad news from home, have you?"

If anyone knew how devastating that could be, it was her.

Lester shook his head. And then he gave a weak smile. "Can't a man just want to sit and talk with his fiancée?"

"We're not engaged. Not yet," Virginia corrected him. She studied his face though. "Is it your violin? Maybe you should ask your sister to send it out here. I know how it is to want to play music and not have an instrument to express all you're feeling."

"Oh, I couldn't ask her to do that," Lester said.

Was it her imagination or did his face turn a little white? In any event, he didn't look at all welcoming of the idea. Maybe he didn't understand.

"It's not that difficult to send things by steamer," she explained. "You don't need to fear for the safety of your violin either. Just get your sister to pack it well. You probably have some sheet music, too, that you'd like sent with it. And that wool vest your sister mentioned in one of her letters. I'm sure she would be more than happy to send you a few things to make your life more comfortable out here."

Lester felt the same way she did about the harshness of these small Western towns. A few comforts from home would be most appreciated.

Virginia tried to remember where his sister lived. She couldn't recall him saying. She knew the other woman was a lady though because she used the most beautiful lavender paper to write her letters. Lester was very protective of the letters themselves or she would have asked to read one just so she could feel the paper.

"She can't send anything," Lester said with a gulp. "She's sick."

Virginia chided herself as he abruptly stood up and walked away. No wonder the man had been acting peculiar these past few days. He was devoted to his sister and must be terribly worried. And, instead of being a comfort to him, all she had done was add to his troubles by criticizing him.

Well, it wasn't too late to show she was a supportive almost-fiancée. She would not only sit with him while they ate, she would encourage him with every breath she took.

Colter was sitting beside Reverend Olson and chewing on a piece of fried chicken. Elizabeth Hargrove had asked Patricia to eat with them so she could get acquainted with Spotted Fawn, and the girls were starting to say a few words to each other. Danny had eaten and was outside, no doubt throwing snowballs at some of the other boys.

"We have such bounty," the reverend said as he lifted up a piece of corn bread.

"Yeah," Colter said and tried to smile. His stomach felt sour though, as he kept his eyes focused on Virginia fawning over that worthless fiancé of hers. She had been like that through the entire meal. She had practically cut his meat for him. He would never understand what women saw in men like him.

"I don't suppose God has changed His mind about shooting people?" Colter asked.

The reverend saw where Colter's eyes were going and he started to chuckle.

"Women are strange creatures," he finally said. "But you have to be careful. Sometimes they take to the man who's wounded and not the one who did the shooting."

Colter grinned. "I guess they do at that."

The reverend finished his corn bread.

"Do you know of anyone around here who has a violin?" Colter asked him then.

"Can't say offhand that I do. Maybe Wells has one—his wife is real fond of music. And, his sister, too, with her school and all."

"I'll ask him. Thanks."

He decided there was more than one way to compete with Lester. Virginia seemed impressed with the fact that Lester could play the violin. Colter had never seen anyone play the instrument, but he knew his hands were nimble enough to learn anything that required quickness. He'd practiced many techniques to train his fingers to move with sensitivity because a gunman needed nimble fingers. He'd seen Lester fumble around outside just trying to get a leather knot tied so his horse would stay where it was supposed to be. If Lester could play the violin with his clumsy fingers, Colter decided he could, too. All he needed was a violin and a few pointers from someone.

Just then, there was a rush of boys through the door into the schoolhouse and it looked as if Danny was in their lead.

"We found it," Danny announced in triumph. "The empty can for the kerosene."

"Ah." Colter noticed that got the attention of everyone in the place.

"I forgot about the fire," the reverend said in the silence that followed. "I meant to pray about it this morning in the service. We can't have that kind of mischief in our town."

There were murmurs of agreement from some of the men present.

"It could be an old can," Lester said from where he sat on the far side of the room.

"It's got no rust from the snow," Danny said.

Colter figured there wasn't much to be proved from an empty container, but he liked Danny's enthusiasm for finding out what happened. So he stood up. "Let's go take a look."

Halfway to the door, Colter decided he wasn't ready to leave Virginia there with Lester. There was no telling what would happen.

"Maybe Virginia can identify it," he said loud enough for the crowd of men to halt and look over at her.

"She was the only one there when it happened." Old Petey spoke out from where he stood on the side of the church. After he spoke his piece, he grinned back at Colter.

Colter nodded. He owed the man.

"So, is she coming?" another of the old men took up the cry.

By that time, Virginia had stood up. She didn't look reluctant to leave, not if the eagerness with which she wrapped her shawl around her shoulders was any indication.

"I don't know what you can tell them," Lester said. He was speaking to Virginia, but his voice carried throughout the room.

"It's the fire," she said to him as she walked toward the door. "We can't be too careful about fire."

And, with that, Virginia paused briefly as she came up even with Colter and the two of them walked out of the church, leading the band of men and boys.

Colter felt victorious.

The day was warmer than anyone had expected, and he stopped along with Virginia at the foot of the church steps. Snow covered the ground, but the winter sun was shining down. A path had been trampled from the church steps down the main street in town.

"I don't want you to get snow in your shoes," Colter said as he knelt down to make sure her shoes were securely buttoned. "Who knows where those boys are taking us."

Colter figured he couldn't be blamed if he lingered a bit. Virginia's high-topped shoes fitted a trim ankle. And the ruffle of her underskirts teased against his hands as he tugged on the fasteners to be sure they held strong. The fine wool of her dress rubbed lightly against his cheek and he forgot all about the kerosene can. He practically forgot his name.

"Hey," Danny shouted from someplace ahead. "Where is everybody?"

Virginia reached down and put her hand on his shoulder. "We need to catch up."

He guessed she was right, so he stood and brushed the snow off his knees. He figured if he knew who wanted to burn his saloon to the ground he would sleep easier tonight.

Chapter Six

As the sun went down that evening, Colter lit all the lanterns in his saloon. Then he opened the front door and waited for his friends to arrive. What a day he'd had.

The dark red kerosene can had turned out to be one the mercantile had left outside last spring. It had apparently gotten dragged around by a dog or a coyote and lodged up against a clump of sage in back of the livery stable. Boys and men alike examined the can, trying to decide if it had been used in the fire, until Colter eventually stepped forward and sniffed at the can's spout. The kerosene smell was so faint he voiced his opinion that it hadn't held anything recently.

By then the men and boys were having a fine time stomping through the snow, looking for clues about the fire and throwing a few snowballs. Finally, the owner of the mercantile declared that, in honor of the boys finding his missing can, he would offer up chocolate enough to make cocoa for any children around if someone had milk to go with it.

Jake Hargrove offered to ride back to his farm and

bring in a bucket of milk. By then Colter was feeling affectionate toward the town he'd missed those long months he'd been gone, and he invited everyone over to his saloon. They'd make up the hot chocolate for the children, he said, and there'd be plenty of hot coffee and tea for the adults. He even had some hard biscuits in a couple of tins he'd brought back with him from Helena. He remembered after he made the invitation that his place had been a saloon and some people might not be comfortable going there, but no one hesitated, not even the women carrying babies.

The graciousness of it all made Colter feel glad to be home. He had wandered all over this country in his younger days, and now that he'd seen the last of his twenties he was fortunate to have friends and neighbors like these. The truth was he had come home in more ways than one during this past year. God had become an anchor for him. And the children—he hadn't asked for either one of them, but they had become his and he planned to raise them as best he could.

When everybody had something warm to drink, they convinced Virginia to play the piano. She started out with some Irish ballads about ill-fated lovers and swollen rivers. Half of the men sang along as she played "Danny Boy." The women shed a tear or two when the song changed and Virginia herself sang "The Orphan's Prayer."

The light of the lanterns flickered on the intent faces of everyone as they listened to Virginia sing of the child who had been ignored and left to die. More than one person looked over to the corner where Patricia was sitting with the other children, so Colter figured her story had been passed around. He tensed up at first, but then he saw the glances were all kind. He wondered if the emotion he heard in Virginia's voice was because she, too, recognized the song as being repeated in Patricia's young life.

There was respectful silence when Virginia finished the orphan song, and then a man yelled out from where he stood at the bar, "Play us the mountain one. The she'll-be-a-coming-around one."

Virginia's fingers started again with a changed tempo and the men began to clap and stomp. Colter felt deep contentment as he sat there and listened. He'd been the last to sit down and he was alone at a table in the back until Petey came and sat down next to him.

"She sure is something," Petey whispered as he nodded his head toward Virginia. "And not just with her piano. She's been real nice to me and the boys this winter. Had us over for soup on many a cold night."

Virginia paused at the end of her song to catch her breath and everyone applauded. As the sound died down, Colter turned to the older man. "Soup, huh?"

Petey grinned at him and continued in a low voice. "She can't cook worth much, but she always asks after us like she cares about whether we have holes in our socks and things like that. It does my heart more good than the soup. I'll tell you that much. I never have had the courage to tell her I don't even have socks. I just wrap an old piece of something around my feet when it's cold."

"Ah," Colter said with a nod. He wasn't the only one halfway in love with Virginia Parker.

"I've been asking around," Petey continued. "It seems Lester wasn't in that back room over at his saloon when we smelled the smoke coming from over here. I was holding a pretty good poker hand so I didn't notice, but Shorty was working at the bar then and he went back to check about something. The door to Lester's office was open, but he wasn't in it. He's usually there that time of the day."

"I see." Colter had watched as people came inside the saloon earlier and Lester hadn't been among the crowd. Colter thought the other man hadn't come because they were rivals, but maybe there was more to it. Now he felt cautious as well.

"I know it doesn't prove anything," Petey continued. "But that morning Shorty had just said he thought he saw Virginia walking down to the mercantile, too. Lester was there to hear it. I don't see him wanting to hurt Virginia. He seems real set on marrying her, but—"

His voice trailed off.

Colter nodded. He had the same questions.

"I think we need to keep an eye on things, is all," Petey finally finished.

"You won't get any argument from me on that," Colter said. "In fact, if you want a job helping fix this floor here, let me know."

"It might be nice to be close," the older man agreed.

"And if you see Lester doing anything else peculiar, let me know," Colter said.

Petey nodded.

The music continued for another hour or so and then the children started to get tired and parents were bundling up their families for the ride home in the cold. Even though the snow hadn't melted much today, there was no wind and everyone would do fine if they had a blanket to wrap around themselves in the backs of their wagons.

Virginia went around wishing everyone a good night. Colter wasn't sure everyone here tonight had even realized how talented she was until now. People were all complimenting her. He thought she would be exhausted, but, when the children had both gone off to bed and he was the only one left, she went back to the piano. That's when she started to play the Bach music.

Colter had taken some of the used cups into the kitchen so he didn't clearly hear the first chords she played. He'd put some hot water on to heat and offered to do the dishes in Danny's stead tonight. The boy was tired.

The music coming from the other room pulled Colter back from the kitchen. Empty cups were still stacked at tables around the room, but he sat down anyway at the table in the shadows. He didn't want to interrupt Virginia. She was playing a song that had haunted him during the months he'd been gone. Many a night, he'd tried to figure out why he was drawn to the thin loneliness he heard in the echoes of that song. Virginia had played it twice when she was working in the saloon. Both times she'd looked sad, as though she was remembering things she'd do best forgetting. When he'd been gone, he'd regretted not asking her about it before he left.

How could a song say so much, he wondered, and not use any words?

Sorrow wasn't comfortable for Colter, but he let Virginia take him there with her. She played the song with her whole body as she stretched out to reach keys far from the center of the piano. He had no illusions that Virginia was playing for him or even was aware he was there; he knew she was playing for herself. He was just blessed to be carried along with her.

Time passed and Colter continued to listen as Virginia played through many classical tunes. A few of them she'd played before in his saloon, but most of them were new to him. Finally, the music stopped and Virginia looked up from the piano.

"Oh," she said when she saw him sitting there.

"That was beautiful."

"I didn't know anyone was still here." Virginia apologized and then smiled. "I try not to play quite so many classical pieces when someone is listening."

"Never stop yourself for me. You play—" He did not know how to explain the depth of it all. "Very well. You obviously love what you're playing and it's very special."

For the first time, Colter wished he was a man with a smooth tongue. A man like that could put the feelings inside him into words telling her what her music inspired in him. He felt a jolt—maybe that's what Lester could do. Maybe that's what she saw in the other man.

Virginia pushed back the piano stool and stood up. "Thank you for saying so, but I'm sure you're tired, too."

"There's still a little hot chocolate left." Colter had held back a couple of cups of milk in hopes she'd drink some with him after everyone had gone. She hadn't had a chance to enjoy any since she started playing the piano.

"That would be nice," Virginia said as she walked toward the kitchen. "Just tell me where it is and I'll get it."

"I can put the milk on to heat," Colter said as he stood as well and picked up the small lantern from his table.

They walked to the back room together and Colter set the lantern on the top of the cupboard where he'd stored the chocolate. Warm shadows made the plain workroom feel like home. He poured milk into a cast-iron pan and set it on the stove. The coals from the previous fire were strong enough to heat it although it would be slow.

"Oh, the dishes," Virginia said as she looked at the large cast-iron kettle on the back of the stove that was steaming with water ready for washing.

"I figured you'd want it hot," Colter said, as he picked up a towel and reached over to move the kettle to the side of the stove to stop its boiling. "But we'll do the dishes in the morning. Tonight is too—" Again he was at a loss for words. "I'd rather have you tell me about your music tonight. I can tell you love it from the way you play."

Virginia smiled. "I forget sometimes that I had to grow to love it. My father was the musician in our family. His teachers always praised his skill. When he was sixteen, he was invited to tour Europe with some older musicians and everyone said his future was bright. Then there was a fire in a friend's house where he was sleeping. He survived, but his hands were burned badly. He went to the best doctors, but when his hands healed there were deep scars. He could still play, but it was no longer the same. He'd lost some of his movement. Another student replaced him in the concert tour and there was no more talk of Europe."

There was silence for a moment and then Colter realized something. "I'm so sorry. It must have been terrifying for you—with the fire here," he said. "Just remembering what happened with your father."

"I did not even think of it." Virginia looked up at him

ruefully. "I was too upset about someone burning down your building when I was supposed to be protecting it."

Colter felt the vise's grip around his heart tighten. "I'd never want you to risk getting hurt to save any building of mine. Promise me you won't do anything like that. Just get yourself and the children outside and call for help."

He'd rather lose everything he owned than to have her try to fight another fire by herself. How terrible it would be if she burned her hands. Or worse. She could have died if that kerosene fire had had more time to burn before she noticed it. What if she had been asleep upstairs?

"Maybe you should get a room at the boarding-house," Colter said. "I'm sitting guard, but a fire— I'd pay for the room, of course."

"I have money. Besides, I couldn't leave without the children. And it's too late tonight to get a room at the boardinghouse anyway."

"We'll look into it tomorrow then. For you and the children, too."

"We don't even know if the person who set the fire is still in town," Virginia said. "Besides, my father—he wouldn't want me to be a coward. He was quite strong on that point."

Colter noticed that Virginia had started rubbing her hands when she talked about her father. Maybe she was just beginning to realize the damage the fire yesterday could have done as well.

"It must have been frustrating for your father not to have the use of his hands," he probed further.

"Yes, it was hard. He missed so much," Virginia agreed.

By now all the joy had drained out of Virginia's face. The pleasure she'd had in playing her music had gone still.

"Maybe it was hard for you, too," he guessed.

Virginia looked up at him as if she was surprised at his question. "Yes, but it was different. He'd lost the place that was to be his. It was only hard for me because I couldn't give him what he wanted. I knew he wanted that place to be mine. He'd trained me for that since I was a small girl. But I was never good enough. I used to think I was when I played in a room alone looking out at the trees, but when someone else was there—my fingers just didn't work right."

Colter nodded. "I've seen the same thing with men who want to be gunfighters. When a man's alone with a tin can, it seems easy. But it takes some getting used to pulling a trigger when someone else is around."

He could see by the shocked expression on her face that he'd picked a bad example.

"All I mean to say," he said quickly, "is that you might just have needed some time to get used to the people listening. I've given up guns, just so you know. I did that even before I bought the saloon here. And then when I walked forward in church—well, I'm not planning to go back to living by my guns."

"I'm glad," Virginia said simply.

By then the milk was steaming in the pan and Colter reached over with the towel he'd been holding to pull the pan to the side of the stove. Then he stepped over to the cupboard and brought down two clean cups. He poured the milk into the cups and Virginia put the chocolate in it.

"It must have been hard for you to lose your father,"

Colter said a few minutes later as they sat down at the table in the main part of the saloon. He'd left the one lantern in the kitchen and there was only one other in the room so the shadows were deep.

"I would have died in his place," Virginia said. "Or at least taken his scars onto my hands if it would have been possible. But there was no way—"

Colter nodded. "I wish I had known my parents. To feel that way about them."

Virginia didn't answer so Colter took a long sip of cocoa.

"Playing snowballs with the boys this afternoon must have reminded you of things you did with your family?"

"Oh, no," Virginia said abruptly. "We never did anything like that."

That surprised Colter, but he didn't let it show. "Well, I suppose each family does different things."

"I wanted to learn to ice skate, but my father was afraid I'd fall and hurt my hands."

"But surely—"

"That's why I'm just learning to cook. I wasn't supposed to be near a stove either."

Colter had to restrain himself from standing up and going over to take Virginia in his arms. What kind of a childhood had it been if she had to worry all the time? Even he had been allowed to grow like a wild weed.

Virginia bit her lips. She'd never told anyone that much about her childhood and she was regretting it already. She didn't want to make her father sound unfair. He had his reasons for protecting her. He envisioned great things for her. It wasn't his fault that she wasn't good enough to step into the life he wanted her to have.

"I was allowed to plant a tree outside my window," Virginia finally said. She wouldn't admit that it was actually the gardener who had handled the shovel. The tree had been hers in the way that mattered.

"That must have been fun," Colter said.

She eyed him carefully to see if he was mocking her, but he wasn't. His eyes gazed at her with kindness though, and a hint of pity.

"I've always loved trees, too," Colter said. "I plan to plant a whole bunch of them when I find a place out by Dry Creek. Cottontail grass grows strong there so there's water for trees."

"Is that where you plan to move?" Virginia was happy to leave behind the subject of her miserable childhood. After all, many people had far worse childhoods. She'd had everything she needed. Food. Clothes. Music lessons.

Colter nodded. "I've got my eye on some land out by the Hargroves. Jake says there's talk of cattle coming to the area. Longhorns coming up from Texas. They'll do good in the sagebrush land out there."

"It'll be nice for the children to have a home." Virginia felt a wistfulness rise up in her. "You'll plant the trees by the house, won't you?"

Colter nodded. "Just as soon as I get a house built."

"Ah," Virginia said. She shouldn't have gotten so caught up in the dream. "There's not much around there to build houses out of."

The steamer from Fort Benton brought in cut timber and the boards were freighted down to Miles City in wagons. But it was expensive. If Colter built a house out by the Hargroves it would likely be built of sod. Even that wouldn't happen until the snows melted.

"I'm sure the children will appreciate any house you build them," Virginia said. And then she drained the last of her cocoa from the cup.

"I can afford to build a house," he said sharply.

"You won't be getting any income from the saloon for a while," Virginia pointed out. "And you'll have other expenses. The children will need shoes before long. And probably a new winter coat for each of them. Not to mention food."

"We can't keep living at the saloon though," Colter said. "Not if I'm out at Dry Creek getting things ready to buy a herd of longhorns."

"At least wait until spring," Virginia said. "They get snow drifts six or seven feet tall out there. I was out to visit Elizabeth Hargrove one day and couldn't get back to town for two days. The Hargroves don't suffer because they've spent months filling in every gap in the walls. And they are a family—"

Virginia stopped. She had no right to be concerned about any of this.

"And the children and I aren't?" Colter asked, obviously misunderstanding her stumble. She couldn't explain her feelings about his family though. She hardly knew what it meant herself.

Virginia looked down. "It's just I don't think Patricia has really decided to stay. In fact, I think she wants to leave and go looking for her mother."

"That'd be a disaster," Colter muttered.

"I don't want her to go either," Virginia said. "But I think I understand why she wants to. Her mother is all she has."

"She has me now."

Virginia looked at the determination in Colter's face.

His jaw was set, his eyes flashing. He'd protect Patricia with his life.

"Yes, she has you," she agreed.

Virginia hadn't intended for the forlorn sound to be in her voice. She looked up at Colter, her eyes stricken, and saw him gazing back at her with kindness on his face. And something more that she wasn't sure about.

"She has you, too," Colter said gently. "If you want, you can be part of our family—me and the children."

Virginia swallowed. She didn't know what to say to that. She had her plans. Her dreams. And what about Lester? It was all going to make her cry, and she didn't want to do that in front of Colter. So she stood up.

"I find I'm a little tired, after all," she said.

And with that, she stood up and walked over to the stairs leading up to the second floor. The tears started to fall after she had taken a step or two up, but she kept her head high. She knew Colter couldn't see her tears and would have no idea she was crying unless she dipped her head.

She reached her room and closed the door before her tears blinded her. She realized it wasn't thoughts of Lester that brought the tears. He might be her destiny someday, but he wasn't the one who broke her heart.

It was Colter. What was she to do? The one thing she had learned from her father was that it was crippling to try to live a life for which she didn't have the natural talents. She had not been able to play the piano as well as her father wanted, but with Colter her inadequacies would be even more glaring.

Just watching Elizabeth Hargrove in the past had made her aware of how much a woman needed to know to make a comfortable home for her family in this land.

Virginia didn't know how to can vegetables, or grow vegetables. In fact, she realized with a final sob as she threw herself on her bed, she didn't even know how to cook vegetables. They always ended up burnt or mushy. And often both. She could brew a good cup of tea and make a passable kettle of soup, but— Oh, dear, she just realized… Colter loved fried chicken. She'd seen how many pieces he'd eaten at the church dinner. She'd be hopeless at cooking chicken.

She wasn't sure even God could cure her deficiencies. Her gaze was drawn upward anyway. She didn't know who else to turn to with the churning inside her. It was as though hope was shining somewhere, but it was out of reach for her. *Please, Lord,* she prayed, *make your grace shine upon me.*

The thought came to her that maybe her desire to move back east was only hiding the real longing of her heart—to have a home where she was loved and accepted.

Chapter Seven

Colter woke to the sound of a dog barking. The sky was still dark outside, but the sun was struggling to come up. He couldn't find any enthusiasm to greet a new day. His back hurt and the rest of him felt worse.

He had slept in a hardback chair so he'd be ready to stop anyone from entering the saloon. He'd bolted the back door so no one could get inside that way without making enough noise to wake him. He hadn't counted on the stray dog going between the front and back doors all night whimpering as if he knew someone was inside.

Finally, Colter put the rest of the milk in a dish with some scraps from dinner and opened the door. The dog came up to him, its gray fur matted in places and a rib or two showing. Dogs generally protected the places where they ate and Colter reasoned the animal would earn the food by barking if anyone came close. He might have even said something like that when he bent down to let the dog smell his hand. He stayed to rub the animal's ears.

Now that dawn was showing up, Colter figured he might as well stretch his legs and see what the day held.

The air was chilly and he could see thin layers of ice along the dirt street where the snow had melted yesterday. He set his feet down softly so his boots wouldn't make any noise as he walked around the side of the saloon. He heard a low growl from the dog before the animal passed him by and raced around to the back of the saloon. Colter flattened himself against the side of the saloon and got ready to fight.

It was the cat. Colter was glad it was still dark enough that no one could see him make his legendary fast draw on a scrawny yellow cat. Although when he saw how the cat managed to outrun that dog, Colter concluded he wouldn't want to underestimate the furry ball of fur as an adversary.

Since the morning was growing lighter, Colter decided he might as well check around the saloon for footprints. The only tracks in the snow between his saloon and Lester's were from the dog and cat. He wondered if Lester ever put food out for them in back of his saloon.

Naw, Colter shook his head. The other man had never struck him as the generous type. Or really any kind of a good type. Which was why it was such a mystery to him that the man had won over Virginia.

The thought was enough to sour a man's morning. Virginia couldn't have left him any faster last night if the place had been on fire. It was downright discouraging when even a hint of a proposal drove her away from him that quickly.

He stood for a bit, looking down the alley to be sure no dark shape was hiding in the shadows. He'd spent a night or two stretched out in an alleyway himself years ago and it wasn't the worst place he'd laid his head.

Colter turned to go back to the front door when he

saw the dog coming back down the street toward him again. The poor fellow looked as discouraged as Colter felt with his mouth open and his tail hanging low. Colter figured he might as well wait and greet the dog before he went back inside. Maybe it would cheer them both up.

Neither one of them had an easy life. He'd bet that dog had been the runt of the litter. Colter hadn't been small, but he'd always been the one to get the least at his uncle's table. Not that he blamed his uncle. As the man had said many times, he'd been under no obligation to take Colter in when his parents had died. His uncle counted every bite of food Colter ate and made sure he paid for it through his work.

"Hi ya, fella," Colter said as he crouched down to scratch the animal's ears.

The chill of the morning felt good on Colter's face as he stood up. The sun was growing brighter and he could see clearly down the street now. The quiet of night was over. Colter opened the door to the saloon. He'd expected the dog to slip in and it did.

"Lookin' for something more to eat, are you?" Colter said as he followed the dog inside. "You just had a bite. Let me get my own breakfast first."

He'd noticed there was a side of bacon in the storeroom. Virginia looked like the kind of woman who would keep fresh eggs in the cupboard, too. First, he needed to get the water heating for a shave. And put the coffeepot on. He'd even go ahead and make those flapjacks that he hadn't made yesterday.

Back on his uncle's farm, flapjacks would have brightened his whole day. He guessed he wasn't so easy to please anymore. It was hard to admit that he had nothing in his life now to satisfy the longings that had overtaken him in the past year.

When he'd walked forward in church last winter, he had figured it was good to make his peace with God since he was planning a better life for Danny. The church folks had been kind to the boy and Colter wanted to be sure he kept his place in their affections. Colter thought it wouldn't do him any harm, but truthfully, he wouldn't have bothered if not for Danny.

But somehow things had gotten tangled. He'd started reading the Bible the reverend had given him. No one had warned him God would crack his heart wide-open. And now he just didn't know what to do about people. Danny. Patricia. And then Virginia. She was the one who troubled him most right now. He didn't want to press her about marrying him, not if it made her unhappy. She had looked stricken as she'd walked up those stairs last night.

Before he'd left for Helena, he had felt a stirring toward her. But last night when he saw the scars in her life, he knew he'd devote his life to protecting her if she'd let him.

Ah, that was the problem, he thought as he bent down to scratch the dog's ears. A man didn't always have control over how close another person let him get to them.

He heard the sound of footsteps overhead. That must be Virginia getting up.

"Danny." Colter gave a call toward the storeroom. They might as well all face the day together.

When she awoke, Virginia got out of bed and determined not to spend any more time wishing things were different. The distress of the night had passed. In the morning light, everything seemed clearer. The truth of the matter was that she had lived most of her life without the things she most wanted. Her concert-pianist dream had eluded her. She'd lost her home amidst the trees. Her father had never said he was proud of her or that he loved her. Her mother had been a gray shadow urging her to work harder. But what was the point in feeling sorry for herself? Virginia suspected it was about the same for everyone. It seemed that most people learned to be content without being happy.

There was no reason to expect her desire for a family would come easily. She was about ready to give up on trying to love Lester. She couldn't marry him. But she didn't think she would make Colter happy either. When he knew how inept she was at the usual things women knew, he would regret marrying her even if he ever made her an offer. No, her best plan was to hope to receive an offer for the job at the school in Denver. Sometimes having half of a dream come true was better than nothing.

As she washed her face, she remembered the feathered bird that had been waiting for her yesterday and she decided it was only fair to give Patricia a morning surprise, too. Years ago, she had purchased a shiny gold pin in the shape of a bird. It was little more than a trinket really, but any girl would enjoy it. So she tiptoed into Patricia's room and pinned the golden bird to a scarf and then draped the scarf over the back of a chair facing the girl's bed.

Following that, she tiptoed out and returned to her room to wait.

She dressed quickly in her old cotton day dress, the one she used when she needed to haul water or scrub the floor downstairs. Then she added a clean apron. A life of work held satisfaction and she would be busy today. First, she needed to take a better look at the scarred floor and see if scrubbing and mopping would make it any better.

Just then there was a squeal from Patricia's room and Virginia went out into the hall.

"Thank you, thank you," Patricia said as she threw herself into Virginia's arms. "It's a present. I've never had a present before."

Virginia nodded as she bent down and kissed the top of the girl's head. "Just for you. Your own little bird."

For a sweet moment, Patricia leaned into her with a hug. Then the girl moved back and looked up in excitement.

"I can't wait to show it to my mother," Patricia said, her eyes shining. Her longing to see her mother was written plainly on the girl's face.

Virginia ignored the pang of jealousy she felt. What would it be like to be loved like that by a child? "It's time to get dressed. We have a busy day."

Patricia nodded. "We need to go to the stage office. My mother promised that she'd send me a letter. It should be here by now."

And with that the girl danced her way back into her room.

Virginia shook her head when the girl shut the door to her bedroom. She, too, had known the tug of loving a difficult parent. It was a peculiar thing—sometimes the less love the parent had to give the more love the child offered them in return.

Well, Virginia thought as she started down the stairs, all she could do right now was to pray Colter had the wisdom to help the girl when she realized her mother was never coming. He'd shared with her some of the conversation he'd had with the girl's mother and Virginia was appalled.

There was nothing she could do about it now though. In the meantime, she could stack up the rest of the dirty cups from last night and take them into the workroom. She could smell coffee brewing so she assumed Colter, and maybe even Danny were up already.

"Good morning," Virginia called out as she took several cups in her hands and headed toward the workroom door. "I'm bringing dishes."

She leaned against the door and pushed. It was unlatched so it swung in easily. "I have—" She stopped and looked. "What'd you do?"

There was a big splotch of coffee on the wood floor and Colter was holding a towel over his hand. He was obviously in pain and that stray dog from yesterday was looking at him with mournful eyes.

Colter winced. "I'm just clumsy."

"You scalded yourself," Virginia said as she set the cups down on the nearest surface and started looking in the cupboard. "I know we have something in here to make it better."

When Danny had scraped his arms while climbing a tree last summer, Virginia had bought an ointment at the mercantile.

"I'll be fine," Colter muttered.

"Here it is," Virginia said as she spied the green tin. She pulled it out and started to take off the lid. Then she turned to Colter. "You'll need to open your hand so I can put this on it."

Virginia wasn't prepared for how blistered his hand

was. The skin was an angry red. She dipped her finger into the ointment and reached out to put it on his hand when the dog gave a short bark that settled into a deep growl.

"It's fine, old boy," Colter said as he reached down to put his good hand on the dog's head.

"Looks as if you have a dog."

Colter shrugged. "I guess he needs a home, too."

The pain started to ease and Colter looked down. Virginia was concentrating on his hand just like she did on every task. Her movements were precise and controlled. He'd had a gunshot wound or two in his life that had been treated with less compassion.

"It must be because you play the piano," he finally said. "That you have such gentle fingers."

Virginia looked up at him with a small frown on her forehead. "Your hand will be all right, won't it? I wouldn't want any scarring," she added.

"I'll be fine." Colter gazed right back into her eyes. They were the color of fall grass, where the browns and sun-striped greens melted together on the flatlands. The colors suited her eyes, letting her hide what she was feeling. Even now, despite the concern filling them, he had a feeling secrets lurked behind her eyes. "Whatever that ointment is, it feels good."

Virginia nodded and started walking around the kitchen. "I'll need a strip of cloth to wrap around your hand. It'll keep the ointment on and the dirt out."

She found an old piece of cotton cloth in a drawer in the cupboard. Colter figured it had been part of a shirt at one time, but it was clean enough to be useful.

"Now you be sure and keep your hand free," Virginia

said as she wrapped the cloth around his hand. "Don't use it for anything if you can help it."

"Well, I'm going to need to get to work around here," Colter said. Besides, his hand did feel a lot better now that it had the ointment on it. "I have supplies that came in down at the mercantile a couple of days ago and I need to get them in the storeroom."

"The other men can help you," Virginia said. "I'll ask Lester to spread the word that we could use some help over here."

Colter snorted. "Lester? I think we'd do better to ask Petey."

"I can do that," Virginia said. "Later. The men won't be at Lester's yet anyway. Noon is when they show up."

"I suppose the supplies can wait that long."

"If you're going over to the mercantile, you might want to get a length of cotton cloth for a dress for Patricia. She can wear her boy clothes, but she'll need a dress for church." Virginia stopped. Then she took a deep breath and continued. "I wish I could do the sewing on it, but I'm afraid I'm not very experienced at that. I apologize. I'm sure Elizabeth would help if we asked her, though. I wish Patricia had something better for school, too."

"What are you apologizing for? I'm the one who neglected to buy her a dress before leaving Helena. Besides, don't they have some ready-made dresses at the mercantile?"

"Not many. Most of their dresses are for women. Usually mothers make the dresses for their daughters." Virginia hesitated. "I think every woman around can sew well enough to make a girl's dress, except for me."

Colter knew Virginia was trying to tell him something important. Her whole body was tense as though she was expecting some reaction from him. "I don't see what it matters if other women know how to sew," he said.

Virginia glared at him. "Of course, it matters. How's a mother supposed to clothe her children if she doesn't sew?"

"Didn't we buy a shirt at the mercantile for Danny?"

"That's not the point," Virginia said after a pause.

"What is the point?"

"I can't sew!"

Virginia looked like she was on the verge of tears, but the dog must have heard the cat outside because he'd raced to the door, a low growl in his throat.

"Stand away from the window," Colter ordered Virginia. It might not be the cat and no one else would be at his back door before dawn unless they were up to mischief.

He gripped the butt of his gun at the same time Virginia whispered, "Your hand."

Colter looked over to see she'd moved closer to the cupboards and wasn't visible from the window. Then he walked to the door and gently opened it.

The dog shot outside before Colter could even see the cat. He heard a furious meow though so he figured that as the end of it. He turned to go back inside when he glanced over and saw that the dog had run right past the cat and headed over to the back of Lester's saloon. There in the snow was a red kerosene can. The dog gave a triumphant bark when he stood guard over the can at Lester's back door.

"Good dog," Colter said as he started over to the other man's saloon. He wanted to know what the man had to say for himself now.

Chapter Eight

Colter headed back to his place within minutes, his gun holstered and the skin on the palm of his hand tight and painful from straining against the cloth Virginia had wrapped around it. The dog followed at his heels, looking as defeated as Colter felt.

"What happened?" Virginia asked when he stepped into the workroom. He saw that the spill on the floor had been wiped up and another pot of coffee was on the cookstove.

"Lester says the kerosene can isn't his," Colter admitted.

"Of course it's not his—I mean, not if you're thinking it's the kerosene can from the fire. What possible reason would he have to harm me?"

"From what you told me, he probably didn't know you were in the saloon at the time." Colter walked over to a stool by the cupboard and sat down. "I smelled the can's spout and the odor was strong. That can was full not too long ago and now it's empty. Who else would have used so much kerosene in the past day or two?"

"Yes, but still—"

"I know," Colter acknowledged. "Not even Lester would be fool enough to drag that can out there and leave prints in the snow going to and from his own back door. That's what I can't figure out."

"Someone just wanted you to think it was Lester," Virginia suggested.

Colter nodded. "Could be."

Then he looked at her. It pained him to see her defend the other man. Loose strands of blond hair fell from the bun she had on top of her head. And her skin put him in mind of pearls, all white and pink. "We need to ask at the boardinghouse and see about a room for you."

"First, let me look at your hand," she said. "You probably worked that bandage loose with all of your moving around."

Colter figured it must be the Bible reading he'd been doing of late. He'd turned poetic. That had to be it, because all he could think of was that the ointment she used smelled like spring grass. He figured he'd remember her standing in the morning sun like this with her brow furrowed with worry as long as he lived. He'd heard an old man once talk about how he could remember the exact color of the dress his wife had been wearing when he first met her. This morning would be that memory for him. He was trying to think of the words to tell Virginia all of this when Danny walked into the workroom.

At first the boy was sleepy and then he was wide-awake. "We've got a dog!"

"It's the same one that was here yesterday morning chasing that cat," Colter told him. He didn't want him to think he'd gone out in search of a dog, as if they needed a dog or anything.

That fact didn't seem to dim Danny's enthusiasm. He knelt down and wrapped his arms around the gray dog. The old mutt lifted his eyes to Colter, although whether for rescue or forgiveness he couldn't tell. Colter figured it was the latter when the dog moved in closer to the boy and settled in as if he was planning to stay.

"You'll have to feed him." Colter decided he might as well give up any claim to the dog gracefully. "That way he'll know who his master is."

Danny nodded. "He likes roast beef."

"You've already been feeding him?"

"He was hungry."

"We'll talk about what to feed the dog after we have breakfast," Colter said. "So why don't you bring out that slab of bacon that's hanging in the storeroom. We're all hungry by now."

"I'll get Patricia," Virginia said as she stepped toward the door leading to the main room. When she got to the door, she glanced back. "But wait to cut the bacon until I can do it. You shouldn't be using knives with your hand the way it is, anyway."

Colter nodded as she slipped out of the room. He liked having someone worry over him.

She just needed a moment to think, Virginia told herself as she stopped on the other side of the door. The big black circle in the middle of the floor reminded her that this whole building could have burned down and her with it. As Colter had been talking, she remembered that Petey and some of the other men had taken to sleeping behind the bar in Lester's saloon. They boasted that he couldn't see them and he had no idea they were enjoying the warmth of his establishment long after he'd gone to bed. She wondered if one of the men had found the kerosene can. Maybe they even knew who had started the fire.

She didn't get a chance to walk over to the stairs before Patricia came out of her bedroom.

"Look," the girl demanded as she stood on the top landing, pointing at the bird pin on the collar of the shirt she was wearing—Danny's old shirt.

"You have to come closer so I can see," Virginia said and the girl obligingly started down the stairs.

"It's a singing bird," Patricia said as she reached the bottom. "I didn't see it right off, but see its beak? It's singing. It loves music just like me."

"Why, yes, it does," Virginia agreed in satisfaction. This must be how it would feel to teach in that school down in Denver. To awaken young people to an appreciation of music would make a worthwhile life for her. "Don't forget we have a lesson this afternoon."

"On the bells?"

"You need to start on the piano, that's what Colter—I mean, your father requested."

Virginia noted the surprise on the girl's face. She had probably not heard anyone call Colter her father until now. Besides, as far as Patricia was concerned, he was just someone temporary in her life until her mother came for her.

"But couldn't I just do something with the bells?" Patricia asked.

"The Wells girls are coming over to practice them later this afternoon. Maybe you can ring one of the bells with us."

The deepest bell didn't have to be rung very often

and Patricia would probably enjoy that one because it had the most sliding echo to it.

The girl beamed.

"But first we need to cook breakfast," Virginia said as she led the way to the workroom.

Virginia told herself that she might not be as good a cook as Colter, but at least she had the use of both of her hands.

She looked around as she entered the other room. Danny had set the bacon on the counter and Colter had pulled the butcher knife down from the shelf. He was obviously considering how to go about slicing off some of it.

"I can do that." Virginia walked over to the cupboard.

"Thanks. I should be able to do it, but—" Colter apologized.

"There's no shame in being wounded," Virginia said as she took up the knife and started slicing the meat.

Patricia, meanwhile, was standing in the middle of the room, studying Colter. "Are you Danny's father, too?"

Virginia turned around and noticed Danny stop patting his new dog. The boy looked up with a flash of longing on his face and then bowed his head down again.

"I just do the dishes," Danny mumbled.

"You do more than just the dishes," Virginia said indignantly as she set down the knife and put her hands on her hips. Then she realized she'd said that wrong. Danny was still looking down and she could see his misery from here. "I mean who you are is more than just someone who does the dishes."

There was a moment's silence and then Colter cleared his throat.

"I should have said it earlier," he said. He looked a little awkward and that melted Virginia's heart. "But I'd be honored to call you my son."

Virginia blinked back a tear.

Danny lifted his head and nodded shyly. "I'll work hard."

"It's not about the working," Colter said firmly. "You're my son, no matter what."

Patricia furrowed up her face where she stood. "He doesn't have to be my brother, does he?"

"Well, now," Colter said, his voice low and easy, "I'd say that's up to the two of you. I figure you might like to be kin though. I never had a brother or a sister and there were many times I wished I had someone on my side who claimed me as family."

Neither Patricia or Danny said anything, but at least they weren't scowling at each other.

"I had a brother," Virginia offered as she slid the bacon slices into a cast-iron skillet. "And I'd be happy if I could sit down and talk with him today. I never appreciated him as much as I should have when he was alive."

Virginia took the skillet over to the hot cookstove and set it down. "Now for some eggs."

Colter went out to the other room to put the plates on one of the tables for breakfast. Virginia had told him where to find the cloth she used to cover the table and he brought that out from behind the bar. He got it a little crooked because he just had the use of the one hand, but he knew it didn't matter. She'd also suggested napkins and he pulled four of those out as well. If it had been growing season outside, he'd be half a mind to go pick a rose or two from the bushes that the last owner had planted behind the saloon.

Colter liked setting the places for four people. His family.

Before he knew it, Virginia was bringing a platter of fried eggs and bacon through the door. The two children followed her, one carrying a plate of biscuits and the other a crock of butter.

"Elizabeth Hargrove made the biscuits," Virginia said as she set the eggs and bacon on the table. "And the butter, too."

"Everything smells good," Colter said.

They were all seated, faces scrubbed and hands clean, when Colter asked if everyone would bow their head so he could pray. "Our Father, thank You for these provisions and the hands who have prepared them. Protect us today. In Jesus's name. Amen."

Colter didn't think he could grow more contented. He felt like a true father when he could put food on the table and lead his children in a prayer of thanks for it.

Virginia dabbed at her mouth with a napkin. Her words had been going around in her mind since she'd spoken them earlier this morning. If one of the men next door did know something about the kerosene can, she needed to find out what it was. After all, she had been responsible for Colter's building when the fire was set.

"I can go get Petey when we're finished," Virginia said as she picked up her last piece of biscuit. "He said he'd help with the floor."

Colter nodded. "I'm happy to pay any of the men next door to come over and work—as long as they're sober anyways."

"Of course, they're sober," Virginia rebuked him. "It's not even nine o'clock."

Colter raised an eyebrow at her statement, but he didn't contradict her. It reminded her that she knew better though. She hadn't even considered that the man who had dragged the kerosene can out in back of Lester's saloon might not have been sober when he did it. She knew she wouldn't rest easy until she solved the mystery of the fire. She had told Colter that she was sure Lester would never do anything like that, but little things were coming to mind. Times when he wasn't the man she thought he was. She knew he was worried about his sister so she didn't want to judge his recent behavior severely, but what if he were the kind of man who could attempt burning down his competitor's establishment?

The good thing about asking Petey and his friends to come over and work on the floor was that she could pose her questions subtly without raising anyone's suspicions.

"I'll go next door and ask them for you," Colter offered as he stood up from the table. "I'd worry about you going into a saloon alone."

"What do you mean? I worked in a saloon and I was fine."

"Yeah, but that was my saloon and I was here all the time."

Virginia would have protested, but she suddenly realized that the men would be more likely to come if Colter asked them. She didn't really care how the men got to be here, she just wanted a chance to talk with them, especially Petey.

"After I get back, we can all head down to the store,"

Colter said. "It'll take a while for the men to get themselves in shape to work."

"And the mail," Patricia spoke up. She had been quietly finishing her eggs. "I want to check to see if I have
a letter from my mother."

Virginia saw Colter's lips tighten, but he didn't say
what he was thinking.

"That's not a problem," he said instead. "We can
check on the way to the store. The stage office handles
the mail."

"My mother." Patricia turned to Danny. "She promised to write to me."

Danny just nodded. Virginia thought perhaps he was
so awestruck at acquiring a father and a dog today that
he wasn't too concerned about not having a mother.

The smells were what Virginia liked best about the
mercantile and she took a deep breath as she stepped
across the doorway. Patricia and Danny had gone in
ahead of her and Colter was following. The shelves at
the back of the store held spices and teas from distant
places. On the left side of the counter in front of the
shelves was a tobacco cutter. Bolts of calico and un-
bleached muslin were arranged on a table on the right-
hand side of the room. Another shelf to the side of the
counter contained face powders and hand mirrors.

The children headed straight for the jars of hard
candy. There were red and green ribbons of spun sugar
for Christmas. Virginia had already made mittens for
Danny, but she didn't have Christmas gifts for Patricia and Colter yet. And Christmas Eve was just two
days away.

"Annabelle Bliss," Colter called out as they stepped farther into the store.

The woman was past middle age and had some slight graying in her hair. She wore a freshly ironed white blouse and a gray wool skirt. Virginia had always found Annabelle to be extremely fair-minded—maybe it came from weighing goods so often. Something was always sitting on top of Annabelle's swinging scale. Even the crackers were sold by weight here.

"It's about time you got back in town," Annabelle said as she stepped around the counter to shake Colter's hand. "I know Virginia has been waiting for you for a long time now."

Virginia felt herself panic. She didn't want Colter to think she'd hung around like a schoolgirl waiting for him to return home.

"Well, fortunately, I'm back now." He didn't seem taken aback by Annabelle's remark. "We were hoping that you might have a ready-made dress for my daughter here, Patricia."

Virginia watched the girl look up and beam. Even Christmas candies couldn't compete.

Annabelle cocked her head and studied Patricia, then she turned back to Colter. "Almost all of our ready-made dresses are for women. Even the smallest dress would be too big to cut down that much. You'd be better just to buy material and start fresh."

"It's just that school is going to start again soon," Virginia said. "We were hoping—"

"I understand," the store clerk said. "You might talk to Elizabeth Hargrove. She bought a length of yellow calico here a week ago for a dress for Spotted Fawn. The two girls look almost the same size. She might let you buy the dress from her. If I know Elizabeth she probably has it almost sewn by now."

"We're also interested in shirts for boys," Colter added. "To fit my son here."

Virginia noticed that those words distracted Danny from the jars of candies as well. The boy was too far away to hear though as Colter quietly asked Annabelle to wrap up a pound of the candies and put it aside for him to pick up later.

"What else do I need?" Colter leaned down and asked. "For the Christmas stockings."

"Add a pound of those walnuts, too," Virginia whispered back. "And maybe some hair ribbons for Patricia and a pocketknife for Danny."

Colter nodded for Annabelle to include those things as well.

As it turned out, there was a blue shirt that fitted Danny and Colter was able to order two more to come in with the next shipment. By then, Patricia was anxious to go to the stagecoach office and see if there had been any mail for her.

The stage office had its own smells, too, Virginia thought as they stepped inside the wood-frame structure. Wet leather seemed to predominate, but she could also smell faint traces of horses and sweat. There was a long counter with a clerk seated behind it and on top of that were various letters. Virginia had never actually received a letter here; Colter had said he would always telegraph anything to her so she hadn't even checked. She hadn't realized that the letters sat out in batches so people could look for any mail that was to go to them.

That's when Virginia noticed a familiar lavender envelope. She didn't even need to read the address to know who it was going to. Lester was getting a message from his beloved sister. Even if he had been difficult lately, Virginia did want him to have reassurance that his sister was all right. At least, she prayed that's what the letter said.

Unfortunately, there was no letter for Patricia even though she looked though the stack twice.

"It's still coming," Patricia said defiantly. "You'll see."

"There have been some bad blizzards this time of year," the clerk behind the counter said. "Some roads are blocked, but I'm sure it'll get here in a couple of days if you're expecting it."

They thanked the clerk and Colter led them out of the stage office and down the street to home.

The air still smelled of bacon when they got home and the first thing Danny did was to go call his dog from the back of the saloon. Colter went after him. Virginia took off her hat and took it upstairs to her bedroom.

When she came back down, Patricia was sitting alone at one of the tables. Her dark hair was hanging down and hiding her face. Virginia wondered if it wasn't also hiding her tears.

"I'm sorry you didn't get your letter," Virginia said softly as she went over and put her hand on the girl's back. She could feel a quiver as the girl swallowed back a sob.

"It must be the snow," Patricia said as she wiped a hand across her face.

Virginia didn't know what to say to that. "It's hard to know what to think when a parent disappoints you."

Patricia kept her head down.

"With me and my father," Virginia said, sitting down

and making another attempt, "I never did make him happy."

That made Patricia lift her head. Her cheeks were blotchy and she still had a lone tear trailing down her cheek. But she was listening intently. "What did you do?"

"I just kept trying harder and harder to please him," Virginia said. "He wanted me to be a special kind of pianist and I made too many mistakes."

"He shouldn't count mistakes," Patricia protested, her eyes snapping. "That's not fair."

"No, it's not." Virginia was quiet for a minute. "He was nothing like your father though."

Colter seemed to accept the girl no matter what she could or couldn't do. Virginia envied Patricia because she was facing a life of encouragement rather than scolding.

"I like my father," Patricia said quietly. "But I still want my mother to write to me."

Virginia nodded. She hadn't really expected to be able to spare Patricia the rejection she was bound to feel at some point.

Just then Petey knocked on the front door to the saloon. Virginia called out for him to enter.

"The others will be over when they're able," the older man said as he shifted the mop he carried on his shoulder. "I don't know what we need to use to clean up that burn, but I figure we'll have to mop it up at some point."

"I expect so," Virginia said as she stood up.

She decided she didn't want to wait for the other men to get here before she talked to Petey so now was her chance. She looked and saw that Patricia was walking toward the stairs.

She stepped over and quietly asked the older man, "You know about the kerosene can? The one with tracks from Lester's place?"

He nodded.

She didn't know how to do this except to be straightforward. "Do you think someone over there wanted us to think it was Lester who had set the fire?"

"Well, now, I reckon there are several men who'd like you to think that—"

"But why would they want to cause trouble like that? It just makes everyone upset."

Petey was quiet for a minute. "I know there's no reasoning it out as to why someone loves someone else. I've seen women grieve something fierce for men who are locked up in prison and not likely to live free again. And I've seen men who were desperate in love with women who didn't want them. But it's a misery. I don't want to see you take up with someone like Lester. He'll break your heart."

"He doesn't have my heart—" Virginia stopped. "But I still don't want everyone to be unfair to him. His sister clearly thinks he's a man with deep—"

"Lester?" Petey said incredulously. "He doesn't have a sister. At least not one who'd claim him."

"Sure he does. He's read me parts of the most wonderful letters from her."

"Letters, huh? Shorty mentioned something about letters he'd seen over there. Purple things."

"That's them," Virginia said.

"Humm, we'll see."

"I wanted to know if anyone knows about that kerosene can."

Petey got a belligerent look on his face. "Shorty

found it in Lester's back room. That's why he rolled it out of there this morning. He wanted Colter to know."

"But no one really knows?" Virginia asked. "It's all just suspicion."

"Well, now that depends on how you figure it. I trust Shorty."

Virginia wanted to say that she trusted Lester. And she did, sort of. It's just that she was no longer sure. Could a man hide his real nature from his sister, who had known him his whole life though? Unless the woman wasn't his sister. Still, some things she knew. "Lester would never set a fire when I was in the building."

"That's just it. Shorty had just remarked that you must be walking down to the store. He saw the back of a gray dress out the window and thought it belonged to you, but I noticed in church that Mrs. Baker has a dress that exact same color, too."

Virginia only had time to clear her throat, before the other men burst into the room all carrying brooms or hoes or some utensil. At the same time, Colter came back inside, too.

"Well, you're ready to work," Colter said with satisfaction as he saw everyone.

"You can count on us," Shorty said.

The older men looked steadfast and honest. *How does a woman know the truth of the matter, though?* Virginia asked herself. Her father would criticize her for being in a muddle like this, but she would give anything if she could ask for his opinion. She felt a surge of sympathy for Patricia. Sometimes even a very imperfect parent could be deeply missed.

Chapter Nine

Christmas was new to him, Colter thought as he sat at the table farthest from the piano. Oh, he'd passed the day of December twenty-fifth before, but usually the only joy to it was a friendly game of poker with whoever happened to be around and, if he was fortunate, a sip of brandy from their not-yet-empty bottle.

And now, all the music of Christmas was ringing around him. The two Wells girls were lined up next to the piano and Virginia was demonstrating how to hold the clapper inside the bell to mute a note. She wanted the bells to fade out when they played "Silent Night."

"Just go soft at the end," Virginia said as she demonstrated it with a bell.

Patricia was standing on the other side of the piano and ringing one of the bells, too. Colter couldn't have been prouder if he was up there doing it himself. Even from back here, he could see the shine on those brass bells. The Christmas Eve service was tomorrow night and Colter wanted to watch the faces of the townspeople as they heard the music.

He'd never seen bells that rang out songs, but then he

hadn't seen many Christmas celebrations. When he was a boy at his uncle's, he remembered once or twice having a dinner of roast beef and hard potatoes on the day. There were never any presents or decorations though. Or even any kind words passing from one to another.

This Christmas, though, it was going to be different. He was going to celebrate with everything he had in him. He finally understood the miracle that had happened on that night long ago in the manger. He saw just a glimpse of the hope it brought to everyone, including him.

This year his family was going to honor that by celebrating.

"Lift the bells higher on that note," Virginia said from the piano as she showed with her hand where it needed to be.

He liked that Virginia and Danny had already put some red ribbons around and brought in the little pine tree. Tonight they were all planning to make popcorn strings and hang some shiny pennies on the tree before heading over to the boardinghouse to sleep.

He'd arranged a room for Virginia and the children. He hoped they wouldn't have to stay there for long, but he didn't know. In the meantime, Christmas was coming.

On Christmas Eve, after the service at church, they would light the candles Virginia had saved back for the tree and read the story from the Bible that talked of the blessed baby.

Only after that would they open their presents. He knew Virginia had gifts for the children and he had some, too. For Patricia, he'd bought a hat that was halfway between the boys' hats that she liked and the girls' hats that she needed to wear. Danny had been a little more difficult until Colter saw the picture frame sitting on the shelf in the mercantile. He'd bought the frame and planned to give it with the promise that the two of them would go to a photographer after Christmas and get a photo taken together.

With the two children taken care of, Colter had sat down to think about Virginia's present. He hoped to find some inspiration by watching her play the bells with the girls. He noticed the way Virginia bent her head down, listening to each of the girls, as though they were the only ones in the room. And when she stopped to rest her hands on Patricia's shoulders, he could hear the murmured words of praise even where he sat. His new daughter glowed after Virginia talked to her.

"Let's do it again," Virginia said from the front to the girls. "You're doing an excellent job."

He knew Virginia was convinced Patricia had a special ear for music, but Colter figured some of that was simply Virginia. She knew how to open the world of sounds to the girl. He had caught Patricia yesterday in the workroom, beating a rhythm on the metal tub hanging on the wall. She was listening to hear the sounds as she beat it in different ways. He knew she was adjusting to her life here because she hadn't asked for a drink of whiskey since that first day they got here. And she wore that bird pin from Virginia everywhere she went.

Colter looked down at the paper on the table. None of that gave him any ideas on what to give Virginia for a present though. He knew she liked his piano and he'd wrap that up and give it to her, but it didn't seem personal enough. He wanted a gift that told her she'd become close to his heart.

The music lesson ended and the girls put their bells down on the piano cloth. Colter put his pencil down and started to clap. Which made the girls giggle—and Virginia blush.

Just then Danny banged open the door from the workroom, holding something wrapped in his jacket. His dog trailed in behind him, making sharp quick barks.

"What's the matter?" Colter said as he stood up. He figured Danny wouldn't have given up his jacket on a cold day like today if something wasn't wrong. And he'd never heard the dog as frantic. Virginia was walking across the room to help, too.

Danny laid his bundle down on the nearest table. "The cat's hurt."

The folds of the jacket fell away and Colter could see the yellow cat had been in a vicious fight. He looked up. "Get the dog away."

Virginia gasped as she walked up. "Is the poor thing alive?"

"Barely." Colter reached down and started examining the cat. Then he looked back at Danny. "The dog."

"The dog didn't do this," Danny protested. "It was another cat. The dog saved our cat's life."

Colter figured now wasn't the time to debate the point about who the cat belonged to. It was a stray. "You're sure? Because this dog has been chasing this cat around for the past few days at least."

"They just like to chase," Danny protested. "They're really friends."

Colter had found a deep scratch along the cat's side and a bite along its leg. He turned to Virginia. "Do we have any more of those strips of muslin?"

"I'll get them," she said as she walked to the workroom.

"And bring that salve, too. The one you used on my burn."

By now Patricia had walked up to the table and the Wells girls had left to go home.

"Is she going to live?" Danny asked.

"I expect so," Colter said as he reached out to put his hand on the boy's shoulder. "You did the right thing to bring her here."

"I could go kick that other cat for you," Patricia offered as she stood beside Danny.

"No kicking," Colter said with a smile to the girl. "But I appreciate you offering to help your brother."

"Well, it won't do any good to talk to the cat," Patricia muttered. "I know that much."

Virginia came back into the room with strips of muslin draped over her shoulder and a tin of the ointment in her hands.

"Here," she said as she laid it all out on the table in front of Colter.

Ten minutes later, Virginia was standing at the cook-stove heating up some milk for the poor cat. She thought of Danny's words about the dog and the cat really being friends and it appeared to be true. Colter had wrapped the bandaged cat up in a piece of wool blanket and laid her in a warm corner of the workroom. The dog had lain down next to her looking as if he was going to stand guard for the day.

"My days back home were never like this," Virginia muttered to Colter as he put another stick of wood in the stove.

She sensed him stiffen up at her words, but then he

took a deep breath. "You're still planning to go back east then?"

She nodded as she poured the warm milk into a bowl she had sitting close. "The only reason I'm going to Denver is to make enough money to go home again. I have friends there who would help me get started teaching there."

"How much?" he asked. "What would it cost to go home?"

"Fifty-six dollars for the steamer down to Kansas City. Then eighty-four for the train to Connecticut."

"One hundred and forty dollars then?" he asked.

She nodded. "When I came out, my brother bought my ticket. Otherwise I don't know what I would have done."

"Sometimes home can disappoint you," Colter said as he picked up the bowl of milk and walked over to set it down by the cat.

It wasn't until Colter left the room that Virginia realized she hadn't included Lester in her plans. Even if she were more enthusiastic about him, she probably would not have counted him. She was used to thinking of herself as being alone when she thought of going back east. Oh, she'd had family back there—her father, her mother and her brother—but she had spent most of her time with the piano. Sometimes she felt she knew the hearts of the composers better than those of the people living around her. Until now she had always considered herself fortunate to have the music. Now, she wondered.

She had been consumed with becoming a pianist worthy of her father. She had never thought how much that quest had cost her. She'd never even had a pet. She glanced over at the cat and dog. She had friends, but not one who felt strongly enough about her to dive into a fight and rescue her if she needed it. Her friends would help her get students and a place to live. But that would be all.

Suddenly, the thought of being in a home like the one where she'd been raised made her feel lonely. She looked a little closer at the cat. Maybe when she went back she would get a kitten.

Colter went back to the piece of paper he'd left lying on the table. He didn't need to spend any more effort thinking about what to give Virginia for Christmas. There was one thing she wanted more than anything— a way to go home.

By the time she came out into the main part of the saloon, he had reined in his feelings.

"The floor is looking good," he said when she glanced over at it. "I think we have one day left with the scrapers and we'll have all the dead wood gone. Then we can replace it with new lumber in the spring."

"The men are doing a good job," Virginia said.

"Yeah."

Virginia just stood there and it suddenly occurred to him that she wanted to tell him something. For a wild sweet moment, he wondered if she was going to say she didn't want to go east after all. That she wanted to stay right here.

"I was wondering," she started. "About Christmas. I've never cooked a holiday meal, but I was hoping. That is—the men who came to help with the floor... I know most of them. They don't have any Christmas dinner planned and I was thinking maybe we could invite them here."

"All of them?" Colter did a quick calculation. "That must be twenty men."

Virginia nodded. "I'm not a good cook. But I was thinking if we did something easy."

"Of course," Colter said. He didn't know why he hadn't thought of this. "It's not the food, it's the company anyway."

"And they love canned peaches," Virginia said.

"I can make a pretty good biscuit," he said.

"I can make soup."

Colter stood there and smiled. A woman who was willing to cook for her friends might just be persuaded to stay with them. He couldn't help checking though.

"Do you have a lot of friends back east?"

Virginia shrugged. "Some of my schoolmates are close enough friends to recommend me as a piano teacher. I was already giving lessons before I left and several of them offered to help me get set up again when I come back."

"Well, that's good."

She nodded. But Colter consoled himself that she looked uncertain. If she were going to be happy there, he would let her go and wish her well. If there was any weakness in her resolve to move back though, he intended to find it.

"What kind of soup?" he asked.

"If I can find a chicken, I can make soup with that," she said and then looked at him anxiously.

"Jake Hargrove told me they have some chickens for sale. I could ride out and get a couple."

Virginia nodded. "You could pick up that dress for Patricia, too. We wanted her to have it for the Christmas Eve service when she plays her bell."

"So she is playing with you for the church service?"

Virginia nodded. "She loves the bells."

"She loves her teacher," Colter said softly.

Virginia blushed slightly at that. "I only show her how to play the notes."

It was quiet for a moment. They just stood there companionably. And then Colter felt his skin break out in a sweat. That was his first clue that he was going to climb up on the cliff and jump off.

"Come with me," he said. "I can rent a buggy from the livery and we can take a ride out to the Hargroves. It's not a spring day, but it's not freezing. No storms anyway. I have a buffalo robe in the storeroom we can use to keep warm. You'll want to pick out the chicken yourself."

Come with me, come with me, his heart sang.

"But what about the children?" Virginia looked bewildered.

"I'll ask Petey to come over here. We'll be back before supper anyway."

Virginia didn't answer. For a long minute Colter just stood there worrying that the sweat on his face would become obvious. A fair number of grown men would pay to see him sweat, he thought to himself. They'd be surprised, but they'd pay.

"Why, I think that would be lovely," Virginia finally said.

"Good. That's good." Colter decided he'd best not give her time to change her mind. "I'll go get the buggy and be right back. I want to show you the place I plan to build my house, too."

Colter muttered to himself the whole way to the livery. Had he made it too obvious by telling her he wanted to show her where his house would be? He wasn't sure if she would be flattered or alarmed if she knew how much he wanted her to come with him.

By the time he got back to the saloon with the buggy, he'd convinced himself that he needed to wear a suit. He had most of the pieces for a suit, but not a tie, so he went next door to ask Petey to watch the children and lend him a tie. Fortunately, Petey had worn his tie today as a salute to the coming holiday so he could just hand it over when Colter asked.

Petey wished him well and advised him to be a gentleman.

"She sets a great deal of store by manners," the older man said. "See you mind yours."

Colter was careful to take Virginia's arm and escort her to the buggy before lifting her up so she could sit. Once she was settled, he tucked the buffalo robe around her knees. Then he patted her hand and asked if she'd like a peppermint.

"I didn't even know they had such a nice buggy at the livery," Virginia gushed and turned to Colter as he climbed up into the buggy, too.

The smell of peppermint floated over to him and he breathed deeply.

"We can be fairly civilized out here," Colter exaggerated. It might be more accurate to say they'd be civilized when the railroad came to town. At least, that was what he'd heard. But now was not the time for a man to be timid.

The road to the Hargroves' place was sprinkled with old snow. For most of the winter, the sides of the road had been piled high with drifted snow. But today the sky was blue.

"I haven't been out of town for months," Virginia said.

"Any time you want to go, just let me know," Colter replied. "I'm planning to buy a buggy like this now that I have Patricia to take around."

"She'd rather ride a horse."

"Maybe, but I want to see her turn out to be a fine lady—like you."

"What?" Virginia looked up at him and squeaked. "She'd hate that."

"Well, I do figure that being a bachelor father, I'm bound to make some mistakes with the children. There are things that women just seem to understand easier."

He gave a heavy sigh after those words and let Virginia sit in silence for a bit. He hated to use guilt, but he hoped it would work.

"Just don't force Danny to play the piano." She finally couldn't stand it. "I already gave him quite a few lessons and he hated it."

"Patricia though—"

"Patricia should have the best lessons you can buy," Virginia said. "On any instrument. She's a natural with it."

Colter congratulated himself. The conversation had flowed in the direction he wanted it to. Maybe Petey didn't need to worry so much.

"I could use your advice. When I build my house out here on the Dry Creek, should I plan to keep the piano in the parlor or in its own room?"

"Oh, don't put it off by itself. The person playing the piano misses out on too much that way. Patricia needs to have others around."

Colter asked her more questions and, before much time had passed at all, they were making the turn to go into the Hargrove place. Jake had added corrals around his place since Colter had been here last. And there were a row of chokecherry bushes growing along the lane leading to the wood-frame house Jake had built after he married Elizabeth. There were snowdrifts melting along the south side of the house and a couple of sheets hanging on the clothesline to the north.

They didn't even need to knock at the door. Elizabeth had heard them and came outside before he'd finished pulling the buggy to a stop.

"Well, what a wonderful surprise," Elizabeth shouted out as she wiped her hands on her apron and smoothed back her dark hair.

Colter studied Elizabeth. She was wearing a brown cotton dress and her dark hair was swept back into a bun. Her cheeks were pink, and he could see her breath in the cold air. She looked so happy he could only believe she was. She'd come from the east just like Virginia had. Granted, Elizabeth had been more of a servant than a lady, but she had found happiness on the banks of the Dry Creek. If she could do that, couldn't Virginia, too?

Chapter Ten

Virginia had never envied her friend as much as when she was in her kitchen. And it wasn't the string of dried onions that hung from a hook by the far cupboard or the jars of spices and herbs that lay so colorfully on the small shelf. It was that Elizabeth knew how to use the onion and the spices. She could probably make a wonderful meal out of dried grass for her family if she had to.

The kitchen smelled like cinnamon. A plank table stood below a small glass window that was frosted over. The heat from the cookstove made the room comfortable. Colter was with Jake and Spotted Fawn out in the shed catching chickens.

"You came just at the right time," Elizabeth was saying. "I was going to go and get a chicken ready for our dinner tomorrow, too. I should have thought about Petey and his friends. You'll need—what? Six chickens?"

"Goodness, no. I think one old hen will be enough." Virginia closed her eyes and added, "I plan to make soup."

"Oh." Elizabeth stopped pulling jars off the shelf by the cookstove. She turned to look at Virginia. "Soup?"

Virginia had been afraid of this. "It's all wrong, isn't it? I don't know what I was thinking. I was talking to Colter and before I knew it I had said we should invite Petey and his friends to dinner. Of course, you know all I can make is soup and—"

"You make a lovely pot of tea, too," Elizabeth interrupted to proclaim loyally.

"I know this Christmas is special for Colter and I wanted to give him—" Virginia spread her hands in despair. "I wanted him to remember this Christmas forever."

"He can remember soup."

"He's going to be wishing it was fried chicken with every spoonful he eats," Virginia said as she went over and sat down in a chair by the table. "He's even going to have to make the biscuits."

"There's nothing wrong with a man cooking. Jake does it sometimes."

"And you're kind, too," Virginia said, half wailing the words. "You're the one he should marry."

Elizabeth started to laugh at that. "I don't think Jake's ready to give me up quite yet."

"Well, you know what I mean."

"I sure do," Elizabeth said as she came over to the table and sat down. "And I'm all for it. I always thought you two should marry. I was going to say something, but Jake said I should mind my own business."

"Oh, no. You don't understand. We're not getting married. I just want him to remember me."

"But why aren't you getting married? I've seen the way you two look at each other."

Virginia blinked back a tear. "I can't make soap either. Children need soap."

Elizabeth reached over and put her hand over the one Virginia had resting on the table. "You can manage soap. The big question is—do you love the man?"

"I don't know. We're just so different."

"It's this place, isn't it? I know when you first came, everything was so new and you missed your home. But how is it now?"

"I've gotten used to a lot of things. And I do know that if I go back, I won't be here to celebrate when the railroad finally makes it to town and when the church gets their own building."

"Then stay. Find out if what you feel for Colter will grow."

Virginia took a shuddering breath. "It's not that simple. I worked all my life to please my father and all I did was disappoint him. What if it's the same with Colter? I keep thinking I should take the job in Denver if I get the position. I just— It would certainly be safer. I could save enough to move back east. And I love music."

Elizabeth stood up. "Virginia Parker, I know you love music, but I never thought you'd scare easy. Don't give up so fast. I say it's time you learn to make fried chicken."

"Colter loves your fried chicken," Virginia said as foolish hope rose in her heart. "I think he ate three pieces at the church dinner."

Elizabeth laughed again. "Then, when we're done with you, you're going to make it even better than I do."

Elizabeth walked over to the cupboard and pulled out a piece of paper and a pencil. "Just do everything the way I write it down. When you've made it a couple of times, you can change things to your taste. I'm giving you some spices, too. Pepper, salt, ginger, cinnamon."

By the time they heard the men walking back to the house, Elizabeth had managed to write instructions for frying chicken, making gravy and mashed potatoes, as well as cooking gingered carrots. Virginia confessed she was not to be trusted with vegetables, but Elizabeth assured her she had written every step down so simply a child could do it.

"We'll still let Colter make the biscuits," Elizabeth said as she stood up from the table. "Just so he doesn't come to expect all this every day."

Virginia thought nothing would be more wonderful than to be so competent he would expect meals like that. But she knew Elizabeth had cooked and waited on people for years before she married Jake. The other woman didn't know what it was like to have men rush to do the cooking because hers was so bad.

"I'm sending some pickles back with you, too," Elizabeth said as she handed her several small cloth bags with spices. "It's not Christmas without my dill pickles."

Virginia put the spices in the pocket of her dress.

When the men came in, their hands cold and their boots muddy, Elizabeth insisted Colter take Virginia over to see where he was planning to build his house. She and Jake would bring the chickens to town with them on Christmas Eve.

Virginia folded up the sheet of instructions Elizabeth had given her and put it in her pocket next to the spices. Then Elizabeth put the yellow dress for Patricia in her hands and handed the jar of pickles to Colter.

"I can't thank you enough," Virginia said.

Elizabeth grinned. "Spotted Fawn is happy to give it

to her. She remembers how it was not to have the same kind of clothes as the other children."

Virginia nodded. "We'll see you soon."

Colter felt nervous as he drove the buggy farther down the road. He'd only shown a few people besides Jake and Elizabeth where he hoped to build his house. A person had to be able to see what the place would look like when it had trees around it in order to truly appreciate the site.

"You're still warm enough?" he asked Virginia as he turned the horses off the main road and headed up the nearby rise.

Virginia turned to him. "I'm stronger than I look. I don't need to be coddled."

So much for Petey's advice on being polite, Colter thought. If he kept this up, she would think he was a snake-oil peddler.

"Of course you don't need to be coddled."

They topped the rise and Colter pulled the buggy to a stop. The area was covered with light snow, but it would be green in the spring. The soil was good.

"We have to go a little way for water," he started to explain, "but I've always liked to be a little higher than what is around me." He knew Petey would despair of him. "I suppose it goes back to my gunfighting days."

Virginia nodded. "I can see that."

Colter had known many women and their response to his mention of being a gunfighter had either met with fascination or repulsion. Virginia showed neither. She just looked at him straight across, like she could accept it, even if she didn't like it.

"Not that anyone who lived in my house would have

to worry much about men coming to gun me down."
This was the reason he'd mentioned it. He'd wondered
if she was worried about this and it was holding her
back. "I entered a couple of shooting contests and lost.
It took the shine right off my reputation."

"That was a clever thing to do."

He gave her a quick glance. "Not many people understand that."

"What way will you have the house facing?" Virginia asked as she turned to look around.

"Northeast." Now that the buggy was at a complete
stop, he was free to watch her reaction. She had a smile
on her face, which he figured must be good.

She nodded. "If you're going to put in a kitchen, take
a good look at Elizabeth's first. I've never seen one so
well-organized."

"Jake plans to help me with the house."

"Good."

The sun was shifting as they sat there in silence.

"I figure two stories with the top for bedrooms."

Virginia nodded. "The children will like that."

Colter let her look around in silence for a bit. Then
he figured that if she looked too long at the area she
might find some reason to not approve of it. Besides, it
was best to leave now so they'd get back to town before
dark. He knew Petey would stay with the children as
long as they were gone, but he would still worry until
they were back.

Virginia saw that lanterns were beginning to be lit
in the windows of Dry Creek as Colter drove her back
to the saloon.

"I don't mind walking from the livery," Virginia said. "If you want to just go there with the buggy."

"There would be no end to the scolding I would get from Petey if I didn't bring you back to the saloon. Besides, it's as easy to go to the livery afterward."

"It's just…" She hesitated. "I wanted to stop by Lester's for a minute."

"Oh."

"I need to talk to him," she added.

Colter looked over at her face. She looked miserable.

"I appreciate you coming with me. I don't think Lester should mind if you go out driving with a friend."

"He has sensitive feelings."

Colter grunted at that. A buzzard could look mighty sad; that didn't mean his feelings were honest. It was just a ploy to fool his dying prey. Colter pulled the buggy to a stop in front of the livery though. If the lady wanted to walk, she could. He swung himself down from the seat and walked around to offer Virginia his hand.

"Thank you," she said as he took her hand.

Colter could feel the tremble in her fingers. "It'll be fine."

She looked up at him with worried blue eyes. "I just have to talk to him. It won't take long."

He nodded. The way the men gossiped in Lester's saloon the man would have probably heard about their drive. "If he gives you any trouble, let me know. I'll talk to him."

"I don't think…" Virginia looked alarmed.

"Not to argue," Colter explained. "Just to let him know we went to the Hargroves' to order chickens."

He helped Virginia step down from the buggy. "I

can walk with you. I don't like you being on the streets at dark."

"It's still light enough," Virginia said as she pulled her shawl around her shoulders more securely. "I'll be home before you know it."

Colter nodded. Nobody could stop him from keeping watch over her as she walked down the street. For the moment, she called his saloon home. That meant she was his to protect even if she planned to give her heart to another.

He stood there until he saw her enter into Lester's establishment.

By then the livery owner had come out to get the buggy.

"How'd it work for you?" he asked. "Have a nice ride?"

"I can't fault the buggy," Colter said as he paid the man.

With that, Colter started walking down the street, too. In his past life, he'd follow Virginia into Lester's place and either start a fight or get roaring drunk. In the morning, he'd wake up sore and sick. Now he was learning a new way. He'd go back to his place and see how that old cat was doing. And make some supper for his children. God would have to help him accept Virginia's decision if she agreed to marry another man.

Chapter Eleven

Virginia stepped inside Lester's saloon and squinted. It was almost too dark to see. She could make out a couple of men standing at the bar though, and she could tell it was Shorty serving them drinks.

"What's happened here?" she asked. "There's no light."

"Virginia!" Shorty said as he set down the bottle he held and walked around the bar, heading toward her. "What are you doing here?"

"I just wanted to talk to Lester. Is he in back?"

"He's trying to find another can of kerosene," Shorty said. "I keep telling him there was only the one and it— well, it's empty."

"The lanterns are dry?"

Shorty nodded and lowered his voice. "I don't think he knew it was the last can when he— Well, Petey said you don't believe it was him that did it, but—"

Shorty looked behind his shoulder into the dim room. "I think I hear him coming out."

"I'll just sit over here," Virginia said as she pointed

to a table. No one was sitting at any of the tables so it would be quiet.

"Petey said you were asking about some letters." Shorty's voice went even lower. "There was a miner who came by here last fall. His sister has been sending him mail in care of Lester's place since then. I haven't read them, but I noticed some of the letters are opened."

Virginia nodded. She supposed if Lester would set fire to a building, it wouldn't be much of a stretch for him to lie about some letters. But she was still disappointed. It had all been such a pretty picture, thinking of him and his sister and that wonderful violin. "Did she write the letters on lavender paper?"

Shorty nodded as he stepped away.

Lester was walking toward them. "Virginia! What a pleasant surprise!"

"We need to talk," Virginia said as she walked over and sat at the table. Lester might not be the gentleman she had thought he was, but she would treat him like one as she kindly explained why she could never marry him. She refused to let the emotions she had for Colter keep growing when there was another man who seemed to feel she belonged to him instead.

Lester might be willing to deceive someone else, but she wasn't. She would have her talk with him and then go next door and try to find something for the children for supper. *This,* she thought to herself, *is how civilized people handled their lives. Orderly and with concern for others.*

Colter had one of Virginia's aprons tied around his waist. He had just sliced some onion and put it in the cast-iron skillet. He'd added some wood to the fire a few minutes ago and when the blaze got higher he would put some bacon in with the onion. He'd sliced some potatoes and had them ready to add after the bacon.

The cat by the cupboard meowed. Colter had checked her bandages when he first got in and they were in place. Petey had left a note on the table saying he and the children would be back soon. Patricia wanted to check on the mail from the last stage of the day.

Colter told himself he had put the apron on so he could wrap it around his hands when he moved the skillet. He didn't want to injure the skin on the hand he had scalded. But, the truth was, the apron reminded him of Virginia.

He was getting ready to put the bacon in the pan when someone knocked loudly on the back door.

"Come," Shorty said when Colter opened up. "Hurry."

Just then, a woman screamed. It sounded like it came from Lester's place.

"Let's go," Colter said as he reached back and grabbed the gun holster he'd left hanging from a peg on the wall. It was dark outside, but both men moved swiftly to the open back door of Lester's saloon.

Shorty stood back so Colter could enter first. The hall to the main room was dark, but there was one lantern lit by the bar. A couple of the regulars were staring at something in the corner of the room. The fact that they weren't moving made Colter worried enough to draw his gun.

He slid around the corner and his heart stopped. Lester was standing there with a knife in one hand and an arm wrapped around Virginia's neck.

"Let her go," Colter said as he stepped farther into the room. *Please, Lord,* he prayed.

Lester laughed. "And let you shoot me? No, she stays with me."

"You're frightening her." Colter kept his voice even. Desperate men were easily spooked.

"Well, that's her own fault," Lester said in disgust. "Coming here and accusing me of setting that fire. Saying she was going to tell you all about it. That you would handle it. I know what that means. And I'm no match for your gun."

"I meant he'd talk to the marshal in Billings," Virginia said. Colter was glad her voice still had a little starch in it.

"And then she played me for a complete fool by saying you'd given up your guns."

Colter knew there was enough light for the other man to see what was pointing right at him. "Let her go, Lester. That's the only way for you now."

The other man didn't move.

"You've heard of me." Colter knew the longer he talked the less chance there was of violence. At least, as long as he kept his voice steady. "All the stories are true."

"I heard you'd been beat in some shooting contest over by the Rockies," Lester said. "Heard you weren't as fast as you used to be."

"Let Virginia step outside and you won't have to worry about how fast I am."

"It's not my fault anyway. I thought everyone was gone. I wasn't going to hurt anyone. I just didn't want to lose all my business when you got back."

"You did this over *money?*"

"You could have burned up that piano," Virginia scolded the man. Colter noticed the color in her face was a little better. Her hair was falling down, but her eyes were fierce. She'd managed to move a few inches away from Lester and was using her hand to reach into the pocket of her dress.

Don't do it, Virginia. He didn't know what she had planned, but anything was too dangerous.

"I did it for us." Lester turned to Virginia, his voice pleading for understanding. "If business stayed good, I thought I could sell the place when the railroad came in. It was for our future. With those friends of your father, I could have made something of myself in politics."

Colter didn't like Lester talking to Virginia. "If it's money you want, we can talk."

"Huh?"

Colter nodded. He'd gotten the man's attention back. Now all he had to do was get Virginia away from him before she used whatever it was she'd grabbed from her pocket. He could see her fist had closed over something even if it was still hidden. He wondered if she had one of those little guns women carried. He hoped not. So many things could go wrong with them.

He spoke clear so Lester would hear. "I have three hundred dollars over at my place. How much would it take for you to let Virginia go?"

"Three hundred?"

Colter nodded. "Let Virginia go and we can go count it."

Lester snorted.

Colter saw Virginia take a deep breath and he knew the talking was over.

He steadied his gun as he saw her hand move. Lester must have felt her turn and he looked down just in time to have seen Virginia throw something. Then Lester sneezed. Virginia slipped away from him and dropped to the floor.

"Hands up." Colter stepped closer.

He saw Virginia crawl under one of the tables.

"Drop the knife," Colter added, in case the other man didn't believe it was over.

Lester sneezed again and the knife fell to the floor.

"Anybody have some rope to tie him up?" Colter asked without taking his eyes off Lester. He heard footsteps so he knew the men who had been standing at the bar were getting what they needed.

"What's going to happen?" Virginia said as she pulled herself up off the floor. She'd managed to put several tables between her and Lester.

Colter took a deep breath. He'd grown up thinking men settled their own differences with a gun. Those days were over for him though. "We'll hold him in the back room at the stage office until the marshal can get here. There's no windows and a good lock on the door."

"We'll get him there," Shorty promised and a few of the other men nodded as they came back with rope. "I just saw Petey outside and he says— Well, he'll tell you. He's next door at your place."

Colter walked over to Virginia as the men started tying up Lester.

"Are you all right?" He brushed back the hair from her face. That's when he felt the grains on her skin. He looked closer. "Pepper?"

She nodded. "And some ginger. I think I still have the packets of salt and cinnamon."

"Well, if that doesn't beat all." Colter smiled as he

brushed the spices off her face. "I'm sorry. I guess this territory is still a little rough."

"There's greed everywhere."

Once Colter finished getting rid of the spices, he didn't have any reason to keep on touching her except that—he pulled her into his arms. "I was so afraid something would happen to you."

"I know," she said and he felt her head move against his chest as she nodded.

Then there was a man clearing his throat.

Shorty spoke up. "Petey said it was kind of urgent—I know we've had our own problem going. But Patricia—"

Colter nodded. Virginia had already turned to the door.

Dear Lord, what now? Virginia prayed as she walked over to Colter's place. At least kerosene lamps were lit in the place, which meant someone was home. She supposed Patricia was upset because there hadn't been a letter from her mother. She heard Colter's footsteps coming behind her and it was a great comfort to know they were both there to help with the tears.

Before Virginia opened the door to the saloon, she heard the dog barking excitedly.

"What's wrong?" she asked as she stepped inside. She didn't need anyone to answer to know that something was happening. One of Patricia's trunks was halfway down the stairs, with its lid locked tight and Danny standing over it with a scowl on his face.

"Patricia's moving out," Danny said.

By then Colter was in the room, too.

"She can't be that upset." Virginia turned to Colter. His face looked as worried as she felt. "Can she?"

Virginia looked up and saw Patricia come out of her bedroom. She was dressed in the clothes she'd worn when she arrived. She had a big smile on her face. "I got my letter."

"From your *mother?*" Virginia asked in astonishment.

Patricia nodded as she bounced down the stairs. "I need to get everything packed and down to the stage. She's not at the Golden Spur anymore, but she's not with that man either. It will be just her and me again. Like it's supposed to be."

"It can't be," Virginia said as she turned to Colter.

"I won't let her go," Colter vowed as he walked over and crouched down by Patricia. "Now, tell me everything."

Patricia started to talk, sounding more excited than Virginia could ever remember hearing her. Not even when she was playing the bells. It seemed that her mother had indeed written a letter, telling Patricia that she had parted company with Rusty the miner.

"He completely ran out of gold," Patricia told Colter. "So my mother isn't going to stay with him anymore. But she sent me her address. So I can bring her trunks to her. She's already paid the money to the stagecoach place in San Francisco."

That's when Patricia turned to Virginia. The girl's face was beaming and she ran over to Virginia with her arms wide. "I'm going to live in San Francisco. I'm sure my mother will take me to the opera."

Virginia opened her arms and held the girl close. Then she looked over at Colter. He seemed as stunned as she was. Virginia bowed her head and kissed the top of Patricia's head.

Then Patricia drew back and looked up. "The stage leaves tomorrow so I won't get to play the bells."

"I'll miss you," Virginia said as she drew the girl into another hug.

Meanwhile, Colter had stood up again.

"I'll get supper ready," he said and then walked into the workroom.

Virginia wondered how anyone could think of food even if the children needed to eat.

Colter braced himself against the cupboard. He'd never felt so powerless. He hadn't thought Rose would ever send for Patricia. Not after the things she'd said. But Rose was the girl's mother. He knew he didn't have any legal rights to keep the girl here. He wasn't prepared to let her go either though.

How could he be losing all the people he loved? The next thing he knew Danny would remember a grandfather that he wanted to live with. Colter knew he had pieced his family together from various places. That's just the way it had happened. But it never occurred to him it could be taken apart so easily.

The cat meowed and Colter remembered supper. He'd pulled the skillet to the back of the cookstove so the onions were not burned. He added the cut-up bacon to the onions and put it back on the front of the stove.

Petey came in the door. "I've been up in her room trying to get the second trunk ready to go."

"She really got a letter?" Colter asked as he reached back for Virginia's apron.

Petey nodded. "The clerk at the office said something about prepayment made from San Francisco. He had some official form that he'd gotten on the same stage that Patricia's letter had come."

Colter nodded. He must not know anything about families. It wasn't surprising given his childhood, but he was still astonished. "Did it say what stage she's to go on?"

"Tomorrow morning."

"I'll miss her."

The other man came over and put his hand on Colter's shoulder. "You know, I'm going to miss her, too. And from what she's told me of that mother of hers, I'm spitting mad that the woman has the nerve to ask her daughter to come live with her again. After leaving her there in that saloon all by herself. Doesn't she know what kind of things can happen to a little girl in a situation like that?"

Colter nodded. "She knows."

The cruel fact was that love could be very selfish. It might be true that, in her own way, Patricia's mother loved her. But it wasn't a love that ever considered what was best for the other person. Colter knew how easy it must be to fall into the trap of loving like that. All he wanted to do was to take Patricia and Virginia and lock them in their rooms upstairs and never let them go.

The door opened again and Danny and the dog came inside.

"They're just crying out there," the boy said in disgust.

Colter turned to the boy and gave him a fierce hug. "Tell me you're not leaving me, too."

"Me?" Danny looked alarmed as he squirmed his way out of the hug. "Where would I go?"

"Nowhere, if I have my say." Colter turned around

to tend the skillet. It was time to add the potatoes. "Go ahead and put some plates on the table in the other room."

"I hope they're done crying," Danny said as he walked over to the cupboard.

"They were both crying?" Colter asked.

"Yeah. Girls," the boy said in disgust as he pulled down some plates.

Colter looked over at Petey. "Is that good?"

The older man shrugged. "I don't know for sure. But at least she must be sad at the thought of leaving everyone here."

"She'll miss the dog," Danny said as he balanced the plates and opened the door.

Colter heard the sizzle coming from the stove. If he had his way, she'd also miss the cooking.

Chapter Twelve

When Virginia woke the next morning, it took her a few minutes to remember why she held a handkerchief in her hand. She'd gone to sleep with tears in her eyes. Everyone had been gloomy last night as they ate supper together, except for Patricia, who had been feverish with excitement.

Before they went to sleep, Virginia had given every gentle reason she could think of to make the girl change her mind about taking the stagecoach to San Francisco. Colter had assured everyone that if Patricia was set on going, he would go with her and make sure she made it to her mother's place.

His declaration had made Virginia cry even more.

She did not want to send Patricia off with memories of tears though so she dressed and went downstairs to make breakfast for everyone. The morning light was just coming into the main room as she made her way down the stairs. The trunk that had been sitting on the stairs last night wasn't there any longer. Neither was the one that had been dragged to the door.

The smell of coffee was coming from the kitchen

and before she walked across the room, Colter opened that door and came inside. He looked as exhausted as she felt.

"I thought I'd help get breakfast," she said.

He nodded. "I have batter made for pancakes. I just haven't—"

He sent her a look so bleak her heart broke.

"She'll be fine," Virginia whispered as she walked toward him. "She's bright. And tough."

Virginia opened her arms and he stepped into them.

"The stagecoach had someone come and take the trunks," Colter said as he wrapped his arms around her, too. "Patricia was up. I don't think she slept at all last night."

"Is she in her room?"

"I think so."

Virginia's heart slowed. She'd never grieved like this before, with someone to hold her who knew the same anguish. She could feel the strength in Colter's arms as he held her, but it was the tenderness in his heart that comforted her the most. They stood wrapped together for a few minutes and then Virginia stepped back.

"I wanted to play some music for her before she leaves," Virginia said as she looked over at the piano.

"Oh." She stopped then looked up at Colter. "I have a bell missing."

Virginia walked over to make sure she was right. She looked all around, but there were only nine bells instead of ten. "The one that's missing is the one Patricia was going to play in the Christmas Eve service tonight."

"Well, I think we need to go upstairs and talk to her," Colter said.

"Maybe she took it upstairs so she could practice."

When Virginia and Colter knocked on the girl's door, there was no answer. They looked at each other and Virginia slowly opened the door.

"Patricia," she called softly but she already suspected what she would find. "She's not here."

Colter followed her into the bedroom. Everything was gone. Patricia's old hat. Even the rope she'd worn cinched around her middle for a belt. The closet was empty except for the yellow dress Elizabeth had made.

"She's probably down at the stage office," Colter said as he turned to go.

Virginia followed him down the stairs. She was surprised that Patricia would try to leave without saying goodbye. Unless she was ashamed for stealing the bell. Virginia knew the girl would never enjoy the bell either since she'd stolen it. Which was such a shame with her ear for music.

"Wait a minute," Virginia said as she went back upstairs.

When she came back down, she was carrying ten small pieces of linen and some cord to tie them together. She went to the piano and quickly wrapped the remaining bells in the linen. Then she tied them together with the cord.

"You're not going to…" Colter asked when she walked back to him.

Virginia nodded. Music had separated her from those she loved when she was a child. She didn't want it to come between her and Patricia now. "Let's go."

The morning air was cold and gray clouds promised snow later today. There were a few people on the street, but it did not take long to arrive at the stage office. Virginia looked in the window and she saw Patricia sitting on a bench inside with a small bag nearby.

"She looks so forlorn," Virginia said as she glanced up at Colter.

"Yes, she does," he agreed as he opened the door.

A rush of warm air greeted them as they stepped inside. Patricia looked over and, when she saw them, shifted farther away on the bench.

Virginia put her hand on Colter's arm. "I'll talk to her. She's feeling guilty."

He nodded.

"We're just coming to see you," Virginia said softly as she walked slowly toward Patricia. "We missed you and your father is making a wonderful breakfast. Besides, I wanted to bring you these."

By now Virginia was standing in front of the girl and she held out the bundle of bells. "One bell is lonely by itself. It needs others to make music. If you want them, they're yours."

Patricia looked up wide-eyed. "But you need them for the songs tonight. For the church service. For that lady with the school."

For the first time that morning, Virginia remembered Cecilia Wells was coming tonight to make a decision about whether or not Virginia could be a music teacher at the school. If she didn't have the bells, she wouldn't appear like a worthy teacher at all. But her heart told her it wasn't only bells that got lonely. She looked down at Patricia's scared face and hoped the girl would remember she was loved when she played those bells.

"I still want you to have them," Virginia said as she sat down on the bench next to the girl.

"But—" Patricia began and then she burst into tears.

Virginia put the bells down on the bench and opened her arms to the girl. "Come here."

"I was talking to the clerk," Colter said as he came over and joined them on the bench. Patricia stopped sobbing in Virginia's arms long enough to look up at Colter.

"He's made a mistake. That's all," Patricia said as she pulled away from Virginia. "My mother sent money for me to go, too. Not just her trunks. He just made a mistake."

Patricia sat with her arms crossed on the bench.

"Oh, dear," Virginia said as she glanced up at Colter.

"Well, you will always have a home with me," Colter said as he opened his arms to the girl, too. "There's no need for you to go anywhere."

The girl started to weep again, this time even harder. Her face was pressed against Colter's shirt, but her voice was clear. "My mother didn't send for me."

Then Patricia looked up at Virginia. "I was going to bring the bell back. I know they're yours."

Virginia shook her head. "In the future, we'll share them."

"But we'll use them tonight for church, won't we?" Patricia asked as she wiped her eyes.

Virginia nodded. "We'll need to practice some later today."

Colter went to the church an hour before the Christmas Eve service was set to begin. He brought a load of firewood over because he had volunteered to heat the room up so everyone would be comfortable as they remembered the day Jesus was born. As long as he was heating the church, he decided he might as well provide some green boughs and a few red ribbons to make everything look festive.

When he was done, he sat on one of the benches to pray. It was about this time last year that he had walked up to the pulpit in this very building, pledging to become a Christian. He figured it wouldn't hurt to begin this next year with prayer either. His family was just beginning to find themselves. Patricia had spent the rest of the day without mentioning her mother. Danny had welcomed Patricia back with a pat on the back and an offer to let her name the cat since he had already named the dog. Virginia—well, she was the one who might be leaving.

Tonight the woman from the school would hear the bells ringing out those Christmas carols. Colter had heard the practicing that had taken place this afternoon. The girls could play those songs flawlessly. He had no doubt Virginia would be offered the job. All he could do was pray that God blessed her and gave her the desires of her heart. He'd never felt so helpless.

A few hours later, Virginia and Patricia carried the bells over to the church and arranged them on a table before anyone else was there. When they opened the door, warm air welcomed them. Virginia knew that was because of Colter's thoughtfulness and she appreciated it. The girls would not be able to ring the bells right if their hands were all freezing.

"May I?" Patricia asked. Virginia nodded and the girl picked up one of the bells and rang it. The sound of the note filled the schoolhouse and the girl grinned.

Reverend Olson and his wife were the next to arrive, but then families started to arrive in clusters. The

Hargroves were there. The Bakers. Annabelle and Higgins. Mr. Wells and his daughters. And, with them, a woman dressed in black silk, who had to be his sister.

Virginia saw Mr. Wells nod for her to come over and she went to greet them.

"This is my sister, Cecilia," Mr. Wells said. "With the school in Denver. We've been telling her all about you."

"I've heard some wonderful things," Cecilia said as she offered to shake Virginia's hand.

"I'm so glad you could come," Virginia said as she accepted the woman's hand. "This is a special service for us tonight."

By the time the Wells family was seated, everybody was ready for the Christmas Eve service to begin. Higgins began by reading the story of the baby's birth from Luke. Then Reverend Olson and his wife sang a duet. Spotted Fawn recited a Christmas poem that she had written. And then it was time for the bells.

Virginia barely had to prompt the girls. They knew their songs so well and the intense sweet smiles on their faces probably moved the listeners as much as the clear tones of their bells. Whichever it was, the building was completely silent as the bells rang out. Virginia wondered if there wasn't some of the wonder with them tonight that had been present thousands of years ago. She could almost hear the sigh from the listeners when the deep tone of the last bell finished ringing.

The girls walked back to their places on the benches and no one made a sound.

At last, the reverend stood. "After that beautiful reminder of the spirit of Christmas, let us pray."

Everyone stood and bowed their heads. "Bless us

on this beautiful Christmas Eve. May You give peace and joy to us all and be with us on our journeys home."

When the prayer was done, people rushed over to tell the girls how much they enjoyed the bells. And to tell Spotted Fawn that they thought she should have her poem published in one of those magazines from back east.

Cecilia Wells came over to Virginia as she started wrapping the bells up in the pieces of linen.

"Those bells of yours are magnificent," the woman said. "And my brother tells me you've only given lessons on the bells for a couple of months. It's truly remarkable what you've managed to teach. I just want you to know that the job is yours if you want it. I'll be in Miles City for a few days, so think of any questions you want to ask about the school. I'll invite you over for tea before I leave and we can talk more."

"Thank you," Virginia said with a nod of her head.

She had never thought it would be that easy. Surely the woman should ask her questions about her character and her references and— Virginia stopped. She wasn't ready to make a decision yet. She looked over at Colter. How was she ever going to decide?

"Can we do that again?" Patricia asked as she came over. Her eyes were bright and her smile radiant.

"Not right now," Virginia said with an answering smile. "Maybe for New Year's Day."

Elizabeth and Jake came up to tell them how much they enjoyed the bells.

"And you're worried about frying chicken?" Elizabeth whispered in her ear as she gave her a hug. "When you can make music like that? You don't even need to cook to put a smile on everyone's face."

"It was a pleasure to hear those bells," Jake said as he offered Virginia his hand.

By then most of the people were leaving and Colter came up to ask if he could walk them home.

Virginia nodded yes and put her shawl around her shoulders.

The moon was shining high in the sky when they left the schoolhouse. The clouds from earlier had moved on so they could see the stars, too.

"Chilly?" Colter bent down and asked her when they stepped onto the street. He didn't wait for an answer, but put his arm around her. She liked feeling his warmth so close beside her. Patricia and Danny raced on ahead. The night was peaceful and Colter didn't seem in any hurry to get home. Neither was she.

"Quite a day, wasn't it?" Colter said as they walked along.

Virginia nodded. Maybe that's why she wasn't as excited as she'd expected to be about learning she had the position at the school in Denver. When she remembered the panic she'd felt when Patricia was going to leave, her heart still raced. But now that those she loved were safe, she would have to consider the school position. But not until after Christmas. Tomorrow she didn't want any distractions. She planned to make a feast that everyone would long remember, whether she was here or not.

Chapter Thirteen

The carrots were sticking to the bottom of the skillet. Virginia had her best apron on and she'd banished everyone else from the kitchen. This was part of her Christmas gift to those she loved. She'd coated the pieces of chicken with flour and spices, just like Elizabeth's instructions said. She had the potatoes boiling on the back of the cookstove. Colter had mixed up the biscuit dough, but she was determined to bake them.

"I need more spoons," Patricia said as she put her head inside the door. She was wearing the hat Colter had given her last night along with the locket Virginia had given her. She was dazzling as she set out dishes for twenty-four people on the gaming tables in the main room. Virginia didn't have enough tablecloths so she had suggested Patricia use a couple of old sheets from upstairs.

"Come in then," Virginia said.

Colter had suggested the two of them exchange gifts tonight, but they had given their gifts to the children. Virginia enjoyed seeing Patricia display her treasures proudly.

"You have to keep everything secret that you see when you come in here though," Virginia added.

Colter still thought she was making soup. Danny probably did, too. Although the boy was so taken with his picture frame and new mittens, he probably didn't care what he ate.

When Patricia came in the workroom, the cat slipped in behind her.

Virginia went back to reading her directions.

She was ready to start frying the chicken. She put some drumsticks in the skillet because Elizabeth said she always did these first to test the heat. Virginia smelled the chicken start to cook. She looked up at Patricia. "Keep Colter away from the door. If he smells this he'll know for sure what we're having. Better yet, send him outside for something."

"What?" Patricia looked blank.

"Oh, one of those things men do," Virginia said. "He could go get something for dinner. Maybe more wood."

Patricia opened the door to go back into the other room and that was when it happened. The dog raced through the opening and the cat arched her back and hissed. That signaled the dog to begin the chase. The cat jumped up on the counter and knocked the plate of seasoned flour on top of the dog. Which made the dog growl at the cat so it ran over and took up a position on top of the pans holding the unbaked biscuits.

"Scat," Virginia said to both of the animals as she waved her apron at them, trying to get them cornered. Unfortunately, she was the one who caught the handle of the skillet and knocked it off balance. None of the drumsticks fell on the floor but they landed on top of the cookstove and started to burn until smoke started to rise up.

Virginia didn't know what to do first so she went to the cause of the problem. She picked the cat up by its fur and took it to the back door. She opened the door, getting ready to throw the cat on the porch, when the dog ran out first and Colter came around the corner carrying a load of firewood.

"I heard you need more wood," he said as he looked around. "What happened to the dog? It's all white."

"That dog is destroying our Christmas dinner," Virginia said, her voice full of outrage.

"I see." Colter stood there looking sympathetic.

If he hadn't looked so calm, Virginia might have been able to keep it in. "No, you don't see at all. I have to be able to make Christmas dinner."

"I'm happy to help."

"But you shouldn't have to do that," she said as she stepped back inside and closed the door. She could get really frustrated at the way Colter acted when she couldn't do something. He didn't criticize. He didn't blame. He didn't— It hit her so hard she had to lean against the door. He didn't act the way her father did even though she kept expecting it. She did not have to worry about disappointing him with every action she took.

Realizing this gave her added determination. A man like that deserved his Christmas dinner. She went over to the counter and smoothed out the piece of paper that had her instructions. The problem was that everything was off course.

She opened the door to the main room and saw the man she needed.

"Psst! Petey," she hissed. Fortunately, the man was close enough to hear her and he came without causing anyone else to look up and see who was calling him.

Petey slipped into the kitchen.

"You can cook, can't you?" Virginia demanded. "I need help with dinner."

"Well, why didn't you say so?" the man said in delight. "I can make a pot of soup that will make your tongue dance."

"We're not doing soup," Virginia said. "It's fried chicken."

Colter checked his watch again. He had expected Virginia to be out of the kitchen an hour ago. How long did it take to put together a pot of soup? Granted, it would have to be a large pot of soup to give everyone a bowl, but it shouldn't take this long.

Patricia was the last one he knew of who had spoken to Virginia, so he called the girl over.

"Do you know what's taking so long in there?" He nodded toward the workroom.

"I don't know a thing," Patricia said emphatically as she backed away.

Just then, the doors opened. Virginia came out bearing a platter of golden fried chicken. Petey followed with a couple of bowls of something that looked like potatoes and carrots.

"Merry Christmas," Virginia announced. "From Petey and me."

The older man ducked his head in a slight bow and Virginia went to the head table and set down the platter. Then she went over to Colter and looked him in the eye.

"I don't know a thing about frying chicken," she

said. "I'm trying to learn, but what you see here is because of Petey."

"Well, I'm grateful to whoever made it."

"And," Virginia continued, "I don't know how to make soap. Or sew up a dress. Or make bread. I'm willing to learn, but you may as well expect me to be hopeless until I do. I've never churned butter or raised chickens or milked a cow."

Virginia was halfway through her list of what she couldn't do when Colter realized what it meant. At least, what he hoped it meant. "You're going to marry me?"

Colter hadn't meant to say it that way. His words had no grace or beauty to them and Virginia set great store by both those things. But before he could take the words back and put new ones out there, she was answering him.

"It seems so," she said. "If the offer is still open."

"Of course, it's still open," Colter said as he swung Virginia into his arms and lifted her up before bringing her down and kissing her.

Virginia was breathless. Her heart was pounding in her. Her feet were still not touching the floor. And she thought a herd of buffalo had found its way into the building and was stampeding until she realized it was the men stomping their feet on the floor and throwing their hats in the air.

It took a few minutes for everyone to be calm enough to eat, but Virginia wasn't about to let this dinner grow cold. It was their first Christmas together and she knew both she and Colter would remember it forever.

"Everyone may take their places," she said. Which,

of course, was the wrong thing to say because suddenly no one knew where they were supposed to sit.

"The bride needs to sit by the groom," Patricia announced as she pulled two chairs out from the table.

Virginia wasn't sure she could eat, but she felt a definite need to sit. Then Patricia seated Colter on the chair next to Virginia.

"We should visit Denver—or San Francisco," he muttered to her as he reached over and held her hand. "I promise I'll be a good husband. That's it—we'll honeymoon in Paris. I know how you like other places."

The noise faded as Virginia met Colter's eyes.

"We don't need to go anywhere else," Virginia said softly. When had his face grown so dear to her? She smiled at the anxiety she saw. "You and the children. That's all my heart needs."

"I love you, Virginia Parker," Colter said as he leaned over to kiss her.

"And I you," she said just before his lips met hers.

* * * * *

Dear Reader,

By now you probably know I love a Christmas story. Whether it's snow or bells or lights, the sight of Christmas decorations makes me feel festive. Part of the reason is that I take great joy in celebrating a day that brings people around the world (and through time) together to remember one central fact—that God came to earth to show us He loves us.

I hope this book reminds you of that love. During this season, with all the decorations and the sounds of carols, take time to reflect on the reason we even have a day such as this to celebrate together. May you also hear Christmas bells at some point and remember they have been used for generations to remind people of God's church and His love.

If you are feeling lonely during this time of year, find a church to attend where you can share the story of Christmas with others who hold it dear. I pray you have a joy-filled holiday.

And, if you get a chance, I would love to hear from you. You can e-mail me at my website at www.janettronstad.com. Or send me a note in care of the editors at Love Inspired, 195 Broadway, 24th floor, New York, NY 10007.

Sincerely yours,

Janet Tronstad

THE CHRISTMAS SECRET

Sara Mitchell

To all who march to a different drummer
and keep tripping over their feet.
May you learn to hear the divine rhythm of
God's voice, and keep time with Him.

Come to me, all you who are weary and
burdened, and I will give you rest.
—*Matthew* 11:28

Chapter One

Canterbury, Virginia
December 1895

An eye-watering sun beamed from a sky the color of her favorite blue hydrangeas—a deceptive bit of nature hoodwinking housebound humans, whose calendars proclaimed the month December. Shivering, Clara Penrose buried her face in her muffler because the sturdy thermometer she had mounted beside the cottage's door read thirty-six degrees Fahrenheit. The air smelled metallic, with a bite that stung her nostrils as she made her way along the uneven flagstone path toward the garden shed.

For Clara, winter remained a difficult season, despite the determined jollity of Christians preparing throughout the entire month of December for the annual Christmas celebration. This particular Christmas, however, promised to be more than difficult. She tried with little success to convince her racing heart that it was doomed to disappointment, that a woman her age should have outgrown girlish dreams.

Her heart refused to listen to reason.

Congressman—no, now he was *Dr.* Harcourt—was moving to Canterbury. And…if the gossip was true… his wife was dead, and he had never remarried. Nobody knew what he'd done with his life over the past three years, including Clara's brother Albert, who had known Dr. Harcourt when the gentleman was a congressman. Albert might be an annoyingly officious lawyer, and three years earlier he might have bullied Clara into attending that Christmas fete…but if she'd resisted, she never would have met the most fascinating man ever to cross her path.

He won't remember you, Clara, the relentless voice in her head repeated. There had been a crush of guests at Senator Comstock's Annual Christmas Gala, over four hundred of them. Dr. Harcourt had still been a congressman, and couldn't take a step without someone demanding his attention. As for his wife… Clara grimaced. An undeniably stunning beauty, Mrs. Harcourt certainly knew how to draw heads, as well as lop them off: she scarcely acknowledged Clara with a single dismissive glance. The skinny old maid in her four-year-old evening gown was about as memorable as a grain of sand. Her only conversation with Congressman Ethan Harcourt had meant nothing to him, nor had she nurtured—until now—any false expectations. He had been married, he had been kind to a clumsy gawk of a woman, and the connection Clara had briefly enjoyed was the natural consequence of someone not used to such kindness from a man, married or not.

She wished she could remember more details about his wife's tragic death. There had been a scandal—something about a fire, and an affair?

When she reached the pile of leaves heaped at the back of the garden shed she sank down on the rough bench her brother Willie had fashioned the previous summer.

Clearing her throat, she invested as much cheerfulness into her voice as she could muster. "Good afternoon, Methuselah. I trust you're enjoying your hibernation. Sometimes I wish I were a turtle like you, especially this time of year. Hibernation strikes me as one of God's most…tidy inventions. So much easier to crawl into a nice hole and close up inside my shell. Do you realize how many homilies human beings have fashioned around the habits of your species?"

Her cat, NimNuan, his coffee-tipped tail swishing, darted past the bench and pounced upon the leaves.

"Nim, you scalawag!" Laughing, Clara shoved to her feet to scoop up the feline, who instantly draped his forepaws on Clara's shoulders and purred in her face. She hugged him, scratching behind his ear while she scolded. "How many times have I explained to you that you're my very favorite companion? Methuselah's a fixture, not your rival. He's turtled around here at least forty years. Granddaddy used to talk to him when he and Grandmother lived here, you know. Methuselah's the perfect listener—unlike the very demanding puss I'm holding."

Talking to a turtle she couldn't see but knew was there, hidden in those leaves, offered Clara a bridge to a faith she struggled with daily to live. Most times, when her mind pretended she was talking to Methuselah, her spirit understood she was actually baring her heart to God. "So behave yourself," she ordered Nim. "No more pouncing in the leaves."

"Clara!" Her younger sister's voice dimmed the crystalline air, sundering Clara's hope of communion with a hibernating reptile and the Lord. "Where are you? Botheration! Your rosebush is attacking me. Clara!"

"I'm behind the garden shed." Clara set Nim down, inhaled a bracing breath. Nim wisely disappeared around the opposite corner. "At least the rosebush was trying to respect my privacy."

Louise peeked around the corner. "I was afraid of that. You were out here talking to that stupid turtle again. Do you realize how bizarre your habits have become over the past years? Bad enough, moving out of the house to this decrepit little cottage, acting like an eccentric—"

"I'm not in the mood for one of your scolding rants." Clara dusted her gloves and gave her sister a look. "Actually, I'm never in the mood for your scolds, but on this day in particular either tell me what you've come for—or leave me alone to my peculiar habits."

Louise blew out an exasperated breath. "Sometimes I have to agree with Mother. Grandfather never should have encouraged your independent notions by bequeathing you this cottage, along with Grandmother's trust fund. If only you could be more sensitive to how others perceive your—your…"

"Don't spare my feelings, now. We bluestockinged spinsters must develop thick skins."

"Clara." Abruptly Louisa reached for her hands and gave them a quick squeeze. "I'm sorry. I didn't mean to hurt your feelings, thick skin or no." They exchanged relieved smiles, the tension between them fading. "But never mind all that. I came on Mother's behalf, to invite you to dinner Tuesday night. There's to be a guest. Would you like to guess who it is?"

"Ha. That doesn't require guessing. I'm sure it will be Canterbury's new physician and ex-congressman, Dr. Harcourt. Albert's been gloating for a month now."

Louise's face fell, her mouth pursing in an unattractive pout while she studied her sister. "I suppose he has. But I'd never heard of the man until last week. You sound almost as though you know him already."

Clara shrugged. "I give piano lessons to children who gossip more than their parents," she began, picking her way through the words. For some reason, she didn't want to reveal the circumstances of the Christmas Gala three years earlier. Her sister would invest more importance in an insignificant event than prudence dictated. Worse, Clara's rebellious heart might tend to believe it.

She began walking back toward the cottage with her sister. "Since you and Mr. Eppling are engaged, I fail to see why you're so excited over having the town's new physician over for a meal."

"I'm excited," Louise stated with exaggerated patience, "because he's asked Albert about *you.* This morning Bertha brought the children over to visit, and she told me Albert mentioned as much."

"Did Dr. Harcourt mention my name specifically, Louise?"

Her sister ducked her head. "All right, no, he didn't mention your name. He knows Albert has two sisters. Bertha did say Dr. Harcourt said he looked forward to meeting them. I thought—I just thought if you thought he was interested, you'd at least…" Her voice trailed away into a thick silence. "I'm sorry, sister."

Disappointment, sharp and bitter, coated Clara like

sludge. She'd known, she'd *known* her sister's penchant for tweaking the truth, but that downy feather of hope had persisted in tickling her heart anyway. And the rush of memories about her first meeting with Dr. Harcourt buffeted her until her legs all but trembled. *She'd escaped the crush of elderly statesmen plying her with questions and slipped outside, onto a relatively uncrowded corner of a massive stone terrace. Dr. Harcourt had been sitting on a bench, invisible in the shadows until Clara, still night-blind, tripped. Hard arms had materialized out of the darkness, clasped her waist, gently steadied her. They had shared a* conversation, *not merely exchanged pointless social trivia.*

With an effort she focused on her sister. "Louise, I can no more turn myself into a curvaceous, green-eyed, golden-haired girl like you than I can fly to the moon."

"You could stop thinking of yourself as an ugly old stick. Because you're not, Clara. If you'd look through some of the ladies' magazines, let me help you with your hair, you'd be surprised by how pretty you are."

Disconcerted, Clara brushed off some dead leaves clinging to her old corduroy jacket. Pointed advice for the family spinster had evolved into family tradition. With Louise gazing at her with sisterly shrewdness, subtlety was useless. "Louise. Whatever you're thinking, abandon it at once. Please, for my sake, accept that I am content with the lot God has designed for my life. Some people, like the apostle Paul, are not meant for marriage."

"My aunt Mitty! If we're going to quote scripture, then I'll remind you that the Lord also declared it wasn't good for the man He'd just created to be alone."

"Well, that may be so, but at my advanced age of

thirty-one, I'm convinced that God forgot to create the man who would relieve his aloneness with me."

"Perhaps we'll be eating dinner with him Tuesday night."

After Louise left, bearing Clara's reluctant acceptance to put in an appearance ("And whatever you do, please try to dress appropriately for the occasion, just this once."), Clara wandered about the cottage, ruthlessly suppressing the tickling feather of hope. Emily Dickinson should never have written such an evocative poem.

More likely than not, instead of perching on her soul, the feathers would make her sneeze.

On the Sunday morning of his first week as a new resident of the town of Canterbury, Virginia, Ethan Harcourt reluctantly attended the same church as his old friend Albert Penrose, who had also extracted a promise from Ethan to come to dinner at his parents' home on Tuesday. Ethan dreaded the socialization necessary to resurrect not only his former life, but a medical practice. Yet…he craved good friends and food again, he was starving for spiritual sustenance, and he needed to fully embrace what used to be his first calling from God.

Of course, over the past three years he'd fallen back into doctoring in spite of himself, patching up broken miners out west, delivering babies to hardscrabble women, and mopping feverish brows. For two interesting months down in Nevada Territory, his medical skills had kept him alive—a notorious gang of thieves had ambushed the stage he was on. When they saw his doctor's bag, they kidnapped him instead. He spent the next nine weeks patching up gun and knife wounds, and prayed over graves of thieves and murderers with considerably less charity than Jesus had dispensed from the cross. When the gang drank themselves into a stupor one night, Ethan helped himself to a horse and escaped.

The stately little community of Canterbury reminded him of his western Pennsylvania roots, with its neat rows of clapboard cottages and brick homes in Virginia's gently rolling hills and lush woodlands. Despite its proximity to Washington, Canterbury suited him down to the bone. He was weary of roaming the country like a homeless brigand.

Two nights ago he'd finished transforming the first-floor rooms of the rambling old house he'd bought into his medical offices. After this morning's appearance at church, he'd officially be back on public display again. A kernel of dread tickled the back of his throat. Time hurled him backward three years, to the memory of a hotel engulfed in smoke and flames. Thirty-six guests had perished, one of them his wife—found next to the newly elected senator from one of the midwestern states. *Public display...*

His stride slowed as he walked the last block to the church, and he wondered if he would ever be free from his abhorrence of public humiliation. The mysterious letter that had arrived the previous evening hadn't helped:

So…you've returned at last. I knew you couldn't hide forever. How convenient that you've chosen the town of Canterbury.

That was all. Penned with careful precision in plain black ink and plain lettering. No signature and no return address, though the postmark was Washington, D.C.

Ethan spared a few moments puzzling over that note, then tossed it back onto the pile of other welcoming missives. The writer would identify himself eventually; a doctor was almost as public a figure as a congressman. When Ethan made the decision to stop wandering and set down roots again, he'd accepted the associated risks.

All the same, the brief note niggled his mind at odd moments.

When he arrived at the hundred-year-old brick church, the congregation was already singing the second verse of a Christmas carol. Ethan slipped into a pew near the back, beside an elderly couple who gave him their hymnbook.

People rubbed shoulders and shared hymnals in every pew, no doubt because this was the first Sunday in December—Advent, the beginning of the Christmas season. Pine boughs, sprigs of holly and dozens of lighted candles filled the sanctuary with their fragrances. Tensed muscles slowly relaxed as Ethan trained his gaze upon the minister and tried, mostly successfully, to hold bittersweet memories at bay.

The sermon was delivered well, he decided, with enough punch to keep listeners awake without firing off points like a cannonade. Been a long, long time since he sat in a church pew and heard the gospel preached with honesty as well as passion.

"...how we shared in last week's message, the celebration of God's gift of His Son does not always sit well within our private lives. Many of you carry such a heavy sack of burdens you've no room in the inn of your hearts for Jesus. Instead of tidings of great joy, this season prompts naught but despair and resentment and pain. You cannot accept the Almighty's gift, much less present gifts of your own to the Christ child, as did the Magi—the gift of your time, your service. Your very selves. So..." palms planted on the lectern, the minister leaned forward, and a portentous aura filled the church "...how many of you remembered, and brought a symbol of those burdens this week? How many of you have the courage to come forward, leave them at the altar, with the One Who promised to help carry them? Only when you release these burdens can you truly celebrate Christmas."

He spread his robed arms in an inviting gesture. "Come, come, ye faithful yet fearful. Come while the organist plays 'Come, Thou Long-Expected Jesus,' place your symbols in the manger, leave with hope in your hearts, and on Christmas Day, when we sing 'Joy to the World,' the words will resonate with truth...with the birth of your new life in the newborn Christ."

Movement and murmurs rippled through the pews as the organist began to play. Ethan watched, feeling a hollow sense of detachment shadowing his soul again. What would his symbol have been? The wedding ring he'd never been able to throw away? The stiffly formal letter accepting his resignation from Congress? Or perhaps the blank-paged Morocco-leather memorandum still tucked inside his coat pockets that stood for three wasted years wandering about the country in search of a cure for past mistakes?

The elderly couple beside him excused themselves to join the growing stream of people filling the aisles. Ethan slipped out, moving to the back of the church, and watched the progression. The manger rapidly filled with objects. He watched a woman tenderly lay a doll on top of the hay, which was soon covered by a man's shirt…a small string-tied journal…eventually the objects had to be placed around the feet of the manger, spilling across the dais.

"Come, thou long-expected Jesus, born to set Thy people free;
From our sins and fears release us;
Let us find our rest in Thee…"

When the organist launched into the hymn for the fifth time, Ethan's restless gaze fell upon the tall figure of a woman who glided from a side door across to the pile of "burdens." Winter sunlight streamed through the stained-glass windows, highlighting the solemn curve of her cheekbone and a wide unsmiling mouth. Her dark hair was worn in an uncompromising knot on the top of her head. Unlike most of the ladies present, she wore no hat. Something about her struck Ethan as both poignant and proud.

A frisson of memory rippled through his mind.

He knew this woman. Someplace, somewhere, he remembered her. Scalp tingling, he followed her every movement, from the soft swaying of her skirts to the slight tilt of her head when she reached the front of the sanctuary, to the taut line of her spine beneath her gaudy green overblouse.

She laid her object down a little apart from the raggle-taggle mound of other objects. Then, still within an invisible pool of isolation, she melted back into the shadows beyond the sunbeams. The music ceased at last, the minister spoke the benediction, and with the conclusion of the service people gathered around Ethan to speak with him, to shake hands with the stranger.

He smiled and responded politely, all the while keeping the corner of his eye on the woman in green. She wove her way across the sanctuary, and the sting of recognition now prickled Ethan like hundreds of tiny needles. She reminded Ethan of—himself. Acknowledged, but apart. Known by all, understood by none. On the surface, serene and confident.

Her eyes would be deep pools the color of bitter chocolate, a mysterious blend of intelligence and... He blinked, impatient with the nebulous wisps of memory.

"Do you know that young woman?" he asked Otis Skelton, a merry-faced little man who had introduced himself and for some reason refused to budge from Ethan's side. "The one with the dark hair, wearing the bright green overwaist?"

"Ah, she's wearing the green one today, then?" Otis gave a dry laugh. "That would be Miss Clara Penrose, Albert's sister. She's a strange one, right enough. Seeing as how you've only arrived a week ago, might be Albert wanted you to settle in a bit, before he trotted her out your way. He's a good man, is Albert, but his sister has a way that seems to twist his bow tie in a knot."

Albert's sister? A "strange one"? The revelation teased him with an even stronger sense of déjà vu, almost as vexing as a welcome note from someone who hadn't bothered to identify himself. "What do you mean by *strange?*" he asked Otis.

"Well, now." Otis ran a finger around the bow tie strangling his throat, slid a sideways look as though to see who was close enough to overhear, then jerked his chin once.

Seemed Miss Penrose was the family oddity, a public-spirited young female with a mind of her own, smart as a whip but who dressed more like a floozy than an old maid, much to the despair of her elegantly turned-out family. Never married. Nobody quite knew what to do with her.... "Spends her days teaching younguns piano, and doing good works. Myself and the wife, we always had a soft spot for the girl. Brings us vegetables from her garden, fresh-baked bread. I remember one time when she—"

Someone called Otis's name, and with a faint air of wistfulness the man left Ethan's side. Clusters of parishioners still stood about talking, one of the groups including Albert Penrose. Not wanting to intrude, Ethan debated briefly before making his way to the other end of the aisle. If his calculations were correct, when Miss Penrose finished speaking to a pair of fidgety girls, she would have to pass him to reach the door.

Sure enough, after the two girls darted off, Miss Penrose walked toward him, one hand idly brushing over the ends of the pews, her step brisk and her gaze focused inward.

She would have run smack into Ethan if he hadn't pointedly cleared his throat. "Miss Penrose? We haven't officially been introduced, but—"

"Yes, we have." Startled dark brown eyes searched his face with unnerving intensity. A flicker of some deep emotion stirred, then vanished. "Dr. Harcourt, formerly Congressman Harcourt of Pennsylvania." Her voice was a clear contralto, unforgettable. "We met several years ago, at one of those holiday levees in Washington. I don't expect you to remember."

Like the Red Sea, the veil that shrouded Ethan's life parted in another rush of memories, once again sweeping him three years into the past, only this time to a vast terrace behind a mansion filled with people. He'd been sitting in stupefied misery on a garden bench, and a willowy woman dressed in a plain blue gown had materialized out of the night.

"But I do remember, Miss Harcourt." He smiled down into her wary eyes while the tug of that encounter filled the air with the same brilliant colors as the sunlit stained-glass windows. "Back terrace, Senator Comstock's Annual Christmas Fete. I rescued you from a nasty tumble." Without warning his palms tingled from yet another memory—the feel of that stiff, slender waist beneath his gloved fingers.

"Yes. I don't see very well in the dark."

His gaze swept over her with sufficient thoroughness to infuse the pale cheeks with color. "You mentioned as much that night. I escorted you to a patch of moonlight, and we enjoyed gazing at a moon as round and white as a pearl. We...talked."

"I understand you've lost your wife. I'm very sorry."

"Don't be. It was a long time ago."

She flinched at the curt tone, but to his surprise—and relief—did not retreat. "She was...very beautiful."

"You were more honest three years ago," Ethan returned quietly. "Lillian was also shallow and insensitive." Among other, far more reprehensible flaws. "I apologized on her behalf, and you told me not to, that I was not responsible for my wife's lack of manners."

The flush in her cheeks deepened to rose, and her mouth half parted. "I—I— You really do remember. I never expected, I mean there was no reason... There were so many people— *Fiddlefaddle.*" Ethan watched in fascination as her hands clenched into fists, and a vein in her forehead pulsed. Her chin lifted, and before his eyes she transformed from startled doe to a proud lioness on the verge of attack. "This is ridiculous. We shared a brief conversation. That's the end of it. There is no reason to attach any importance to the exchange, Dr. Harcourt."

Lightheartedness, an emotion he almost didn't recognize, sawed at the rusted bars around his heart. "Until a moment ago I would have agreed with you, Miss Penrose. Now... I'm thinking that brief exchange on the terrace might turn out to be one of the most significant in my life."

"Miss Penrose!" A coltish girl of about fifteen bounded up, a mass of curls bouncing around her indignant face. "Molly says you told her she could play 'Jesu, Joy of Man's Desiring' at the recital. I wanted to play that one. I've been practicing...."

"We can continue our conversation Tuesday, over dinner," Ethan murmured. He stepped past Clara and the young girl with a buoyancy he hadn't experienced in, well, longer than he remembered.

Tuesday suddenly promised a lot more than succulent pot roast. A soft chuckle slipped out; Ethan shook his head, then turned his attention to the three sober-suited gentlemen and a plump-cheeked lady who were gathering the last of the "burdens" from the altar. Not until they departed, arms full, did Ethan notice they had missed the object left by Clara Penrose. Keeping one eye on Albert, he strolled over and picked it up—a small pill box holding a dull silver watch charm of... the Capitol Building.

A charm of the Capitol?

He didn't know what precipitated the impulse, but instead of following the gather-uppers and handing over

Miss Penrose's offering, Ethan tucked box and charm inside his vest pocket. When Albert Penrose finally extricated himself from a clutch of parishioners and turned with effusive apologies to Ethan, the same inexplicable impulse restrained him from handing the charm over to Miss Penrose's brother.

She had left this burden at the altar, her private symbolic gesture of renunciation, and Ethan could not betray that privacy, especially to a family member. By confiscating it he had already trespassed enough, though anticipation dulled the sting of guilt.

He hoped that over dinner on Tuesday he would gather more insight into the personality of a woman he suddenly wanted to understand—very much.

Chapter Two

Clara wore her scarlet shirtwaist with her black watered silk evening skirt for the Tuesday dinner with her family. She convinced herself the bold red was her acknowledgment of the holiday season, and when uncertainty wove hairballs she defiantly tied an equally bold red ribbon around her topknot. Then, to prove her nerves weren't strumming over seeing Dr. Harcourt again, she spent half an hour revising her latest treatise on the efficacy of setting aside vast tracts of land for national parks.

As usual, the distraction made her late.

The Penrose family was famous for its hospitality. Though this particular meal was considered a "family" dinner, Louise had reminded her that a half dozen other guests were invited along with Dr. Harcourt. "Don't worry. I've made sure you're seated beside him. But do please try to remember this is a dinner party, not a debate."

Her sister's heavy-handed matchmaking usually elicited a barbed retort on Clara's part. But it was disingenuous to protest when her heart whirled and her mind spun at the prospect of seeing Ethan Harcourt again. She had even made a stab at flirtation, with Nim as her masculine representative. Since the cat already adored her and, being feline, considered himself master of their small domain, the exercise only proved how silly she could be over a man. Pragmatism nagged her to quit weaving dreams out of dandelions.

One puff of reality would blow them away.

When she reached the stately Georgian brick house three blocks from her cottage, her mother was waiting.

"Clara, dear! Late as always, but I'm grateful you've at least— Oh." The flow of words ceased as Mavis Penrose took Clara's hat and cloak. Lips compressing into a straight line, after a final motherly perusal she gestured toward the hallway behind her. "Well, you're here now. Everyone's in the drawing room. You might want to rescue Dr. Harcourt. I'm afraid Patricia Dunwoody's monopolizing his attention."

Patricia Dunwoody, Clara thought, determination faltering. "Where's Willy? He's been panting after her for a year now." The mayor's daughter was a dainty debutante with lustrous black tresses and a helpless air that seemed to attract men the way navy serge attracted cat hair.

"Your brother is amusing himself with Mr. Pate, arguing the opposite political view. Ever since he joined the debating team, he's become almost as obnoxious in his public discourse as you."

"I've trained him well."

Her mother sniffed, but a rueful smile flirted at the corner of her mouth. "All this intellectual energy must be from your father's side of the family. Sometimes I despair of the two of you, at least in a social setting. If only you…" She stopped, waved a graceful hand. "Never mind, let's join everyone before the dinner bell rings."

Clara's first task upon joining the fray in the drawing room was to rescue Mr. Pate. When she waded in, he was thumping his ivory-handled cane on the parquet flooring while he berated her youngest brother.

"…nothing but a glib-tongued young whippersnapper! You listen to a lecture delivered by some musty professor who hasn't left the classroom in forty years, then consider yourself knowledgeable enough to tell me how this country can recover from the Panic?"

Willy grinned down at the elderly gentleman. "Yes, sir." At fourteen, Willy had been a mischievous brat; at twenty-one, his lanky frame might be elegantly draped in a black dinner jacket and striped trousers, but the mischievous brat remained. Clara inserted herself between him and Mr. Pate, one elbow administering a sisterly jab to Willy's ribs. "Welcome home. Still arguing about free silver, are we?"

"Still insist on wearing garish colors, do we?" Willy lifted her hand and gave it an exaggerated kiss. "As always, you brighten the room just by walking into it."

Clara gave his cheek a sisterly pat. "Trifle warm in here, isn't it? May I fetch you a glass of the famous Penrose Christmas punch, Mr. Pate? Mother's given it a new twist this year, adding grated orange peel to the cloves and cinnamon in the cider."

"I'm fine," the man retorted testily. "If I want to be coddled, I'll fetch Mrs. Pate. I'd rather hear your opinion on Secretary of State Olney's accusation that the British violated the Monroe Doctrine in British Guiana."

Across the room, Clara saw Dr. Harcourt say something to Miss Dunwoody, then begin weaving his way through the crowd, directly toward Clara.

Her hands turned damp, and a tight sensation squeezed her middle. "I know England...ah...feels we're overstepping our sovereignty," she began, distracted by the approach of the man who would now be comparing her to Patricia Dunwoody.

"If you want to talk foreign affairs, addressing the problem of Spanish oppression in Cuba is more important, I'd say," Willy put in, his chin jutting.

"Whole world's headed for a fiery destruction," Mr. Pate grumbled. He peered around Clara. "Dr. Harcourt. You're looking fit as a fiddler's fiddle tonight, young man. And that tonic you insisted I take seems to be doing the trick. Mrs. Pate won't let me hear the end of it, I tell you."

"Glad to hear it. Are you taking those daily walks I mentioned?" Tall and imposing in his evening wear, the town's new physician ran an alert gaze over Mr. Pate before turning to Clara and wishing her a pleasant evening. Instead of replying in kind, Clara's throat locked, and every polite social response drummed into all Penrose children from the time they could sip cider from a cup vanished in a fog of uncertainty.

Willy was staring at her strangely. Worse, Dr. Harcourt looked as though he were—bored? Amused? Contemptuous?

"No need to bother spouting pleasantries with this young woman," Mr. Pate broke the awkward silence. "Don't know if you've noticed, Doctor, but Miss Penrose here's possessed of a mighty adroit mind. In fact, last time I was here she trounced me at a game of chess."

"Dr. Harcourt." Patricia Dunwoody floated up beside

him, a vision in peach-colored silk and lace, her shining ebony tresses artfully piled in cascades of ringlets interwoven with strings of seed pearls. "I've come to rescue you."

"From what?" Willy challenged.

"From you and your sister," Patricia returned, smiling a white-toothed smile as sincere as a panhandler's. "The two of you do like to go on and on, about matters much too serious for a dinner party." She turned back to Dr. Harcourt. "I'd very much like to finish telling you about the Christmas Festival this coming Saturday. I'm sure you're used to fancy galas, having been a congressman, but we acquit ourselves quite adequately here in Canterbury. Miss Penrose and I are on the planning committee, of course." She laughed lightly. "It's quite the battleground on occasion."

Clara exchanged glances with Willy, and wondered if her own emotions were as easy to read as her youngest brother's. *She's not worth it,* she longed to warn him, love and the instinct to protect finally unlocking her throat. "My brother and I believe God endowed human beings with the ability to think, and to make reasoned decisions. We enjoy lively debates, even when it's over a seemingly simple issue, such as whether to include Sousa and Stephen Foster melodies along with Christmas carols at the town's annual Christmas Festival, in an effort to allow unbelievers as well as believers to feel that they're part of the community. I love Christmas carols, but I'm also partial to a lively march or a nostalgic folk melody."

"Clara, really, the matter was settled weeks ago!" Patricia glanced up at Dr. Harcourt. "Do you see what I mean? She's always so serious, one can't enjoy a simple tête-à-tête without Clara Penrose turning it into a verbal jousting match. Besides which," she added, "the committee agreed with me. Sousa and Foster are more suitable for the Fourth of July, not Christmas. How like you, to keep badgering an issue when you've already lost."

Losing did not necessarily equate to being wrong, Clara almost whipped out—except she would only prove Patricia's point. Stung, she lifted her chin and forced her lips to curl up in a smile. The couple looked good together, Ethan Harcourt's restrained virility the perfect foil for Patricia's dainty femininity. Clara might have been whisked backward to Senator Comstock's party, when Dr. Harcourt's wife stood impatiently beside her husband, her gaze passing through Clara as though she were invisible. Which was worse, she wondered bleakly—invisibility or condescension?

Why did beauty always win over intellect? "Willy, why don't you and I go find Albert?" She finally patched words together to form a sentence. "I haven't been able to annoy him in almost a week now. How about you?"

Willy managed a laugh. "I told him just last night I always thought the word *pettifogger* was coined because lawyers fog the facts with petty notions. I annoyed him just fine then, but I'm always open for more opportunities."

Ethan Harcourt emitted a deep-throated chuckle that caused Clara to gape at him in astonishment. "No wonder Albert warned me about you," he told Willy. "Frankly, I think I might prescribe a daily dose of brother *and* sister."

His eyes twinkled down at Clara, and for the first time she noticed their color—green, with flecks of amber when they twinkled. Surrounded by dense black eyelashes, and attractive laugh lines at the corners...

Willy loudly cleared his throat. "I beg your pardon," she mumbled. Her cheeks burned like chilblained skin. "I'm afraid I didn't catch that."

"I said," Dr. Harcourt responded congenially, "your older brother's a good friend and a conscientious attorney, but—" He stepped close enough for his coat sleeve to brush against Clara's shoulder, and finished in a conspiratorial whisper, "I'm afraid Albert's a bit stuffy, isn't he?"

Overhearing, Willy grinned. "Like the moose head hanging in Father's study. Well, doc, since you brought it up, I'll go administer another dose. Tell you what, Miss Dunwoody, how about if you join me? You can make sure I don't slip up and administer an *over*dose."

"I need to speak to your father about a, ah, matter," Mr. Pate announced. Cane thumping, he effectively herded Patricia and Willy along ahead of him, Patricia with a backward look of ill-concealed vexation, Willy with an irrepressible smirk.

Clara and Dr. Harcourt were alone.

"Smile, Miss Penrose," he commanded her softly. "And stop comparing yourself to Patricia Dunwoody."

"How did you—" Clara bit her lip, then gave up and allowed a pent-up sigh to escape. "It's an exercise in futility, at any rate, isn't it? Comparing oneself to another person?"

"Yes, but I've done so myself," Dr. Harcourt admitted. "Usually to my disadvantage...except for the time when I was a reluctant member of a gang of outlaws."

"Are you trying to divert me from wallowing in self-pity, Dr. Harcourt?"

"Absolutely, Miss Penrose. From personal as well as professional experience, I guarantee that self-pity is not conducive to good health." His expression turned reflective. "You have no need for such feelings toward yourself, you know."

There it came again, that disorienting sensation of being flung into dizzying mist. She fiddled with the ruffles on her basque, stalling, then gave herself an impatient mental pinch. "Do you talk with such familiarity to everyone you meet, Dr. Harcourt?" The breathlessness in her voice made her wince.

"Not for a very long time, Miss Penrose." The melodic tinkling of the dinner bell sounded behind them. He offered his arm, and after a panicked internal skirmish Clara laid her hand on it. "I'll share some particulars over the meal, if you like. I've had it on good authority that you're to be my dinner partner."

"My younger sister, Louise." Clara sighed. "I'm sorry. My family is famous for many admirable traits, but subtlety is not one of them. I'm their thorn in the flesh, a spinster of independent means who scribbles prose nobody reads. They all think if they could procure a hus—"

"You're a writer, Miss Penrose?"

Loose-tongued, empty-headed…*twit*. Nobody outside her immediate family knew about her secret pastime. "Not really. Please forget I said that. I'd really rather hear about that band of outlaws you mentioned."

For some reason the twinkling green eyes had turned frozen as hoarfrost and his expression— No. She realized as she pondered his face that it was wiped clean of any expression at all. "Dr. Harcourt?"

"Mmm? Oh, sorry." With a dismissive headshake

he resumed speaking, and the skittish fingers scraping down her spine disappeared. "The outlaws. Yes. As Albert may have told you, for the past several years I've been wandering about out west. Last summer I was on a stage, bound for some tumbleweed town in the Nevada Territory. Gang of bandits ambushed us. Killed the drivers, threw open the doors and started on the passengers—an old miner, seventy-four years old, on his way to visit grandchildren he'd never seen…a young couple from Missouri. Homesteaders—they shot them dead, every one."

The quiet words spoke of brutality and horror, of actions inflicted by humans upon fellow human beings. "I read a lot," Clara murmured, self-consciously glancing around the room. In its hundred-year history, this dignified old Virginia home had survived war, financial chaos and illness, yet somehow retained its atmosphere of Christian charity and decency. "I've seen greed. I've witnessed poverty and hopelessness and helplessness in tenement housing. But I've never witnessed cold-blooded murder. I won't even try to pretend to understand." Dr. Harcourt's story reminded Clara anew of her privileged circumstances, rekindling the lifelong tussle between pride and inadequacy. "Why didn't they kill you as well?"

"I happened to be holding my doctor's bag on my lap. I was searching through it for some ginger drops for the young woman, who was feeling ill. One of the brigands realized the significance of that black satchel. Their leader had been shot a week earlier, so they kidnapped me. If he died, they promised after I dug his grave they'd hang me, and leave my body for the buzzards." He paused, adding dryly, "According to the U.S.

Census, as of 1890, the Western frontier no longer existed. Someone forgot to tell those villains."

"Dr. Harcourt." Her mother spoke from the entry to the dining room, "I see you've found my older daughter. I trust she'll allow you to enjoy the meal, and not try to monopolize the conversation."

In her pearl-gray evening gown, Mavis Penrose epitomized the Penrose heritage. The diamond pendant she'd received for her sixtieth birthday gleamed against the *poult-de-soie* fabric; matching earrings—an anniversary gift—perfectly complemented her silvery-blond hair. How could this vision of sophisticated elegance inhabit the same world as a band of soulless murderers?

Mavis pointedly cleared her throat, and with a start Clara pulled herself together. "I'll try to be on my best behavior," she promised. "Confine my remarks strictly to the weather."

"Clara, really..."

"I'm afraid I'm the one who has been monopolizing the conversation," Dr. Harcourt interposed with the suavity of a seasoned diplomat. "We were reminiscing about old times."

Her mother arched one eyebrow. "I see. Well. The holiday season does seem to evoke feelings of nostalgia, does it not? I hope you enjoy the decorations as well as the meal, Dr. Harcourt." With a final lingering glance she turned to a sprightly couple in their seventies whose property abutted the Penroses'.

"Mother loves to decorate for holidays," Clara murmured as everyone was seated. She gestured to the centerpiece—a footed silver bowl brimming with fruit, sprigs of holly and gilded pinecones, all trimmed with red ribbon streamers which drifted around a matched pair of silver candlesticks. "Every Sunday in December she creates a new centerpiece for the dining-room table. The one for Christmas Day is the most extravagant. Some years ago a ladies' magazine wrote an article about them. Ever since then the centerpieces have grown more elaborate and outlandish."

"Did you notice that the ribbons match the one in your hair?"

Clara made a production out of arranging the lace-edged napkin in her lap. Her appearance had never been compared to the centerpiece on a dining-room table, particularly one in which her mother had invested weeks of preparation. "It wasn't deliberate. Are you still seeking to divert me from self-pity? If so, I'd rather hear more about your saga with outlaws."

Unexpectedly he laughed, a rich, deep sound that attracted attention from the entire assembly of twenty-four guests. Clara's father immediately reclaimed control with an authoritative announcement that everyone bow their heads for the blessing. But in the respectful silence that descended before he spoke, Dr. Harcourt leaned sideways, toward Clara. "I can see," he whispered next to her ear, "why you're able to beat Mr. Pate in a game of chess."

So while her father thanked the Lord for His bounty and the food they were about to receive, Clara offered a quiet addendum, asking God to protect her heart from a man who was dangerously close to stealing it completely.

Chapter Three

That night Ethan had trouble falling asleep. The quantity and quality of the four-course meal he had consumed at the Penrose home was only partially to blame. At three o'clock in the morning, with a stifled imprecation he threw aside the covers, snatched on a Turkish smoking jacket foisted upon him by a grateful saloon girl whose life he had saved in Leadville, Colorado, and stalked down the hallway to his study.

After dropping down in the creaky old rocking chair in front of his desk, he turned on the banker's lamp, then moodily rocked for several moments while he contemplated a small locked drawer. Finally, his gut knotting, he unlocked the drawer and retrieved two envelopes and read the notes yet again. But no definitive proof that Clara Penrose was *not* the author revealed itself.

Clara Penrose, who liked to write yet who didn't want anybody to know she…"scribbled prose."

Clara Penrose, whose relations with her family contained inexplicable overtones of disapproval.

The rocker groaned as Ethan leaned back, his hands absently shuffling the notes. All sorts of welcoming missives had been delivered over the past weeks, some several pages long, others merely a line or two of greeting—"looking forward to meeting you," "relieved another physician available to help old Doctor Witherspoon," etcetera, etcetera. But at least the senders signed their names. All right, yes, his reaction to these anonymous notes stemmed from an admitted hypersensitivity to intrigue of any sort. Between backdoor politics and an adulterous wife, Ethan had choked down a bellyful of human deceit. If the stupid notes had been signed, he wouldn't be sitting here at three o'clock in the morning, stewing over the motives, their mysterious tone or the sender.

Which brought him full circle back to Clara Penrose.

After running a weary hand around the back of his neck, Ethan sat forward, snagged a magnifying glass and spread the sheets across the desk.

So you've returned at last. I knew you couldn't hide forever. How convenient, to have chosen the town of Canterbury.

The letters were written with a steady hand and a good pen. No blobs of ink, no dribbles or scratched-out misspellings.

The second one, which he'd found tucked inside the curved brass handle on his front door when he returned home this evening, was shorter, only a single line:

This Christmas will be one you'll never forget.

Was the ink darker, were the letters broader? Or was his mind manufacturing the threat?

Ethan was no detective; based upon the quality of the stationery and the cryptic messages, however, he felt confident they'd been written by a woman.

Clara Penrose, the elderly Mr. Pate told him, was possessed of a fine mind, which Ethan had seen for himself during the course of the evening.

Well, she did have a fine mind, a mind sharp enough to win at chess and carry on intelligent conversation. But secretive? Devious? A short laugh rumbled in his chest. A woman who wore a scarlet overblouse to a dinner party could not be accused of subtlety, much less deviousness...unless her design had been to capture Ethan's attention.

Like writing anonymous letters.

Of course, over the past week he'd learned that Clara's love of bright colors and indifference to fashion was the bane of her family. Clara dressed to please herself, not others. It would be the height of arrogance for Ethan to assume her eye-popping attire had been designed solely to attract his attention.

Clara Penrose was not Lillian, he reminded himself. She was not the sort of woman who would stoop to subterfuge, who would— With a snort of disgust Ethan sat up straight. All women resorted to subterfuge when it came to men. He had learned that dismal truth through the crucible of humiliation.

And yet... With a groan he propped his elbows on the desktop and rested his head in his hands.

The Clara Penrose he'd met three years earlier had been different from any woman he'd ever known. Forthright in manner and word, she had also projected an aura of uncertainty that appealed to every one of Ethan's chivalrous instincts. Unlike tonight's, three years earlier her evening costume had been forgettable, drab and dark. If she hadn't tripped over his feet he might never have known she existed at all. Lillian, he remembered in a sharp stab of recall, had tossed out some contemptuous remarks, though her character assessments tended more toward character assassination.

Within the quiet yellow lamplight more memories sprang forth, as vivid as they were painful.

"You always were a stick, preaching compassion and common sense, when if you possessed an iota of either you'd tell Albert Penrose he should have left his sister at home, knitting socks for orphans. She's pathetic, Ethan."

"The woman I chatted with on the veranda is far from pathetic, Lillian. On the contrary, I found her well-spoken, with a rare sense of humor. You could learn a thing or two."

"I've found a much more agreeable sort to teach me a thing or two." With a final flick of a glance that had the power to break a bone, Lillian strolled off into the crowd, boldly linking arms with the man who burned to death with her forty-eight hours later.

If it weren't for the two notes, Ethan might have thanked God for resurrecting the memory of his first encounter with Clara Penrose, reminding him that something good had happened that bitter night.

All right, these days he was a bit rusty on thanking God for anything. He'd strayed from his faith, not renouncing it, but certainly not living it. Ethan hadn't felt much like *living* for a long time…until Albert had convinced him to settle in Canterbury, and re-establish a medical practice. Until he'd met Clara again.

If he hadn't found the second letter stuck in the door

handle, Ethan had been planning to intensify the flirtation he'd initiated at dinner.

Admit it, man. You enjoyed the evening. Despite her own heavy-handed attempts to return his flirtation, he enjoyed Clara Penrose's company. Tonight he had discovered another side of this fascinating woman, one he would not have expected—in her own milieu, she was a social lioness. Regardless of her family's ill-concealed disapproval, Clara Penrose transformed dull dinner chit-chat into a broad range of discussions that commanded the respect—and participation—of every guest at the table within hearing distance.

All right, so he enjoyed her company, and admired her. Didn't mean he was planning to offer a proposal of marriage.

Ethan's hand closed in a fist.

He despised the needy part of his heart Lillian hadn't succeeded in killing, the part stubbornly tempted to risk that bond of connection again.

Eventually fatigue coated his brain; he fumbled the notes back into their envelopes and relocked them inside the drawer. Either the notes were innocent, or they were threats. Eventually he would discover which and who. For now, he was finally too spent to care.

The wall telephone in the hallway rent the silence before he reached his bedroom. "Dr. Harcourt?" The operator's tinny voice was threaded with urgency. "Mrs. Brown's gone into labor, and Mr. Brown told me to tell you the pains are three minutes apart."

"I'll be there in twenty minutes."

In an instant his exhausted mind clicked into place; in eight minutes he was on the way, all thoughts of Clara Penrose and mysterious notes banished.

* * *

The following Saturday a snow squall dusted Canterbury with two inches of powder-fine flakes, then blew out to sea. Distracted, for most of the day Clara flitted around the cottage, baking pies in the kitchen, tying red ribbons around white peppermint sticks and cutting out the last of the paper bells to hang around the Meeting Hall for the Annual Christmas Festival.

Sometime in midafternoon her best friend Eleanor Woodson arrived to help load everything into baskets.

"Brr! It's nippy outside. Good thing this snowstorm seems to have passed. Maybe we should have the Christmas Festival in September instead." She glanced around the parlor, her merry brown eyes widening. "For heaven's sake, Clara. Are we having it here instead?" Shaking her head, she turned to give Clara a brisk hug. "You do realize you're supposed to look like an upstanding member of Canterbury's finest families, not the local washerwoman?"

"I still have time to change. I've spent most of the day in the kitchen. Mrs. Brown's baby came a week early, and her mother couldn't make the pies she promised." Dr. Harcourt had performed the delivery, which from the little bit Clara gleaned had been a difficult one. CoraMae Brown and her baby daughter were alive only through the skill of the attending physician. Ethan Harcourt, it seemed, was fast replacing Clara Penrose as the favorite subject of Canterbury conversations.

Clara gratefully ceded him the honor. She was befuddled, however, over the discovery that her heart gave a little jump every time Ethan's name was mentioned. Best not mention that weakness to Eleanor. "I volunteered to make the pies," she explained. "I don't have a husband or children."

"Spinsters are so convenient to have around, aren't we?" Unrepentantly plump, cheerfully accepting of her status, Eleanor maneuvered her way around a stack of evergreens woven into long ropes, pausing by the chair to give Nim a pat. "You do realize we're society's slaves, relegated to any and every task nobody else wants to do?"

"There's not enough time to engage in one of our discussions, Eleanor. Frankly, I'm too weary to care one way or the other."

"What?" Eleanor charged back across the room, her heavy serge skirt hem narrowly missing a stack of cookie tins. "Clara? Are you ill? No, of course not. You're never ill. Wait…oh, no. Tell me what I've been hearing isn't true."

Clara offered a vague smile. "There's always gossip. Some of it might actually be true. Um…if I'm going to make myself presentable enough to prevent more of it, would you mind organizing everything? Everything is labeled, decorations are all on the sofa or stacked here on the hall tree, except for those tins full of gingerbread men. I'd just brought them out when you arrived. The rest of the food is in the kitchen by the picnic baskets. Gifts for the orphanage children are by the fireplace. Willy's supposed to be here at five to be our pack mule, but if you—"

"As usual, Willy's late. It's five-twenty, Clara."

Clara threw one appalled look at the prosaically ticking wall clock, then fled toward her bedroom with Eleanor jabbering at her heels.

"Bathe your face and hands in scented rosewater,

you'll feel better and smell clean even if you're not. I'll weave a sprig of holly in your hair. Why don't you wear your red overwaist?"

"I wore it for dinner on Tuesday." Stupid mistake, one she wouldn't make again. If she'd been thinking properly instead of like a besotted schoolgirl she would have saved the red for tonight. "The green will do. No—wait. When Louise dropped by yesterday, she mentioned something about leaving me a dress. I was up to my elbows in flour at the time, and haven't bothered to look. If she did what she threatened, a totally unsuitable gown, dripping with geegaws and ruffles and lace—" something Louise herself preferred "—will be in my wardrobe."

"She can't help it, Clara. Louise has succumbed to the concept of femininity preached in *Godey's Lady's Book,* in part because she's undeniably lovely."

"I know. Everyone loves my youngest sister." Perhaps someday the thorn of wistfulness would not jab so deep.

"Pooh! Half of those everyones prefers stimulating conversations and crowd around you. I'm sorry I missed dinner at your home the other night." A good friend, Eleanor always knew when to change the subject. "Seems I missed more than a good meal and your mother's decorations. What did she do this year?"

"Gilded fruit and pinecones, trimmed in red ribbons." And Dr. Harcourt had told her that her hair ribbon matched the table decorations.

Eleanor followed Clara over to the dressing table and unfastened buttons while Clara tugged pins out of her hair. "Well, underneath the scent of gingerbread your hair still smells clean, at least. Gracious, you have a lot of it." She shoved the unpinned tresses over Clara's shoulder. "No wonder you just stuff it up in a bun. Myself, I'd hate to deal with your horse's mane." Two years earlier, much to her old-fashioned parents' outrage, Eleanor had cut off her baby-fine hair. Now it framed her face in silky ringlets that scarcely covered her ears. "There. All unbuttoned. I'll find the dress, and you tell me about the dashing Dr. Harcourt."

Clara had been waiting for it, and barely flinched. "There's nothing to tell. He came, Louise contrived for us to be dinner partners and, yes, he's a charming gentleman who can hold his own in a conversation. One would expect as much, him having been a congressman."

Eleanor made a rude sound. "You can't do a Methuselah with me, Clara. You may enjoy your reputation as Canterbury's most colorful maiden lady, but I'm the one who knows every jot and tittle about every soul. And, dear one, I've learned from no less than five individuals that Dr. Ethan Harcourt spent most of Tuesday evening watching you. He even, I understand on good authority, leaned close enough on a couple of noticeable occasions that you couldn't pass a hairpin between the two of you."

She plucked an errant pin from Clara's hair, dropped it into the china jar on the dresser. "Besides which, the moment I mentioned his name you colored up like a tea rose. Clara Penrose, please tell me you haven't gone and allowed your heart to sweep away all your common sense. Look at us! We're never going to have husbands, nor should we even want them. You own this charming cottage, and when my parents are gone, I'll own Tavistock Farm and, by jingo, I'll turn it back into a prosperous one."

By jingo? "You've been attending too many lectures, Eleanor." Unsettled, Clara walked over and flung open the old oak wardrobe. Sure enough, a flowing gown of dark blue watered silk hung on a padded hanger. Two wide bands of lace decorated the bodice, overlaid by a strip of velvet ribbon. Surprised, Clara lifted it out of the wardrobe and carried it over to her bed. "Shoo, Nim." With absentminded gentleness she lifted the cat off the counterpane, hugged him a moment, then placed him on the floor.

"Well," Eleanor admitted, "for once I think your sister matched the dress to you, instead of herself."

Nerves made her fingers tremble as Clara lightly stroked the velvet bow set at the waist. "Yes. She did. It's a lovely gown. But all the lovely gowns in the world aren't going to transform me into a vision of grace and sweetness."

"I hope not! The world would be a dull place without you, Clara."

A thunderous knocking sounded on the front door, followed by the sound of Willy's voice.

"I'll go help your brother," Eleanor said. "Pull yourself together. And if you have to wear a corset with that gown, whatever you do keep the stays loose so you can breathe."

She would breathe just fine, Clara muttered to herself, if Dr. Harcourt stayed away from her.

Chapter Four

He was enjoying himself, Ethan realized with a seismic internal shock as he strolled among the townsfolk at the drafty lodge hall. Red and green crepe ribbons draped from the ceiling, evergreens filled the window ledges and the band dutifully produced joyful tidings of the newborn King of Kings. Hundreds of paper cutouts in the shape of bells dangled…everywhere.

Clara, he had learned, was responsible for the bells, not to mention half the baked goods and the Christmas-stocking charity bazaar in one corner to raise money for an orphanage.

"Good to see you, Dr. Harcourt. Heard you were a mighty fine replacement for old Doc Witherspoon. Say…" the gentleman pumping his hand leaned closer "…I've got a small matter to ask you about. Won't take but a second…"

Ethan knew better than to succumb. "A good physician never takes 'just a second.' Come by my office, and we'll take it from there. Hours are daily nine until six, except for Tuesday, when I'm off at noon." Giving the man a final warm handshake, Ethan turned to compliment the mayor's wife on her eggnog.

Over the course of the evening he caught glimpses of Clara, but after three hours he had still found no opportunity to speak directly to her. Either she was bustling around displays, ladling punch and slicing pies, or surrounded by a mostly male crowd, talking animatedly in loud voices. All Ethan glimpsed was her head, with her hair confined in its severe bun.

Eventually he worked his way over to a long row of tables that overflowed with gifts and toys peeping from the top of a bulging red flannel sack. Momentarily alone, Clara seemed to be counting—Ethan watched her lips moving silently as she ticked off numbers with her fingers. Above a flushed face, beads of perspiration slid along her temples. Her ears, Ethan noted, were free of earrings, offering a tantalizing view for any male astute enough to give them a closer inspection. Delicate and pale pink, they were, with a strand of rich brown hair dangling around the left one. Ethan clenched his hands against a tug of yearning strong enough to tempt him to do something too risky to contemplate.

Before he succumbed to her lures, Ethan moved until he stood directly in front of her, his back to the room. "Well, Miss Penrose. You're a popular and busy lady. I was losing hope of enjoying another conversation together."

Her head jerked up, and a plethora of emotions chased across her face. "Dr. Harcourt."

"May I say you look quite fetching this evening?"

"Why ask permission when you've already said it?" She turned scarlet, and bent her head to straighten one of the huge red velvet ribbons fastened to the table's edge. "But...thank you. You should compliment Louise. She's responsible for my costume."

"You're the one wearing it." He'd learned that any compliment, however deft, flustered her, so Ethan changed the subject. "Charming party. I like Canterbury very much, and you've done a wonderful job with this Christmas Festival. I think everyone in town is in attendance."

"Except for the Browns. I heard about the delivery. You saved Mrs. Brown's life, and the baby's. Albert was right. You're a wonderful doctor, and everybody I've talked to is mighty glad to have you hang your shingle outside old Mr. McLean's house."

Unlike Clara, instead of shyness Ethan tended to respond to compliments with suspicion, particularly ones proffered by women. On the other hand, Clara might simply be telling him the truth. Weary of the incessant internal battle, he shrugged. "Most of the time I think God is the primary healer. Good doctors just offer a bit of assistance." Bad ones, on the other hand, usually ushered their patients along to the pearly gates, and blamed God's will for the patient's demise.

"A humble attitude in a physician. But if everyone left the healing up to God, you'd soon be out a medical practice."

He studied her curiously. "You sound more like a skeptic than a believer, Miss Penrose."

"Only occasionally, Dr. Harcourt. I no longer blindly believe anymore. No matter how hard you pray for healing, people die. No matter how faithfully you follow the tenets of your faith, eventually you'll feel..." she hesitated, then looked him in the eye "...betrayed, or the fool."

"Mmm. It's a tightrope, isn't it—trying to find a healthy balance between life's cruelties and faith? Jesus was the Great Physician, but even He didn't heal everyone." He paused. "My early years as a doctor, back in Pennsylvania, I struggled a lot, especially with cases where neither prayer nor all a physician's skill reversed an inevitable course."

Clara was looking at him strangely. She opened her mouth, shut it, then shook her head as she gestured toward the room behind them. "This is much too serious a conversation for the occasion. But... I wouldn't mind pursuing the topic, some other time." Her next words emerged far more rapidly. "When the band starts playing 'O Come Little Children,' Reverend Miggs brings the children in through the front door, and St. Nicholas will arrive through the back door, to dispense these gifts to all our orphaned little ones. It's loud and confusing and great fun. I...ah... I need to finish counting these gifts, make sure we have enough to go around."

Ethan nodded. "I'll help." Without giving her an option to refuse, he strode around behind the table to join her. Warning bells clanged in his head, but he couldn't ignore this compulsive need, a need that intensified with every encounter. He wanted to find out who had betrayed *her,* and whether her life was fueled by courage—or a bitterness tightly restrained beneath a personality that, if pushed beyond measure, would erupt, destroying everyone in its path.

Like Lillian.

Stubbornly he reached for one of the wrapped boxes. "Where did you leave off?"

For several moments they worked without speaking, until the awkwardness between them gradually settled into comfortable congeniality. Occasionally they exchanged pleasantries with passersby, and one time Ethan even caught Clara humming beneath her breath. The blue gown flattered her, he thought, casting a surreptitious appraisal over it as he handed her the last gift to stack around St. Nick's sack of treasures. She was not a beautiful woman, nor would she command instant attention in a crowded room. But the more he was around her, the more he wanted to know about those contrary flashes of wistfulness that clashed with the sharp-edged wit, and blunted the edge of bitterness she'd let slip earlier.

"What do *you* want for Christmas?" he inquired casually just as she intercepted a young boy dressed from head to toe in Scottish plaid, complete with Tam o' Shanter, as the sprout sidled around the table.

"You know better, Charlie," she scolded the child with a smile. "These gifts are for boys and girls at the Home—those with no families. You're helping St. Nicholas hand them out this year, aren't you?"

"Yes, ma'am. I was…um… I just wanted to see…"

"Never mind, Charlie. Here." Clara produced a peppermint stick tied with a red ribbon, and winked at him. "Don't tell anyone where you got this." Grinning, the boy departed, and she turned back to Ethan. "What were you saying?"

"I asked what you wanted for Christmas."

Bewilderment flickered across her face. "What *I* want?" she repeated, shaking her head. "Why would you ask? I'm not a child, expecting a stocking full of goodies to magically appear Christmas morning."

Ethan glanced around; the orphans had arrived, and the din practically set Clara's paper cutout bells to ringing. Several adults herded the children into place while everyone's attention focused on the door at the end of the hall, where old Vladimir Cherkorski, the town blacksmith, would momentarily appear. Clara promised Ethan the blacksmith would look the spitting image of the Santa cartoonist Thomas Nast first created for *Harper's Weekly,* during the War Between the States. After Vladimir and the town children handed toys out to the orphans, he would recite *'Twas the Night Before Christmas* in a splendid bass voice.

For the Christmas Eve pageant in the town square, however, Vladimir played the part of Joseph. "A lovely harmonious blend of faith and tradition," Clara finished before adding with a twinkle in her solemn eyes that "Most of the children here believe Santa Claus speaks with a Polish accent."

She needed to smile with her eyes more often.

Ethan leaned close, his lips almost brushing the delicate ear. "You're wonderful at giving to others, Clara. But have you ever stopped to consider that an equally significant portion of the Christmas message is learning how to receive?"

To his astonishment she flicked him a raw look bristling with hurt, then half turned her head to stare blindly across the room. "Too much is made of gift-giving. The custom may have originated from those gifts the Magi offered the Christ Child, but it seems to me that every year more attention is focused on presents than on Jesus's birth." Abruptly she hugged her narrow waist. "I beg your pardon." One hand briefly fluttered toward the bulging sack. "Considering what I'm—what we're doing at the moment, you must think me the worst of hypocrites."

The door at the end of the hall burst open, cheers and delighted shrieks erupting as a great hulk of a man dressed in cherry red, with a flowing white beard, ho-ho-hoed his way into the room.

Clara's hand, Ethan noticed, had balled into a white-knuckled fist that pressed against the midnight-blue velvet bow at her waist. Turning slightly to screen his actions, Ethan reached for that fist, cupped the chilly curled fingers inside his. "I think a lot of things about you, Clara Penrose." He ran his thumb over her knuckles, then lifted his other hand to prise her fist open, gently spreading the cold fingers across his palm. "But a hypocrite is not one of them. You do have more facets than a prism, so what I'm thinking is that I want to see every one of them in the sunlight."

"There's nothing colorful about me, other than my choice of attire. I can't imagine why you'd think otherwise." Her fingers trembled. Guileless brown eyes reflected honest confusion.

"I don't understand all the whys," Ethan admitted honestly. "And I know neither of us is ready for me to admit this." She did not return his crooked smile, nor even blink. He resumed stroking the trembling fingers because he couldn't quell the need to soothe. "When I look at you I see a woman of extraordinary strengths, but I also see questions and loneliness and...well, something that strikes a chord inside me. I see a reflection of myself." He no doubt sounded idiotic, and if she told him so he'd no one but himself to blame.

Instead she stared at him, looking both confused and sympathetic.

The noisy mass of humanity would be upon them in less than ten seconds. Ethan gently squeezed her hand, then with a lingering caress slid his fingers free. "Time to be Santa's helpers. But we will definitely continue our discussion later."

"You might discover that familiarity breeds contempt, Dr. Harcourt."

"Ah. Since you're familiar with Aesop and his fables," Ethan replied, "perhaps you recall his observation that it is not only fine feathers that make fine birds."

Chapter Five

What to do, what to do? Clara spent most of the Sunday service alternatively trying to determine how to respond if Ethan approached her after church, or how to approach him herself if he didn't. Frequent mental whacks of self-disgust could not discipline the tenor of her woefully girlish dreaming.

The previous Sunday, heeding Reverend Miggs's sermon, she had renounced her prideful longing to be Someone of Significance—grand hostess for a literary group, or the benefactress of a much respected Washington philanthropic organization—endeavors suitable for the eldest daughter of Clarence Penrose. The family old maid. Until today, that solitary walk up to the dais with the little silver charm of the Capitol Building clutched in her hand had been one of the most painful experiences of Clara's life. But now... *Lord? You must know I never intended to cultivate a prideful heart, or a silly one.* Had she unwittingly become a coward as well, unable to admit her attraction for a gentleman?

She should write an article about it: "Death of a Spinster's Sensibilities."

No, what she should do was focus on *worship,* set her mind and heart on things above. On the moment in time when the course of history changed forever because God transformed Himself into flesh, and moved among the flawed human creatures with whom He longed to connect.

People constantly hovered around Dr. Harcourt, vying for his attention. Not only was Ethan Harcourt an attractive, erudite, respected man—he had a past. Thus, being a widower of marriageable age, a former congressman *and* the town's physician, every single female in Canterbury, from Clara's giddy piano students to several widows in their early forties, fluttered about him in hopes of making a favorable impression. *You're just another flutterer, Clara.* Last night signified nothing—he was merely being courteous, helpful.

Patricia Dunwoody had twice now inveigled his presence for tea. "He was quite impressed with our Festival, and made a point of complimenting me on the smoothness of the arrangements," she preened before the service. "By the way, Clara…a teensy bit of advice? Last night, I couldn't help but notice your attempt to monopolize his attention, when Vladimir was giving out gifts to the orphans. Nothing annoys a gentleman more…"

Her friend Eleanor was probably right. The prospect of courtship rendered all participants desperate, or diabolical. "So you need to watch yourself with this one, Clara. All you're doing is making yourself miserable. Life's too short to squander on a man." For all her cheerful demeanor, Eleanor tended to prefer persimmons to plums, and pragmatism over romance.

The congregation rose to sing "Break Forth O Beauteous Heavenly Light." Fumbling the pages, Clara ignored the surreptitious glances the family cast her way. She fought an irreverent smile: in a desperate attempt to include the Almighty in her mental meanderings, she began to pray. *Lord, You did create male and female. Contrary to Eleanor's opinions, You indicated they are better off together. But as of course You also know, everyone seems to have made a fine mess of things these past few thousand years. I don't seem to be able to do much better, Lord. I'm not an Eleanor, and I don't want to be a Patricia. Frankly, Lord, I don't know who I am these days.*

Louise tugged her skirt. "Clara, sit down!" she hissed. "The hymn is over."

After Reverend Miggs pronounced the benediction, her sister immediately launched into speech. "You've been behaving strangely ever since last night. Willy said when he took you home you acted—and this was the word he used—*moonstruck.* He told me he couldn't even provoke you into a quarrel." With an impatient wave of her hand, she grabbed Clara's arm and pulled her to the end of the pew, out of the way. "The dress worked, didn't it? Everyone in town saw the way Dr. Har—" hurriedly she lowered her voice "—Dr. Harcourt's attentiveness. Tell me, what did he say to you?"

"Louise, I've admitted the gown turned out very well, and I thank you. But if you think that entitles you to pry into any conversations I might have with Dr. Harcourt, I'll tell you—again—they're none of your business."

"Piffle. Of course they are. I'm your sister. You like him. Don't even try to deny it."

"Of course I like him. So does every other woman in town, and all the men with whom I've chatted. Every person in Canterbury likes Dr. Harcourt. For once Albert deserves to gloat." She smiled at several ladies from the missions committee, thanked them for their contributions to the Festival.

"Clara— Oh, botheration. Now Eleanor's headed this way. I might as well try to stop a steamship. Very well. Mr. Eppling's waiting for me, anyway."

"Honestly, Louise. You're marrying the man in four months. Can't you refer to him as Harry, at least with me?"

"You know what Mother would have to say about that level of familiarity."

"I know that for all our lives Mother has used convention and manners to distance herself from any form of familial intimacy with her children." Frustration with everything—her sister, her family…with life—pushed through Clara in a strong gust of rebellion. "As a matter of fact, I think of Dr. Harcourt as Ethan. I might even ask him to call me Clara, since I'm thirty-one years old and quite capable of establishing my own set of conventions."

For a moment Louise gaped at her, then she reached up and pressed a quick kiss against her cheek. "Good for you, sister. I shall take courage from you, and promise to at least call my affianced Harry when I'm alone with you." After a brief but fierce hug, she slipped past, smiling at Eleanor but not stopping to speak with her.

Before Eleanor managed two sentences, several piano students surrounded Clara, followed by more townsfolk wanting to compliment her on the success of the Christmas Festival. By the time Clara extricated herself, promising to visit Eleanor later in the afternoon, Ethan was nowhere in sight. Hurriedly she fastened her coat, all but running down the now-deserted aisle to the church's front doors, and almost ran smack into him.

"Whoa! Is the sanctuary on fire, then, Miss Penrose?" he teased, his hands steadying her shoulders. In her flustration Clara probably only imagined that his grip lingered before he set her free and stepped back. Eyes narrowing, he examined her with what Clara thought of as a physician's analytical intensity. "Is something wrong?"

"I thought you'd left," she stammered, stupidly. "I wanted to… I wanted to, ah…thank you for your help. Last night, at the Festival. With the gifts. It's always a melee, as you saw…" Finally she corralled her tongue and lapsed into silence. Regrettably she could not corral her thoughts. Even now the memory of their closeness the previous night produced a surge of warmth. Under cover of all the joyful confusion she and Ethan had shared an unnervingly personal conversation. *He had held her hand.*

"It was my pleasure," Dr. Harcourt commented easily. "Miss Penrose—Clara? Are you sure you're all right? You're flushed, and—" he hesitated, then added with slight smile "—you're not acting like yourself."

"I know, and I despise myself for it."

Flirting, she had instructed Louise since her little sister first let down her dress hems, was degrading to both parties. Honesty was preferable to artifice. Since Clara had spent the past twelve hours rehearsing the latter, either God wanted to administer a dose of humility, or He was indulging in a bit of divine comedy. Very well, then. She would try her hand at both honesty *and* artifice. "I did enjoy your company, last night—Ethan." She fluttered her eyelashes as much like Patricia Dunwoody as she could manage, and summoned what she hoped was an inviting smile. "I look forward to seeing you this coming Thursday. Bertha told me that you're joining the rest of our family for dinner with her and Albert. She tries hard to emulate my mother's formality, but with my nephews and niece you're more likely to feel like you've tumbled back to last night at the Festival."

"I'll try to look forward to the experience." Perhaps it was only a cloud passing in front of the sun, but to Clara his face seemed to darken. "I must go. I promised to stop by the Browns' after church, to check on Mrs. Brown and the baby." After touching the brim of his hat, he turned and rapidly departed, disappearing around the corner of the church.

"So," Clara murmured aloud, shivering a little in the nippy winter day, "was I too obvious, or too subtle?"

Scowling, Ethan climbed into the buggy, his scowl deepening because he was forced to shove aside several more envelopes, along with a brightly wrapped mason jar full of pickled cucumbers. He had never been the kind of man who believed he understood women, except from a medical perspective, and Clara Penrose was tempting him to go search out that band of outlaws in the Nevada Territory.

Last night she had been everything he'd ever wanted in a woman—and he'd come dangerously near to making a fool of himself again. He had felt safe with Clara. Free. Unlike most women, including and especially Lillian, Clara did not dissemble, or batter him with admiring glances and honeyed words.

Until today.

Ethan seldom swore, but he was tempted to now.

What was she trying to do, anyway, batting her eyelashes like a professional floozy, flashing him those
bright and utterly artificial smiles? On the church steps,
of all places! And to think he'd been entertaining the
notion of courting her. Angrily he rifled through the
scattered missives beside him, thinking with the only
portion of his brain still capable of rational thought that
he needed to calm down before he visited the Browns.
After sucking in a deep breath and holding it for a moment, he picked up the note on top and read the cheery
Christmas greeting. By the time he made it through another two unpretentious notes he felt his pulse slowing
down to a healthier rate.

Then he opened the envelope with the fourth note,
and the hair on the back of his neck lifted as he removed
the neatly folded vellum: *Somebody plans to give you
something special this Christmas.* As with the other
two notes locked in his desk drawer, there was no signature, no other greeting.

Had Clara been running because she'd slipped out
the side door, left the note in his buggy, then dashed
back out the front door to waylay him? The prospect
sickened his gut. He wasn't sure which of them suffered from a mental malfunction—Clara or himself—
for believing she was capable of such aberrant behavior.

Enough, Ethan vowed to himself. He'd endured quite
enough. On Tuesday afternoon, when he closed the office at noon, he would pay Clara Penrose a visit. In his
thirty-seven years he had suffered enough from the clandestine intrigues of females to last thirty-seven lifetimes.

Tuesday, in the way of weather in this corner of Virginia, dawned mild, with skies the color of aged pewter.

"Rain by tomorrow," Mrs. Gavis pronounced stoutly when Ethan finished his examination. "My shoulder's set to aching. It's never wrong when I get that ache."

"Mm…" Ethan had learned which patients to coddle, which to lecture, and which few to simply agree with because he would never change their minds.

"You're a bit down in the mouth today, Dr. Harcourt. Something besides my lumbago troubling you?"

"I'm fine," he lied, courteously cupping her elbow as he escorted her down the hall to the door. "But I will take my umbrella tomorrow, when I do my rounds."

After Mrs. Gavis departed, Ethan turned off all the lights and, eschewing the buggy, set off for Clara Penrose's cottage at a brisk walk.

A block away a woman watched from the one-horse trap she'd rented at the livery stable. Her hands, slippery and trembling, clutched the reins too tightly; the livery horse backstepped, his tail swishing. The woman spoke to the animal, apologizing, then nervously edged the trap closer to Dr. Harcourt's office after his tall figure disappeared around a corner several blocks down the street. Her movements clumsy with haste, she set the brake, secured the reins and, after climbing down, turned to pick up a large basket from the floorboards. The putrid odor of rancid fruit brought tears to her eyes. She darted several glances around to ensure that nobody was in sight before carrying the basket down the brick path, up onto Dr. Harcourt's wraparound porch. One of the broad planks squeaked when she stepped on it. She froze, holding her breath. She'd never seen a servant loitering about the place on Tuesday afternoons.

The daily maid he hired to clean and cook meals was allowed Tuesdays off, she'd discovered.

She was safe, if she hurried.

Carefully she set her gift down directly in front of the door, where he'd be sure to see it—or, perhaps better, to trip over if he returned after dark. After wiping her eyes, she reached into the pocket of her long overcoat and tugged out the note, which she placed between two brown-specked, soggy apples to ensure a breeze wouldn't blow it away.

All the way back to the livery stable she sang, her heart pounding with victory and grief.

Chapter Six

Clara lived in a quaint stone cottage with tall brick chimneys at either end. She didn't answer Ethan's knock, but as he turned away from the door a slender cat with the most unusual markings he'd ever seen materialized from beneath a pruned-back rosebush at the corner of the cottage. Wide, myopic blue eyes appraised Ethan unblinkingly. Fascinated, Ethan knelt, stretching out his hand. "Hey, fella. What kind of feline might you be?"

As though his voice was a signal, the cat strolled over, sniffed Ethan's hand, butted its head against the fingers, then commenced purring.

"You sound like a sawmill," Ethan remarked, obliging the animal by scratching its seal-colored ears and then under the chin. "Where's your mistress?"

The cat turned and whisked with silent grace around the corner. Slowly Ethan stood, dusted the knees of his trousers and followed, telling himself that the animal was *not* responding to the question, but for whatever reason had decided to run off. When he turned the corner he stopped, his mouth dropping open. Though it was winter, he could still see the gifted hand of a loving gardener everywhere he looked. Beneath several massive oaks, an English-styled garden had been laid out, with neatly pruned-back shrubs and mulched flower beds lying dormant, waiting for spring. The grounds were tidy, as scrupulously tended as Ethan's examining rooms.

The cat waited for him in the center of an ancient flagstone path. When Ethan approached the friendly feline greeted him with a meow that was part growl, part purr and part an indescribable conglomeration of sounds that nonetheless emerged as though the cat were, well, speaking to him. Then it darted down the path, chocolate-tipped tail waving.

"Lewis Carroll must have used you for his model in *Alice in Wonderland*." Smiling despite himself, Ethan trod along the uneven stones half buried in the ground to the rear of the cottage. An immense thicket of lilacs crowded the back corner of the structure. Peering around the branches, Ethan glimpsed a small shed, a large pile of composting leaves—and Clara Penrose. Her back was to Ethan, but he could hear her talking, and assumed it was to the cat until the animal burst from the lilacs, streaked across the dead grass and leaped into the pile of leaves.

"Nim! You are such a spoiled-rotten boy! Bad kitty. You know this is the first time I've been out here in a week." She picked up the cat—Nim?—and despite the scolding hugged him close. "Go along now, and let me have a few more moments. Methuselah was about to provide some illumination, I believe. I haven't perfected turtle talk, so you're just going to have to be patient."

Methuselah? Turtle talk?

Head shaking, Ethan stepped around the lilacs. "I'm afraid Nim's not the only one you'll need to scold."

She'd been sitting on a crude bench, and sprang to her feet so rapidly the cat panicked. With a hiss and a yowl Nim catapulted from Clara's arms, then vanished behind the garden shed.

"Sorry I frightened everyone," Ethan began as he walked over to her. "I knocked on your door first. You didn't answer, but your butler showed me back here."

"I don't have a butler. Oh…you mean NimNuan." She grimaced. "He'd be insulted if he heard himself relegated to the status of a servant. He's a new breed of cat known as Siamese. It's my understanding they were originally bred by royalty to guard the temples of Siam. A friend of our family knows the British Consul General. The King of Siam gave him a breeding pair of the animals. Nim's descended from them, and he takes his royalty seriously."

"I'll humbly beg his pardon the next time I see his majesty. Here—what's this?" He dropped the banter and reached for Clara's arm. "Don't flinch away. I'm not initiating an improper advance. But you have a scratch on your neck, courtesy of your royal cat Nim—Noon, did you call him?"

"Nim*Nuan.* It means *supple and graceful* in Siamese, despite what you just witnessed." She drew in a sharp breath as Ethan took hold of her chin and turned her head so he could examine the scratch. "I— It's nothing, I'm sure. He's usually very careful not to use his claws on people."

The skin beneath Ethan's fingers felt soft as a newborn's. The chin he held, however, was an uncompromising one and her eyes, the same dark bitter chocolate as her cat's paws and ears, searched his with alert wariness. He reminded himself forcefully that this woman might have left him three very disturbing anonymous notes over the past two weeks, and the purpose of his visit was to have a serious conversation with her, not only as a man, but as a doctor.

He dropped her chin and stepped back. "You're right. Skin's a little puffy from the scratch, but unbroken. You still ought to clean it before bedtime. Cat scratches can turn nasty—they're actually more open to infection than a dog bite."

"Unless it's a rabid dog. Why are you here, Dr. Harcourt?"

Ethan contemplated his answer, finally countering with a question of his own. "Do you often talk to piles of dead leaves, Miss Penrose?"

"Only when a box turtle is hibernating in them."

A box turtle? "You're telling me you were talking to a *turtle?*"

A faint blush dusted her cheeks. "I inherited this place from my grandparents. My grandmother loved gardening. When I was a child, I helped her plant over a thousand daffodils imported from Holland. Come spring—"

"Clara..." he emphasized her name deliberately "... answer the question."

"I'd rather not. You might conclude I'm dotty, not eccentric."

Despite his suspicions, Ethan smiled. "Possibly. But I'd like to know about Methuselah anyway. That's what you called him, isn't it?"

"He's a biblical and godly man in the Bible who

lived for a very long time." The color in her pale cheeks deepened.

His mouth twitched, but Ethan clamped down the laughter. Her evasive manner might be shyness, but it could just as well be shrewdness. Thoughtfully he studied her. She was tall for a woman, slender—almost bony, her skin pale as alabaster. As usual, her hair was scrunched up in the unattractive bun. More unusual was her attire. In stark contrast to the bold jewel tones to which he'd become accustomed, and especially to Sunday night's elegant gown, today she wore a plain gown faded to an unattractive gray, with only a shawl woven in equally depressing shades of gray over it.

There was nothing about her of glowing beauty or curvaceous femininity or elegant sophistication.

Yet Ethan didn't care a flea's whisker about her appearance, fashionable or not. He did care about self-preservation, which seemed to evaporate around Clara. Something about this maddening, confusing woman appealed to him on such a visceral level he was rapidly losing any semblance of control. He needed to reclaim his objectivity, immediately. After finishing his appraisal, he folded his arms and drawled, "I have the afternoon off. I'm quite content to stand here until dark. Since I'm blocking the path, we might as well indulge in a useful conversation. Learn a bit more about each other."

Her gaze flicked over her shoulder.

Uh-uh. No escaping like your cat. "Don't bother dashing around the garden shed," he warned. "Come now, Clara. You were more intrepid three years ago, not to mention the other evening. Here—I'll start. I'm intrigued—and irritated—by you. And I'm not feeling noble. I came to have an honest conversation without interruption. Now it's your turn. Tell me about the turtle."

For a moment she stood in silence, hugging the shawl closer around her shoulders, her hands restlessly smoothing over its fringe. Finally she shrugged. "Box turtles can live half a century or more. The one hibernating under those leaves was already a permanent resident thirty-odd years ago, when my grandparents moved into the cottage. I named him Methuselah. Sometimes I need to—to clear my head. After I moved here and started gardening, I used to meet up with Methuselah quite a bit. Some years ago, when I was having trouble praying…" she stopped, searched his face and finished simply "…I started talking to Methuselah instead of God. I've come to believe neither of them mind." Her chin jutted out. "I warned you that you'd think I'm dotty."

Not a single individual out of all the people Ethan had ever known—not one of them—would share such a bizarre confession, even with their physician. A decade earlier, he might have been smug and insensitive enough to label that person as mentally deficient.

Life, however, tended to beat the starch out of a body; he was also coming to accept that while God usually didn't prevent the beating, He at least dispensed grace to make it possible to survive it. "I don't think you're dotty," he told Clara, his voice gruff. Because she stood there as unmoving as one of the old oaks around them, he reached for her hand and looped it through his arm. "Introduce me."

"I assume you mean to Methuselah, since you've indicated at least a passing acquaintance with the Lord."

"Let's say I'm interested in pursuing a deeper understanding of both."

Her tart response sparked the fire that had been smoldering inside Ethan for weeks. The woman might be
unpredictable as a dragonfly, but regardless of her eva-
siveness and his own wariness, she always made him
feel alive. At this moment his doubts seemed more the
product of an embittered mind than the observations of
a man honed in the world of political chicanery.

Watching her, he lifted the hand resting on his forearm and pressed a kiss against her knuckles. "Perhaps
talking to you and a turtle will provide it."

Clara yanked her hand free. "Are you making sport
of me, Dr. Harcourt?"

"I only make sport of ladies who talk to goldfish, not
turtles." In a quick move he recaptured her hand and
tugged her over to the leaves. "After Saturday night, I
was hoping you'd think of me as Ethan."

"I did, until you provoked me. Frankly, I don't know
what to think. You're not acting like the congressman I
met three years ago, nor the thoughtful gentleman who
helped me with gifts the other night. You—well, you're
acting more like my brother, the way you're—"

"Clara—" he bent so his lips brushed the shell of
her ear "—this is not how brothers behave toward their
sisters."

"The last time Willy nibbled on my ear he was eight
months old and teething."

Her voice had gone breathless. Ethan could hear the
light rapid exhalations, feel the pulse skittering beneath
his fingers. And the way she looked at him...

*If she kissed him, he'd be lost. For months Lillian
enticed him with bashful gazes and half-parted lips*

*until he would have followed her off the edge of a cliff.
After that fateful evening when she'd pulled him behind an urn bursting with greenery and pressed those
lips against his, he'd asked her to marry him the very
next day.*

He'd been twenty-three, and an idealistic fool.

"Ethan…you're hurting my fingers—"

"Sorry."

He dropped her hand as though it were a bundle of
thorns. Silence thickened between them until he finally
scraped up the courage to meet her bewildered, half-
angry gaze, the eyes grown dark as the dregs at the bottom of a cup of very bitter coffee. Swallowing hard, he
ran his hand around the back of his neck and prepared
to abase himself. Then Clara spoke.

"She really hurt you, didn't she? Your wife?"

In three years, no one had dared broach the subject,
even indirectly. Yet this indefatigable woman, a woman
he had just manhandled and frightened, sliced through
all the polite social fabrications to offer him something
he'd forgotten existed—honest empathy.

"Yes, she did." The admission still stung. In a flash
of insight Ethan realized how much he'd needed to talk
about Lillian with someone, instead of immersing himself in mindless flight to a place where nobody knew
him from Adam's house cat.

Festering wounds to the heart required lancing as
much as boils on the skin. "Can we sit down on that
bench? Perhaps Methuselah will listen in, and have
some helpful counsel."

"I've learned that most times, just listening is enough."

Chapter Seven

T hey sat on the damp wood bench, shoulders almost touching. Thin silver-gold sunlight washed over the yard, and a stray wisp of breeze twirled a couple of leaves. Somewhere a bird twittered. Clara sat quietly, her mood contemplative, her gaze steady on the pile of leaves. She kept her hands folded in her lap, and didn't speak or even clear her throat because she didn't want to distract Ethan. He had indicated a need to clear the air between them. While her heart might palpitate with fearful hope, his behavior toward her was erratic; one moment he was tender, solicitous—the next moment he was crushing her fingers, his expression cold as a winter wind.

She could not afford to trust this troubled man.

All of a sudden he began to talk, the words halting at first, then escaping in a geyser, and Clara forgot about the need for caution. "The adulteries were humiliating enough—but what hurt more was her vindictiveness. I wasn't the man she'd wanted me to be, I refused to turn a blind eye to her infidelities, so she delighted in making them as public as possible. I think by the time

she died, I—" he turned slightly, watching Clara with
fierce intensity "—I think I hated her. I wouldn't have
wished her to die like she did, but I was glad I wouldn't
have to deal with her anymore. It's a desecration of the
spirit, allowing that poisonous emotion to take root."

"Oh, Ethan… Even if you did grow to hate her, you
never acted on your feelings. Based on what I saw at
Senator Comstock's party, and what I've learned since,
you're a private man with a reputation for personal integrity. Of course you'd need to build a wall around
yourself to try to cope with a wife who possessed neither. I'd say your hatred was over the circumstances
and your wife's behavior, not a reflection of your true
feelings toward—her name was Lillian?"

"Yes."

He chewed over that a while, then shook his head.
"I never should have gone into politics. I'm afraid I've
spent the past three years avoiding the whole blamed
mess because I don't want to forgive either her, or myself for being relieved that she's dead."

"Obviously I've never been in your position. If anything, at times I know all too well *I'm* the embarrassing
weed in the Penrose family garden. But…" she relaxed
her guard, even as common sense stridently warned
against it "…but Ethan, I can tell you I'd probably feel
the same way you do—did, if I'd had to step into your
shoes." He flashed her a grateful look, and Clara told
her common sense to hush and go sit in the corner.
"She betrayed you, in every way, publicly and repeatedly. I'm so sorry."

"A lot of people said that to me, back then. You're
the first one I actually believe."

Oh! His compliment sang through her. "One of my

more awkward flaws is my inability to dissemble to spare someone's sensibilities. You may have noticed?"

"The trait has manifested itself upon occasion."

She had always appreciated dry humor. "I've tried to…ah…control it by…by writing." A nervous gulp of air shuddered through her body as she confessed details of her most closely guarded secret, one she had not shared even with Eleanor. The sense of fellowship with this man was a potent elixir, and Clara had been thirsty for a long time. "I spent most of my childhood with a leaky pen, holed away in nooks while I scratched ponderous thoughts on papers I scrounged from my father's study."

Pausing, she glanced up at him, wondering vaguely about the aura that seemed to have gathered around him like a cold gray mist. *Don't dry up now, Clara. He's listening closely to you, not searching for ways to shut you up.* "The habit's never changed," she plowed ahead. "Writing, I mean. I believe I mentioned nobody outside the family knows about my eccentricity? My parents never approved—my mother deplored my ink-stained fingers. Father was annoyed every time I pilfered through his desk looking for paper, even more so after he gave me an allowance and I spent most of it buying journals and foolscap instead of hairpins or hat pins or other feminine fribbles. When it became apparent that I—that I…" she stumbled a bit, then finished matter-of-factly "…that I was destined for spinsterhood, they sent me off to college, mostly because they hoped it would at least retrain my energies on something of value, like teaching or nursing. I disliked both. I now have a useless degree gathering dust in a trunk, and my parents have given up hope of reforming me into a proper Penrose. It was a relief, moving here to the cottage, where I can indulge myself to my heart's content."

"So you've never outgrown your...writing habit?"

"Well, no. And I probably wouldn't have told you, except I'd already mentioned it at my parents' dinner party." Self-conscious now, she forced the rest out before fear froze her tongue. One bared heart deserved another. "I wondered...you might want to try writing yourself? It's very therapeutic, you know. Actually, most of what I write these days are letters to editors, offering unsolicited my opinion on, um, everything. I've always admired the courage of men like you, who sought public office to proclaim their platform. Albert told me you were one of the few men he knew who believed women should have the right to vote. I've wished ever since that night we'd been able to discuss the subject. Of course, I don't have the courage to flout *that* much convention, so I write letters." After clearing her throat, she finished sadly, "Even then I use a pen name so I won't embarrass the Penrose family name."

Letters. *She wrote letters, using a pseudonym.* Despite his unwillingness to accept the obvious—Clara possessed the time, the convoluted mind and now, the predilection for the medium—he did not want to believe she was the author of the notes. It required a tremendous effort of will for Ethan to keep his voice uninflected, stripped of emotion, yet warm enough to avoid spooking the young woman sitting beside him. "So you have no secret ambition to emulate the Brontë sisters or Jane Austen? Write charming stories of life in American towns instead of English villages?"

"Heavens, no! I've little use for fiction. Why waste

all your energy making something up, when real life offers more challenges?"

"Point conceded. But if you write make-believe stories, you retain all the power of the creator, where with the stroke of a pen you bless, or curse, your characters."

"A rather Machiavellian-esque touch in your mind, Dr. Harcourt? Well, I already know I'm too opinionated. Whatever characters I might create in a work of fiction would be held hostage to my own will, so I don't create them at all. Letters, on the other hand, leave the option to be blessed, or cursed, upon the reader."

Feeling trapped, Ethan casually shifted sideways. "So what do you write about, in your letters to editors?"

"Hmm?" She blinked several times. "Lots of things. Political, religious, social issues—sometimes I chastise them for their abuse of their responsibilities as journalists to, well, strive for objectivity and truth. The written word holds power, would you agree?"

Ethan managed a short nod, and Clara continued, her pale face lightly tinted with apricot. "Since I use a pseudonym, I'm fearless. My family of course would be horrified. For them public decorum and private discretion are nonnegotiable. I have a dear friend, but I've never shared this secret with her. She's a born debater and we engage in lots of lively discussions. But I don't want her reading over my shoulder. She'd argue about every phrase."

An awkward pause ensued until Clara finished lightly, "You're the only one who knows my secret vice. You'll have to promise either to be Methuselah, who certainly knows how to keep a secret, or Nim, who thinks paper was intended to be scrunched into balls and chased."

"I don't know whether to feel honored or intimidated."

Beside him Clara stiffened, and Ethan couldn't blame her; his response sounded as friendly as a trapped wolf. He wanted to bang his head against the garden shed. This was neither a stupid nor a silly woman; her candor left her particularly vulnerable, through no fault of her own. He felt like a clod, being angry with her when he was still unwilling to confront her with the suspicions that fueled the anger. Obviously she sensed something of his internal violence. Tone of voice, his expression... women possessed a sensitivity to atmosphere God had not seen fit to pass along to the male of the species. Or perhaps God just wanted to teach Ethan Harcourt a lesson in—what? Hadn't he eaten enough humility pie?

Inside the pocket of his trousers, the tiny charm of the Capitol Building seemed to scorch through the layers of fabric to burn fresh shame on his soul. *Be a healer, Ethan, not a blasted judge and jury. You've learned that at least over the past three years.*

"I've bored you, haven't I?" Clara announced. Her hand jerked in a half-abortive gesture. "Made you feel awkward, prattling away about a girlish habit I should have outgrown years ago. Forgive me. Would you like some apple cider? I still have some leftover Sally Lunn bread from the Festival I can offer as well. The cottage is woefully untidy, but you're more than welcome. Don't worry about the lack of a chaperone. I'm too old and too contrary to care. If you're uncomfortable being alone with me, Nim's pretty efficient at the task of maiden aunt." Her quick laugh emerged too high. "Which of course I am already. You needn't feel confined by convention, Dr. Harcourt... Ethan."

She stood, forcing Ethan to follow suit. *What do I do here, Lord?* "Convention is pretty necessary, under some circumstances," he returned slowly. "But not between us, hmm? We've never been conventional, have we, Clara, even three years ago? Some cider sounds pretty good."

Clara nodded without looking at him, then set off toward the front of the cottage. When they reached the door, Ethan quickly stepped in front of her to open it. She was correct—the cozy rooms on either side of the minuscule entryway *were* a mess. Comfortable horsehair furniture feminized with lace antimacassars was covered with dozens of embroidered and needlepoint pillows; sheet music spilled onto the floor out of an opened music cabinet by an ebonized grand piano; stacks of newspapers and periodicals bulged from several walnut stands. A faded oriental rug covered the wide-planked floors. To Ethan's left, the other front room bulged with bookcases filling two of the walls, and a ladies' desk in the far corner. Wads of crumpled paper littered the floor, and a colorful paisley shawl draped forgotten over the spindle desk chair.

Not a single sign of Christmas, not even a sprig of holly, was on display.

Clara wandered across the parlor to the right, surprisingly turning on a pair of electric floor lamps before she lit the fire in the fireplace, laid with old-fashioned wood. With more force than finesse she gathered up an armful of sheet music and stuffed the pages into the music cabinet before finally returning to Ethan.

"Well? Would you like to sit by the fire while I prepare a tray, or shall I invent an engagement I've forgotten and allow you a graceful exit?"

He had hurt her. Now he could either inflict the coup de grace and level his accusation—or he could heed the remnant of idealism still clinging to life in a corner of his soul. "Clara…" Her name emerged on a long sigh as he surveyed her carefully expressionless face. "How about if we flout all the rules further, and I follow you to your kitchen? While you serve us up some cider, you can tell me why there's no evidence of the Christmas season inside your home."

Some indefinable emotion flickered across her face, and her erect posture seemed to droop. Then her chin lifted. "Just because I don't decorate for Christmas doesn't mean I don't celebrate the occasion."

"You have lots of habits I'm coming to know. One of the more annoying is avoiding a direct answer when you don't like the question."

"Why should you care one way or the other? Is your home fragrant with ropes of evergreens? Do you have heaps of gifts all wrapped in ribbons and sprinkled with stardust, waiting to be delivered on Christmas Eve? Is there a crèche on display in your waiting room?"

"Perhaps you should come see for yourself."

"I'm not sick."

Ethan cocked his head to one side while he sifted through the passionate outburst. "You feel you can't compete with your mother or, for that matter, your sister-in-law? Is that what this is all about?"

Clara swiveled on her heel and marched over to poke at the fire. "Don't be ridiculous. I don't decorate because it's a distraction, a sentimentalization of what should be a reverent, holy celebration."

"Hmm. I suppose a manger full of straw, surrounded

by smelly cattle in a dark stable, does lend itself to reverence."

"Now you are mocking me."

"Only a little." His mood turned contemplative as he chewed over thoughts that had jigged about in his brain for a while. Here with Clara, they finally settled into place. "I've always considered the birth of any baby a miracle, worth celebrating whether the birth takes place in a stable or a castle. Perhaps all the lavish decorations folks like to display for Jesus's birth merely reflect their inadequate attempts to acknowledge what God gave up when He squeezed Himself into human form. Doesn't matter whether they live in a castle or a stone cottage, it's a way of saying, 'Welcome to the World, we're glad You stopped by.'"

"It's not the decorations God looks for, Ethan. It's how people decorate their hearts."

"Well said. Point conceded. Ah… I enjoyed the decorations you made for the Christmas Festival."

"Since you obviously enjoy debating, perhaps you shouldn't give up on running for public office. For the record… *Congressman,* I do enjoy decorating—for others." She stabbed at a log with enough force to send a shower of sparks shooting up the chimney. "For the present moment, however, let's leave it that the dearth of decorations here is because I simply don't have time, and this cottage is cluttered enough."

"You may rest assured I won't run for public office. I'm not interested in debates—except with you." The quip elicited nothing but silence. His voice gentled. "I think I understand more than you realize, Clara. A year ago I barely noted the Christmas season at all, much less sang 'Joy to the World' in a church."

Floorboards creaked as he made his way to the fireplace. The flames cast brooding shadows over Clara's face, accentuating the strong bones of her cheeks, the straight uncompromising line of her nose. But the wide mouth was trying not to tremble. Compelled by a force he no longer wanted to ignore, Ethan waited until she hung the poker on its hook, then lifted her to her feet and clasped both her hands in his. "This year, I'm finding my way back to Christmas. Your family, this town—and you—are part of the reason. Grace seems to be a concept we human beings have trouble accepting, as well as dispensing—except at Christmastime. Your outside is full of grace, Clara. Over the past weeks I've watched you scatter it freely over everything and everyone, except yourself. A little bit ago, outside, I felt that grace when without any censure you allowed me to share secrets that have festered inside for years. Trouble is, I think you're nursing a secret pain or two of your own, hiding it deep, somewhere inside where nobody can see."

"I don't want you to believe I—"

"But you let *me* see it." He talked over her, ignoring the interruption. "Clara…you let me see a part of you I've never known." Before he could regret the impulse, he lifted her hands and brushed a kiss over the backs of her knuckles. "I'll take you up on your offer of refreshments another day. I've some thinking to do, about you, about me. About…" he released her hands so he could trace the furrow between her brows with his index finger "…things." When Clara opened her mouth he shook his head at her, adding softly, "While I'm thinking, perhaps you would write a letter—to me? Only sign your real name, this time. Write me a letter, Clara."

Chapter Eight

Write Ethan a letter. For the next two days Clara crammed so many activities into the hours between sunrise and midnight she scarce had a moment to eat, or even scribble a recipe for Eleanor. Nim padded after her whenever she was home, meowing pitifully and snuggling close, the tilted eyes reproaching her for her neglect.

At one o'clock on Thursday morning, after lying sleepless while the cat kneaded her shoulder and groomed her face with his rough tongue, in order to salve her conscience Clara got up and darted through the cottage, robe and gown flapping as she pulled a piece of string for the cat to chase until they both collapsed back into bed.

She could find time to placate her pet, but Ethan Harcourt was another ball of string entirely.

No matter how busy she stayed, the string *he* had cleverly dangled kept tickling her nose, no matter how many times she pushed it out of the way. Tonight she would see Ethan again, at the dinner with Albert and Bertha. Sure as oaks dropped acorns Ethan would find a way to bring up his bizarre notion that she should write him a letter.

Write Ethan a letter… How about: *Dear sir, your request for a letter, sharing personal intimacies similar to those you confided out by my garden shed on Tuesday past, exceeds the bounds of social convention even for someone who prides herself on ignoring them. If you desire written correspondence—you go first.*

Her imagined sauciness prompted Clara's first laugh in days, and she dressed with a pinch less trepidation for the evening. Her peacock-blue dress costume further bolstered her confidence—with its oversize leg-o'-mutton sleeves and figured silk skirt she might light up the room brighter than Albert's hundred-light chandelier, but nobody could accuse her of looking like a drab mouse with a drippy nose.

Words possessed such power. A soft tongue, Proverbs warned, could break a bone. And a careless tongue could wound a heart forever. *You're nothing but a dull, skinny, brown beetle, and your pointy nose always drips… I'd rather kiss a mouse in a mud hole than Clara Penrose.* Her first introduction to boys, Albert's best friend Petey Fitzsimmons, should have offered sufficient warning. But at thirteen… Clara absently smoothed her fingers down the bright blue sleeve, over and over. At nineteen, older but no wiser, the man her parents selected for her husband should have cured her forever of all romantic notions…. *No man will ever want a bag of bones with a tongue like a cheese slicer…* Those had been Mortimer's parting words. The taunts had lost their sharp sting, but even now the memories could not always be silenced.

And apparently she still hadn't learned to accept what couldn't be changed.

Defiantly Clara pulled on her cloak, pinned her hat over her topknot, then dashed out into the cold December night to the carriage Albert had sent to fetch her.

By the time the coachman turned the ostentatious brougham into the equally ostentatious drive leading to the three-storied masonry mansion Albert had had built five years earlier, an idea had sprung forth in Clara's mind to counter Ethan's suggestion that she write him a letter.

Come morning, she would set her mind as well as her feet to the task.

"Clara! How colorful you look!" Bertha greeted her with plump, moist hands and a bosomy hug. "I've always envied a woman who could carry off that shade of blue— Nan! Come out from behind that urn at once. You know your papa warned you about slipping downstairs after bedtime."

"Want to see Auntie Clara." At six years, the youngest daughter, Nan, with her flaxen hair and blue eyes, bore an uncanny resemblance to her aunt Louise. Yet she was a studious child who preferred reading to dolls. Clara adored her.

"Hello, sweetkins." She knelt and cuddled the slight form. "You should obey your parents," she whispered in her ear, "but I'm very glad to see you."

"Papa says you wear clothes that re-resemble Joseph's cloak of many colors," Nan whispered back, and above them Bertha choked. "But I think you're beautiful, like a rainbow." After pressing a damp kiss to

Clara's cheek, the child scampered back up the wide staircase. *The power of words...*

"Don't look so mortified," Clara reassured Bertha. "I rather like the comparison to a rainbow. Might even pass that one along to Albert."

Confidence intact, she sailed down the hall toward the salon, and the sound of Ethan's deep baritone voice.

Dinner was a disaster.

For some inexplicable reason Ethan was remote, even austere, not revealing by word or expression his visit with Clara on Tuesday. In fact, for most of the evening they scarcely exchanged a sentence. Because he was seated beside Louise's fiancé, Mr. Eppling, on the same side of the table as Clara, little opportunity arose at dinner to engage him in conversation, intimate or challenging. After the meal Albert promptly herded the men into the library. Bertha was summoned by the children's nanny to check on three-year-old Abner, who had woken up and refused to go back to sleep without his mama.

Clara's mother and Louise pounced upon her the moment Bertha disappeared.

"Really, Clara, challenging your brother and Mr. Penrose on pro bono counsel for the poor and elderly? Must you always trot out the radical bent of your mind and beat us over the head with it?"

Louise smacked a dramatic hand to her brow. "Mother, for goodness' sake, let it rest! Why not brag about her generous heart instead. Despite her peculiar personality and 'radical mind,' she still has one, you know."

"Hmmph. And people are forever taking advantage of that as well." Mavis Penrose lifted the lorgnette she'd taken to wearing the past year and examined Clara. "Are you eating properly? You look as though you've lost weight. I'll have the cook send over some chicken soup, but you really should consider curtailing some of your charitable activities. I won't have you sicken with a cold or something more unpleasant, like influenza, for Christmas, Clara."

"I wouldn't dream of it, Mother."

"You know Clara," Louise observed dryly. "The more charity work she does, the healthier she grows." She gave her mother a brief peck on the cheek, then stepped back. Mavis Penrose discouraged affectionate displays of any kind. "At this point there's little we can do to change her inclinations. However—" in a gentle swirl of rose-colored taffeta Louise turned to Clara "—I do refuse to give up trying to instill at least a paragraph of style sense in your book-crammed brain. This evening offers the perfect illustration. I don't know how many times I've explained to you that that shade of blue—unlike the gown I picked out for you to wear at the Festival—is not good for your complexion. Turns it frightfully sallow." Louise shuddered. "Remember how Dr. Harcourt couldn't take his eyes off you last Saturday? That's hardly been the case this evening. He's not even looked your way. I wanted to kick Har—um, Mr. Eppling, for prattling on about the best fishing spots on the Potomac. We can't do anything about your costume, but let me at least refashion your hair, and I promise you'll command the doctor's undivided attention. You'd look stunning with a simple Grecian knot, sister. It would soften your face, possibly even help with that sallowness."

Clara batted her sister's hands away. "Don't touch

my hair. I know you well. The last time I submitted to your pleas I looked like a—"

She stopped, her mind churning. Hadn't she decided on the drive over here to call Ethan's hand, by pursuing *him* with the same disregard for decorum he had displayed? Already her head was full of plans—baking him gingerbread men, leaving a basket full of Christmas greens anonymously on his porch, and yes, she planned to write him some kind of note on the most over-romanticized Christmas card she could buy at the stationer's. Perhaps he regretted his display of affection on Tuesday. Equally possible, however, Clara had not adequately signaled her reciprocal feelings, hence his distance this evening. Men, Louise reminded her frequently, might avoid overtly flirtatious females, but they still required sufficient encouragement to fan the flame. "What's the point in striking a match to wet wood?" she'd pointed out several days earlier.

Time to prove you're not *a coward, Clara.* Swallowing hard, she lifted her hands, tugging out combs and pins until her hair unfurled down her back and shoulders. "There. Do your worst. Consider this a Christmas gift."

For a humming span of time her mother and sister gawked at her as though she'd...well, as though she had announced her intention of playing the part of Delilah, with Dr. Harcourt an unknowing Samson.

"Hurry up," she said, thrusting pins and combs at Louise. "The gentlemen won't linger in the library indefinitely, suffering through Albert's and Father's ponderous speeches. Imagine the scandal, all of them trooping in here and me with my hair down." Her mother would suffer apoplexy for sure if she knew

Ethan Harcourt had held her hands in his, had even brushed a kiss against her knuckles when they'd been at Clara's cottage, alone. Unchaperoned.

Or that Clara longed for more.

Fifteen minutes later, the sound of masculine voices swelled, echoing down the hall into the sitting room. Louise frantically stuffed the last pin in place. Clara had no idea what her sister had fashioned, since there was no mirror available, but she figured her hair now looked as different from her usual topknot as Louise could manage. The stage was set. She would maneuver herself close enough to force Ethan's attention, then commence whatever appropriate feminine behavior her panicked brain divulged, to indicate her reciprocal interest.

The gentlemen filled the entry, resplendent in their black tie and tails, Dr. Harcourt in the middle of the group. The hard planes and angles of his face looked more relaxed than when he first arrived. He half turned to her father. "...and I look forward to speaking with you on the matter soon."

"Anytime, sir," Clarence Penrose replied, clapping a hand on Ethan's shoulder. "Canterbury's fortunate to have acquired such a knowledgeable healer of bodies. But I must say again, Doctor, that Congress has lost a powerful voice. Perhaps in a few more years, you'll reconsider."

Bertha rejoined the party. Chatting and smiling, she wove her way through the men, urging them to partake of dessert and coffee. Then she spied Clara. Her mouth dropped open in dumbfounded silence. Close to bolting, Clara fixed what she hoped was a congenial expression on her face.

Dreamlike, she watched Albert frown when he

glanced down at his wife, watched Harry hurry over to Louise, Willy to the plate of Christmas petit fours on the sideboard.

Watched Dr. Harcourt finally turn away from her father to face the ladies—and Clara. His eyes flared wide, then narrowed to slits that reminded Clara more of a rattlesnake's stare than an admiring gentlemen struck dumb by a lady's beauty. A muscle in his jaw twitched. "Ladies." Ignoring Clara as though she had melted into the wallpaper, he bowed to Bertha. "Thank you for opening your home to a newcomer, Mrs. Penrose. Mr. Penrose is fortunate to have so accomplished a hostess for a wife."

"Clara?" Holding a delicate china plate piled with confections, Willie elbowed his way past the other men. Though twenty-one, he had not perfected the fine art of dissembling. "What in the name of Abe's aces have you done to your hair? You look like—you look…."

"Absolutely lovely," Mr. Harcourt finished smoothly, his eyes darkened to a fiery emerald green. "And now, I must beg your leave. It's late."

He turned on his heel, nodded to the others and strode down the hall, leaving behind him a widening pool of silence.

Chapter Nine

Friday morning, before he opened his offices for morning patients Ethan paid a visit to the sheriff's office. After the rotten fruit basket Tuesday evening and Clara's transformation the previous night, he could no longer justify a private investigation on his own. But as he drove the buggy through the almost deserted streets he continued to second-guess himself.

He should have tried harder to secure a few moments' privacy with Clarence Penrose, subtly pick his brain about Clara's childhood.

He should have conducted the Tuesday afternoon visit with Clara like a medical visit, not a blasted confessional.

If only he knew *why* she'd transformed herself the previous night—a joke on him, for ignoring her most of the evening? A ploy to force his attention? Prove he was as helpless against feminine wiles as the next man?

He had spent another sleepless night, fighting all those 'if onlys,' shadows he couldn't touch, feelings he couldn't ignore.

Whatever alchemy Clara had contrived with her hair,

the result had taken his breath away. She had looked...
beautiful. Bewitching.

And he was questioning her sanity.

God help me, he prayed the last four blocks to the
town hall, where the sheriff's office resided.

Canterbury did not have a jail; on the infrequent occasions when confinement was required, law enforce-
ment transported miscreants to the jailhouse in the town
of Fairfax. Ethan pulled the horse to a stop in front of
the sturdy redbrick building, for several moments staring blindly between the horse's ears before he heaved
himself out of the buggy. Sheriff Millard Gleason's office was on the first floor, where tall windows allowed
him to survey the busiest blocks of Main Street. When
Ethan pushed open the door, the sheriff had just poured
himself an earthenware mug of eggnog.

"Morning, Dr. Harcourt. What brings you to town
so early in the morning?"

"My first appointment's at nine, so I'll need to head
back shortly. But I..." he fought, and lost, the final battle with his heart "...I need to alert you about a... I'll
call it a situation."

The sheriff's congenial expression disappeared.
"What are you saying here, Dr. Harcourt? I take it this
is an official call, then?"

Ethan crossed his legs, fingers hovering at his waistcoat pocket before he reluctantly pulled out the notes.
"I might have a problem. But my, ah, dilemma, seems
to have progressed from mischief or medical, to legal,
and I don't like my conclusions. Someone's been leaving me these notes." With a sinking sensation hollowing
his gut, he handed them to the sheriff. "No signature,
no return address. Only the first one was postmarked."

Gleason swiftly read them, shaggy eyebrows drawing together. "Hmmph. By themselves, benign. Read all together, I can see why you're concerned. One with the postmark's from Washington, D.C. Inconclusive as far as tracking it down. What happened to this one?" He held up a discolored, rumpled note.

"Tuesday night when I returned home from evening rounds, I almost tripped over a basket of rotten fruit. That missive was stuck between two rotten apples. There were also rotten potatoes, moldy bread—and two rotten eggs. The stench was so bad I had to hire a man to scour the entire porch."

"I can imagine. Note still stinks a bit, too." Scowling, Gleason read through all three again, grunting a bit over the last one. "'More will be coming, because you deserve more,'" he read, his frown deepening. "Considering the mode of delivery, I'm inclined to agree with you, Doc. This constitutes more of a threat than a malicious prank. So why didn't you bring this to my attention first thing Wednesday?"

Ethan shifted. The back of his neck felt as though an iron spike was shoving its way to the base of his skull. "Because until the rotten fruit, it was just the notes, and they're phrased very...ambiguously. I tried to fob them off as trivial incidents, annoying rather than posing any sort of problem. When I was a congressman, this sort of thing happened all the time—the price one pays for serving the public. You learn to ignore most of them unless a specific threat is tendered."

"You're no longer a congressman." The sheriff's fingers, thick as cigars, were nonetheless nimble as he spread each note out on the desk. "So. I think the reason you've waited until now to bring those notes to me is because you have an idea who's behind this."

"I do." Ethan sat forward, while inside the sickness swam in tightening circles. "Evidence is circumstantial, a bit of conjecture. The last thing I want to do is impugn the reputation of a lady."

Gleason rumbled an agreement. "Handwriting's definitely female. From what I hear and see, there's not an unattached woman in Canterbury who hasn't eyeballed you for potential husband material, you being a fine-looking fellow and a widower. You don't strike me as a man who deliberately tramples a lady's delicate feelings, but it appears you have ruffled a feminine feather or two?"

"Not intentionally, except for...one."

"Ah." The sheriff picked up his mug of eggnog. "Well, get on with it, then. Do what you came here to do. Who's the suspect, Doctor?"

Ethan closed his eyes, braced himself, then faced the sheriff and stated flatly, "Clara Penrose."

"What!" Gleason choked on the eggnog. "Clara Penrose?" he spluttered after he quit coughing. "Clara's about as sly and secretive as a brass band. Woman's got a mouth on her, that's a fact, and she's never been shy about stating her opinion. But she's a *Penrose*. I mean, the family helped found this town. Their roots go back to the Revolution. Her father's law firm is one of the most respected on the east coast."

"Don't you think I know all that?" Ethan stood, paced the room. "Albert Penrose is my friend. I've eaten meals with the family, I've observed them in social settings. I worship with them." He whirled around and pounded his fist on top of Gleason's desk. "I feel like a Judas! But she's…she's… There are indications. Habits—"

He couldn't do it. He simply could not break confidence, not with Clara. *Even her family doesn't know.* Yet she'd bared her heart's passion for writing…with him. *But why? God? Why?* "I'm a physician," he ground out. "Regardless of the improbability, if Clara Penrose wrote those notes, my first priority is to determine the motivation. To diagnose whether her actions are malicious rather than medical. Then, if possible, to help her. But without proof, provided by trained officers of the law, I can confront neither her nor her family with any authority."

"Take it easy, Dr. Harcourt. I see your point. You're in a difficult position. Come on, have a seat. Drink some eggnog. I'll tell you what I'm going to do." The sheriff snagged a second mug from a shelf, then poured some eggnog out of a large mason jar. "I won't mention any names, but I'll have a word with Donald Fitzwalter—he's Canterbury's postmaster. Ask him to keep an eye out for any correspondence mailed to you without a return address. Also, either myself or one of my deputies will immediately commence keeping an eye on your place. Discreetly, mind you. No names will be mentioned to anyone but my two deputies. If anyone comes snooping around, we'll catch 'em in the act. But I can pretty much guarantee it won't be Clara Penrose."

By Saturday afternoon, while carefully packing fruitcake, snickerdoodles and two jars of preserves into a basket, Clara finally admitted the truth—she had fallen in love with Ethan Harcourt. Instead of the heavens opening with golden trumpets, her eyes stupidly teared up.

Her fingers fumbled with a silver ribbon she was weaving around the handle of the basket; twice she had to wipe her cheeks with the back of her hand. Despite Louise's overly romantic soul, despite the evidence in literature, poems—even Bible stories—Clara had never believed love rendered a person brainless. Yet what else could account for her stubborn refusal to scrap her "counter-courtship campaign" after Ethan had left the dinner party Thursday night with that barely civil departure?

"Intolerably rude," her mother had pronounced after the door shut behind him. Then she turned a glacial stare upon her two daughters. "As for you and your sister, I trust there will be no repeat of this ill-timed and inappropriate conduct."

"But, Mother, did you see the look on Dr. Harcourt's face?" Louise unwisely pointed out. "I think Clara poleaxed him. That's why his leave-taking smacks of rudeness."

After her mother had excoriated Louise for her vulgarisms, she'd swept out of the room. Clara had hugged her sister and escaped to the sanctuary of her cottage.

Miserably, she finished her first "secret gift" basket by covering it with a bright red tea towel, newly decorated with green holly leaves embroidered in each corner. She'd stayed up until three in the morning doing the needlework, her eyes burning along with her heart.

She wanted to believe Louise was right about Ethan's expression; it was difficult, however, when Clara felt more like the ugly duckling who had grown into an equally ill-favored duck instead of a swan. Here she was, thirty-one years old, supposedly content to be the erudite spinster of the family. *Quit lying to yourself, Clara.* Ethan's ice-tipped comment, shorn of any emotion—*She looks lovely*—had wounded her deeply. If she hadn't cared so much, if his earlier honesty and tenderness had not tricked her into trust, she wouldn't have cared two figs about his indifferent reaction to Louise's handiwork.

Love. One either soared on its wings, or sank like a stone into a bog of self-pity.

Rubbish. Next she would pen bad poetry instead of competent prose. Sigh over sunsets, weep by a window—a reluctant smile at last brightened Clara's mood.

Well, then. Tonight she had promised to join a group of carolers, comprised mostly of members of various church choirs, along with other townsfolk who, like Clara, possessed some level of musical training. Unless she quit mooning over her basket of goodies and instead set about delivering it, she wouldn't make it to the meeting spot on the front steps of the town hall by seven o'clock.

Moments later she let herself out of the cottage and set off down the street. The afternoon was cold, but not unpleasant. With sunbeams slanting sideways through the elms, Clara made her way to the livery stable on the edge of town, basket clutched firmly in her gloved hand. She could have walked the mile or so to Ethan's house, but she risked being seen by too many people, all of whom would ask too many nosy questions. She also refused to borrow the family runabout, because a family interrogation was worse than good-natured nosiness. Amos Todd would rent her a hack, no questions asked. She would simply tell any loiterers who perpetually gathered around the stable to gossip that she had walked to town, then decided to follow up on some duty calls which required a buggy.

Truth sometimes served better than sleight-of-handing explanations.

By the time she pulled the trap to a halt a block away from Ethan's house, streaks of red-orange and salmon pink fingered across the western sky; shadows had lengthened, allowing Clara to dart from tree to tree as she approached the house from the side opposite the door to his offices. A fine sense of the absurd fluttered beneath her breastbone, along with a recklessness that throughout her life presaged nothing but trouble.

She ducked behind the screen of some unpruned English boxwood, waiting for a carriage to roll by in the street, then two schoolboys furiously pedaling bicycles to disappear around the corner. Perhaps she would write her next letter to the editor of a ladies' magazine, warning about the irrational behavior precipitated by a heart in the throes of love.

Her family and friends…heavens, the entire community, would never believe that Clara Penrose could skulk through the bushes outside a gentleman's home. Grinning now, she hurried across to Ethan's front porch. It was half past four, and she knew his Saturday hours ran late, usually until almost six. He would still be busy with patients, all of whom would use the door on the other side of the house, leaving the front porch nicely deserted.

After some swift internal debate, Clara deposited the basket in the middle of the porch, beside the afternoon paper. The recklessness shimmied through her in a delicious shiver; she dashed back toward the boxwoods, her mind on her next "Ethan Project" until from the corner of her eye she spotted movement in the shadows off to her right. Seconds later Deputy Michael O'Shea stepped out from behind the trunk of a white pine. Arms dangling, mouth half-open in disbelief, he gawked at her as though he couldn't decide whether to socialize—or flatten her with his billy club.

Thoughts scattered, Clara gathered her skirts in her hands and ran for the rental buggy.

Chapter Ten

Saturday proved to be a viciously long day for Ethan. First patient of the morning was Saul Porter, who had to be told the pain was due to an incurable cancer. After that he treated seven cases of chicken pox, two of mumps, set one broken arm and two broken fingers, then puzzled over an inexplicable rash. A little past five o'clock he was about to draw his first deep breath of the day when Patricia Dunwoody dropped by with a trumped-up complaint about a dry cough.

"Tonight I'm going caroling. I was afraid not to see you, in case there's something wrong."

Ethan avoided the sweetly smiling eyes, examined her and pronounced her in perfect health, the cough likely due to dryness in the air. "Suck on some peppermint drops," he suggested. "Take in as many fluids as possible. Nonalcoholic, of course."

She colored up prettily, and a coy smile tipped the corners of her mouth. "Of course, Dr. Harcourt. Um… would you like to join us with the caroling this evening?" she tried next. "We're always in desperate need of gentlemen who can carry a tune, and I've heard on good authority that you've a fine tenor voice."

Now his face heated. "I don't think so, Miss Dunwoody."

"Please reconsider. There's something wonderful about singing Christmas carols on a clear winter's night, bundled up with all your friends and neighbors, strolling the streets." She paused before adding casually, "Clara will be there. She doesn't have much of a voice, but she does have a good ear. You know she teaches piano?" Ethan managed a nod. Patricia finally picked up a fur-trimmed wool coat and slid her arms into the sleeves. "It's none of my business, of course, but I've known Clara all my life. Underneath her bluestocking ideas and annoying habits is a very nice person, Dr. Harcourt. She and I butt heads a lot, but… I wouldn't want her to be hurt by misunderstandings, or expectations fueled by erroneous gossip."

"I don't know, or care, about town gossip." Teeth grinding, Ethan restrained his temper. Barely. Protestations and denials would only fan the flame, so he mustered up a smile. "I'm pretty rusty at it these days, but I used to enjoy singing. Perhaps I'll join you after all, Miss Dunwoody. Thanks for the invitation."

Surprise flared in her face. While he maintained the upper hand Ethan, plying her with questions about the caroling, managed to usher her out to her waiting runabout. Dusk had fallen, the air turning colder. Streetlights threw out yellow smears of light against a darkening sky. Shivering a little, Ethan waited until Patricia expertly backed the horse, and waved as she drove away.

Clara will be there, Miss Dunwoody had slyly in-

formed him. Might as well slice open a vein and let his
blood drip down the middle of Main Street, since apparently nothing about his life passed unnoticed. In a burst
of unspent fury he scooped up a couple of acorns, and
hurled them across the street. He was no longer a poli-
tician—he was a physician, for crying out loud. What
gave these people the right to poke about his private
life, speculate on his personal relationships with others? Skin crawling, Ethan stalked around to the front
porch to fetch the afternoon paper, and found Mick
O'Shea, the deputy sheriff, sitting in one of the old
cane-bottom rocking chairs the previous owner had
left with the house.

O'Shea tipped his bowler back and nodded to Ethan,
a grim look carving deep lines on his weather-beaten
face. "Dr. Harcourt. Been waiting for you a spell."
Lackadaisically he struck a match on the bottom of
his shoe, lit a kerosene lantern sitting beside the chair.
Light spilled across the porch, limning a wicker basket
covered with a red cloth, sitting beside the paper some
six yards away from Ethan. "Saw the person who left
that there basket, I did. And I wouldn't be wanting to
alarm ye, but 'twould seem you had the way of it. Miss
Clara Penrose left it, and she wasn't wanting to be seen
committing the act."

If O'Shea had punched him in the solar plexus with
his billy club, Ethan couldn't have felt more sickened.
With a feeling of unreality he walked across to the basket. A perky silver ribbon had been wound around the
handle, ending with a fancy bow at one corner. The faint
aroma of some kind of spice tickled his nose when he
hesitantly picked the thing up.

He supposed he should be grateful that she hadn't left rotten fruit this time.

"You wanting me to examine that for you first, Dr. Harcourt?"

He hadn't even noticed that the deputy had approached, and now hovered at his side. "No, thanks. I'll do it. Put the lantern on the railing, if you don't mind, so I can see." Fingers numb, Ethan fumbled the cloth aside, then stared at the contents, a lump swelling in his throat. Silently he carried the basket back over to the rocking chairs and sank down in the one O'Shea had vacated. One by one he lifted out the objects, holding them where the lantern light fell. A sack full of cookies, dusted with sugar sprinkles. A loaf of fruitcake, which he quickly set aside, his stomach turning over. Fruit… Two jars of preserves.

No note.

"Thanks for waiting," he told the deputy. "I'll come by in the morning to talk to the sheriff. I'd appreciate it if you wouldn't mention this to anybody."

"I'm to stay hereabouts till midnight. If you're of a mind, I'll ask the sheriff to send along a replacement. Don't be needing mischief to befall ye, Doc."

"That won't be necessary. And you may as well go home to your wife. I'm…not going to be here this evening. I'm going caroling." Bitterness lapped over him at the prospect of singing merry Christmas melodies elbow to elbow with Clara.

Bitterness, however, was preferable to despair.

After the deputy reluctantly clumped down the porch steps and vanished into the gloom, Ethan carried the basket inside. In the silent house, the steady tick-tock of the handsome cherry wall clock he'd inherited from his father only magnified his isolation. Ignoring the time—he needed to leave in half an hour to make it to the town square by seven—he dumped the contents of the basket on the kitchen table. For some moments he sat, chin resting on the heel of his hand while he contemplated the condemnatory evidence.

Eventually he gave in and selected one of the cookies, sniffed it. If she'd laced it with some kind of poison, or any of several noxious substances designed to incapacitate but not kill, he wanted to find out now. Memories danced in ethereal will-o'-the-wisps around his head—Clara, talking to a pile of leaves with a real or imagined turtle buried in them; Clara, walking in graceful solitude to the front of the church to lay the charm on the corner of the dais; Clara, listening to him bare his soul…. *Dear God. I don't know what to do.* He had no choice but to believe O'Shea, yet he could not abandon entirely his own observations, or yes, blast it, his feelings, which insisted that Clara Penrose was not capable of this level of deceit. All the evidence accumulated against her remained circumstantial, not definitive enough to convict her of any crime but driving *him* crazy.

If amoral thieves and murderers hadn't hanged him in the southwestern desert, surely God did not intend him to perish at the hands of a spinster who talked to cats and turtles. A spinster whose personality shone with the brightness of the North Star… His free hand fumbled inside the pocket of his vest, closing around the tiny silver charm.

Abruptly he bit off half the cookie, chewed and swallowed.

Flavors exploded in his mouth—of nutmeg and sugar

and vanilla, a delicious concoction too irresistible for a man who hadn't eaten since breakfast, not to mention a man who stood on the brink of destruction. Five minutes later he'd eaten every one of the cookies. As he poured himself a glass of tepid limeade from the bottle the housekeeper had left in the icebox, he finally faced a truth far less palatable than the cookies.

He'd fallen in love with a woman who baked like an angel, yet who might very well be clinically insane.

Clara shifted from foot to foot, shivering a little despite the smothering confines of coat, hat, muff and a muffler wound at the moment over half her face. It was five past seven and Jeremiah Fiske, choir director at the local Catholic church, was, with limited success, attempting to arrange the milling carolers.

"...so that each group of four comprises a harmonious whole. Please remember this endeavor will offer much more musical satisfaction to the listeners when sung in harmony."

"I only know the melodies," one of the men called out.

"Can I stay with my aunt? She sings off-key if I don't help her..."

"I have to leave by nine...."

Finally everyone was collected to Mr. Fiske's satisfaction. Clara was paired with another alto because her voice, though true, possessed little carrying power. The other three members of her little ensemble worshipped at the Methodist church; Clara had a nodding acquaintance with them but set off gamely despite learning on their first carol—"Lo, How a Rose e'er Blooming"—

that Mr. Klausner, the tenor, sang with more force than purity.

It looked to be a long, chilly night.

Halfway through "O Little Town of Bethlehem" she sensed movement in the darkness to her left, and Mr. Klausner's voice faltered. She heard the rumble of a whispered exchange as another man pressed against her shoulder close enough that she felt him inhale a deep breath before he joined the carolers with a magnificently pure tenor that tripped Clara's heart. Almost unconsciously she angled her head to better blend her light alto with the new man's voice. *"No ear may hear His coming,/But in this world of sin,/Where meek souls will receive Him still/The dear Christ enters in..."*

She lost herself in the sheer joy of singing beside a man who surely must have Irish in his blood, so reverentially soaring was his voice. When Mr. Fiske signaled the carolers to move along, Clara twisted her head to compliment the newest member of her little ensemble. "You've a marvelous tenor," she began, except the group passed beneath one of the wreath-decked streetlamps, and she caught a glimpse of the singer's face. The rest of the words caught in her throat.

"I'm glad you think so," Ethan returned, light and life now stripped from his tone. "You're a marvelous cook, Miss Penrose. I ate every one of the cookies, which is why I was late arriving. I, ah, persuaded Mr. Klausner that his services had been requested for a section lacking a strong tenor voice, because I wanted to let you know my feelings about your anonymous gift."

The cookies? He must have discovered the basket, then. Should she be warmed or piqued that he had instantly divined the identity of the giver? "How do you know I left the basket?"

Above her head a sound like a hiss escaped. A strong hand clamped down on her shoulder. Even through the thick wool caplet draped over her long coat she felt the commanding strength of his grasp. "I'd like to say I recognized your handiwork. But the truth is—"

"All right, everyone," Mr. Fiske announced. "For our next song, 'It Came Upon a Midnight Clear,' we'll start with just the ladies. Gentleman, join in on the second verse."

He hummed the starting note, and all female voices save one launched into the song. Ethan's hand slid down her arm, burrowed beneath the cape so that he could grasp her elbow. "We're going to have a little chat," he whispered into her ear as he relentlessly herded her away from the carolers.

Chapter Eleven

"What are you doing?" Heart thumping hard enough to make her dizzy, Clara stumbled over a crooked brick, and Ethan's hand tightened. "Ethan, I can't see well in the dark, and you're walking too fast—oomph!"

He stopped with a suddenness that made her smack straight into him. But even as she tried to pull back, his arm wrapped around her, coat and all, then he half guided, half carried her past the Gordons' house, Mrs. Brenders's boardinghouse and a packed-dirt cross street until they reached the livery stable, now deserted. Obscured by the night, a horse and buggy waited in front of the hitching post.

"Get in," Ethan ordered, his hands insistent as he virtually shoved her up onto the narrow cloth seat.

Clara might have leaped out while he walked around to untie the horse, except she was almost as curious as she was furious. The seat springs squeaked when he climbed in beside her. He jiggled the reins, setting the buggy in motion. "I've never dealt well with officiousness," she began levelly enough.

"Right now, I'm not dealing well with anything."

While Clara sputtered her way through that retort he tossed a heavy wool lap robe over her. "Bundle up. I'm the only physician around Canterbury these days, and in my present mood you wouldn't want to fall sick."

"I never get sick of anything but surly high-handed males." She was grateful at the moment for the thick shroud of darkness, otherwise Ethan would be able to see her face. Surely the hurt would show—how often had he told her about her expressive face? Worse yet, tears stung her eyes.

Clara was not a weeper. One more reason she never should have fallen in love with this difficult, confusing man, she decided as one of the puddled tears finally slid down her cheek. If it wouldn't have involved fighting her way free of muff, coat and heavy lap robe, she would have swatted his arm. "Now that you've successfully abducted me, where are we going?" she asked instead.

For a sickening moment Ethan didn't respond. The horse trotted along, its hooves and the jingle of the harness the only sounds other than the rattle of the buggy wheels. Clara's vision blurred no matter how many times she blinked the moisture away.

Without warning he swung the horse to the side of the road, under a bare-branched elm whose immense trunk, when combined with the starless night, plunged them into invisibility. "I don't know where we're going," he growled before muttering some inaudible phrase. "For three years I've been doing my best to go nowhere. When I finally scrape together the courage to try living again, you come along and resurrect feelings I thought atrophied a long time ago."

"So sorry to hear you have feelings. Since you've trampled all over mine, I'll try to return the favor."

Struggling furiously, Clara worked one hand free of all encumbrances, swiped her face, then attacked the lap robe. "Ever since we met again you've behaved like an India-rubber ball, bouncing helter-skelter in all directions. One moment you're a charming gentleman, the next you act as though I'm a noxious insect in need of squashing. You compare me to a *table arrangement,* but when I try to alter my appearance to look more... more womanly you storm out of the house without a word. You call unannounced, bare your soul, and now you're dragging me off in the night like a pirate! So to reassure you, *Dr.* Harcourt, I will abandon all the plans I've made, and promise to pretend you don't exist even if we have the misfortune to sit beside one another at a dinner party. And if I'm ever unfortunate enough to need a physician, I'll find one in Washington!"

"You want to talk about erratic behavior? Very well, let's look at yours. You're an educated, intelligent woman, yet for all intents and purposes your family acts as if they're embarrassed by you. You're also a striking woman, yet you seem set on hiding the beauty. You live alone, you write anonymous letters to editors that you don't want anyone to know about. You talk to me with perception and sensitivity, then turn around and...and— *Dear God in heaven.*" His voice turned hoarse, even anguished. "This is too much. I can't—"

All of a sudden his hands burrowed beneath her cape to clamp over her upper arms. "Clara, why didn't you include a note with the basket?"

She passed her tongue around dry lips and tried not to cringe. "What difference does it make? You apparently knew instantly I was the giver. I planned to include a note with my next surprise." When Ethan jerked as though she'd jabbed him with a hatpin, Clara couldn't control a reflexive flinch.

Thick silence froze the air between them.

Then slowly, his movements almost caressing, Ethan slid his hands up her arms to her face. Like Clara he wore gloves. The faint scent of expensive leather burned her nostrils and the careful touch burned her heart. "I've frightened you, haven't I?" he asked in a voice gone soft as kidskin. "I'm sorry. Shh…don't say anything. It's all right."

"No, it's not." She sniffed loudly. Where had her righteous indignation disappeared to? "I don't understand you."

"The feeling's mutual." There was a pause. "Clara? Why, you're crying, aren't you?"

"What if I am? You drag me off into the night, hurt my feelings, then you—you…" The words dribbled to a halt because he removed his hands long enough to tug off the gloves, then skimmed her cheeks with his bare fingers. Though chilled by the winter night, his touch set off torches that heated Clara's skin and shot Chinese sparklers along her veins.

But his gentleness intensified her confusion. More tears spilled over. She heard Ethan's breath catch. "Here." He pressed a handkerchief into her hand.

Silently Clara mopped her face and wondered if she possessed the strength to maintain her composure until she reached the privacy of her cottage. "I'm cold. I'd like to go home. Please."

"Will you at least answer a question? I know I don't have the right to ask, but… I need to. Badly."

She peered through the darkness, but could scarcely discern the faint glitter of his eyes, much less his expression. But she sensed the desperation rolling off him in waves, desperation and a profound weariness that mirrored her own. Love, Clara decided, truly left one's soul too vulnerable to pain, and all the joys promised in the Bible were not strong enough to counter it.

Yet she could not refuse Ethan's plea. Perhaps that in itself was from God—this longing to dispense reassurance, to offer comfort despite the fear of enduring further hurts. *Comfort ye, my people...*

Hesitantly, Clara allowed the tenuous emotion to fill her up, praying that her own fractured faith would still be heard with compassion.

If Ethan asked her something improper or salacious, however, she'd wallop him with the buggy whip, assuming she could find it in this ink-blot darkness. "What do you want to ask me, then?"

A short laugh was the response, followed by another moment of strained silence. "I'm probably shooting myself in the foot, but at this juncture I don't care anymore. Clara...over the past several weeks have you sent me other notes? Anonymous ones?"

Mystified, she tilted her head, straining to catch at least a glimpse of his expression. "No. I know you asked me to—" and she'd spent days fretting about it "—but I've never sent you any sort of note, anonymous or otherwise. It might sound contradictory, considering the basket I left on your porch, but it would be rude to send an unsigned note, don't you think? I don't write many personal letters—don't have time."

"You do write letters to editors, using a pseudonym."

"Which is why I don't have time to write personal notes. As you pointed out, I'm already an embarrassment to my family. They would be—I'll call it indignant—about the tone of some of my letters."

"I never should have said what I did, about your family. Will you forgive me? My sister harped about my stupidity in marrying Lillian. My dad never understood why I wanted to leave medicine for politics. But they still loved me. So does your family." He paused, then heaved a long sigh. "Never mind. I know you're still confused. I'd like the chance to explain. Actually, if you're willing to trust me enough, I'd like to show you something."

Gathering fortitude about her like chain mail, Clara cautiously responded, "I trust the man I met in a garden three years ago. I trust the doctor my brother convinced to open a practice here. As for anything else…"

"That will do for now. Whether you believe it or not, I understand. You might say I'm not the trusting sort myself, when it comes to women." He gave another bitter little laugh. "You tell yourself you'll heal, that time and God's grace will eventually do its work. You finally lower your guard—and get thrashed."

"What have I ever done, that you believe I could deliberately hurt you, Ethan?" The question burst forth, but she no longer cared a fig what emotions she revealed. Later she would work through any regrets—much later, when she was a tottering old lady who only faintly remembered what it felt like to have been seared by unrequited love. She would write her memoirs, then burn them to ashes.

"God help me," Ethan said, "but I hope the answer to your question is nothing at all." He gathered the reins and they continued down the street. "What I want to show you is in my desk drawer. If you prefer, we can stop by the sheriff's office, and have him or one of the deputies accompany us."

The sheriff's office? A niggle of alarm quickened her pulse. "Does this have something to do with Deputy O'Shea lurking around your house?"

"Yes."

"So he's the reason you know who left the basket."

"He saw you leave it, yes."

When he didn't elaborate, Clara leaned her head back against the seat and closed her eyes. Sometimes, picking at the scabs of a person's hurts left deeper scars. Lord only knew she bore a heart full of them herself. "Do whatever you want," she told Ethan.

He murmured something in response. She wasn't sure, but she thought it sounded like *If only I could.*

Chapter Twelve

On the short and silent journey to his house, Ethan tried to pray. His thoughts had scattered like windblown snowflakes when Clara claimed she'd never written him any notes. She'd even offered an explanation, one quaintly Clara-esque, and because he wanted to believe her so badly he'd behaved like the most boorish of clods.

He had frightened her. What sort of man bullied the woman he loved into a buggy and drove off into the night with her?

Don't ask the question if you can't face the answer.

After securing the horse, he assisted Clara down, unsurprised when she marched down the brick walkway without once looking his way. Fortunately a streetlight illuminated the path to his front porch. Once inside, he hung their coats and mufflers on the coatrack, then led her down the hall to his office. "This won't take long," he promised, reaching for a scrap of paper and a pen. "Please sit down." She stiffly perched on the edge of the chair while he dipped the pen in ink, then handed it to her. "Would you write a sentence, anything you think of—a line from a Christmas carol, a poem? Even a shopping list will do."

"You want to see if my handwriting matches the notes, don't you?"

He nodded, noting absently that his blood pressure had given him a headache, and his insides felt as though he'd ingested an entire block's worth of bricks.

"What on earth do those notes say?" She stared blankly at the pen, then up at Ethan, comprehension draining her complexion of color. "Someone's *threatening* you, aren't they? That's why Officer O'Shea was here. He's guarding you. So where is he now? If you've been threatened, what are you thinking, to wander around without him? Ethan, why haven't you— Wait. Wait." Her gaze slid back to the pen, then the paper on the desk.

When she lifted her head again, Ethan planted his feet square on the floor and stood unmoving, shoulders braced for the killing blow. A hurt, angry woman inflicted more injury with words than any hurled stones. His hands, sweating now, curled into fists, and he could feel the nervous tic in his left eye he'd developed the year Lillian began her first affair. *God, I don't want to run anymore. Help me face her like a man.*

So he stood still while she searched his features with excruciating thoroughness. Stood while she wrote several lines on the sheet of paper, then solemnly thrust it out.

Their fingers brushed; he watched in stupefaction as color rushed into her pale cheeks, and the pen dropped with a clatter onto the desk. A blob of ink splashed onto the blotter like drops of blood. Slowly Ethan forced himself to look down at the words.

It is easy to go down into Hell…but to climb back
out again, to retrace one's steps to the upper air—
there's the rub, the task.

"It's from Virgil's *Aeneid*. I could have written it
in Latin, but I was afraid you'd think I was showing
off. Well?" She stood abruptly, chin tilted imperiously.
"What do you have to say, Dr. Harcourt?"

Ethan tossed the paper onto the desk, then carefully
reached for those cool, slender fingers. "I say thank
God, and will you forgive me?"

"Amen. And…eventually."

A gust of pure relief weakened his knees. He brought
her hand to his mouth and pressed a fervent kiss against
the inside of her wrist. "Would it help if I confess that I
love you, that these past few weeks have been eating me
alive…and your quote could not have been more accurate if you'd been inside my head?" He smiled, loving
the sight of her rapid descent into flustered confusion.

"I… What did you say?" she stammered out. "Is this
another trick?"

"No, dear one. It's the declaration of a man teetering
on the verge of destruction, because he was terrified the
woman with whom he'd fallen in love had instead fallen
into a mental abyss where I couldn't save her." Wrapping his fingers around her delicate wrist, he tugged
her closer. "Not only are you inside my head, you're
inside my heart."

Because he'd come to better understand her, Ethan
quietly held her hand against his thudding heart and
waited for her to sort everything out. The wait was not
devoid of pleasure; for the first time he felt free to absorb her features—the line of her jaw, the shape of her

ears and the soft tendril of seal-brown hair that had escaped to dangle along her temple. Her incredible eyes brimmed with intelligence and uncertainty and shyness.

After a while the prolonged silence began to erode his nascent confidence.

God, I don't deserve her. But I can't bear the thought of her turning away. He should have waited, should have kept his fool mouth shut until he gained her trust again. He should have—

"Ethan?"

"Ask anything you want, sweetheart." He brushed his index finger, which trembled slightly, to the pulse throbbing in her temple. "I understand why you're confused, and I can only apologize—the rest of my life if necessary—for ever believing you'd be capable of writing threatening notes, no matter how vague the threat."

Unbelievably, Clara shrugged. "If I'd been married to a man who repeatedly betrayed me, I'd feel the same suspicion toward all other men. Without evidence to the contrary, of course you'd wonder if I'd written…whatever was written in those notes. Then for Mr. O'Shea to witness my delivery of a basket—" her eyes crinkled at the corners "—which I'm afraid was carried out in a noticeably clandestine manner, well, I'd be suspicious of me, too. You don't have to apologize. You've made it…ah, abundantly clear that I'm no longer a suspect."

Abruptly the wisp of humor vanished. "I just can't believe… I never dreamed a man, especially someone like you, would…would…"

Her voice trailed away and her eyelashes swept down to screen her expression. When she started shaking, Ethan with scant ceremony tossed convention aside and drew her into his arms. "Shh…" he whispered, pressing her head against his shoulder. "Shh…"

Her hands clutched fistfuls of his waistcoat. "You're a former congressman, a respected physician. You can't possibly lo—" She stopped.

"Love you?" he finished it for her. "Well, now that I'm convinced I'm not going to have to have both of us admitted to St. Elizabeth's Asylum, how about if I spend between now and Christmas convincing you that, if you'll have it, my heart is yours, Clara Penrose?"

"You don't know me!" She thumped her hands against his chest. "That's why you suspected me in the first place. I'm eccentric. I live alone. I love animals and treat them like people. I have absolutely no fashion sense as you know, and I never know what to do with my hair. That's why I just stuff it in the bun. What you saw that night at Albert's house is impossible for me to duplicate. My fingers can play a Bach fugue but they don't know what to do with hairpins. And…and I believe that women really should have the right to vote and that— Mmph."

He stilled the panicked flow of words with a kiss, a brief but thorough kiss that ripped through his wavering control like a scalpel slicing cheesecloth. When Clara turned boneless in his arms, he forced himself to lift his head. "I refuse to apologize for my gross impropriety."

"Mmm. Me either," she mumbled dazedly, then blushed a lovely shade of rose.

Charmed, he cupped her chin. "As for your character condemnation—a trait we'll have to work on—I happen to believe God knew precisely the sort of woman I needed to clear the scales from my eyes. And that woman, dear one, is you."

"I always heard love was blind." Her fingers crept up to his face. "I've never been kissed like that before," she whispered. "Is it different, when you love someone?"

All the breath sucked out of his lungs. Throat tight, Ethan hugged her, dropping soft kisses to her eyelids, her nose, forehead, then finally eased her back down into the desk chair to avoid the temptation of her tremulous mouth. "What are you saying, Clara?" he asked, the words husky.

She swallowed several times, but the dark brown eyes didn't so much as flicker. When at last she spoke, the words emerged soft yet clear as a cloudless winter night. "I'm saying that I love you back, Ethan Harcourt. I'm not sure what we're supposed to do about it, though."

All the Christmas bells in the world could not equal the joyful clanging in Ethan's heart. He wanted to shout, wanted to sweep this precious woman back into his arms and never let her go.

Instead, because she was Clara, he knelt on the floor beside her, lost himself in those great dark eyes and allowed himself one last kiss, repeating his avowal of love against her lips.

Tomorrow he would address the unknown woman's identity, and contact the sheriff. But for tonight, he needed to embrace the one he was convinced had been heaven-sent, at just the right time, for all the right reasons.

Thanks for the best Christmas present You could give me, Lord.

Outside, a dark figure slowly sank to the cold ground, one fist pressed against her mouth to stifle the scream clawing to escape. How could he? How *dared* he bring a woman to his house, late at night, without even a butler or housekeeper in residence? He knew better. And the woman—she knew that woman. She'd seen her face in the streetlight when the doctor helped her out of his buggy. Of all the women in this self-righteous little community, Clara Penrose should know better than to engage in such scandalous behavior.

Except she *was* Clara Penrose, who, despite her unconventional ways, was considered practically a saint. Oh, she'd heard all the stories in the boardinghouse. It was Miss Penrose this and Miss Penrose that. They might talk behind their hands about her eccentricities, but they still thought she set the moon and stars in place.

Well, perhaps Clara Penrose's reputation deserved a readjustment.

Her previous warnings to Ethan Harcourt had not achieved the desired effect. She had been too cautious. Too…squeamish.

Huddled on the bone-chilling ground, she rocked back and forth, awful memories swirling around her in shades of scarlet and orange and black. It wasn't fair, wasn't fair, *wasn't fair*.

Gradually a thought formed deep inside, gathering force until it dispelled the ugly memories. A slow smile spread across her cracked lips and chilblained face.

Yes. The idea offered a perfect solution, though she didn't have much time to gather everything. She risked one last peek through the window, which revealed two silhouettes still at the desk. The Penrose woman looked to be reading something while the doctor stood close by her side, his hand resting on her shoulder.

The woman slipped away from the window and melted into the night.

Chapter Thirteen

Despite the chilly December night, Clara decided she felt like an icicle in sunshine. Shiny but brittle, soaking up the warmth, and melting into a blissful puddle. No wonder Louise wandered about with a glow on her face.

Love might be worth the painful uncertainty after all.

After they left Ethan's house, he drove the buggy back to the town square, where other carolers had parked their conveyances, instead of taking her directly home. When he lifted Clara down, the tingling warmth from the firm touch of his clasp around her waist permeated all the way through the layers of heavy fabric. Clara Penrose, the skinny town spinster, was strolling down Main Street with a man, a man who was *holding her hand*.

A man who claimed to love her.

Her heart skipped a beat, and so did her feet.

"Easy." Ethan's grip slid to her elbow, his voice murmuring low in her ear as he steadied her. "Remind me not to take you on a hiking expedition at night."

Clara stifled a laugh. "Disastrous," she whispered back.

A dozen yards away the carolers launched into the first verse of "As with Gladness Men of Old." Without a word of communication both she and Ethan began singing along. By the time the first verse ended, they had eased into a clutch of singers at the back of the group, Ethan's hands now clasped behind his back, Clara's burrowed deep inside her muff.

Perhaps it was only her imagination, but—did the singing sound richer, the harmony a perfect balance of voices proclaiming the good news of Jesus's arrival? The delicate icicle feeling melted into the gladness of men of old as Clara blended her voice with Ethan's and those of the smiling carolers around them.

Two songs later, after a rousing chorus of "Joy to the World," with effusive expressions of gratitude for their splendid performance, Mr. Fiske dismissed everyone. Clara and Ethan were immediately surrounded, and spent several chaotic moments fending off invitations to thaw out in friends' homes while everyone wandered back to the town square. Finally only a handful of people remained, most of them choir members from another church who were noisily piling inside an old wagon.

"Did you walk from your home, Miss Penrose?" Ethan inquired politely.

"Why, yes, I did, Dr. Harcourt," Clara responded with reciprocal cordiality. "Every year I remind myself that I'll regret the decision by the end of the evening. But when the weather's clear and not too frigid, I enjoy being out in it." She had to bite the inside of her cheeks to keep from breaking into a fit of giggles.

"Miss Penrose." From behind Ethan, Mr. Fiske loomed out of the darkness. "Might I have a brief word with you, please? I would be more than happy to offer you a ride home in my trap while I discuss my plans for an ecumenical hymn sing on the twenty-third. I was hoping you'd be the accompanist, since my organist is unavailable."

"I... I..." Her usually nimble brain seemed to have frozen like her fingers and toes.

"I'm afraid Miss Penrose has already accepted my offer to take her home," Ethan declared, pulling her hand through his arm.

The streetlight illuminated Mr. Fiske's face. He looked from Clara to Ethan, and a little smile softened the disappointment in his eyes. "I see. I won't keep the two of you any further then." His smile broadened, and before he turned away Clara thought he winked at Ethan.

"Oh, dear." Clara laughed. "The gossip will ignite now. Mr. Fiske loves to talk about folks almost as much as he loves singing with them."

"Good. Let the whole world know." He lifted her back into the buggy, tucked the lap blanket around her and, after settling beside her on the seat, his arm came round her shoulders. For a moment he didn't move, just hugged her in the darkness.

"Ethan? What is it?"

"Nothing, my sweet. No," he corrected, and his lips pressed a soft kiss against her temple, "no more evasions between us. I was loving the lilt in your voice, and wondering how many years it will take for me to get over feeling guilty for thinking *you* were..."

Ah. The notes again. "I know about guilt." Sighing, she settled back against the seat, the warm but unfamiliar weight of his arm more comforting than the most luxurious of fur stoles. "It never solves anything. I told

Methuselah once that guilt reminds me of mildew. No matter how hard I scrub the floor, there's a corner near the back door where I can never seem to get rid of it. The odor permeates everything. I try not to put anything on the floor there."

"An apt metaphor." For a little while they rode in silence, the steady clip-clop of the horse's hooves beating with metronome precision. "What guilt are you wanting to scrub away?" Ethan asked finally, the arm around her shoulders tightening again. "It's not writing letters to editors, is it?"

"No." She'd wondered when he would ask, but until this moment she had not been sure of her response.

"Will you tell me about it?"

Because God had apparently decided to give her a man who said he loved her for Christmas...and because she loved the man back, Clara told him. "When I was nineteen, my parents informed me they had arranged for me to be introduced to the man I was to marry. After sifting through a number of candidates, they'd picked a state senator with congressional aspirations. I was young, with grand ideas of my own. I didn't fret overmuch about love. Marriage, we Penrose children were informed frequently, was about suitability, not sentiment." A little laugh more close to a sob escaped and she hurriedly finished, "I agreed without a fuss. I was... I had my own dreams..."

"We all do," Ethan observed, his voice comfortably matter-of-fact. "What happened to you and your perfect candidate for the office of husband?"

"Oh!" She rubbed her cheek against his forearm, the only part of him she could reach. "I've always believed a sense of humor offers one of God's most effective tinctures against life's hurts. One of the reasons I eventually refused Mortimer was because he didn't have one. He considered laughter a 'vulgar expression of the bourgeoisie,' was how he phrased it."

"Met a few of those myself. Insufferable snobs, aren't they?"

"My parents didn't see it that way. He was wealthy, attractive and willing to overlook all my flaws. I was, of course, expected to overlook all of his, which, along with advanced snobbery and no humor, included an insatiable thirst for liquor. I never saw him drunk, but I also never saw him without a drink of some sort in his hand. When I queried him on the matter, he reminded me that only one opinion counted—his own." After a brief internal debate she added sadly, "But the main reason I finally couldn't agree to the marriage is one I never told my family, because I…because…" She swallowed hard, annoyed that even after all these years the raw spot hadn't completely healed. "It's a silly reason, I expect. I don't know why I can't just spit it out and be done with the subject."

"I doubt *silly* is the appropriate application," Ethan said. "It's all right, Clara. You don't have to tell me anymore right now."

"Yes, I think I do." She stared straight ahead, into the silvery-black night that no longer made her feel safe. "Because it's one of the reasons I struggle with guilt. You see… I discovered Mortimer was a—a mean-spirited hypocrite. Quoted scripture, prayed unctuous prayers and promised my parents that our children would grow up in a Christian home. I discovered the truth by accident. Overheard him tell one of his friends he was marrying a bony Christian chit with too much virtue and not enough vanity. He supposed he'd have to attend church, but faith in God was a waste of time. Jesus might have existed, but He was no more the Son of God than Mortimer's valet, who at least knew the difference between a Windsor knot and a four-in-hand. I tolerated the slurs against me. But I challenged him about his faith, and was again ordered to keep my mouth shut, or after we married he'd turn my life into— Well, never mind what he said. I ended the engagement. Six months later he married a debutante from Richmond. For months Mother badgered me about her disappointment or ignored me completely. My father shrugged, told me to ignore my mother back and proclaimed to everyone he talked to that he was resigned to his eldest daughter's status as the family old maid."

Without warning Ethan pulled the buggy to a halt, right in the middle of the road. "We'll see about that," he snapped, the arm around her shoulders hauling her so close she felt the huff of his breath on her face. "I've had a bellyful of people inflicting their warped opinions on others, particularly the ones they're supposed to love. I wish Mortimer and my wife had met. They certainly deserved each other." Once again he cupped her face in his gloved hands, his thumb brushing the sensitive skin beneath her jaw. "I think it's time we both let the past go, don't you?"

His touch soothed, yet set every nerve to jumping. "Yes." Her voice broke on the word. "I don't care about Mortimer, and I've made peace with my parents, Ethan. It helped when I moved out, and Louise has softened my mother's attitude. It's just that… I don't want to be a hypocrite myself. I believe in God, I do. I believe Jesus is His Son, that He willingly sacrificed His life for me.

But sometimes…sometimes I feel like I'm only saying words, especially at Christmas. I wouldn't marry a hypocrite—I'm terrified I'll become one."

"Mm. So…no decorations in your home. No dreams of Santa filling your stocking with oranges and nuts and candy canes…"

"Yes. I know it's silly, but—yes. It's just I… I have all these questions without answers. I feel when I should be thinking, and think when I should be feeling."

She pulled her hand free of the muff and blindly reached to lay it against *his* cheek, drawing strength from the beard-roughened skin, the firm line of his jaw. "It's exhausting, trying to live my faith. Some days, I'm tempted to stuff it in a box, because no matter how many letters to the editor I write, no matter how many 'good works' I perform to help people, there's all this pain in the world. So much evil. Yet right now…"

The words trailed away in confusion and she paused, astonished at herself, a little afraid of Ethan's reaction. But his head merely shifted against her hand and, rumbling vague encouraging sounds, he brushed a kiss against the palm resting on his cheek.

No condemnation, no condescension, not even a lecture.

Drawing in a grateful breath, Clara shared the last of her thoughts, one in particular that had churned in her mind these past few hours. "The woman who's writing you those letters? I recognize the implied threat, and I'll do everything I can to assist you in discovering her identity. But she hasn't physically harmed you. If she did I…well, I'd drag her by her hair to jail myself—ooh, *this* is what I was trying to explain! There's this unruly piece of my heart that isn't very Christ-like toward this

woman. But the rest doesn't want her in jail, particularly over a few malicious letters. I—I want to help her."

"I believe what that makes you is human, not a hypocrite, Clara. I've struggled with similar thoughts myself, and some worse. Want an example?" When Clara
nodded her head he continued, his voice wry, "How
about... I used to believe that service to my fellow
man—whether as a doctor or a congressman—was
sufficient for God to overlook my less-than-pure at-
titudes and behavior. See? My badge of faith is every
bit as dented and tarnished as you perceive yours to be.
What's more, if this unknown woman hurts *you,* I'd be
tempted to dispense with jail altogether, and administer
my own brand of justice." The arm around her shoulders jostled her a little. "We both know that we'll do
the right thing, in the end. Sin isn't the temptation—it's
giving in to those base urges and impulses."

A feeble star twinkled to life inside her. "You're
right. You make a much better confidant than a turtle,
Dr. Harcourt." When he laughed, the starlight burned
even brighter. "I feel much better. And when we discover the identity of this unknown woman...? I think...
I think perhaps that's how to live our faith when we
don't feel the words. Help someone else who's hurting inside."

"I think you're right, and that I should buy you a
camel, Miss Penrose." He dipped his head and pressed
the lightest of kisses against her half-parted lips. "But
instead of offering gold, frankincense or myrrh, I recommend some of those cookies like the ones you left
on my doorstep. I love you very much, Clara," he continued. "All of you, especially the struggling parts. I
understand why you don't quite trust my love, that you

don't quite believe it's going to last. That's all right. I've squandered a good many years of my life, so I figure I can invest some time in pursuing what I believe is God's personal gift to me for Christmas this year—you."

He released her and set the buggy in motion once more.

"But…that's how *I* feel!" Clara exclaimed. "While we were singing those carols to the townsfolk of Canterbury, I really singing them to God, because I wanted to thank Him for giving me the most wonderful gift I've ever received for Christmas. For the first time in a very long time, I was feeling the words as well as singing them."

"I know exactly what you mean." Ethan pulled the horse to a stop by the path that led to the cottage.

Wrapped in wonder, Clara floated out of the buggy onto the frost-stubbled grass, one hand inside the muff, the other nestled securely in Ethan's.

The stench assailed their noses before they walked half a dozen paces down the flagstone path to the front door.

Chapter Fourteen

An unnatural pall hung in the air. The noxious odor flooded Ethan's senses even as warning pumped through his veins. "Get back in the buggy," he ordered, stepping in front of her.

"I will not!" Clara shot back, the words crackling in the still night. "This is my home. What *is* that horrid odor?"

"Rotten garbage, among other equally putrid things. Dumped on the path just inside your gate." Muscles taut, he peered through the stygian darkness, searching for movement, ears straining for sound. "Clara, I haven't told you everything about the woman. Last week, she left one of those notes in a basket on my front porch, only, unlike you, she'd filled hers with rotten fruit. So please, love, get in the buggy. Let me search—"

"No wonder you've had such a miserable few weeks, and don't be ridiculous." When Clara stubbornly shoved past him he grabbed her even as he conceded the battle. "At least hold my arm so I can guide you. I don't want you stepping in the mess."

Gingerly he led her around it, his skin prickling.

"There's more, I'm afraid. Looks like it's all over your front stoop."

"It's her, isn't it? Only this time I'm the victim, not you. She must have been spying," Clara hissed the last sentence from the side of her mouth. "When you took me to your house, to show me the notes, she—" A gasp choked off the words. "Ethan, *what if she went inside? I never lock my door. Nim… NimNuan!*"

Frantically she struggled against him, her breath ragged with fear. "I have to find him. Nim. P-please, God. Please…"

His own heart slamming against his rib cage, Ethan clamped both her forearms, trapping her inside her cloak against his chest. He pressed his face close against hers. "We'll find Nim. But you have to calm down. You told me you have a back door?" He barely made out her nod. "All right. We'll go inside that way. Hold my hand, there you go…shh. He'll be all right, Clara."

"You don't know that." She choked on the words, and Ethan could hear her teeth chattering. Even through their gloves he could feel the pulse galloping in her wrist at breakneck speed.

No, he didn't know what might have happened to Nim. But he did know Clara was on the verge of shock, and the last thing he wanted right now was to confront a deranged woman when he was administering aid to an ill one. Grimly he lifted her completely off her feet, swinging her over a stinking mass of garbage, then led her down the flagstones to the back of the cottage.

The door gaped wide-open.

A whimpering cry burst from Clara's throat. Ethan forced her behind him and used his body to block the entrance. He could see a bit of light coming from the kitchen, and his nostrils stung with the mildewy odor Clara had described earlier. Slowly, one arm stretched like a bar across the threshold, he eased into a minuscule mudroom, his gaze swiftly searching the dark corners for movement.

"Ethan. Please…" Clara pushed against his arm, her hands digging into the wool of his overcoat. "I can't bear this…"

Grimly he stepped forward and forced himself to peer into the kitchen, dread and fear and determination tangling his own insides into knots.

A square oak kitchen table with four press-back chairs sat in the middle of the floor. An oil lamp had been lit and placed atop the table. A woman dressed in black widow's weeds sat in one of the chairs. Another oil lamp sat beside the sink, its light shining on a pile of damp rags from which the putrid odor emanated, though less strong.

Purring noisily, NimNuan sat on the widow's lap, his blue gaze trained upon Ethan.

Suddenly Clara shoved her way past him to charge into the kitchen, where she came to a dead halt. Ethan came to stand beside her.

"Nim!" she cried brokenly. The cat leaped down and streaked across the floor. Clara scooped him up into her arms and buried her face in the cream-colored fur.

Ethan scratched behind one chocolate ear, then skimmed his fingers soothingly down one of Clara's tear-dampened cheeks; all the while his gaze remained trained upon the other woman.

"I wouldn't have hurt him," she spoke into the charged silence, her voice surprisingly refined.

"That's good." Approaching her carefully, he

watched her eyes, which after a moment flickered before she turned her head away. Her hand, reddened but scrubbed clean, lifted to her throat. Ethan pulled out one of the chairs and eased down beside her. "What's your name?" *Stay casual,* he repeated to himself, while his trained gaze noted the gaunt, paper-white cheeks, the tremor in her hands and the eerily calm rise and fall of her breathing.

"Velma Chesterton."

She met his gaze, and even as he sifted through his memory he automatically catalogued the dilated pupils in her light blue eyes—and the expression of shame. Deranged individuals did not manifest an awareness of inappropriate behavior.

"You don't remember me, do you?" she asked, her voice resigned. She lifted one hand to wearily press her fingers to her temple, and the lamplight caught on the dull gold of her wedding band.

Shock jolted Ethan's heart as the name finally clicked into place. "Chesterton," he repeated with lips gone numb. An amalgam of memories poured through him. "Your husband was Senator Chesterton, from... Indiana?"

"Iowa." The haunted gaze moved beyond Ethan to Clara, then returned to Ethan. "I've always loved animals. I grew up on a farm. When we moved to Washington, my husband promised I could have a pet to keep me company, because he would be gone so much. But he died. *He died and it's your fault.*"

Ethan's muscles tensed, instinctively ready to defend Clara, or himself, from physical attack.

Seemingly impervious to the seething atmosphere, with Nim draped over her shoulder in a limp purring bundle, Clara sat down opposite Mrs. Chesterton, then transferred Nim to her own lap. "What do you mean, it's his fault? Why have you committed all these acts of vandalism against Dr. Harcourt?" she demanded. "What has he ever done to you?"

Clara was not a woman to beat about the bush.

"He didn't control his Jezebel of a wife!" The words spewed across the table. "He stood by and watched while she seduced my husband. Never lifted a hand, never made her leave him alone. If he'd done his duty by her, I wouldn't be a widow, haunted to this day by the scandal of it all. I'd still be a wife. I'd have a husband who loved me."

Tears glazed the fever-bright eyes, their gaze locked on Ethan. "I heard when you returned, heard all about the congressman who went back to doctoring in this idyllic little town in Virginia, only an hour's ride from where you failed your wife and turned your back on your duty to your country. It wasn't fair. Your wife ruined my life, and here you are, cool as you please, setting up a medical practice, buying a home." The long fingers curled into fists. "And then…and then you have the audacity—*both of you*—to engage in the same sordid behavior that robbed me of my husband."

Rage scorched Ethan's body in a conflagration. "Madam, you may level any attacks at me and I'll answer to them. But you will not impugn the character of Miss Penrose." He planted his palms on the table and stared the woman down until she turned her head aside. "May I remind you that my wife, like your husband, is dead. I am legally and morally free to pursue any unmarried woman I choose. And if that woman accepts my attentions, you *will not* accuse either of us of less-than-honorable behavior."

Clara soothed an alarmed Nim with one hand while she stretched her other across the table, resting it on Ethan's forearm. "Mrs. Chesterton, I think you should be careful about painting a scarlet letter on my back, when you're the one who's guilty of trespassing, not to mention vandalism."

The other woman's face crumpled. She fumbled a black hankie from her sleeve and dabbed her eyes. "You're right. I'm sorry, so sorry. I don't know what came over me. Ever since that awful night when my husband perished, I haven't been myself." She glanced at Ethan with streaming eyes. "I couldn't bear returning home to Iowa in shame, nor could I stand the gossip and the looks of pity. For the past three years I've been living in a one-bedroom apartment, so full of anger and bitterness I could scarce swallow a bite of food. The day after I learned you'd returned to Virginia, I took the train here. Took a room in a boardinghouse. I s-saw when you put out your sign. Watched all week how patients flocked to see you. It was as though you had erased the past, while I…" she twisted the damp handkerchief into a gnarled rope "…I couldn't escape from it."

"So you decided Dr. Harcourt deserved to be as miserable as you?" Clara asked, though her tone remained mild. The hand stroking Nim never wavered. "Hence the letters?"

A sigh shuddered through Mrs. Chesterton's body. "I never intended any real harm. I was just… The anger… It was choking me alive. Writing those notes—it seemed harmless enough. It…helped."

"And the basket of rotten fruit?" Ethan put in, eyeing her without sympathy. "The garbage all over Miss Penrose's front porch and path?"

"I shouldn't have done that. I do realize now. But the feelings... For the first time I was focusing on something other than my own suffering. I even slept at night. Except the notes...after a while, they weren't enough. I knew I needed to stop, but I couldn't. I...couldn't."

"Why did you come into my house?" Clara suddenly blurted. Nim stretched his front paws up on her shoulders, as though he were embracing her, and let loose a plaintive meow. Clara's eyes teared, and she tucked the cat against her like a small child. "Thank you for not hurting my cat," she whispered. After clearing her throat, she finished more strongly, "My house—why *did* you stay?"

"I'd frightened your kitty, when I was—" Her shoulders hunched, and her feet shuffled nervously. "He came up behind me, out front, and meowed. I was so startled I dropped the, um, well, the sack, and your kitty ran off. I felt so bad. I followed him, and he was there, at the back door. Sh-shaking." She covered her face with the handkerchief, but after a moment managed to continue. "I opened the door for him, and he ran inside. I wanted to reassure him, but my hands were filthy. So I washed them in your sink, and while I was washing them he came over and sat at my feet. He's so beautiful, and he started purring, and making strange sounds, almost as though he were..."

"As though he were talking," Clara finished. "He was. Nim's not your ordinary barn cat. He's from Siam, and he thinks he's supposed to converse with humans. He's also discriminating about his company. Normally he doesn't take to strangers, particularly ones in the process of slinging garbage all over my yard."

"After I washed my hands, he let me hold him." She glanced from Clara to Ethan, deep lines scoring her forehead and cheeks. "I know what I've done is dreadful, unforgivable. But you must believe me about the cat. I would never hurt him, or any other animal. And even when I wrote those notes, I knew it was wrong. I knew, but I couldn't stop. I'm sorry. So sorry."

A strange sensation feathered through Ethan, like the brush of warm invisible fingers. The outrage seemed to swell like a cresting wave before it receded into a widening pool of...peace. "I know a thing or two about guilt, and lack of forgiveness," he said, and had to clear his throat before he could finish. "I've spent the past three years hating my wife, feeling guilty because I wasn't the man she wanted me to be. Those injurious emotions almost cost me the love of a good woman."

When Clara's hand lightly slid over his shoulder, he turned toward her—and instead found himself inches away from a pair of myopic blue eyes. A smile that started deep in Ethan's belly whooshed up and tugged at the corners of his mouth. "Not to mention the love of a good cat." When Nim more or less poured his agile feline body into Ethan's arms, all Ethan could do was accept the lithe bundle and grin. "Tell you what, Mrs. Chesterton. Tomorrow morning you clean up the mess you made out front, then you come with me to the sheriff. I think we'll be able to clean up the rest of the mess you've made of your life without too much trouble. As for the past—" over Nim's head he and Clara exchanged a warm look "—perhaps Miss Penrose and I can help a bit with how to let it go. Some things aren't worth hanging on to."

For the first time he looked at Velma Chesterton with compassion, and saw enough of himself to realize Clara was right—sometimes living one's faith simply meant helping a hurting person, regardless of the state of your own emotions. "I've also rediscovered the love of God," he confessed, his skin suddenly prickling with that indescribable sensation of warmth infusing his heart—his soul, his spirit. "I'd say it's long past time to quit toting the coffins of our respective spouses on our backs. I believe, with God's help, I can dump mine in the grave where it belongs. Then between the two of us, not to mention the help of a good woman and her cat, we ought to be able to do the same with yours."

"I don't deserve... I don't understand." As though she couldn't help herself, Mrs. Chesterton reached a trembling arm out, her fingers barely skimming Nim's furry belly. "You have no reason to be kind," she whispered.

Clara rose and walked around the table. "It's Christmas," she said, leaning down to give the other woman a hug. "It's the perfect time of year for kindness. Forgiveness. And new hope. Some weeks ago our minister gave the congregation a task. We were to bring symbols of our burdens, and lay them in the manger, renouncing them in order to celebrate the Christmas season. I had broken dreams, just like you, dreams that were never realized. So... I listened to our minister, and I let them go—and God supplied me with something infinitely more wonderful."

"After we take Mrs. Chesterton home," Ethan commented, gently depositing Nim on the floor, "I have something to share with you about that Sunday and the symbol you left at the altar."

Epilogue

On a blustery afternoon two days before Christmas, Clara was busily writing when someone pounded on the door. When Clara opened it, Ethan stood grinning on the freshly scrubbed stoop, his thick hair wind-tossed and a glint sparkling in the clear green eyes. "Good. You're not busy. I've brought something, and I'll need your help with it."

"Ethan, what on earth—? And I am busy. I'm writing."

"Your letter to the editor can wait."

"It's not a letter," Clara began, but he had turned aside and leaned down. When he straightened, his arms were full of a fragrant little fir tree.

"You'll need to clear off that table under your window. I think this tree will look quite nice on it." And with Clara dazedly trailing after him he proceeded into her parlor, set the tree on the floor, then strode back outside to return with a large gift-wrapped box tied with a huge red ribbon. "Here. Open this while I clear the table."

"You brought me a Christmas tree."

"I've always known you were an intelligent, observant woman. Open the box, sweetheart."

A whoosh of sentimentality gummed up her throat, paralyzing her vocal chords. Clutching the box to her middle, Clara watched while Ethan cheerfully cleared the tabletop and plonked the tree—to which two strips of wood had been attached crossways, forming a stand—right in the center. A fresh, resiny fragrance permeated the air.

Nim strolled in from the bedroom, instantly going over to strop himself against Ethan's legs before rising up to sniff the tree. Smiling, Ethan gave the cat an affectionate pat before walking back over to Clara. "Looks perfect, doesn't it?" Gently he removed the box from her unresisting hands. "Like Christmas has finally arrived at Clara's cottage."

"You're impossible, and I love you." She reached for the box, her heart fluttering at the same time the rest of her seemed to be dissolving like the sugar glaze she'd applied to a batch of cookies she'd made that morning. "Your present isn't ready yet."

"This isn't a present, it's decorations. Hurry up and open the box. This will take some time."

So Clara ripped off ribbon and paper and lifted off the lid, to discover dozens of tissue-wrapped objects nestled inside. The objects turned out to be tiny charms, like the one of the Capitol Building she'd relinquished weeks earlier. Only these charms were made of gold. "Ethan... You... I don't know what to say." Eyes filling, she held up the first one, a long-tailed cat with a mischievous smile. Bright blue-colored glass eyes winked in the December sunlight pouring through the window. "It's Nim!"

"Keep going. Methuselah's in there somewhere."

Until this moment, Clara had never experienced the child-like joy possible only at Christmas. Each charm elicited a happy gasp, a delighted laugh, a sigh of contentment. Ethan helped her tie them to the tree with strands of red ribbon—a turtle, as promised, a piano, a key...

"The key to my heart," he told her as he brushed a circumspect kiss against the nape of her neck, sending a wave of goose bumps all over Clara's skin.

"I love you, Ethan Harcourt," she replied. "And I'll cherish my Christmas tree forever. But don't delude yourself for an instant if you think I plan to consider any garlands, or gilded angels, or magnolia leaves and sprigs of ivy, or— What's that?" He had reached inside his waistcoat to tug something out, which he shielded from Clara with his other hand.

"I thought I'd defer negotiations on appropriate Christmas decorations until after I gave you your Christmas present."

"But... Christmas is still the day after tomorrow. You were supposed to wait. I told you I haven't finished—I mean, I'm not ready to give you— Oh, padiddle!" Eyes narrowed, she lunged for his hands. "What is it, then?"

Ethan held his hands up high, way beyond her reach. "Are you sure you don't want to wait for another forty-eight hours?"

"If you'd wanted to wait, you shouldn't have teased me." Exasperated, she picked Nim up, then turned her back on Ethan, ostensibly to study her lovely tree, proudly displaying the dozen gold charms amongst its fragrant branches. "I can't wait for everyone to see this. Albert will take all the credit for introducing you to me in the first place. Eleanor will probably kiss you—no, she'll shake your hand, firmly. Willy will offer to take you to his favorite fishing spot and Louise will enlist your aid on the sly, to hang a few greens and some mistletoe."

"I like the mistletoe part. What about your parents?"

For a second the old defensive misery dimmed the present glow. But as she absorbed the kindness in Ethan's eyes, the defensiveness transformed into an extraordinary lightness. "Mother will rearrange the charms to her liking. Father, as he comments every visit, will suggest I either rid myself of half the furniture, or move someplace where he won't trip over a footstool or something. They might congratulate you on reforming their daughter."

"Well, their daughter *transformed* me." Slowly he returned whatever he'd been holding to the pocket of his waistcoat. "Perhaps I'll wait until Christmas Day after all. I want your whole family to witness how much I love you."

"Ethan... Louise has been matchmaking from the first time she heard about you. Our feelings for one another, especially after you and Mrs. Chesterton talked with Sheriff Gleason, by now fuel every conversation in Canterbury from dawn until dusk." After putting Nim down, she approached Ethan, grateful when, without asking, he took her hands and tugged her closer. "Speaking of Mrs. Chesterton... I learned she was a church organist before she married. Oh, and she's no longer wearing widow's weeds."

"I know. She stopped by yesterday to offer me another basket, this one filled with fresh oranges, nuts and a mince pie." He grinned down at Clara. "She's not as good a cook as you, but it was nice seeing her looking the way a woman ought to look, delivering food fit for human consumption. She also included a formal note of apology, on the same stationery, only this time she signed it."

"Feels good, doesn't it, watching her bloom?"

"Mm. Not as much as watching the woman I love bloom." His gaze wandered lazily over her. "Your hair looks nice today. I like the way you moved the bun from the top of your head to the back of your neck. I especially like the strand of hair dangling by your ear. Have I told you how much I love your ears?"

Clara blushed and took refuge in a geyser of words. She wasn't sure she would ever entirely believe Ethan's effusive blandishments, but she hoped he'd never cease giving them. "I, um, I took Mr. Fiske to Mrs. Chesterton's boardinghouse after church this past Sunday. They developed an instant rapport. She's playing for the community hymn sing tonight. From the gleam in Mr. Fiske's eye within an hour of meeting her, I've a hunch he won't be inquiring about my services as an accompanist much longer."

"Good."

They stood together in a puddle of sunshine, listening to the wind rattle the shutters and the fire crackle in the parlor fireplace, holding hands and basking in a transcendent peace.

"Ethan?"

"Hmm?"

"I don't want to wait for Christmas Day."

"I know. I don't either." He reached back into his waistcoat and withdrew a small box. "Here."

Fingers suddenly unsteady, Clara took the proffered

box and fumbled it open. Nestled in a bed of midnight velvet was the small charm of the Capitol she'd laid on the altar. "I don't understand." She lifted uncomprehending eyes to Ethan's.

"The first Sunday I went to church was the Sunday when the minister asked you to leave your burdens. Yours was accidentally left behind, so I picked it up. I've been carrying your secret burden ever since. Now I think it's time for us both to follow Reverend Miggs's counsel, and lay this at the foot of the manger."

As he spoke he produced a slender red ribbon, took the charm out of the box, threaded the ribbon through the hole and handed it back to Clara. "There's a nice spot on that branch, just below the manger charm."

Feeling as though she were dreaming, Clara carefully looped the ribboned ornament so that it dangled close by the charm depicting a manger with the Christ child sleeping peacefully in the hay. "I had no idea," she whispered. "All this time…"

"Even back then I found myself needing to protect you, wanting to discover all your secrets. Though I didn't comprehend God's fine hand at work, I couldn't shake you loose from my mind. Now that I understand why…" he plucked the box from her hand, removed the scrap of velvet, then handed the box back to her "…I'm hoping to replace your old burden and lost dreams… with this."

Speechless, Clara stared up into his face until with a little laugh he clasped her chin with his thumb and index finger, gently forcing her to look down into what she'd thought was an empty box.

Instead of a tarnished silver charm of the Capitol

Building, a ring holding a diamond surrounded by sapphires lay in the bottom, waiting in splendid silence.

"Is that for me?" she stammered.

"Well, I suppose it might fit Nim's tail, but I'm not sure it's his style." Laughing, he waited with more patience than Job until Clara finally scraped together the wit to gingerly clasp the ring.

"Does this mean—?"

"Yes. Now it's your turn to say the word. Would you like some help with the placement? Custom dictates that you slide it onto the fourth finger of your left hand...shall I help?"

Like a flock of birds freed at last from their cages, joy and happiness and hope soared upward, filling the small cottage with heavenly light. She could almost hear the angels singing. "Yes," she managed, and held up her hand. "Yes and yes and yes!"

She watched with an overflowing heart as Ethan slid the ring onto her finger. Almost reverently he bestowed a kiss upon her lips. "Merry Christmas, sweetheart."

"I love you." In a rapture of emotion she flung her arms around him and hugged him fiercely, then stepped back. "Wait here." Whirling, she dashed across to her sitting room, over to her desk. Before she lost her nerve, she gathered everything up in a messy bundle and returned to her—to her fiancé.

Shyness tugged, but she thrust it aside and handed Ethan her offering. "It's very rough," she told him breathlessly, "and will take a lot more work. But— I've already sold it." A pang of sheer nerves turned her palms hot, filmed with perspiration. She watched in an agony of suspense as Ethan accepted the pages and began to leaf through them.

"'Joy of Every Longing Heart. A Story of a Spinster. Why a Believer Should Never Lose Hope in the Power of Love. By Clara Penrose,'" he read the title aloud.

"I started it weeks ago, when I knew I'd fallen in love with you," Clara said, quivering inside because she wasn't sure whether the light blazing from his eyes was a reflection of her own joy, or—

He snatched her into his arms, crushing her and the manuscript against his chest. "You used your real name! Clara…you used your name. I love you, love you, love you."

"Ethan… I just thought of something," she managed between the intoxicating kisses he pressed to her brow, her temple, her lips. "Wait…" Laughter wove through the breathless words in an effervescent tumble. "The editor tells me the book won't be published for well over a year."

"Doesn't matter. It will be worth waiting for, like you." He stole another kiss.

"I can't use my name!"

When he froze, she grabbed the manuscript, smoothed the crumpled pages and laid it on the table, beneath the Christmas tree.

"Clara…"

"When were you thinking to marry me?"

"I thought… Christmastime next year? It seemed appropriate. My love, you should be proud to use your name. I know I am. I'll announce it from the rooftops, on every street corner."

"By the time this book is published, I won't be Clara Penrose. I'll be Clara Penrose *Harcourt*."

Ethan threw back his head and shouted with laughter. "So you will be. So you will…" Then he wrapped her back in his arms, and sealed her lips with a thorough kiss.

NimNuan watched unblinking beside the tabletop Christmas tree, a loud purr proclaiming his satisfaction with the arrangements.

* * * * *

Dear Reader,

The working title of *The Christmas Secret* was *Long-Expected Love,* which came from an old Christmas hymn "Come, Thou Long-Expected Jesus." I still can't think of this story without humming that melody in my head and repeating those comforting words—*"From our fears and sins release us; let us find our rest in Thee..."* That's what music, especially Christmas music, does to me, sticking like colorful Post-its in my mind and heart. I love the reverence of all the ancient hymns, the soaring magnificence of Handel's *Messiah,* the irrepressible fun of Frosty and Rudolph (except when the tunes are blared over store speakers in September), the sing-along nostalgia of *White Christmas*—so the very day after Thanksgiving our home is filled with the music of Christmas.

However, like Ethan and Clara in the late nineteenth century, our family has also struggled through difficult holidays, where our twenty-first-century radios and CDs remained silent because our hearts were grieving, and joyful holiday music only drove the pain deeper. Life during the dark times of the soul is somehow harder to bear in the Christmas season. Yet God steadfastly reaches out until He captures your attention. Through that mysterious process called faith, He can heal the soul and lift the heart. For me, most often His Voice speaks through the music. That's why *The Christmas Secret* is filled with references to Christmas carols. My heartfelt hope for each of you who reads this story is that you may experience an hour or two of lightness, that one of the carols mentioned rings a chord within and allows you to look up—and hear the heavenly choir proclaiming joy to the world.

All ye, beneath life's crushing load,/Whose forms are bending low,/Who toil along the climbing way/ With painful steps and slow,/Look now! For glad and golden hours/ Come swiftly on the wing:/O rest beside the weary road,/And hear the angels sing.

Regardless of circumstance, may your hearts this Christmas sing with joy,

Sara Mitchell

WE HOPE YOU
ENJOYED THIS

LOVE
INSPIRED®
BOOK.

If you were **inspired** by this

uplifting, **heartwarming** romance,

be sure to look for all six Love

Inspired® books every month.

Love Inspired®

www.LoveInspired.com

SPECIAL EXCERPT FROM

Love Inspired®

*When a young Amish woman has amnesia during
the holidays, will a handsome Amish farmer help
her regain her memories?*

Read on for a sneak preview of
Amish Christmas Memories *by Vannetta Chapman,
available December 2018 from Love Inspired.*

"What's your name?"

The woman's eyes widened and her hand shook so that
she could barely hold the mug of tea without spilling it. She
set it carefully on the coffee table. "I don't—I don't know
my name."

"How can you not know your own name?" Caleb asked.
"Do you know where you live?"

"Nein."

"What were you doing out there?"

"Out where?"

"Where was your coat and your *kapp*?"

"Caleb, now's not the time to interrogate the poor girl."
His *mamm* stood and moved beside her on the couch. She
picked up the small book of poetry. "You were carrying this,
when Caleb found you. Do you remember it?"

"I don't. This was mine?"

"Found it in the snow," Caleb said. "Right beside where
you collapsed."

"So it must be mine."

Caleb noticed that the woman's hands trembled as she
opened the cover and stared down at the first page. With one
finger, she traced the handwriting there.

LIEXP1118

"Rachel. I think my name is Rachel."

Rachel let her fingers brush over the word again and again. Rachel. Yes, that was her name. She was sure of it. She remembered writing it in the front of the book—she'd used a pen that her *mamm* had given her. She could almost picture herself, somewhere else. She could almost see her mother.

"My *mamm* gave me the pen and the book…for my birthday, I think. I wrote my name—wrote it right here."

"Your *mamm*. So you remember her?"

"Praise be to *Gotte*," Caleb's *dat* said, a smile spreading across his face.

"Is there someone we can call? If you remember the name of your bishop…" Caleb had sat down in the rocker his mother had vacated and was staring at her intensely.

They all were.

She closed her eyes, hoping to feel the memory again. She tried to see the room or the house or the people, but the memory had receded as quickly as it had come, leaving her with a pulsing headache.

She struggled to keep the feelings of panic at bay. Her heart was hammering, and her hands were shaking, and she could barely make sense of the questions they were pelting at her.

Who were these people?

Where was she?

Who was she?

She needed to remember what had happened.

She needed to go home.

Don't miss
Amish Christmas Memories *by Vannetta Chapman,*
available December 2018 wherever
Love Inspired® *books and ebooks are sold.*

www.LoveInspired.com

LIEXP1118

Love Inspired®

Save $1.00

on the purchase of any
Love Inspired® or Love Inspired®
Suspense book.

Available wherever books are sold,
including most bookstores, supermarkets,
drugstores and discount stores.

Save $1.00

on the purchase of any Love Inspired® or
Love Inspired® Suspense book.

Coupon valid until April 30, 2019. Redeemable at participating retail outlets in the
U.S. and Canada only. Limit one coupon per customer.

52616033

Canadian Retailers: Harlequin Enterprises Limited will pay the face value of this coupon plus 10.25¢ if submitted by customer for this product only. Any other use constitutes fraud. Coupon is nonassignable. Void if taxed, prohibited or restricted by law. Consumer must pay any government taxes. Void if copied. Inmar Promotional Services ("IPS") customers submit coupons and proof of sales to Harlequin Enterprises Limited, P.O. Box 31000, Scarborough, ON M1R 0E7, Canada. Non-IPS retailer—for reimbursement submit coupons and proof of sales directly to Harlequin Enterprises Limited, Retail Marketing Department, Bay Adelaide Centre, East Tower, 22 Adelaide Street West, 40th Floor, Toronto, Ontario M5H 4E3, Canada.

5 65373 00076 2   (8100)0 12391

U.S. Retailers: Harlequin Enterprises Limited will pay the face value of this coupon plus 8¢ if submitted by customer for this product only. Any other use constitutes fraud. Coupon is nonassignable. Void if taxed, prohibited or restricted by law. Consumer must pay any government taxes. Void if copied. For reimbursement submit coupons and proof of sales directly to Harlequin Enterprises, Ltd 482, NCH Marketing Services, P.O. Box 880001, El Paso, TX 88588-0001, U.S.A. Cash value 1/100 cents.

® and ™ are trademarks owned and used by the trademark owner and/or its licensee.

© 2018 Harlequin Enterprises Limited

LICOUP44816

Love Inspired®

Inspirational Romance to Warm Your Heart and Soul

Join our social communities to connect with other readers who share your love!

Sign up for the Love Inspired newsletter at **www.LoveInspired.com** to be the first to find out about upcoming titles, special promotions and exclusive content.

CONNECT WITH US AT:

Facebook.com/groups/HarlequinConnection

 Facebook.com/LoveInspiredBooks

 Twitter.com/LoveInspiredBks

LISOCIAL2018